A Portal in Time

A Novel by
James A. Costa Jr.

CCB Publishing
British Columbia, Canada

A Portal in Time: A Novel

Copyright ©2002, 2013 by James A. Costa Jr.
ISBN-13 978-1-77143-062-3
Second Edition

Library and Archives Canada Cataloguing in Publication
Costa Jr., James A., 1931-
A portal in time : a novel / written by James A. Costa Jr. -- 2nd ed..
ISBN 978-1-77143-62-3
Also available in electronic format.
Additional cataloguing data available from Library and Archives Canada

Cover artwork and design by Joseph 'Zugs' Klein. A semi-retired artist, Mr. Klein resides in Placentia, California.

Publisher: CCB Publishing
British Columbia, Canada
www.ccbpublishing.com

For Jeannette, my wife, my love

Chapter 1

Spring 1939

Her Shirley Temple ringlets bobbed in time with her feet descending the wooden staircase.

"Come straight home and don't dilly-dally along the way," her mother called after her. "It will be dark soon."

Dolly stopped and called back. "I won't, Mama."

"And don't talk to strangers."

Dolly started down again. "I won't, Mama."

Day was fading to dusk when Dolly emerged from the old tenement building onto the pavement. Her yellow pinafore was mostly hidden behind a hand-me-down woolen sweater that hung loose on her. "Milk and bread, and a pack of Camels for Daddy," she sang to herself as she skipped along keeping a rhythm with her little black shoes scraping the sidewalk.

The street was quiet and her shadow fell long before her in the dull evening light. The grocery store lay two blocks ahead, not far, and she didn't really know why her mother always told her not to talk to strangers. What would a stranger do anyway, ask how to get someplace or where somebody lived? What was so bad about that? Besides, nobody ever stopped to ask her for anything in her whole life.

Her thoughts turned to the birthday party she would be going to next Saturday at Dante Cosner's house and what kind of present she could get for him. She liked Dante a lot because he was cute, and she knew he liked her too because he was always pulling her hair in class and teasing her. It made her happy just to think of him. Someday maybe she might even marry him! She tittered at the thought of it.

At first she didn't see the man standing across the street. As always, her attention was drawn to the deserted house she had to pass on the way to the store. It was so spooky the way it just stood there covered with shadows, like it was alive and staring at her with its broken windows like eyes watching her go by, and the broken porch posts hanging like arms that wanted to shoot out and grab her. And, as always, she was tempted to cross the street and then cross back again, but that seemed a silly thing to do now that she was older, almost ten. A little closer and she could just dash past it faster than it could ever catch her. She was about to break into a run when the man seemed to appear out of nowhere, a big man wearing a long, black coat.

"Little girl," he said, his voice soft but distinct, "little girl, did you see a little dog around here anyplace? A black and white dog?"

Dolly's first instinct was to glance around. The man stood next to her now, a big man, twice as big as her daddy. "Gee, mister—"

The huge hand he suddenly clapped over her mouth cut off her words and powerful arms hauled her in under the flap of his coat. Her feet came off the pavement thrashing as he carried her down the crumbled walkway alongside the deserted house. Stifled screams swelled her throat, suffocating her. Eyes wide with terror peered out between the thick fingers nearly covering her entire face....

Chapter 2

Spring 2007

Gary sat cross-legged on the attic floor, rummaging through a stack of old magazines and newspapers he had lifted from a wooden crate stamped with the faded name 'Weckerle's Dairy.' The musty smell of the newspapers and the mingled odors of wood planking and stale air seemed to wrap him in a warm cocoon. From a porthole window at the end of the attic, a river of dry sunlight swimming with dust motes streamed in and brightened the floor where he carefully separated the magazines from each other.

Intrigued, he studied the covers, so oddly stylized with snooty-faced men in monocles, and women in furs; cocked top hats, canes and tilted bubbly champagne glasses. It made him a little giddy to look at these artificial images, and filled him with a mixed sense of familiarity and unfamiliarity, of a reality and unreality he couldn't quite reconcile.

The Past! It seemed to beckon him, like the Sirens luring him to some distant home. No doubt his grandfather had much to do with his fascination with the past. Raised by him most of his life, how could he help but be influenced. He was a nostalgic man, Gramps was, a dreamer who longed for the 'the good-old days' right up to the time he died ten years ago. But it was more than that, Gary thought. Something had to run in their blood, a family gene, some little-understood yearning or predisposition of the mind that made the past seductive, compelling, magical.

A veritable museum, the attic was crammed with boxes and

stacks of 78 rpm records, crates of jars and bottles, bundles of magazines, pieces of furniture— everything, from rusty garden tools to tangled fishing tackle to crushed Christmas decorations. Peeking out from under an old canvas bag was the yellowed edge of a newspaper. Gently he slid it out, parting the pages as delicately as he would the damp wings of a butterfly and spread them on the floor.

"Gary," came a quavering voice from the foot of the attic stairs, "Gary, are you still up there?"

"Still here, Gram," he called back, pressing the pages flat.

"Supper's almost ready. Come down now and wash your hands."

Wash your hands. Like he was still a kid.

Except for its crumbling edges, the paper was in excellent condition, and it pleased him to see the date, an old one, Tuesday, September 5, 1939. The headline read, *Second British Ship Is Sunk Off Scotland.* Fascinated, he skimmed the page, reading of Hitler's invasion of Poland; of our proclamation of neutrality; of the war boom sending stock prices soaring. Totally absorbed, he was about to flip the page, when, almost as an editorial afterthought in the lower left corner, the picture of a young girl smiling out to him caught his eye. Beneath the picture the caption read, *Body of missing girl found.* A curious sadness touched him, and he was about to read, when his grandmother's voice jarred him.

"Gary, supper's on the table now. Don't let it get cold."

Knowing full well that he had about a five minute leeway, he folded the paper and tucked it under his arm. Rising, he took a quick look around, trying to decide which chest or old suitcase he would search next. He was hoping there would be a cache of old coins hidden away.

"Gary!"

"Coming," he called back, his feet drumming down the

hollow staircase into the house.

"Did you turn out the hall light?" she asked as he brushed past her on the way to his room.

"I absolutely without fail surely did," he said, tossing the newspaper on his bedroom dresser and heading back to wash up.

"Wash clean now and don't leave dirt on the towel."

"Yes, ma'm."

"And please don't splash up the mirror."

"Who, me?" He scrubbed his hands, ran wet fingers through his hair and dried off. "Lots of good stuff up there," he said, catching the water drips on his forehead as he emerged from the bathroom.

"Half the city library and dump, I'm sure," she murmured, fixing his plate.

"What's that, Gram?" he said, bouncing into the kitchen and patting her rounded shoulder as he threw his leg over his chair and dropped into it. He watched her brush gray wisps of hair from her brow over her ears.

"I think it's time to start getting rid of all that junk."

"Gram, did Gramps save anything valuable up there that you know of?"

"Heavens, don't ask me, but I doubt it." she said, lifting a tablespoon of peas onto her plate. "I know he thought someday all that stuff would be worth money, but that wasn't it. Your Grandpa just loved everything from the past. All his life, ever since I met him, reading about old movie stars, and ghost towns and even going down to city hall, trying to dig up records of the family to find the family roots, when they were born— all kinds of things— what boat they came over on, where they lived, worked. He even talked about going back to the old country someday and looking up the names in the churches, he said, because that's where the only records were kept unless you were royalty."

"He was a real nostalgia buff," Gary said, ladling more gravy onto his potatoes. "I guess I'm like him in a lot of ways. I remember how he used to get me out of bed so I could watch some late-night Western with him."

"He liked the black-and-white movies best. And those jazzy records— oh, my."

"I know. I used to listen to them with him. Goodman, the Duke, Kenton...."

When they'd finished, Gary pushed his chair back.

"I hope you're not going up there again."

"No, Gram, but, you know, there's something about the past. It just grabs me right here." He poked his heart. "Sometimes I feel like I've lived before," he said, looking across to her. "Does that make sense?"

Creases deepened in her pale forehead. "Your grandpa used to feel the same way," she said. "I didn't understand it then and I don't understand it now. It seems to me everybody gets a turn in life. Those people back then had their turn. Today is our turn, yours and mine and, yes, even Grandpa's, though he never could see it that way. It's like giving up something you have for something you can never have. I'm just not so sure it's a healthy thing."

He laughed. "Gram, what harm can come from it? It's like a hobby. Some people like golfing, some like fishing. In a way, it's like collecting, collecting memories— or recollecting them. I can't really explain it. I only know it's a good feeling, like the bitter-sweet feeling you get from hearing a sad song. It's sort of like all the people in the world are on a trip together and some of us would rather see where we've been than where we are, or even where we're going."

She studied him as he spoke, watching his animated hands, seeing his dark hair flop over the bright blue eyes that flashed with excitement, the angular features of his face flush with the joy of someone making a discovery— or maybe it was simply the exuberance of youth— so like his father at his age, God rest his soul.

"I'll say it again, Gary, it's not something I understand." She rose and carried the dishes to the sink. "And something I'm not sure I want to understand. All I know is that people don't walk backwards. They don't drive backwards. You don't see the clock running backwards, that's for sure— too bad for me and my wrinkles. I don't know, Gary, maybe I'm just not smart enough, but it hardly seems natural to me, this hankering after the past. It just never did."

"Gram," he said, sitting back and looking far off, "you know what I really wish?"

"Oh, dear, I'm afraid to ask."

"I'd love to go back, I mean actually transport myself into the past, to…like when you were young, to actually be there and see everything firsthand, talk to—"

"I've lived those times, Gary, and believe me, they're not everything your grandpa made them out to be. I wouldn't want to live them over again, I tell you."

"Want some help wiping, Gram?" he asked, rising and carrying his plate and glass over to the sink.

"No," she said, drowning the dishes in a pan of soapy water. "I'm fine. You're not seeing Shelley tonight?"

"Shelley's busy with homework, some project."

"No homework for you?"

"I'm taking a break. I deserve it."

"Of course you do, dear…Oh, there's a nice movie on tonight. Do you want to watch it with me?"

"Old or new?"

"Pretty old, I think."

He laughed. "'Pretty old' isn't old enough for me, Gram.

Thanks, but I'll take a rain check," he said, going down the hall to his room.

She smiled to herself as she lined the dishes in the rack to drain. Her thoughts turned inward to her husband, Granville, gone ten years ago, just like that, of a stroke, just about the time of his retirement from the railroad...and just when they could have really enjoyed life! And eight years before that, their son, John, killed in a car accident with Debbie, his wife, leaving Gary a six-year old orphan. At first it was hard, not being a spring chicken anymore when they took him in. Now he was the sole joy of her life and her sole reason for living. So much like her husband, Gary almost made her feel that her Granville had never left her, that Gary was there to take his place.

She rinsed the rest of the dishes and dried them with slow, circular motions and stacked them in the cupboard. Arthritis stabbed her shoulder with every stretch, the way it hurt her knees all the time. She was getting older fast, and privately she worried. How much longer would Gary be with her? He was already twenty-three, or was it twenty-four? ...no, not for another few months... and apparently quite serious with Shelley. Being engaged, it was only a matter of time before they— The sudden thought of being left alone or, worse, shipped off to a nursing home so terrified her that she almost dropped the bowl in her hand... to be put in with all those old people!

With the door closed behind him, Gary opened his computer to check his e-mail. "Nobody loves me," he said, shutting it down and making a quick dive onto his bed. His eyes burned from all the reading of record labels, advertisements and magazines earlier in the attic, and his full belly made him sleepy. Turning on his side to get more comfortable, he spotted the old newspaper atop his dresser.

Briefly, he fought the impulse to get up, but memory of the haunting face of the little girl on the front page got the best of him and he gave into it. Sitting on the edge of his bed he smoothed the paper on his lap and began to read.

What Gary didn't realize at the moment was that the newspaper he'd found buried that afternoon would open the door to the past, to a world of danger, mystery and romance.

Chapter 3

The little girl smiled out at him again, seemed to be smiling with bright eyes, despite the shadowy quality of the picture. The story, continued on an inside page, was so disturbing he could hardly bring himself to read it, but after doing the calendar math he comforted himself with the knowledge that the pain and the agony of the murder no longer had meaning to anyone. Sixty years or so was a long time ago. Still, he read through the account quickly:

Early this morning two boys discovered the partially decomposed body of nine year old Dolores 'Dolly' Czarnowski under debris behind a building next to the old First Ward playground, two blocks from where she lived. The girl had been missing since April 21st when she failed to return home from a trip to the grocery store. Sources close to the investigation say that she had apparently been sexually assaulted, bound and gagged and her throat slashed. They speculate that the murder took place inside the building, an abandoned two-story house which, in recent months, angry neighbors have been petitioning the city to demolish. Investigators are asking anyone with information regarding this crime and, in particular, a stranger seen lurking in the vicinity several days earlier to....

It made him sick thinking of the terror the little girl must have gone through before she died. *If I could only go back*, he thought, looking at the picture again. *Back just long enough to save this one beautiful child. And to perform one definitive act in my life, just one!* Wondering if his grandma possibly knew the girl, he tore the article out to show her and shoved it in his pocket.

He was about to set the newspaper aside when an ad for a Hohner harmonica jumped out at him. Only a dollar. That was a good make harmonica, and still around today, if he wasn't mistaken. Wouldn't it be something if... he mused... if...no, it was a crazy thought... but just maybe.... He checked the name and address. Yes, right here in town, Morgan Fisher Enterprises, not far away on the south side, North Division Street.

He chided himself. Maybe he was beginning to lose it, like Grandpa did, near the end. Grandma had good reason to worry that he was becoming too much like him. He cast the paper aside, about to lay back... still...Oh, what the hell! What did he have to lose except for a postage stamp. It was possible the company was still in business here in town and they just might find his order amusing enough to play along:

"Hey, Clarence, look here. Some joker wants to order a base model from a pre-World War II price list.

"You're kidding."

"Naw. Lookee here."

"What a screwball. Throw it—no, wait a minute. Did he send the buck?"

"Yeah, here, see?"

"Fill the order."

"You mean it?"

"Sure, why not? Make the sap happy, and charge it up to good will."

Tearing the ad out of the paper, Gary scribbled a quick note placing the order, pulled a dollar from his wallet and put it all together in an envelope, ready for mailing. He set it on his dresser, then dropped back to relax. He was comforted by the warm smell of popcorn seeping into the room.

Arms akimbo behind his head, he gazed across to the wall he helped his grandfather paint a long time ago: *You hold the brush like this, see, Gary? Then you dip it just so far, like this, see? Run one side flat against the lip of the can so it don't drip all....*

More than anything, he loved the old man, gaunt, forever running an agitated hand through wispy gray hair, moody, sometimes explosive, his hard jaw set in anger against the world and his place in it. But the old man was always good to him, taking him along on his trips to the library and book stores, teaching him to tie knots— the square and the bowline and the sheepshank, regaling him with stories of his long ago youth and his navy experiences in the war.

He brought it all to life the year before he died, when the three of them took a trip to Hawaii and visited Pearl Harbor. He remembered vividly the pictures his Grandpa painted of the attack as they took the launch out to the Memorial, just off Ford Island, more vivid even than the movie they showed in the visitors' center before they boarded. He could still visualize names of the dead sailors engraved in marble inside the Memorial, and tried to imagine the thousand trapped sailors suffocating to death at the bottom of the harbor. Most horrifying of all was the image of them still there, entombed in the hull, directly below where he was standing.

And Grandma, patient despite her exasperation with Gramps, her pale blue eyes expressing an understanding beyond words, serving him dinner as if he were a king, massaging his aching back with a liniment so strong it burned your eyes if you stood too close, tolerating his tantrums that erupted like boiling geysers, and faded away as quickly, like a harmless mist.

For a long time he had been thinking of getting his grandma out of the old house she had lived in for fifty years or more. As a whole the neighborhood still had some vitality to it, but it had been decaying for at least a decade, and here and there boarded up houses festooned with graffiti bloomed like festering lesions. She had no real reason for wanting to stay put, not any that he could see, anyway. Most of her friends had either moved away or passed on. The businesses and shops she had spoken of so often, and one or two that he himself still remembered— Franz's bakery, Jack's grocery store, the tailor shop run by a little hump-backed man they called Hammy, the drug store with the sweet smell of vanilla ice cream sodas— all were gone except the grocery store, which had been replaced by one of the big chain markets, and the closest drug store was now half a mile away. The dark shell of the old Bijou Theater was still standing, and the Kit Kat Klub, his grandpa's old hangout, had long since faded into oblivion.

Over the years everything had changed. No wonder Grandpa yearned for the 'good old days.' They were simpler, happier days. Ironically, in her own way and for her own stubborn reasons, Grandma couldn't give up the past any more than could Grandpa.

In another month he would be graduating from the university and finally be able to give all his time to work. He had several interviews set up with various public schools and had no doubt he'd get hired. His grades were about as high as they could go, and he had nothing in his background that could hurt him. With a full-time teaching job he would easily make enough to buy something nice just outside the city. She was a stubborn lady, his grandma. The times in the past few years when he had broached the subject of moving, she had refused to even discuss it. His uncles Jerry and Wilbur and Aunt Shirley had no more luck talking to her than he did. But eventually she would have to accept the inevitable. Sometimes it was really hard to figure out old people.

Then, of course, there was Shelley. They'd been engaged six months and had pretty much agreed to wait awhile after their graduation to get married. They hadn't really discussed where they would like to live, although it was assumed, at least by her, that they would rent something cheap until they could save enough for a down payment on a house of their own. He had his own ideas, though he wasn't about to air them yet. Shelley apparently assumed his grandmother would live on her own or move in with one of her children, most likely Aunt Shirley, but that wasn't something he wanted to happen. He wanted to take her in himself, to do for her what she had done for him when he had no one, when he was essentially an orphan. He didn't know how he would work it all out, but he would. Somehow. Growing drowsy, he sank back to his pillow and fell into a light sleep. He dreamed:

...*a burning ship, his grandpa shouting something from the rail and holding a child in his arms, a little girl whose shadowy face he couldn't quite make out.....*

Chapter 4

At three in the afternoon, a few days later, Gary bounded up the steps to the university library. Once inside, his eyes swept the cavernous room filled with book smells, where neither the librarian nor the handful of people browsing among the shelves seemed to notice him. His eyes lit up when he spotted her at a long table near the 'mystery' section, hunched over her texts.

"Hi, Shell," he whispered, sliding up a chair across from her.

From between a curtain of blond hair that parted when she lifted her head, her face appeared smiling, coyly. Pleasure or displeasure, he couldn't tell. Her pale eyebrow cocked, she glanced at the clock on the far wall. "Is this two o'clock?"

Displeasure, obviously, but he blustered on, undeterred. "Oh, do I have a story to tell you," he said, laying his hot hand over hers. "When you hear this you'll flip."

"So what has that fertile Walter Mitty imagination cooked up today? Wait, don't tell me...." She pressed her pencil to her lips, thinking... "You were crossing Bardwell Bridge when you had to stop and talk a would-be suicide from taking the fatal plunge."

"Shelley, come on—"

"Or was it a heroic effort to capture a bank robber?"

"Shelley—"

"Don't tell me, you were aiding another poor soul pinned under his car."

He looked indignant. "That accident really did happen, you know. You saw it written up yourself in the newspaper."

She smiled at him, indulgently, warmly, forgivingly. "I

know," she said. "I was only teasing. Actually, I've been so absorbed working on this dumb term paper I wasn't paying attention to the time, anyway." She laid her pencil aside. "So?" she said, flashing a sparkling white smile, "I'm waiting...."

Folding his arms, he sat back with a small pout tightening his lips. "Forget it, it's okay. You'll just say I'm making up stories and laugh at me. You're already starting, I can see it."

"I won't laugh, I promise. Go ahead, tell me."

"You wouldn't believe it anyway, no."

"Try me."

"You'll say I'm making it all up. No, never mind. I'm sorry I brought it up."

Sighing, she reached for her pencil. "Well, all right, if—"

He fairly flung himself forward across the table and leaned close to her. "Look at this," he said, pulling out the harmonica out and laying it in front of her.

She frowned. "You're taking harmonica lessons?"

"No, for God's sake, no."

"You want me to take lessons?"

"Shelley, cut it out, quit joking."

"Well then, what?"

"I'm trying to tell you," he said, glancing around and sliding back into his seat. "Listen, you have to believe this." He raised his right hand and lowered his voice. "I swear it's the truth and I'm not making it up and I'm not hallucinating and I'm definitely not crazy." He whispered, "Promise you won't laugh."

"Promise," she said, glancing away and hiding a smirk.

"Okay. This afternoon, just about the time I was on my way over here, a UPS truck pulls up to our house, the driver gets out, comes up to the door and says, 'Package for Mr. Tyler.' I sign for it, wondering what it is, and take it inside to my room. I plop on my bed, holding it on my lap, staring at it, and I'm almost afraid to open it because now I remember and have a good idea of what it is, or at least what it's supposed to be. I must have sat there like that for a good five minutes just looking at it before I worked up the nerve to do it."

She snickered. "What did you think it was, a bomb?"

"Yeah, right, very funny, sure—although it hit me like one. I said I knew what was in it."

She glanced at the clock. "I'd like to know, too, someday, and where this story's going. Are you going to get to the point or is this a new quiz show?"

He tapped the harmonica. "This was it."

"This?" She pointed a finely manicured finger. "Okay, Gary, what's going on? What game—"

"Listen, this is what happened...."

Gary proceeded to tell her the whole story, from the discovery of the newspaper in the attic, to the ad he answered, his subsequent order and the delivery. When he had finished, he looked at her, hard, trying to read her thoughts before she expressed them.

"Only a dollar, you said?"

"Right."

"For this?" she said, poking it, rather insolently, he thought.

"For that, yes."

She picked it up and turned it in her hand a few times before setting it down and sliding it across to him. "Does it blow?"

He frowned. "Of course it does."

"And you really believe it materialized from out of the past? Mysteriously?"

"I didn't exactly say that."

"You didn't exactly not say it."

"Well, how else do you explain it? What other explanation

could there be?"

She shook her head sympathetically. "Gary, Gary, that imagination—"

"Wait wait wait. At first I thought like you, that maybe it's a company still around and somebody there decided to humor me."

"Isn't that logical?"

"Until I looked in the phone book. Hohner's still around but the company I ordered through doesn't exist anymore. I even asked my grandmother about it and she remembers the place— a friend of hers used to work there. She said it was shut down at least twenty years ago."

"Gary, I know how exciting this is to you and I really hate to burst your bubble, but did it ever occur to you that some mail-order company now uses that address— you did say the building is still there, didn't you?"

"No, but I did look it up and it is."

"So? Somebody there just took your order and filled it. Why make a mystery of it?"

"As far as I know, that building's been empty for years. But if I have to, I can go down and see for myself."

"That wouldn't prove anything. The post office could have forwarded your letter to wherever they moved."

He slipped the ad from his shirt pocket and shoved it in front of her. "Here, look for yourself."

"Why, it's just an ordinary ad."

"Well, it's not. It's from a 1939 newspaper."

"All right, I'm impressed. But what does that prove?"

"It proves I'm telling the truth."

"I never denied you were."

"But don't you see? It's a Hohner. That's a famous German harmonica maker, a reputable company. You don't get those for a dollar, not these days."

She smiled. "Does it play any music, or only German music?"

"C'mon, Shelley—"

She laid her hand over his. "Oh, Gary, Gary," she said, stroking his hand, "can't you see how crazy this all sounds?"

"That's why I'm not telling anyone except you." He pulled his hand away. "I thought you of all people would believe me, especially after seeing the ad and the harmonica itself."

"Gary, the harmonica may say Hohner, but is it a genuine Hohner? What do they call it, bootlegging? when some country duplicates the same product and passes it off as the real thing?"

"And no tax, no sales tax, what about that?"

"I don't believe it's required if the business headquarters is out of state."

Crestfallen, he jammed the harmonica in his pocket, sulked awhile, then straightened up. "Okay, we'll see. Time will tell who's right." A wan smile crossed his lips. "And how's the term paper going?"

She brightened. "Oh, this?" she said, riffling through a sheaf of notes. "I'm getting there, little at a time, I suppose. 'The Psychology of Money and Its Effect on Minorities.' Sound thrilling?"

"Which reminds me," he said, digging into his pocket, pulling out a handful of coins and laying them on the table in front of her. "Pretty, aren't they?"

She picked up a coin. "A dime. So?"

"Look close. That's no ordinary dime that's been minted after 1964, which is really nothing but a slug. It's a 1943 Mercury dime, with real silver in it. How 'bout that?"

"I've seen old coins before. Dad had some." She examined it, set it aside and picked up another. "They're nice, but I'd expect them to be shinier. How much did you have to pay for them?"

"Not a cent, not an Indian Head cent," he said, pushing a penny toward her. "That one's an 1882. I found them all about a week ago while I was scavenging through some old dresser drawers in the attic. I already have a bunch and there could be more. I'm going to keep looking."

"How much are they worth?"

"I've been meaning to find out, I don't know, I'll have to check them out.... Look at this silver dollar, 1922. Isn't that Liberty Head on it beautiful?"

"Do you always carry these around with you?" she said, lightly rubbing her thumb over the surface of the coin.

"I love to hear the jingle. Real silver jingles, not like the counterfeit junk in your purse."

"Heavy, too," she said, bouncing it on her palm.

"Because it's the real stuff," he said, snatching it away and sweeping it up with the other coins. "I have a few more at home."

She studied his face. "This sort of thing really gets your heart pumping, doesn't it, Gary?"

"Not as much as you do," he said, reaching over and squeezing her hand. "Why, does it show?"

"Is water wet? When doesn't it show? Your nostalgia, I mean. What I don't understand is, people usually long for their own past, but you, you seem to be nostalgic for times before you were even born. I always thought nostalgia was for old people."

"Maybe that's why I'm a history major. I can't help it, Shell, I just love anything old— old movies, old books, old songs, things mostly of this century, though. Not that I'm not interested in the more distant past, but... somehow, it's almost as if, as if...."

"As if...?"

"I don't know, Shell. Let's just say it's sort of a hobby. A little more intense than what other people feel about their hobbies, all except maybe golfers."

"Like my brother Bob."

"Like him, yeah, and all the other addicts like him. It doesn't bother you, does it, that I'm hooked on this... this hobby?"

Her smile splashed on him like sunshine. "I guess not, as long as it doesn't extend to *older* women."

They laughed together, a little too loud, and he looked around self-consciously. "How long do you intend to stay here?" he asked, shoving the coins into his pocket.

"Probably until closing time. I really want to get this paper finished by the end of the week."

"Which translates into I won't be seeing you at least till Saturday, right?"

Her hair formed a silky scarf around her neck as she cocked her head slightly. "You're not angry, are you?"

"Just disappointed. I'm going to miss you." He brought her hand to his lips and kissed her fingers, kissed the modest engagement ring with the tiny diamond in the center of it.

"In a week or so it will all be over. Then we can go out and celebrate. It's been a long time since we've done it, hasn't it?"

"Too long," he said, gazing into the blue wonder of her eyes and wishing he could pull her close to him. "I love you."

"I love you, too, Gary," she said, rising a little and stretching for a peck on the lips.

God she smelled like heaven. "Okay, then, I'll give you a call in a day or so. Or you can e-mail me right from the school computer here. That all right?" he asked, getting up and pushing the chair under the table.

She smiled a sweet and glowing smile that would carry him all the way home. It bothered him, though, that she had taken his story so lightly. Of course, what could he really expect. What he had suggested would be regarded as completely mad to any rational person— and Shelley was as rational a person as anyone could ever hope to find. But that was fine with him. He needed her to balance his impulsiveness, his active imagination and maybe his gullibility, too, if that's all it really turned out to be. But if she loved him as much as she said she did, she could at least bend a little and show a little more indulgence toward him. Humor him, anyway.

Excitement stirred his blood as he wheeled along, threading his way through the building dinner hour traffic. Tonight he would order something else, something that would convince her and maybe himself, too, that he wasn't going mad. One way or another, if it killed him, he'd solve this mystery.

Chapter 5

Monday afternoon. He didn't think classes would ever end that morning as he grabbed his books, slid out of his 1990 Honda and hurried into the house. "Any packages come for me today, Gram?" he called, his anxious voice echoing in the kitchen.

"Is that you, Gary? I'm back here in the spare room. I'll be right out."

He headed for his bedroom, saw no package, tossed his books on the bed and stripped down to put on a comfortable pair of pants and a tan Greg Norman golf shirt Shelley had given to him for his last birthday.

But I'm not a golfer!

So? I couldn't help it, I loved the shirt. Maybe it will inspire you.

Stuffing his wallet, a couple of Kleenex tissues and the silver dollar in his pockets, he sat down at his computer to check his e-mail. "Ah, Shelley loves me," he said, seeing the library e-mail address and opening his mail. The message, just a line, put a crease across his forehead and then a smile on his face. Shelley's doing it to him again, playing games, making fun of him. He read the line again:

If you want a future forget the past!

Chuckling, he deleted the message, shut down the machine, slipped on his sweater and left the room, almost bumping into his grandmother outside his door.

"No package for me, I take it?"

"What a day," she said, running her wrist over her tired

23

brow. I've been working like a dog, but you'd never know it. Nothing shows." She went to the cupboard. "You want some lunch? There's some leftover roast beef."

"I'm not really hungry, Gram." He glanced around. "No package for me?"

"Some mail came. The usual junk for me and a letter for you. Even one for your grandpa. All this time, ten years, they don't know he's dead? At least no bills came." She put a plate of cookies on the table. "You feel okay, Gary?"

'I'm fine," he said, straightening up.

"Too much school on your mind?"

"Among other things."

"Worried about your examinations?" she said, sitting across from him.

"Not really."

"A hard day?"

"Not so hard, just boring. I'm glad it's almost over."

"Well, that's good. Your grandpa would be so proud of you, God rest his soul, to see you graduate from college. Nobody in the family ever did before, you know."

"I know," he said, grabbing a cookie.

"He always wanted that for you. I wish he could be here to see it, your graduation."

"I know, Gram. But like you say sometimes, maybe he's looking down, watching us. When the day comes, he'll be there, I'm sure."

"I pray so."

"Gram, when you were young, did you by chance remember reading in the paper or hearing about a little girl—"

The phone rang. "That must be your Aunt Shirley," she said, getting up. "She's supposed to set up my doctor's appointment for me. Your letter's over on the stand by you," she said, pointing and picking up the phone.

A sprinkle of cookie crumbles fell to the floor as he stretched for the envelope.

"What is it, Gary?" his grandmother said, alarmed by the expression on his face when he pulled the letter out. "Wait a minute, Shirley... Gary...?"

"It's okay, Gram, don't worry," he said, scrambling to his feet, jamming the letter in his pocket and rushing for the door.

"Will you be back in time for supper?" she called after him, but he was already gone....

Chapter 6

Gary glanced at his car clock as he tooled down the road—a few minutes past three in the afternoon. He hoped the mail-order office would still be open when he got there. The address wasn't really that far from where he lived, but the route was a little convoluted, and the streets narrow and busier than usual at that time of day, especially with the new road construction all over town.

Wouldn't it be something, he mused as he sped up to make a light, wouldn't it be something if he had really found a way to communicate with the past, to actually communicate with people living in 1939? My God, it boggled the mind just thinking of the possibilities. The things he could tell! The events he could warn them of! The disasters he could help avert! He pondered: Why shouldn't he do it? He could make the world a better place. What a contribution to society that would be!

The more he thought of it, the more appealing the idea became. With a little imagination the possibilities for doing good were endless. Just telling someone back then what to look for could be enormously beneficial to mankind. Don't pacify Hitler, for instance, or make no deals with Stalin. Or don't sail on the Andrea Doria on... he'd have to look up the date. His mind ranged over the catastrophic events he could prevent, the bombings, especially the recent horrendous attacks in New York. Oh, the wonder of it all if these orders he'd placed in the ancient newspaper he'd found in the attic—orders that were filled! —if it all wasn't some kind of elaborate prank.

Maybe he could stick a note in with the next order. Just for the hell of it, to see what response he'd get. Maybe when he got back home later he could look up in the almanac which horse would win the Kentucky Derby back then, or who would win some election, or what movie would win the Academy Award— something simple, some event that would take place a week or so after the date of the order. He could even—

Then again, maybe it wasn't such a great idea. One little change in the past could alter the course of history, or at least that was the prevailing theory. Then again, why should anyone assume that the way things are is the best way. Change could be an improvement. Could the world be more messed up than it's been since cavemen started throwing rocks at each other? Anyway, he'd have to give it more thought, careful thought. For all he knew, this whole mail-order business could be a gigantic farce, and him a gullible dope.

A car moving at high speed around him suddenly veered into his path, cutting him off and driving him over the curb onto the sidewalk. Jolted, he slammed on the brakes and fought the wheel for control. Careening over the sidewalk, barely missing the face of a brick building, the car swerved and spun around, tires screaming, and stopped inches in front of a telephone pole.

"Goddamned idiot!" he cried, blasting his horn at the other car, already long gone.

"Lucky, nothing but lucky," he told himself, realizing he could have been killed or killed any number of pedestrians he saw leaping out of the way. He remembered the e-mail message he'd received: *If you want a future forget the past!* If he had been killed, how funny would Shelley, his skeptical fiancee— how funny would she have thought her little computer joke was then!

Shifting into reverse, he backed off onto the street and eased away, listening for any foreign sounds from the undercarriage. Hearing nothing unusual, he relaxed. For a moment, and only a moment, he wondered whether someone had actually tried to kill him, but dismissed the idea as ludicrous. An average guy just finishing college, no money, no enemies, none that he knew of, anyway, what reason could anyone possibly have for wanting him dead? Of course, he couldn't discount the nuts out on the road these days.

Approaching the neighborhood minutes later, he took the letter from his pocket and read it again, his head bobbing as he glanced from the paper to the road and back again:

Your order, #148, has arrived and may be picked up at the above address between 10:00 a.m. and 3:00 p.m. any day except Sunday. We will hold this item for you for one week, after which time a charge of $.25 per day will be levied. Please present this letter at time of pickup....

Containing his excitement was difficult and he had to be careful his foot didn't get too heavy on the accelerator. Today would be the day he'd get to the bottom of the mystery. The first order, the harmonica, had been delivered to his house. This one wasn't much bigger, so why did he have to pick it up? Crazy. The whole idea of getting packages from 1939 seemed nothing but crazy. He didn't want to think of what he'd say to Shelley if all this turned out to be some kind of prank or hoax... making a colossal fool of himself....

Ahead, the North Division Street sign came into view. What didn't come into immediate view was the time warp Gary was about to enter.

Chapter 7

"Damn," he said, hearing his tires rub against the curb as he pulled up in front of the building to check the rusted metal numbers over the door against the address on the letterhead. They matched: 270. Twisting around in his seat, he looked up and down the street for some sign of life, but saw only a couple of workers climbing out of a landscaping truck nearby. He took his time getting out of the car and, feeling suddenly squeamish, stood there a few seconds, undecided, absently jiggling his car keys. Then he bent down for a quick look at the underside of his car to see if anything was broken or dangling in that near death smash-up, saw nothing amiss, straightened up and surveyed the area again.

Like blank faces, a wall of warehouses with bricked-up windows stretched down the block in both directions. And like all the others, his building looked just as forbidding and, in some subtle, undefined way, even threatening. His instincts told him to run, to get out of there fast, but he refused to give in to them. No doubt it had to be some elaborate joke being played on him, like one of those reality shows that make fools out of people. But somehow that didn't make any sense. He had to settle down; this whole damn thing was making him paranoid. Or just plain nuts!

Dented here and there, the jamb and solid steel door with its drab green paint told its age. Oddly, it had no doorknob or handle of any kind. Alongside the door, beneath the paint-thickened doorbell, was a tin sign with the faded words **Ring For Service** stamped into it. Would it even work? he wondered as he pressed the bell, waited a few moments, shifting from one foot to the other, and pressing again.

Hearing nothing, he was secretly relieved and about to scamper back to his car and get out of there, when the door clicked and suddenly sprang open a few inches. He hesitated, wishing he had told someone where he was going, then reached out and pulled the door open far enough to peek inside. A dim light illuminated a narrow passageway.

Mustering the last of his faltering courage, he stepped inside and stood a moment. He grew suddenly angry, angry at himself for being afraid, and angry at whoever was behind the ridiculous charade. "Hello!" he called. "Anybody here?"

The slam and click of the door behind him sent his heart up into his throat. Swinging around he lunged for the door, feeling for a knob in the shadows, pushing, then ramming his shoulder against the cold steel with all his strength. To no avail. He stood there a moment listening, hearing only his own tight breathing, then turned back into the corridor, his gut twisting, his eyes wide, his ears attuned to the faintest sound.

"Okay, the joke's gone far enough," he yelled, his fist balled, adrenalin pumping, and forcing his leaden legs to move ahead.

Passing several darkened rooms on both sides of the corridor, he read the stenciling on the frosted panes of their closed doors: *Perry Coster & Son, Floor Specialists; H. Clarke, Interiors; Brian A. Castro, Attorney at Law; Geo. Danglos, Restaurant Equipment.* From an office farther down he saw a dim glow and thought he heard the flat, clacking sound of a typewriter. He stood a moment as if scenting the air, then hurried toward it. The faded stenciling on the door read *Morgan Fisher Enterprises,* and below that, *Walk In.*

The coldness of the brass knob mimicked the cold sweat trickling down his back. A half turn, and the door swung open smoothly on its hinges. The room was better lit than the corridor, though not by much, and he could see a row of wooden file cabinets lining the wall.

So the moment of reckoning is here, he thought, taking a deep breath and stepping inside.

"Ahem."

Startled, he almost fell turning around to face a middle-aged woman with deeply rouged cheeks and pinched mouth sitting at a boxy, oak desk behind a clunky typewriter and peering up at him over tiny spectacles perched on her nose like a second set of eyes.

"May I help you, sir?" she asked, looking a bit flummoxed.

He managed to untie his tongue. "You might start with a little better way of getting into this building," he said, still agitated.

"Sir?"

He unfolded his letter and handed it to her. "I'm here for this."

Lifting her glasses to read, she took the paper. "Order number 148, yes, it's here. Our suppliers are very efficient," she said, resetting her glasses and rising from her chair to retrieve a small carton box from a shelf lined with lettered bins. "TA... TH... TR.... This is it." She handed the package over to him. "If you'll just sign here, sir...."

He scribbled his name and tucked the box under his arm.

"Is there anything else I can do for you, sir?" she asked, settling herself behind her desk again and adjusting the white lace collar of her dress.

"You can start by making sure that door opens when I leave here."

"Door, sir?"

He pointed. "The one down near the end of the hallway there."

"Down there, sir?"

"Yes, down there, *ma'm,*" he said, poking the air, "that

way."

"Oh, you must have turned yourself around coming into the office through this door, sir. It happens occasionally. The outside door you're pointing to is non-functional. As far as I know, it hasn't been used in ages, and certainly not in the ten years that I've been employed here."

"Well, I have news for you..."

"I'm sorry, sir. I know it can be confusing getting around all the corridors in this building. It took me awhile to get used to it myself, but I'll be sure to report the need for better wall signs." Smiling demurely, she nodded toward her left. "That's the entrance there, sir. And exit. I'm sure you'll find it easier leaving that way. Simply go through the doorway, bear right and go straight ahead to the end, turn right and you'll see the outside door to South Division Street."

"South—now wait a minute," he said, looking around, confused. "Unless I'm going crazy, I know which way I came in here and—"

"Really, sir, if there is something else I can do for you...."

"All right, all right, we'll do it your way," he said, adjusting his package. "I suppose I'll just have to walk around the block to get back to my car."

He crossed the room, found his way through the corridors and out into the street, a street lined with warehouses washed and freshened with afternoon sunlight, their windows gleaming like mirrors. The world seemed newer, somehow, the buildings sturdier and the air itself had an odd feel to it, a tingling kind of edge to it with a subtle and alien fragrance that sent a chill through him. Shrugging off the peculiar sensations touching him, he concluded that the North Division Street side looked shabby because it was the back side of the buildings.

Looking up and down the street, he saw no signs of life and broke into a quick walk toward the intersection a dozen or so yards ahead.

At the same time a group of four boys, teenagers, maybe sixteen or seventeen, came loping around the corner toward him, laughing, their shoes slapping and scraping the pavement as they shoved each other around. At the sight of him their roughhousing ended abruptly and their raucous voices trailed off and died. They froze, blocking his path, their cold eyes fixed hard on him. Gary tried to sidestep them but they moved with him, like a wall. He stepped to the other side and they shifted with him like a quartet of dancers.

"Excuse me, guys," he said, feeling his heart pump as he tried to get by them again.

"Where you goin'?" the big-muscled one said, the obvious leader of the gang.

"To my car. Now if you don't mind—"

"I don't see no car," the apparent second-in-command said, his nose twitching, "did you, Joey?"

Joey's muscular arms hung loose. He glared out of snot-green eyes. "Nobody did."

"It's around the corner on North Division."

"We just came that way. We didn't see no car there, neither."

"Well it's there anyway, so let me by and let's avoid trouble."

"He doethent want any trouble, Twitch," the beefy one lisped through a set of buck teeth.

"We don't neither," Joey said. Forming a crescent, they backed Gary against the brick wall of the building.

"Whath in the bockth?" the beefy one said.

Despite his rising anger and the obvious threat, Gary couldn't help smiling, recalling Alfonso Bedoya, the big-toothed Mexican bandit asking Humphrey Bogart, "What eez een ze bag?"

"Whath tho funny?"

"None of your damned business."

Joey stepped in close. "We're making it our business."

"Out of my way," Gary snapped, arm-locking the box and sticking out his other arm.

"You ain't gonna let him push you, are you, Joey?" one of them taunted. "He pushed you, Joey, I saw him push you, didn't we see him push him, Twitch?"

Joey shoved Gary up against the building. "What're you doing around here, anyway? This ain't your neck of the woods."

A prickly fear painted sweat on Gary's face. "Look, you guys, I just want to get to my car and get out of here."

"Well, boo hoo, ain't that a damn shame. We can't let him do that, can we, guys?" Joey said, glancing around for approval. "Not without payin' somethin'."

"Whath in hith pocketh, Joey?"

Gary pulled back, casting desperately around for somebody to help. He thought he glimpsed someone on the corner, a man standing in the shadows.

"Get your hands off me and get the hell out of my way! I told you I don't want any trouble."

Hardly had the words left his mouth when he heard the smack of bone on flesh, his flesh. He felt the pressure of the blow on his jaw as his knees sagged and his senses reeled. Another punch to the face rocked him back and slammed his head against the wall behind him.

Tasting the blood choking him as he slid off the wall to the ground, he flailed blindly against the swarming bodies that cut out the daylight and rained punches down on him until his arms fell away and an encroaching darkness threatened consciousness. The sudden fear of being stomped to death, of being killed, brought a new surge of strength. Covering his face with his arm he twisted away, over onto his belly and up to his knees in a blind, instinctive effort to get up, to free himself and run, but a kick, or series of kicks in the ribs flattened him back down on the cement walk. Something hit his head, hard.

Chapter 8

...Seconds, minutes later—Gary never could be sure how long it had been— he was standing on wobbly legs, with two policemen supporting him by the arms.

"Are you okay there? Can you stand on your own okay?"

The florid face of the cop with eyes the kind of blue that could be cold and cruel or warm and sentimental swam into cloudy focus. "I'm fine, I'm okay," he said, struggling to remember...the letter, yes, racing to the mail-order house, the gang circling... menacing....

"Ah, you don't look so good to me. I think a trip to the hospital for a check-up wouldn't hurt."

"No, no, thank you, no hospital," he said, still groggy.

"This package here on the ground," the second officer said, picking it up, "yours?" His lean body looked as hard as the soulless eyes studying him. "Or theirs? Been stepped on."

Gary reached for it. "Yes, that's it. My name's on it, see? I just picked it up..." he gestured..."when... when—"

"We know," the lean one said, appraising him as if he were sizing him up for a suit. "Took off like gangbusters when they saw us coming. We know that bunch."

"No real harm done," Gary said, trying to blink away the cobwebs shrouding his eyes. He brushed off his pants and sweater, anxious to get back home.

Both officers eyed him suspiciously. "I don't know, do you, Ed? It looks to me he could use some medical help."

Ed, the lean one, shrugged.

"A police report wouldn't hurt, either. Show the captain we ain't just out here cruising the streets doing nothin', or mooching coffee and doughnuts someplace."

Ed nodded. "What are you doing in this neck of the woods, anyway? The address on that package you're carrying puts you a little ways off from here."

"Special order. I just came down to pick it up. Honest, officers, I'm fine, really fine. They were only a bunch of kids, a little wild, that's all. You know how kids are these days, too much time on their hands."

"What do you think, Ed?"

Ed shrugged again. "Let's do a report, anyway. Just to cover ourselves."

"Sounds fair enough to me. And you," he said, resting a gentle hand on Gary's shoulder, "we'll drop you off at the doctor's for a quick check-up. That eye and that split lip could use a little fixin'."

Gary wondered if they were playing good-cop-bad-cop as they led him to the curb and helped him into the back seat of the police car. Ed pulled out a clip board and Gary gave his name and address as it was on the package. They pulled away, cruising slowly.

The smell of blood in his nose and the taste of it in his throat nauseated him, and he tried to get his mind off his discomfort by gazing out the window at the houses sliding by. Even through clouded eyes, he could see that the neighborhood was old, older than his, but looked well-maintained and better than his. He thought about his grandmother and how one day he'd get her into the suburbs where everything was clean and new and safe. It could've been her on her way to the post office or someplace today instead of him who got mugged. He thought about the man across the street, watching, and didn't do a damn thing to help!

Shifting position to ease the ache in his ribs, he noticed how cramped the back seat was and, for the first time, really paid attention to his surroundings. *What the hell is going on here?* As a matter of fact, the cops themselves looked somehow out of place, and the uniforms they were wearing— though he couldn't put his finger on it— resembled something actors impersonating cops would wear on a stage. *And this antique car, what's that all about?*

"Is there some kind of a parade or centennial going on today? A special occasion?" he asked.

"Why do you want to know?" Ed said.

Gary shrugged. "This car, for instance."

"What about it?"

"It's ancient. Are you using it in a car show or something?" He let out a nervous laugh. "Or is the police department really that hard-up for funds these days?"

Both officers looked at each other. "I think you might have cracked your head pretty hard there on the concrete. What did you say your name was? ...What's his name, Ed?"

"Gary...Gary Tyler," Ed said, checking his sheet.

"Uh huh. Tyler, tell me, what day is today?"

"Today?"

"Today."

"Today's Monday."

"Monday, is it?" He looked at Ed. "You're sure of that?"

"Of course I'm sure."

"Okay. Well, when you see the doc, you tell him what happened and all your symptoms." He pointed to his head. "Be sure he sees that lump. Doc Goldman's a good man. He'll take care of you. And stay the hell out of that neighborhood! It ain't safe." The car wheeled up to the curb. "Need help getting out?"

"I appreciate the ride, and thanks," Gary said, grasping the handle and stumbling out. He rubbed his head, still foggy from the beating.

Chapter 9

The shingle with black lettering hanging from a white post on a seedy lawn read: **EMILE GOLDMAN M.D.** Holding tight to the wrought iron railing with one hand, and his ribs with the other, Gary limped up the half dozen steps to the door, obeyed the *Enter* sign and walked in. Three people turned to stare at him: two elderly ladies and a shabby man about fifty, with horny, yellow toenails sticking out of a bandaged foot, and a pair of crutches occupying the chair beside him. He was smoking a cigarette.

Seeing no receptionist, Gary eased into a chair opposite the others. After looking around a few moments, his attention came back to the man. Gary pointed to the cigarette curling smoke into the air. "You can hardly do that anyplace anymore," he said.

The man seemed startled. "If it's bothering you..." he said, reaching for the ashtray.

"No, not at all."

The man looked askance at the women, who had stiffened in their seats and were already appraising Gary's dirty clothes with steely-eyed disdain.

Something strange here, Gary thought. Even though this part of town was poor and way behind the times, it seemed oddly strange... oddly out of place. He looked down at the package in his hands and around the room again. No television set? Even in the poorest ghetto you could find a television set. And no magazines, not even the tattered, year-old ones. Then again, maybe not in a doctor's office. Some doctor's office! Hard wooden chairs, wooden floor, lousy lighting, and ashtrays. Four of them.

One by one, the three before him disappeared into the back room, where they seemed to spend an eternity before finally emerging and passing him without so much as a wave of the hand or the courtesy of a nod.

"Next," the voice called from the doorway of the back room.

"Have a seat," the doctor said, motioning him into a cubicle and gesturing toward a chair. Gary took the room in at a glance. It looked primitive and reeked of medicine.

"Looks like you had a bad time," the doctor said, taking up a high stool a few feet away. He had a smooth, boyish face, thinning blond hair and liver-spotted hands.

"It could have been worse, I guess. A gang jumped me."

The doctor smiled knowingly. "Where does it hurt?" he asked, looking into his bruised eye.

"Mostly across here," Gary said, laying a hand on his chest. "And I think my mouth is cut inside. I can still taste blood."

The doctor reached for a tongue depressor and inserted it far enough into his throat to make him gag. "I don't wonder," he said. "Your teeth cut in pretty deep." He stretched for a fat cotton swab, dipped it into a jar of foul-smelling stuff and rubbed it on the inside of his cheeks.

Gary winced with the sting.

"That should be taking care of that," the doctor said, getting up. "Take off your sweater and shirt and give us a look-see."

Gingerly, Gary maneuvered his arms out of his sweater sleeves and pulled his shirt over his head. He clenched his jaw as the doctor pressed and probed, not any too gently.

"I suspect a rib fracture or two, judging by these scrapes and bruises. X-rays will tell for sure." The phone rang in another room and the doctor excused himself.

Gary felt disturbed. Things didn't seem quite right, though

he couldn't tell why. Squinting at the framed diploma on the wall above a medicine stand, he moved closer to read it. So. The doctor was a surgeon as well as a general practitioner. He had to be one of the few general practitioners around; everybody seemed to be a specialist these days. Startled, he read the date again: May 18, 1926. Of course. It must have been the doctor's father's diploma, or his grandfather's. Nice nostalgic touch for the patients, and clever way of showing that he was carrying on the family tradition. Must be quite a man, he thought, foregoing work in some affluent neighborhood to attend the poor like this.

Still...something had been unsettling him for the past hour or more, some idea trying to break through that he was reluctant to see, trying to assert itself. He glanced around the room, looking... looking for what? A plain room in what appeared to be an old converted house. Way behind the times with its green linoleum floor and, no doubt, original ceiling, a tin-like metal with a flower design stamped into it.

Moving over to the window and pushing the lace curtain aside, he took in the row of houses across the street, rather well-taken care of by their owners, he thought, and in surprisingly good condition for their age. No slum landlords here, obviously. A car scooted by down the street, black, with a high top, and another passed in the opposite direction... another old one... like the police car....

The sight of the cars jolted him. His eyes traveled around the room again...the plaster walls, porcelain sink...a radiator? Everything seemed made of wood. No plastic. He knew what he was seeing, couldn't deny what he— Could those blows to the head have affected his mind!

The door swung open and the doctor came in adjusting his stethoscope over his white jacket. "Sorry for the interruption," he said, approaching Gary and pressing the cold metal against his chest. "Sounds fine. I think you should go over to the hospital for those x-rays. Just to make sure."

"What if the x-rays show a cracked rib?" he asked. "What will they do for me at the hospital?"

"They'll tape you up."

"And if I don't go, what will you do?"

"Tape you up."

Gary checked a quick laugh and grabbed for his ribs as pain stabbed him. "In that case, Doctor Goldman, you know my answer."

The doctor didn't seem amused. "I don't have to do it, you know. And without x-rays I'm not absolutely sure it's necessary."

"Can't hurt me if it's not, can it?"

"As you wish," he grumped, his impatient hands rummaging through his medicine cabinet.

"Doctor, is there any chance, do you think, of an infection from these mouth cuts?"

"Infection is always possible," he said, cutting a strip of tape.

Hesitating, instinctively apprehensive, he asked, "Don't you think I should have a shot of penicillin?"

The doctor paused. "A shot of what?"

"Penicillin. You know, to fight off any infection."

"It must be something brand new on the market. Or experimental. If it is you're way ahead of me, lad. I haven't heard or read of it yet."

"Yes, right," Gary said, puzzled, "I probably read about it…somewhere."

"Those ribs will be uncomfortable for a while, but this should help," the doctor said, snipping the tail off the last piece of tape. "And it might be a good idea to report this assault to the police if you haven't already done so. Overall, you're in excellent health, fortunately. You'll heal quickly enough." He gathered some papers. "You can put your clothes on now and come next door to my office."

Gary slid one arm then the other into his shirt sleeves and painfully worked the shirt over his head. His sweater was too filthy to wear and he carried it with him to the next room, where the doctor was sitting at a roll-top desk filling out a form.

"Have a seat," he said. "I just need a little information for my records." He wrote down the nature of the injury and treatment, Gary's name and the false address Gary gave him, while Gary's curious eyes traveled around the room. Everything looked antique, from a dusty fan on a table to a coat rack that resembled antlers, to a tiny corner sink to a shelf with a brass, fist-sized bust of Hippocrates anchored to a cracked wooden base.

"What are you doing in this neck of the woods?" the doctor asked, looking up.

Did everybody say 'this neck of the woods'? "Just running an errand."

"You really ought to be x-rayed, Mr. Tyler. You could have some other damage."

"I'll take my chances, Doc," he said, peeking over his shoulder and seeing the date on the form: April 15, 1939. And his desk calendar said 'Friday.' No wonder the cops.... His hair stood on end. *My God!*

The doctor swiveled in his chair. "Don't do anything strenuous for at least six weeks. Until it heals completely," he said. "That will be three dollars, please."

The penicillin...1939...and he dipped his pen in a jar of ink!

"I said that will be three dollars, Mr. Tyler."

"Three—oh, sure, Doc," he said, his voice shaking as much

as the hands digging into his pockets.

"Are you all right, Mr. Tyler?" he asked, scrutinizing him. "I don't like that bump on your forehead. You have a concussion, too, you understand. You've taken quite a beating." He stood up. "Let me call the hospital and—"

"No, doctor, I feel fine. It's just that…they must have robbed me too," he said, bringing his hands out empty. "But," he added quickly, "I can mail you the money."

A hint of amusement touched the corners of the doctor's mouth, but he masked it with a serious face. "I understand," he said, extending his hand. "When you get a chance you can stop by and pay me."

"Thank you, Doctor Goldman," he said, shaking his hand and turning to leave.

"Mr. Tyler. Your package. Don't forget it."

Thanks again," he said, retrieving it. "Oh, Doc, if someone had a concussion— say, for instance, I did— would it make me hallucinate?"

"What kind of hallucinations?"

"I mean, well, could I imagine I was another person, or in another country? Or time period, like thinking I was living in the future? Or the past?"

"Are you experiencing any such thing now?"

"Oh, no, no, of course not, I was just wondering, that's all, seeing that I did bang my head pretty hard on the sidewalk."

"The mind is a very complex organ, Mr. Tyler. It's capable of almost anything you can conceive of."

"If I do have a concussion, Doc, will it take care of itself?"

The doctor smiled. "You'd better hope it does. But if you feel any dizziness, double vision or nausea, don't hesitate to get to a hospital…. And if you don't mind my asking you a question now, Mr. Tyler, who's Greg Norman?"

"Who?"

"The shirt you're wearing, that," he pointed, "with the name Greg Norman."

Gary smiled. "Oh, Greg. He's just a friend I golf with."

"I see," he said, looking puzzled. "And the name you mentioned...?"

"Name I mentioned?"

"For warding off infections?"

"Oh, that—penicillin, or something that sounds like it...."

Out on the street, Gary looked around, trying to decide the best way to get back to his car. Somehow he'd been caught up in a Twilight Zone nightmare he couldn't wake up from. Maybe he was still unconscious on the sidewalk and everything up to now had been a dream. Or maybe that crack on the head had his mind playing crazy tricks on him. The only thing he was certain of was that he wouldn't be able to walk very long or very far. Just breathing hurt. And he was getting hungry. He should've taken Grandma's roast beef instead of the cookies when he had the chance.

Thirty-five minutes later he found himself staring up at the North Division Street sign. No mistake about it, this is where he had pulled up and parked his car. Possibly towed away? He saw no signs against parking. Although the car was gone the building wasn't. Retracing his steps, he walked back to the door he had entered earlier. Same address, but with shiny numbers, same knob-less door, but with a lustrous coat of green paint, and the sign saying **Ring For Service**. Wary of another encounter with the gang, he caressed his ribs as he hurried as quickly as he could around the block to the door he had exited from. Like the rear door, it was relatively new, but this one had a handle. He tried it but it was locked.

Worry stirred in his gut as he moved off down the street. Edgy, unable to think straight, he tried to calm himself, but everything seemed out of sync, out of place, out of time.

Everything was familiar and nothing was familiar. Most disturbing of all were the few cars that passed him as he walked along. They all looked like antiques. In fact, they were antiques.

He wondered, could he be hallucinating? Could he be going mad? Could he at that very moment be at home in his room, dreaming? What other explanation could there be? It was all much too complex for a practical joke. Unless...unless what he had tried to convince Shelley of was true. Theoretically, going back in time seemed reasonable, possible, but if this actually was... if he had somehow actually slipped back.... His skin prickled at the thought and his blood ran cold.

The world seemed strangely quiet as he headed back downtown. No radios or televisions blared anywhere, no planes roared overhead, no rumbling trucks shook the pavement, no voices crying out or barking dogs. The air itself seemed a calming blanket of silence that had a subtle unsettling effect.

The sun warmed his skin, but the air carried a chill in it. The few people he saw, he saw only at a distance. A stray beagle waddled up behind him, sniffed at his heels and padded off into an alleyway.

On the opposite side of the street, farther down, he spotted a diner and crossed over to it. If this... this dream... this hallucination...this time warp were for real, he couldn't use the paper money in his wallet, not unless they didn't look at it too closely. He did have the silver dollar in his pocket, though. If he had really landed sometime in the 1930s, it would go a heck of a lot further than in his own time. Still, he was going to need some luck, lots of luck. His mind couldn't deny what his senses told him must be true. He felt scared. What in hell had he gotten himself into? And what was even more frightening, could he get out of it?

Going into the diner, Gary failed to see the man observing him from across the street.

Chapter 10

The hinges squeaked when Gary opened the door to Ernie's Diner, and the heavy smell of grease and cigarette smoke nearly closed his windpipe. The diner, an actual railroad car, was as deserted as the street. He debated between taking a padded counter stool or a wooden booth, and opted for the booth, where he had a better view of the outside. A cream pitcher, a sugar shaker, a napkin holder and an ashtray hugged the wall at the edge of the table under the windowsill where a couple of houseflies were dancing against the glass. On the wall behind the counter, in a childish scrawl, the specials of the day were chalked on a slate board:

> macaroni and cheese ....15 cents
> veg soup, roll & coffee.....20 cents
> liver and onions ....20 cents

Another list carried the usual hot dogs, hamburgers, tuna and BLT sandwiches. Here and there other signs were thumb-tacked to the wall:

IF YOU WANT YOUR PRAYERS ANSWERED
GET OFF YOUR KNEES AND HUSTLE
and
IF YOU DON'T EAT HERE WE'LL BOTH STARVE

A slender man with sunken cheeks and dark, gloomy eyes, and wearing a dirty apron rose from the far end of the counter, where he had been whistling softly over a cup of coffee and smoking a cigarette.

"Need a menu?" he asked.

"No, I think I'll have a hamburger."

"One burger coming up," he said, whistling his way over to the grill behind the counter."

"You'd better make it two, Ernie. And a cup of coffee."

"Two burgers coming up," he said, slapping the patties on the grill. "Name's Toby, by the way. Ernie died a couple of years ago— heart attack they said. I took the joint off Mae's hands. Mae's his widow." He moseyed over to a fat stainless steel urn, where he poured the coffee into a white mug and, sticking a spoon in it, carried it steaming over to the table. "Never changed the sign 'cause everybody said it was bad luck. Would've have made no difference one way or t'other, though, not after they shut down the hair oil factory up the street. Hurt the business, but I get by all right." He gave Gary a quick once-over. "Must be new around here."

"Well, it's not exactly my neck of the woods" Gary said, stirring sugar in his cup.

"Looking for work, I s'pose?"

Gary shrugged.

"Like everybody else. Jobs ain't easy to get these days. You got a trade?"

"I'm almost finished with school," he said, blowing on his coffee. "I hope to be a teacher."

Toby's thick eyebrows lifted. "College boy?"

"In the meantime I could use a few dollars to help carry me."

"Not cheap, I hear, them colleges. A couple of hundred a year?"

"At least."

"Quite a hunk of change. You maybe could try your luck at one of the factories in the neighborhood. I heard they might be taking on some help at the cereal company down on Exchange

Street."

"I guess I can try that," Gary said, looking toward the grill.

Toby took the hint and shuffled back behind the counter. "Yep, things are tough all over," he said, talking over his shoulder as he flipped the hamburgers and set them sizzling anew.

Gary watched, fascinated, as, first one, then three more cars passed down the street. If, as he suspected, he had lost his mind and was living in some internal world, then insanity wasn't as bad as he thought. He could think of worse scenarios, far worse. He stretched his neck a little to see a green truck pulling up to the curb in front of the houses across the street. An ice truck. A real ice truck! Just like Gramps described. And there were kids chasing behind and reaching into the bed to scoop up ice chips to suck on, just like he said. Clearly, he could see a man with white hair and a black, long-sleeved shirt sitting behind the wheel of what had to be at best a door-less 1930 model truck. It looked like an antique Ford.

Toby scooped the hamburgers onto the buns. "Anything on the burgers?"

"Just ketchup," Gary said, watching the truck pull ahead a few houses.

Toby set the hamburgers in front of him and a bottle of ketchup. More coffee?"

"If you don't mind," he said, wincing against the cuts inside his mouth.

Toby picked up the cup and carried it around to the urn. "So where you staying?"

"I'm still looking. Any suggestions?"

"Matter of fact, my sister Elsie rents out rooms. Nice place, not fancy, but nice. Only a couple of streets over." He set the fresh coffee on the table and sat on a counter stool across from Gary. "I can't say for sure if she's got any open now, but no harm trying. Just tell her it's me that sent you."

"Thanks, I will."

"Things are tough all over, but Roosevelt's gonna straighten it all out yet, wait and see."

"Him or the war?"

"What's that?" he said, leaning forward and cupping his hand behind his ear.

"Nothing. Just thinking out loud."

"Been awhile since the Crash. I kinda thought by now things would come around, but—"

"That would've been...how many years ago now?"

"Ten years this October. How could anybody forget! Of course, then you had to be just a kid."

"I should know anyway. You'll have to excuse me. I had an accident. It left me a little bent out of shape."

"Bent out of— hey, that's pretty good, saying it that way. College talk?"

"You could say that."

Toby lit a cigarette. "I noticed you looked kinda rough when you came in. What happened... and what's your name anyway?"

"Gary Tyler."

"Tyler...Tyler... Any relation to Bill Tyler, William Tyler? Used to run a garage up on Cherry Street?"

"No, not that I know of."

"Nice guy. Real nice guy. Moved away a couple of years ago, Arizona, I heard. For his health. TB, I think... So what happened, you get run over by a car or somethin'?"

Gary wiped ketchup from his fingers. "I steped in where I didn't belong and a gang of guys let me know it. They took everything except what's in my pockets and my little package here."

Toby looked him over. "Gotta watch those toughs... Those

the only clothes you got, what's on your back?"

The door squeaked open and Toby spun around on his stool. "Sebastian," he said, rolling his eyes up. "Running a little late today?" he said, uncrossing his legs getting up and moseying around behind the counter.

Sebastian settled himself on a stool near the door and folded his hands in front of him. "Late, early, what difference does it make?" he said. "Yesterday, today, tomorrow, before you know it we're all in the marble orchard pushing up daisies and making the worms fat."

"Thanks, I needed some cheering up," Toby said. "The usual?"

"If it's beef barley, yeah, and make sure it's hot."

"How much do I owe you, Toby?" Gary asked, rising and moving over to the cash register.

"Thirty-five centavos."

Gary slipped the silver dollar from his pocket and laid it on the counter.

"This'd burn the asshole out of the Devil himself," Toby said to Sebastian, setting the steaming bowl of soup before him and coming over to the register, where he picked up the coin, pressed the levers that popped open the drawer and dropped it in. "And sixty-five centavos change."

"About your sister's place?"

"Oh, that, yep." He took the stub pencil from behind his ear, licked the tip, drew a sketch on a napkin and wrote down the address. "Big white house on the corner, with a big porch, green trim and a little white fence in front. You can't miss it."

"I'd hate to go up to the door looking like this," Gary said, not unmindful of Sebastian giving him the once-over twice-over. "Is there a clothing store close by?"

"Out the door, steer right and straight toward downtown. Follow your nose and you'll come to it. Before you get to it is a second-hand store, if that suits your pocket book better. Should have most anything you want."

"Thanks," Gary said, heading out, his package firmly tucked under his arm.

Toby called after him. "I don't know who this Greg Norman guy is, but I'll be damned if I let anybody put his name on my shirt or anything else I paid for."

Chapter 11

Two meager light bulbs did little to dispel the deep gloom of the store, and probably nothing could have masked the stuffy odor of old clothes jammed tight on floor racks so closely spaced you could barely move between them. A diminutive man barely five feet tall, with a gray mop of hair and a ragged mustache to match, seemed to materialize from nowhere.

"Yes, sir, can I help you?" he asked, shuffling up behind Gary and rubbing his hands together as if washing them.

"I need something presentable and cheap," Gary said, a little dismayed by what he was seeing as he browsed through the clothes.

"I don't have cheap but I do have inexpensive. There's a difference, you know," the old man said, his blue, marble eyes glistening behind his wire-rimmed glasses, and commenting on every article of clothing that Gary touched. "Guaranteed, like new... ahh, now that one is beautiful," he said, dragging out the 'beautiful,' and gesturing with clasped hands toward a suit Gary was holding up to catch the light. "Just came in yesterday. So good I almost hate to sell it... but a good looking boy like you, such big shoulders... I give you a bargain price, special, you can't beat it, if you take it right now." His puckered mouth made his mustache droop when Gary squeezed the suit back into the rack.

Finally, after much pondering, Gary picked out a tweed jacket and dark brown trousers. He set his package aside and slipped on the jacket. "Looks all right to me," he said, tugging at the sleeves. "What do you think?"

"Ahh, very nice, very nice. Fills your shoulders out, too.

Perfect."

Gary held the pants against his own. "I don't think I have to try these on, do you?"

"Shirts you need now, too, to go with it. Over here," he said, tossing the clothes over his arm and hobbling between the racks to a shelf along the wall. "Beautiful selection here, look yourself, you see."

Gary selected two white shirts and the old man laid a yellow-and-brown striped tie across the jacket. "See how nice this goes with it? Very nice, but not as nice as with the suit over there you saw I would give you a good price on." He shrugged.

"Maybe we better forget the whole—"

"No no no," the old man said fairly jumping out of his shoes and grabbing up the shirts. "In these clothes you look like a duke, I guarantee it, a prince, even."

"I don't need two white shirts. How about one and a sport shirt?"

"I have just what you want right here," he said, hopping to another counter and holding up a blue-and-red checked shirt."

"Okay. How much for the shirts?"

"Twenty-five cents each."

"Twenty-five cents!"

"All right all right," he said irritably, "fifteen cents."

"Good. How much for everything?"

"Pants and jacket—five dollars, two shirts, thirty cents, and fifteen cents for the tie. Altogether, five dollars fifty cents."

"You sure you figured that right?" Gary said, turning sideways to the old man and the light as he pulled a twenty dollar bill from his wallet.

The man slapped his sweaty forehead. "What am I thinking— five dollars *forty-five* cents, of course, not *fifty* cents," he said, squinting at the bill and folding it over the top of the neat wad he took from his pocket. From the bottom, he counted out fourteen singles, squeezing each one between thumb and forefinger before releasing them. "And fifty-five cents," he said, taking the change from his opposite pocket and dropping it in Gary's hand. Packing the clothes neatly in a brown shopping bag he took from beneath the shelf, he handed it over.

"Any time you're in the market," he said, following Gary and bowing him out the door, "any time you need something first-class, I'm here, best prices in town." He called after him. "That suit I was telling you about, believe me, I raise my right hand to God, the honest truth, it would cost you, I swear it, at least twenty-five dollars anyplace else...."

* * * * *

A block down on the opposite side of the street, Gary spotted a Greyhound bus depot sign. So much walking was making him puff, and making his ribs ache. Passers-by looked askance and gave him wide berth as he crossed over and made his way along, shifting the packages from one hand to the other.

Once inside the station, he found the men's room, where he went inside a stall, stripped off his dirty clothes and stuffed them in the bag, and put on the pants and white shirt. The fit wasn't perfect, but not too bad, either. The outfit wasn't exactly color-coordinated, but from what he'd seen others wearing, it was better than most.

Hung high up on the wall above the toilet was a wooden box, *just like the one Michael Corleone found the gun stashed behind in the Godfather movie.* He couldn't resist giving the dangling chain a yank and gave a start with the explosion of the flush. Relieving himself, he flushed again, ready this time for the explosion, washed his hands and face at the sink and ran wet fingers through his hair. He didn't think he looked too bad, all things considered. A few lumps and bruises spoiled the smooth terrain of his face, but being freshened up and with his new clothes, he thought he could get by.

Chapter 12

The walk was hard and seemed especially long, but he found the boarding house without any trouble, climbed the porch steps and knocked on the front door. A hefty, square-faced woman chewing a wad of gum, and looking closer to sixty than fifty years old, opened the door and stepped onto the porch. Her pendulous breasts hung loose behind a baggy house dress with a red-and-black flower pattern. Her lipstick matched her bright-red toenails protruding from her torn slippers. "This better not be no sales pitch," she said frowning.

Unabashedly looking him up and down and side to side, she seemed to be more interested in studying him like a laboratory specimen than in listening to what he had to say.

"…and he said to tell you your favorite brother sent me."

"My ass. Come on, don't let the cold in," she said, holding the door open and leading him down the hall. The room had a single bed over which the bedspread undulated; a dresser; an overstuffed, velvety armchair; a night stand with an ash tray on it; a card table and two folding chairs with *Tanner's Funeral Home* stamped on the back; a sink; an ice box; a makeshift cardboard closet; and a window with limp white curtains over the shade. A skimpy throw rug covered a bare wooden floor.

"Toby wasn't lying," he said. "It is clean."

"He's a sweetheart all right, that kid brother of mine."

"How much?" he asked.

"Five dollars a week? In advance."

Posing it as a question told him she'd take less. "Five dollars!"

"I suppose I could take four," she said, bitterness lacing her words.

He hesitated, looked toward the door and said, "I'll take it for three."

He could see her face flush behind a scowl as she turned her back on him and stepped outside the room. "Okay. Toilet, sink and bathtub's down the side. Don't hog it. And don't leave no ring around the tub when you're done." Her mouth twisted with the words. "Others live here, too, you know."

He dropped his packages on the chair and followed her out. "Could you possibly supply me with a couple of towels and soap?"

"Fifty cents for that."

She tried to peek over his shoulder as he turned sideways and peeled off four singles. "Let's make it a dollar, okay?"

She softened. "If you need anything more, just knock, first door there on the left. That's my apartment." She turned to face him directly. "Turn out the lights when you go out, and no parties, no guests past ten, and no ladies— ever!"

She tried to squeeze a little more information out of him, but he edged himself back into his room and shut the door. Pressing his ear against the door, he listened to her footsteps falling heavily on the wooden floor until they stopped with the slam of a door.

He pulled the key out of the keyhole, recognized it as a skeleton key— one that would probably open every door in the place— stuck it back in the hole, turned it and left it in place, locked. Slipping out of his jacket, he eased himself down on the edge of the bed and bounced lightly a few times to get the feel of it. Then, running his hands at his sides over the lumpy mattress to brace himself, he slowly lowered himself with a long, drawn-out groan. His ribs ached, his mouth was dry and his eyes burned. He closed his eyes trying to let go, to relax, to forget for a while, but he couldn't relax, couldn't allow himself that luxury, not yet, not until he figured out what was going on and what he was going to do to get straight again.

Money. He needed money and all he had left in his wallet was a twenty, a ten, and a single— thirty-one dollars, money he'd have to be exceptionally careful about spending. That, plus the fourteen good singles the old man gave him... and fifty-five cents... and sixty-five cents change from the diner, that's... a dollar twenty more. So, fourteen dollars and a dollar twenty is fifteen dollars and twenty cents, minus the four he paid for the room... leaves a little over eleven dollars in good money to his name.

Thinking tired him out, but he couldn't let up, not now, not yet. Assuming he hadn't gone mad— and he wasn't quite sure he hadn't— he really had found a way to the past, to 1939, to a time long before he was born. All because of a newspaper ad that he'd answered on a crazy whim! For years he'd fantasized over going back in time, just as his grandfather and millions of others had, but actually doing it, having it become a reality, gave it a whole new coloration. Maybe if he had known it was coming, had anticipated it, he could have prepared for it, given some time to thinking of the problems he'd have to face and be ready for them. But this way, he might just as well have been dropped from an aircraft into an alien world. He couldn't even contemplate the kind of pitfalls or the number of pitfalls that lay ahead. No doubt about it, the more he thought of it, the more certain he was that he was walking through a minefield. How did that saying go, 'Be careful what you wish for...'?

The larger question was even more troubling than he ever could have imagined: Am I trapped in the past? So far it seemed so, but he wasn't about to give up on that yet. He would definitely go back to the warehouse where he'd picked up his package, go during business hours. And what of his own time, was it still moving? Would Grandma be worried to death over his disappearance? And Shelley, what must she be thinking?

Then again, how could time be progressing in the future when the future had not yet arrived? The thought comforted him. By the same logic, though, how could he be here if he hadn't yet been born? He let out a small groan, his mind whirling with these contradictions in logic. Or paradoxes. Whatever the answer, he'd have to be alert to what he said and did. Already thinking about it all was driving him crazy. Too much at once! How could he sleep now, with these questions on his mind, his bones aching and that damned gruesome light from the ceiling fixture shining in his eyes. He eased himself up from the bed. A walk, a little walk, casual, not too strenuous, to get out and get the feel of the times, to breathe some fresh air and not think at all, at least not for a while. He grabbed his jacket and snapped off the light.

Stepping out on the front porch, he was surprised to see a girl about his own age sitting in a wicker chair, her legs crossed and her hands folded over her lap. "Hi," he said, pausing beside her.

Startled, she glanced up, her brown eyes wide with surprise. "Oh, hello," she said, pulling a blue shawl down from her chin and tugging at the hem of her skirt.

"I'm Gary Tyler. I took a room here this afternoon." He held out his hand.

"I know. Mrs. Harmon told my—"

"Don't get up," he said, taking her extended hand. "And you're…?"

"Sarah." Her mouth formed a small smile. "Sarah Montera." Her eyes, warm and soft as her voice, lowered to their clasped hands.

He jerked his hand away as if from a hot stove. "Sorry. Have you lived here long… Sarah?"

She stood up, putting a more comfortable distance between

them. "Almost a year, I think. I live in the one of the back apartments with my mother." She gazed into his eyes a moment, then lowered her own with a little-girl shyness he found oddly appealing, so different from Shelley's, whose eyes were never anything but cool-blue and unwavering .

"Well, it's nice to have you for a neighbor," he said, backing off a bit. "Maybe sometime… we can have a talk, that is, when you have nothing better to do… and if you feel like it. You can clue me in on the neighborhood."

"Clue you in…?"

A mistake, he thought, answering her frown with a smile. "You know, tell me where things are around here, like the drug store, grocery store, like that."

"That would be nice," she said. "My mother wouldn't mind, I'm sure." Again she smiled demurely. "I'm not so sure about Mrs. Harmon, though."

"Why should she mind, she's only the landlady?"

Clasping her hands together in front of her pulled her shoulders in, which made her appear even more frail than she already was. "You can't say 'only.' Mrs. Harmon's pretty strict."

"Still, I don't think she'd mind two of her tenants having a conversation on the porch. I mean, she doesn't have the right. This isn't a POW camp."

"A what?"

Damn! "It's still a free country, isn't it?"

Sarah shrugged. "I guess you're right."

"Good," he said, giving a little wave and starting down the steps. "Maybe we can do it soon…if you want to. I'm taking a little stroll right now."

"How long will you be staying here…Gary? If I may ask."

"I don't know for sure. It depends," he said, seeing her smile as he stepped off down the street toward the intersection.

Chapter 13

Conscious of the pain that could spike at any second, he walked stiffly, his feet slapping the pavement, heading toward downtown. His mind wasn't on any particular destination, but on the girl, on Sarah. And she remembered his name, too. The image of her standing there on the porch refused to leave his mind. Something about that girl...not so much the way she stood there like a wraith, nor the nearly black hair that waved down and seemed to secretly shield her pale face, nor the haunting— or haunted— brown eyes, now wide and innocent, now narrow and shrewd, eyes that seemed to take him in little pieces at a time, like quick snapshots, or pixels putting together a composite picture— No, it was something more than all that, something compelling and alluring that seemed to invite him, to beckon him.

At the intersection, he stood looking around, deciding on a direction. Neighborhood taverns took up three corners, one next to a shop with the words **GUS'S SHOE REPAIR** under a picture of a gargantuan, black boot painted on the window. The idea of a drink suddenly appealed to him. It beat walking and would give him a chance to rest the bones already beginning to ache in his chest.

From out of bright sunshine he stepped into a gloomy bar called **WINDY'S**. A honky-tonk piano played under the stink of stale beer, cigar smoke and dirty cat litter that almost knocked him back out the door. The place was deserted except for the bartender, wiping big circles down the bar, a bald-headed man sleeping face down at a corner table with a half a glass of beer at his fingertips, and someone sitting at an upright piano along the wall on the far side of the bar room. Just like the old black-and-white movies, Gary thought.

The bartender, a beefy guy about thirty years old, with thick, hairy arms and a crew cut looked up. "What can I getcha, friend?" he asked, tossing the rag under the counter.

"I'll have a beer," Gary said, leaning against the bar and sliding a foot up on the brass rail.

"Bottle or tap?"

"Make it tap."

"What kind?" His husky voice complemented his husky build.

Gary looked up at the advertisements plastered on the walls. "Iroquois."

"Gottcha."

Gary watched the foam rise in the glass and spill over the sides as the golden yellow liquid swelled up from the bottom.

"New in this neck of the woods, or just stopping by?" the bartender asked, leaving a wet trail with the glass as he slid it over the bar.

"I just moved in down the street this afternoon." He sucked in some of the foam, enjoying the sweetness but not the bitter aftertaste.

The man at the table lifted his bald head. "Hey, Nick, will you play *My Buddy?*"

The old upright plinked out the notes and the old man smiled, teary-eyed.

Gary turned around to look, then said, "I don't see any music in front of him."

"Nick don't need none. Comes right out of his head straight to his fingers. He's here morning to night. You can't tear him away from that piano. He don't talk to nobody, just hears things inside his head and plays. Music's his world."

"Hey, Sam, gimme another beer will ya? for chrissake."

"You already got one, Gordy, right in front of you."

"I do?" he said, looking cross-eyed at his glass before his wobbly head thunked back to the table.

Sam turned back to Gary. "Whaja get a job around here or somethin'?"

"I'm hoping to get a teaching job."

"Oh, schoolmarm, huh?" He almost sneered the words.

"I guess," Gary said, ignoring the hostile note, and tipping up his glass.

Glasses clinked as Sam's hands splashed water over them under the bar. "I always admired college people. I got an education, too, but in the School of Hard Knocks." He smiled a not-too-genuine smile. "How 'bout I test ya, for the helluvit?"

Gary didn't miss the sarcasm. "What kind of test?"

"Questions. A couple of questions. Say, three."

"What do I get if I answer them correctly?"

"You get a beer."

"Three questions, one beer. That's not fair."

"Okay, three beers." He pointed a hairy finger. "But you gotta get all three right to collect."

"And if I miss?"

"See that chalkboard over there?" He pointed across the room. "That's Charlie Modum's famous Wall of Shame. Lose and your name gets put there— in big, bold letters. Then you get the big heehaw from me and anybody else who walks in here. Leo Sorge's name just came off. Stays there a whole week, anybody who loses. Now we're looking for new blood. You still game?"

Gary smiled across to him and took a sip. He knew that, in the eyes of the bartender, he was a country bumpkin, a lamb being set up for the slaughter, a sucker waiting to be taken, but he felt strangely confident in this new environment, and in some odd way, superior, as if he were dealing with children.

He didn't know why, but he exuded a cockiness, even an arrogance that he didn't particularly like in himself, especially since that wasn't his nature, at least he didn't think it was. Apparently getting your name on the wall was pretty disgraceful to these people, but he didn't see it as all that bad. "But your name doesn't go up there if you lose?"

"That's right, kid. I just buy the beers."

"All right, go ahead."

"Hey, you're a sport," Sam said, winking at him. "I like that. Okay." He looked up, thinking or, as Gary perceived it, pretending to think. "Okay, I got one. What planet is farthest away from the sun?"

"Pluto," Gary snapped back.

Sam's mouth dropped open. "That's right, that's right. I guess that one was easy, too easy, especially for a college kid."

"I suppose you're right," Gary said, lifting his glass. "You could have asked me how far from the sun Pluto is, now that would have been really tough."

Sam eyed him suspiciously, vigorously wiping a glass, sensing a trap, then said, "Okay, college boy, how far *is* Pluto from the sun?"

"Is that the second question?"

Sam hesitated, then said, "Yeah, I'll make it the second question."

"Pluto, ninth planet in the solar system, and smallest, 3,500 million miles, or roughly, three and a half billion miles, discovered about seventy— I mean, about nine or ten years ago."

Sam's face went chalky. "Goddamn, I thought you were bluffin'. You set me up for that. Snookered me. You said that would be a tough one."

"It is a tough one, ask anybody, but I didn't say I didn't know the answer." He raised his glass for another sip.

"Yeah, well, besides, how do I know your answer's right, that it's that far?"

"You're supposed to know the answer to your own questions. But it's right. Look it up if you don't believe me."

"I will. You can bet your ass I will."

"That's two down, one to go."

Sam lips went tight and white with concentration. "Okay, here's one for you... you know what a stirrup is?"

"Is that the question?"

"Hell no. I just want to know if you know."

"Sure. That's what you put your foot into when—"

"You got it. And—this ain't no question, neither— you know what an anvil is?"

"That would be a piece of iron blacksmiths use to—"

"Okay, you got it, you got it. Easy, right? Now the question is— and I don't mean those answers you just gave— the question is, whereabouts in your body can you find a stirrup and an anvil?"

"Are they in your body, too?"

"Of course they are! Everybody's got'm." He folded his hairy arms tight across the barrel of his chest and smirked.

"You said anvil and stirrup? Did I *hear* you right? In the body. Is that the question?"

"That's right," he said, shaking his head up and down, the smirk fading.

"Anvil and stirrup. And my *ears* did *hear* those two exact words, anvil and stirrup."

Sam's smirk dissolved to a scowl. "Yeah, I said that's right, anvil and stirrup anvil and stirrup."

"Then I did *hear* what I thought I *heard* and I'm not going *deaf.*"

Sam balled up the towel and flung it down on the bar. "Naw, you ain't goin' deaf. C'mon, c'mon, answer the goddamned question, I know you know it, and quit the crap."

"Hey, Sam," Gordy called, "how's about another beer here."

"Shut up, Gordy, and go back to sleep."

"Bones in the ear," Gary said, draining his glass.

Sam looked at him hard and long, then picked up the cloth and began furiously shining glasses. He glowered and muttered and moped around behind the bar. After a while, he said, half-apologetically, "Y'know, kid, I guess maybe you're all right. Wha' cher name?"

"Gary," he said, noting that he was calling him 'kid,' and he couldn't have been more than a few years older than himself.

"I'm Sam," he said, reaching over and shaking hands. "Yeah, you're okay in my book, Gary. Nobody around here can answer those questions. I get 'em out of almanacs. You're the first time I got to buy. My hat's off to you. I guess I was a little off base there. You're smart all right. I gotta hand it to ya. Smart like my brother. The old man paid for his college, but no dice for me. Haven't seen him in years, my brother, that is."

"Hey, Nick," Gordy crowed, "play *That Old Gang of Mine.* And if I don't get some goddamned service over here, Sam, I'm taking my business someplace else."

Gary looked up at the clock and pushed away from the bar.

"Hitcha again?" Sam said, holding up the empty glass.

"No thanks, Sam. It's five-thirty already." He dug into his pocket. "How much—"

"Forget it," Sam said, waving him off. "It's on the house. Sort of to make up for my being a wisenheimer. And I still owe you three free ones. But I'm warning ya, I'm still gonna check those numbers you spouted off like a scientist. Stop back when ya get a chance," he called after him. "Later in the day is best, when the locals bounce in. Always better on weekends." He laughed. "We get a lot of dummies around here. Maybe you could learn 'em a thing or two." He laughed again and went back to wiping down the bar.

The piano was playing *That Old Gang of Mine* as Gary went out the door, smiling.

Sam had given him an idea.

Chapter 14

Walking cautiously, Gary headed down the street toward his room. Just breathing hurt his chest.

When in pain, distract yourself. That's what his Grandpa used to say when he'd pull him onto his lap to watch a television movie after he had fallen and hurt himself. 'Distract yourself.' So he distracted himself, looking up at the trees beginning to bud, and crowning over the narrow street like a delicate canopy of green, shadowing houses fronting porches upstairs and down, and so closely spaced there was barely room for a walkway between them. Here and there someone popped out and disappeared just as quickly.

A car raced toward him, and close behind it, hugging the curb, rumbled a truck spraying stiff jets of water onto the street. He stepped back between two houses as it roared past in a misty cloud, its huge revolving, whisker-like brushes scouring the pavement beneath it. *A city street cleaner, just like Gramps had described it!* He stepped back out onto the wet sidewalk and watched the truck go by like some huge water beast chasing prey, leaving in its wake cool drafts of its fresh, damp breath.

At the corner of the block, he paused to let a car pass, and was about to step off the curb when he saw a sign farther down the cross street: Adelaide's Delicatessen. He recognized it as what he called a Mom and Pop store. No big supermarkets in this day and age. He remembered too his grandpa telling him of getting the most delicious cold cuts there ever— salami, ham, baloney, liverwurst, *Not like the tasteless garbage they dish out today!* And he smiled remembering his Grandma joking, *That's right, Honey, Grampa likes tasty garbage.*

Stenciled across the bottom of one of the two windows flanking the doorway was an advertisement for *Salada Tea.* Across the bottom of the other was one for *Rich's Ice Cream.* A bell tinkled when he opened the door and, except for the faint odor of saw dust, a bouquet of smells he couldn't immediately identify wafted over him and made him a little heady.

He picked his bread and mustard off the shelves while the young girl behind the counter hefted the loaf of baloney onto the machine and set it whirring.

"Is there a drug store nearby?" he asked, watching the deliberate motion of her pale arms pushing the meat against the blade, its humming forced to a deeper pitch under the load as it guillotined in and lopped off the slices....

She worked just as fast as she spoke, wrapped his order and gave him directions. He paid, took up his package, thanked her and left.

* * * * *

And there it was, Sid's Pharmacy, just as she said it would be. He climbed the few cracked concrete steps and went inside, where he ordered his shaving gear and passed his bad one dollar bill. Within minutes, he was on his way home.

Despite the evening air chilling down, Gary worked up a light sweat walking back to his room. Slowly, he climbed the porch steps, disappointed not to see Sarah sitting there, though he really didn't know why he should feel that way. The air in the hallway was heavy with the smell of cabbage cooking somewhere in the house. Back in his room, he shut the door, snapped on the light and sat on the bed with his packages on his lap. When his breathing had evened out, he got up, pulled the card table close to the bed, sat on the edge of the bed and pulled the table in close. His knees fit just right beneath it. He unwrapped his food and realized he had no utensils. He dreaded having to ask the landlady but he had no choice.

Softly he knocked on her door, waited a moment or so, and knocked again. He stepped back when the door swung open and she stood glaring at him. "I heard you the first time. Don't you have any patience?"

"I'm sorry, Mrs. Harmon," he said, "I don't mean to disturb you, but do you have a knife I could borrow?"

"A knife! What for?" She smirked. "You gonna kill somebody?"

"Just a butter knife or anything I can use to spread some mustard with."

"You eatin' in your room?"

"Well, I didn't get a chance to stop at Toby's, so I picked up some lunch meat. I figured I could make myself a sandwich."

Her eyes narrowed on him as she considered. "If I knew you were going to be staying any length of time, I could've rented you a room with a little kitchen. I still got one left upstairs." She looked him up and down. "But you don't look like the type that can cook. And I don't think you'd want to spend the extra money… Okay, step inside and wait."

The apartment had a close smell of old perspiration and was filled with stuffed furniture made of a velvety material. Embroidered lamps stood on ornate end tables on each side of the couch, above which a picture of a pheasant hung. In a corner near a heavily draped window stood an empty bird cage. A thin carpet of faded colors deadened the sound of her footsteps when she came back into the parlor. She handed over the knife. "Keep it. And any garbage you make, take to the back of the house. Put it in one of the cans and make sure the cover's on tight. I don't want no rats or roaches running around here any place. I run a clean place here."

"I understand," he said, taking the knife by the handle. "Thanks very much."

"You think you're gonna want some ice?"

To his puzzled look she said, "For your ice box."

"That's probably a good idea."

"I should think so. Your box holds twenty-five pounds. That's fifteen cents. He's due on Monday, the iceman, but you can pay me and I'll pay him. I don't intend to get stuck with nobody's bill, not anymore."

"Sure," he said, reaching into his pocket. "Here's a quarter."

"I'll have to go get the change," she said, her sour face contemplating the coin in her hand.

"That's all right, you keep it."

"Well, if you insist," she said, softening. "You want me to let him in, or are you going to be home? He comes early, about ten o'clock."

"I'll be home."

"Oh, and I can let you have a hot plate if you want it. Two-burner. A quarter a week."

"That sounds real good, Mrs. Harmon."

"See me tomorrow. I don't want to be bothered hunting it up tonight."

Back in his room, Gary made himself a sandwich and wolfed it down.

Holding the table to help himself up, he slid it back in place. Stuffing his toothpaste and new toothbrush in his pocket, he grabbed the garbage and stepped out into the dim hallway. He could see light through a glass panel in the door at the rear of the house, and headed back that way, passing the bathroom and a staircase to the upstairs on the way. Outside, he found the garbage can hidden under a little shed-like shelter, dragged it out, lifted the lid, dumped his garbage inside, and placed the lid back tight, per Mrs. Harmon's orders. Surrounding the dirt patch that passed as a yard were crowded together two-story houses with steep roofs and narrow windows, some glowing with soft lights.

Taking a couple of deep breaths of fresh air, he stepped back inside, startling a man just emerging from the bathroom. Standing fixed for a moment, the man stared at Gary, his eyes wide beneath bushy eyebrows, as if too surprised to move, then suddenly, he bowed his head, mumbled some greeting and took the staircase up. Gary stood a moment, listening to his quick footsteps reach the landing and thump down the hallway, apparently toward the front of the house, where they faded and died behind a closing door.

Gary shrugged, took his toothpaste and toothbrush from his pocket, and went into the bathroom. Only then did he remember— he never got his soap and towel from Mrs. Harmon. Tomorrow he'd get them, first thing in the morning. And he'd have to buy a comb for himself, too.

He forgot about the chill he'd felt when the stranger with the bushy eyebrows of old movie star Oscar Homolka stared at him....

Chapter 15

Eyelids fluttering to a baby's urgent cry, somewhere, Gary rolled over and buried his head in his pillow to drown out the noise, but the sudden twist awakened the pain in his ribs, and he rolled back, groaning himself awake. Gradually, his eyes adjusted to the weak light seeping in between the drawn window shade and the sill. For a long moment he lay still, fighting against the images forcing themselves upon him, then, finally, relenting and letting it all come back, all come together, the memory of the events parading before his mind's eye like an Alice in Wonderland dream. He still didn't believe it!

Easing himself up, he looked around at the unfamiliar surroundings. He had to believe. It was that or accept the fact he'd descended into total madness. He wasn't about to concede to madness. Not yet, anyway.

Putting on his new sport shirt slowly, he ran his fingers through his hair, patted down the high spots, and bent carefully to put on his shoes. He raised the shade to let the light in, and saw that the room was both better and worse for it. Better because it chased away the awful gloom of the gruesome ceiling light, and worse because it magnified the flaws in the scarred furniture, the dingy wallpaper, the cracked plaster ceiling. Taking his package off the dresser, he tore the wrappings away, reached in, separated a watch from its cardboard container, pulled it out and tried to put it on, but the band was too small. He put the watch in his pocket, reminding himself to get another band.

From the small shelf above the sink he took his razor, toothpaste and toothbrush and crossed the room, mindful of making no sudden moves that could cause him pain. Closing his door behind him, he headed to the landlady's apartment, but before he could knock— his hand still in the air— the door swung open.

"I heard you coming," she said, thrusting out a towel, washcloth and a bar of soap. "You're not so light on your feet."

He took his things, wanting to say, *Neither are you, lady*. Instead he said, "Thank you, Mrs. Harmon," and went down the hall to the bathroom.

A few minutes later, back in his room, freshened and clean-shaven, he put his things away and slipped on his jacket. He felt intimidated by the prospect of a new day. But what was the alternative. Until he could get back to his own time, he'd have to stay cool, bide his time and, above all, make no mistakes that could get him in trouble. That might be harder to do than it sounds.

Twisting the knob a time or two after locking his door, he shoved the key in his pocket and went out past Mrs. Harmon's apartment, down the porch steps to the street.

* * * * *

Ten minutes later, winded, his ribs aching, he stepped inside the restaurant, where Toby was busy behind the counter, whistling to himself as he flipped the bacon, writhing and spitting grease at him. Toby glanced over his shoulder. "Tyler... Bill?"

"Gary," he said, moving to the booth he'd occupied the last time there.

"What am I talking about, sure, Gary, Gary Tyler....I talked to my sister. She said you're all set up. Glad she had room for you." He chuckled. "Don't let her put you off with her tough talk. She's really a sweetheart."

"That's what she says about you, that you're a sweetheart."

"Hey, sweetheart," a man at the end of the counter said, "this time burn the bacon instead of the toast." He laughed.

Toby dropped his spatula on the sideboard and wiped his hands on the half apron he wore tied around his waist. "Coffee, Gary?"

"Eggs, too, and bacon, well done," Gary said, taking out his watch, setting the time by the wall clock and winding it.

"Hey, Toby, what's the difference between burnt bacon and well-done bacon?" the man down at the end called. He laughed again.

"Funny, Earl, very funny," Toby said, going back around the counter.

"Looking for work today, Gary?" Toby asked.

"Not on a Saturday. Anyway, I have some errands to run first. Maybe you can tell me, is there a store nearby where I can get some odds and ends stuff?"

"Sure," he said, cracking eggs on the grill and covering them with a metal lid. "A little shop that sells all kind of things, only a block from here. You probably passed it and didn't even notice. Kind of pushed back off the street. Used to be blacksmith shop when I was a kid. A couple of doors from the corner gas station." He pointed with the spatula. "You'll see a sign in the window… unless you want to go downtown to a Five and Dime store. Stuff could be even cheaper there but it's a longer walk."

"There you go, Earl," he said, setting his order in front of him. "Like you said, burnt bacon…. More coffee?" he asked, automatically taking up his mug and going over to refill it.

His double chin resting on his chest, Earl picked up his fork and poked at the bacon. "Burnt doesn't mean make it disappear," he said, brooding over the dish.

Toby sneered. "You want me to make you up some more?"

77

"I don't have the time to spare," Earl said, pouting his displeasure.

"One more thing, Toby," Gary said, "is there someplace I can get some clothes cleaned around here?"

"You mean dry cleaning or just plain washing?"

"I'm not sure, maybe both."

"Well, Overnight Cleaners ain't too far, maybe three, four short blocks from where you're staying. Just washing, ask my sister. She'll do it in her cellar for you." He chuckled. "But not for nothing." He chuckled again as he fixed up the plate. "She's a real business woman." He went back to whistling a tune while he finished up Gary's order and placed it before him.

Gary scarfed down his breakfast in record time.

"Why didn't you say you didn't like it," Toby said, his smile showing brown teeth as he cleared the table.

"A quarter, right?" Gary said, reaching into his pocket.

"Twenty-five centavos it is."

Gary laid down the quarter and a dime tip. He motioned Toby close. "Tell your friend at the end there," he whispered into his ear, "tell him that burnt bacon is loaded with carcinogens."

Puzzled, Toby whispered back. "What's that?"

"Carcinogens. Chemical change in the bacon. Can cause cancer. Can kill him." He got up.

Toby took up the money. "Thanks," he said, moving away toward the door with Gary.

Gary stopped near the register to get a toothpick as Toby leaned over to Earl. He was just closing the door behind him when he heard Earl's strained voice: "Who the fuck made *him* a doctor!"

* * * * *

78

Gary found the little sundries shop without any trouble, went inside and picked out what he needed, including a pocket knife he spied at the last minute and thought might come in handy sometime. The lady scrolled up the bag, handed it to him and he left.

Snugging his package against his chest as he walked slowly past rows of neighborhood houses, Gary wondered if his ribs would have popped out by now if the doctor hadn't taped his chest the way he did, good and tight. He slipped his watch from his pocket and checked the time: 9:25. Much as he wanted to see if he could return home, he didn't want to go back yet. He'd hardly tasted the flavor of the period, and he still had a mission. If he was to save Dolly, he needed to stay about a week.

Leaving the neighborhood and entering the industrial area sent a shiver through him. If he were able to fight or run he'd have felt better, but he had to get back to the warehouse and could only hope that he wouldn't run into that wild gang again. Now the world grew quiet, with the stark faces of buildings lining the street, wire fences protecting the open spaces alongside and behind them. Shadows of white clouds in blue skies mottled the pavement before him. He tried to hurry.

Rounding the corner, he saw the building from the North Division Street side where his car should have been parked, the side he had entered the building from. Nervous and out of breath with walking, he approached the door as apprehensively as he had the first time. He rang the doorbell, shifting from one foot to the other, looking around, waiting. Impatiently he stabbed the buzzer again and held it until his finger hurt. *Come on, come on, dammit, open up!*

After a couple of agonizing minutes, he tried wedging his fingers between the door and the jamb where it was slightly dented. In two places he managed to squeeze in four fingers from each hand and pulled, pulled hard, only to have his fingers slip away without budging the door. He tried several more times and, giving up, went around the block to the south side of the building, the side he had exited from only yesterday. Once more he jabbed the bell, irritably, his spirits sagging with a sense of hopelessness and the vague realization that he could be trapped back in time for the rest of his life. His temper rising with his frustration, he pressed on the handle, kicked the door again and again, and pounded it with his fist, the metal panel echoing loud enough to drown out the sound of the car pulling up to the curb behind him.

"Hey!"

Chapter 16

"Hey, you!"

At the bark he wheeled around and saw the face of the same cop who had helped him the day before.

"Yeah, you! What the hell do you think you're doing there?" the lean cop, Ed, said, opening the door and climbing out of the car. "Tyler, right?"

"Yes, right, that's right. I'm sorry, officer, but I...I—"

"You're sorry, all right. Damaging property. That's cause enough to lock you up."

Gary forced himself to think. "I didn't mean to, I swear it. It's just that... that they gave me the wrong package yesterday and I wanted to return it." He held out the bag from the sundries shop. "Nobody answered the door and I guess I just lost it."

"Lost what?"

"My temper. I guess I lost it. Walking all the way here, and to find the door locked like this—"

"Well of course it's locked, you dummy. Something wrong with your head? It's Saturday. Any damn fool knows most businesses close on weekends."

Gary fumbled with the bag. "I guess I thought they might be open half a day."

"Maybe, but not this one, not in these times you won't find many. They're lucky to be open at all."

"I thought we told you to stay out of this neighborhood," the cop behind the wheel said, bending sideways and his head ducked low so he could look out the open passenger door. His face, full and ruddy and hard, was all cop.

Gary saw that the warm and sentimental eyes of yesterday

had taken a vacation.

"Maybe we should lock him up, Ed. If getting beat up didn't teach him a lesson, maybe a couple of days in the hoosegow will."

"I think you got something there, John. We'll have to contact the business on Monday, see what it'll cost to repaint the door where he scuffed it all up here."

"If you just give me a chance—"

"Give you a chance! To what, kick a hole in the door? To let some gang splatter your brains all over the sidewalk? C'mon, you had your chance," he said, reaching over and taking him by the arm. When he tugged, Gary winced. Ed let go. "What's the matter?"

"My ribs." He fingered open a shirt button to reveal the tape. "They're cracked."

Ed looked back toward his partner. "What do you think, John?"

John's anger-flushed face reconfigured to disgust. "Get him in the car."

Gingerly, Gary slid into the back seat and the car moved away. "Thanks," he said. "I really appreciate this."

"Don't thank us yet," John said, glancing over his shoulder, "'cause we're still thinking what we oughtta do with you. So tell us, what's so goddamned important with the package that makes you go kicking in doors?"

"Uh...it was supposed to be a...a statue of the Blessed Virgin... for my mother. She's sick and it's her birthday tomorrow."

Ed and John looked at each other. "Sick bad?" John asked, his voice thawing.

"Pneumonia, but we're praying she'll come out of it all right."

John nodded his sympathy. "How 'bout you, you feeling

okay after that shellacking you took yesterday?"

"Well, my body is sore all over, with these cracked ribs, but that's about it."

"Surprisin', your face looks pretty good compared to what it did. Did you tell the Doc about the bump on the noggin?"

"He said a little mental confusion is normal, but that I had nothing to worry about."

"Yeah, well, still....Where should we let you off," he said, looking over to Ed, who stared straight ahead, his lean jaw taut.

"If you're going past Huron Street, you can let me off at the corner. I have to run an errand."

"Tell me..." John said a few moments later as he pulled over to the curb to let Gary out, "...about the mistake they made, what did they give you instead of the Virgin Mother statue?"

Gary eased himself out of the seat. "A box of Mickey Mouse wristwatches."

"Mick—ga-damn!" he yelled, jamming the gear shift into first and tromping on the accelerator. "I'm telling you, Ed, this country is going to the ga-damn dogs."

* * * * *

Heading back to the boarding house, Gary paced himself to keep from breathing too hard. He purposely avoided letting the police know where he was staying, and let them believe that the address they copied off the package the first time they picked him up was legitimate. Not that he had any particular reason for it, but his instincts told him to reveal as little information about himself as possible. What they didn't know couldn't hurt him. He walked the last short blocks home and could see from a distance the white picket fence sticking out in front of it. As he approached he saw Sarah sitting in a chair on the porch, swaddled in a shawl that came up around her chin. Sitting in a chair next to her was someone he hadn't seen before, someone around his own age, give or take a couple of years.

"Hello, Sarah," he said, using the railing to help climb the porch stairs.

Tucking the shawl around her sides, she pushed herself to a straighter position. "Hello, Gary," she said, a smile lighting her eyes. "Gary, this is Dexter Ried."

Gary leaned forward to shake hands. "Glad to meet you, Dexter," he said, noting the steel grip.

"Same here," Dexter said, his tight lips belying the sentiment and making it immediately clear to Gary that Dexter was not at all happy with his presence.

"Gary just took a room downstairs," Sarah said, trying to loosen Dexter up, but he held to his hard-nosed aloofness.

Dexter had a pug nose and a few freckles scattered over his face. His blond facial hair was almost indistinguishable against his fair skin, and his bony jaw suggested the tenacity of a bulldog. Despite the 'Get lost!' vibes singing loud and clear, Gary couldn't help but feel pity for him. Somehow he seemed a sad soul, the kind of guy who needed to be needed and would devote his life to a woman who loved him back.

"Nice day for a walk," Gary said, opening the front door to go in. "Nice meeting you, Dexter." Dexter, looking the other way, mumbled something in return.

Back in his room, Gary tossed the bag on the table, stripped off his jacket, threw it over the chair and stretched out on the bed with a drawn out, weary moan. He'd overdone it today. That much walking could kill him. If he had his car—but that was impossible. One way or another, he had to find some kind of work. That wouldn't be easy, not with the Depression still on and at least two years to go before it ended. God only knew how long he'd be caught in this time trap. His mind turned sluggish and his eyes closed against the dreary light in the room. He needed a nap, a good nap to clear his head and restore his strength.

* * * * *

A film of sweat cooled his brow when Gary's eyes popped open, a fuzzy awareness of where he was at gradually coming into focus. Reaching lazily down into his pocket, he pulled out his watch and held it close to his eyes. 3:10. Quite a nap, he thought. He had been dreaming, dreaming of Shelley, of her taunting him:

"*...really, Gary, from the past?*"
"*I'm telling you, Shelley, it's the God's honest truth.*"
She threw her head back and laughed. "*When are you going to come down from that dream world you live in?*"
"*Shelley—*"
"*A harmonica! What next, Gary, a hobby horse? Or maybe a cowboy suit or—*"
"*That's enough, Shelley. If you don't believe me—*"
"*Oh, I believe you, Gary. That's the problem. I believe you believe what you're saying, but I think you've been spending so much time in that attic of yours that you're getting a few bats in your own.*"
"*I wish you'd stop mocking me, Shelley.*"
"*And I wish you'd stop coming up with these silly stories. And why are you wearing all those Mickey Mouse watches on your arm? And look at that ridiculous jacket you're wearing. What Salvation Army bag did you dig that rag out of?*"
"*If you don't like what I am, or anything about me, why don't you say so, Shelley. Someone else out there might not*"

think I'm so funny."

She smiled, and her icy blue eyes chilled him to the bone. "Like who? Like who, Gary? Like the girl you've got your eye on?"

"I don't know what you're talking about."

Her face came close, closer, so close he could actually feel her icy breath in his face. "Like the one with the big, brown eyes? Like SSSSarah?"

The name hissing off her tongue like a fiery lash awakened him with a start. He lay there, breathing hard, thinking, waiting for the unsettling effects of the dream to wear off. This trip back in time was becoming a nightmare; he didn't need any more in his sleep. The glamour he had imagined was beginning to lose a little of its luster, in fact, a lot of it. Of course he had come totally unprepared. If he had only known— but that was all past history now.

Simple as this world was, or seemed to be, it posed great problems for him, problems and dangers, seen and unforeseen, problems he'd have to solve if he hoped to save the little girl named Dolly Czarnowski, who had only days to live.

Chapter 17

Needing to freshen up, Gary gathered his things, fished the comb from the bag and put it in his pocket. As he stepped into the hallway, towel over his shoulder, the smell of onions was thick enough to glue wallpaper. Starting for the bathroom, he saw someone emerge and head toward the back stairway. Shadowy at that far end of the hall, the man's face would have been unrecognizable even if he had been facing Gary, but it was definitely a man and, if memory served him right, the same man Gary had run into the night before when he had come in from putting the garbage out. No doubt about it: the same stooped gait and hunched shoulders. The same air of secrecy, or so it seemed. Gary wondered if the man could be a Nazi spy. He remembered reading that there were many saboteurs in this country during those years before the Word War II. What organization was it that was so active at the time...the Bond? The Bund? Bund, yes, that was it.

Back in his room Gary slipped on his jacket and went out down the hall to Mrs. Harmon's apartment. When she opened the door he was properly polite. "Sorry to bother you, Mrs. Harmon, but yesterday you mentioned a hot plate?"

"So I did, so I did. Step inside." Wrapped in a maroon housecoat, ballooned behind with her hefty rump, she padded off in big, floppy, pink slippers into the kitchen. He heard a radio playing somewhere in the apartment. Moments later she returned, carrying the hot plate before her like a libation.

"Thanks," he said, taking it from her and handing over the money.

"There's a plug on the wall down near the floor under the table. Make sure you don't keep nothin' near it that can burn, especially the window curtain." She dropped the quarter into her pocket. "And turn it off when you ain't using it."

"I understand…By the way, what's the name of that tune playing on the radio, do you know?"

"Of course I know. It's *Smoke Gets in Your Eyes.*"

"It's beautiful."

Her eyes flared then narrowed. "You like it?"

"How can anybody help not?"

"I thought you'd be more into that jazz or Dixieland crap, being one of them college boys."

"How did you know I was one?"

"Don't tell Toby nothin' you don't want anybody to know." She laughed. "He's a sweetheart, though, my baby brother, if I do say so myself."

"He also mentioned that you might do some laundry…?"

"I might. So long as it's nothing greasy with oil or got a lot of house paint in them. I ain't wrecking my new wringer washer for nobody." She looked him over. "Depends how much you got to wash."

"Right now just pants and shirt. I think my sweater needs dry cleaning, though. I'll probably have more clothes later on." His underwear and socks he figured he could wash in the sink himself.

"Okay, you bring 'em today and I'll get 'em back tonight. You want 'em ironed?"

"I guess."

"You want me to take care of the dry cleaning? I gotta go there for myself on Monday, anyway."

"I'd appreciate that very much."

She nodded. "Nice to see some manners and respect around here once in a while."

"Thank you."

"Yeah, well, let's not overdo it." She looked up,

calculating. "Okay, let's see. I'll collect for the sweater when I pick the stuff up. Everything, pants, shirt and ironing— forty cents. Soap costs money, you know. I'll throw in the starch if I need it. I'm giving you a break, just to show you that my heart's in the right place. And not to mention because you appreciate a good song. That was one of my husband's favorites, *Smoke Gets in Your Eyes.* He's dead."

"I'm sorry to hear that."

"I'm not. The skunk kicked the bucket after he walked out on me," she said, opening the door for him. "Wait, hang on a minute." Again she padded off with a thunderous display of her haunches and came back holding a metal container hand-painted with daisies. "Here's a bread box to use. I don't want no damn rats feedin' around here."

"Thank you, Mrs. Harmon," he said, turning to leave.

"You can call me Elsie. Everybody else does. You might as well, too."

Back in his room again, he put everything in its place. His dirty clothes were still in the bag and he picked it up, took out his sweater and pants and went through the pockets to make sure they were empty. He remembered how his Grandma always had a fit whenever he forgot to get rid of the Kleenex tissues and they ended up shredded in the water. From the side pocket he felt paper and at first thought it might be money, but it was the article on Dolly, the little girl who was strangled— or who would be strangled on...He read it over... *missing since April 21st.* He counted on his fingers. That would be next Friday. He laid the article on top the dresser, near his car keys, looked around and went out the door, locking it behind him.

Mrs. Harmon's door was half open and she was squatting in a big chair, stockings rolled down around her ankles, and smoking a cigarette. "Just toss them on the floor there," she said, blowing a stream of smoke through thick, loose lips up into the air. Her free arm hung over the side of the chair, a beer bottle dangling from her hand.

"No rush on this, Mrs. Har—I mean, Elsie."

She crinkled her face in what he took to be a wink.

"Oh, one question, Elsie—Could you tell me who the tenant is… a man, not very tall, has a mustache, and I think lives upstairs somewhere here in the front?"

She snorted. "None of your goddamned business!"

He backed off in a hurry and could still hear her yelling when he stepped out on the porch. Seeing no Sarah around, he grabbed the railing and took the half dozen stairs down like a child, one step at a time.

His Mickey Mouse watch showed almost four o'clock. Still early, with a lot of time to kill. He was helpless until at least Monday, when he'd try the warehouse office again to see if he could make it back through when the time came for it. He tried not to think of the two cops, John and Ed, but he had to take the chance. Of all the things he found in short supply in this world, 'choice' was the shortest. Isn't that what they called Hobson's choice, having no choice at all?

He hobbled along, pacing himself, and getting used to the pain that rebuked him when he tried picking up the tempo. Fortunately, he didn't have far to go, but he wasn't done for the day. He still had to stop at the store for groceries and take them back to his room. If his strength held out, he intended to go back to the tavern later on. With no television, not even a radio, no books and no friends, he needed some kind of diversion. Not that he was much of a drinker. Shelley could put him under the table every time. He just couldn't handle the stuff, and he really didn't like the taste of alcohol. Fancy drinks that tasted like milkshakes he loved, but he was always too embarrassed to go that route.

Along the way he thought of Dolly, whose fate would be

sealed if he couldn't help her. Exactly how, he didn't know, but first he'd have to find the abandoned apartment house next to a playground in the First Ward. That couldn't be too far from his place. He still had time. In fact, if he could locate her address, he could stop her from going on her errand in the first place. But that could be the worst thing he could do. How could he explain his knowledge of a future event unless he himself was in on it. He couldn't just go up to her house and say, *Excuse me, Mrs. So-and-so, but don't send your daughter to the store tomorrow night. If you do she'll be murdered.*

How long would it take that woman, or any woman, to scream bloody murder upon hearing words like that! In no time at all he'd be hauled in by the police and grilled. And if the murder actually took place, God knows what they'd do to him in the back room to find out how he knew what he knew. They might even charge him as an accomplice. From what he knew, the police weren't any too gentle with suspected criminals these days.

No, one way or another, he'd have to stop the killing before it happened, and, if successful, stay out of the limelight afterward, or that in itself could result in unwelcome attention from the law.

* * * * *

Gary ambled along, shuffling, changing his gait to ease the wincing pain in his ribs. As he approached the house he saw a figure standing out front at the bottom of the steps. At first he didn't recognize Sarah, standing there and looking so small in the fading daylight hours. She was not looking at him, but straight ahead when he came up on her.

"Hello, Sarah," he said.

She turned toward him, her brown eyes glistening, as

surprised to see him there as he was to see her. "Hi, Gary."

"Kind of cool to be standing out here, isn't it?" he said, noting the threadbare condition of the corduroy jacket she had on.

"Oh, I don't mind. I like the fresh air."

"It's just as fresh sitting on the porch out of the breeze, isn't it?"

"I don't mind. I love cool afternoons like this, with the wind blowing in my face. Our apartment can be so stuffy, but my mother likes it hot. She's always cold."

He saw the way the wind tousled and played with her hair. "You just come out and stand like this every day?"

She laughed, a soft, shy laugh, as if she wasn't used to laughing. "Not every day, but whenever I can. Sometimes I'm so tied up taking care of my mother I don't have time. When I do, though, I usually take a short walk to the corner. When I feel up to it, I go all the way around the block. But that's only if my mother's napping."

"Your mother's not well?" he asked, trying for delicacy.

"She's been sick for a long time, almost since—well, it's hard to say exactly when."

She was shorter than he was, petite, almost pixie-ish, and invitingly attractive the way she seemed to twist a little side to side, and gaze up at him in such an alluring, captivating way.

He hesitated a moment, thinking about Dexter, before saying, "If you want a little company, some afternoon— or anytime— I'd like to take a walk with you."

"I think that would be nice," she said, the tone of her voice a little unconvincing. Maybe she was thinking of Dexter, too.

He looked at her closely. Her pale cheeks had a candy-apple glow to them. "Did you say you just finished walking around the block now?"

"I didn't say I did, but I did. How did you guess?"

"Psychic, I guess."

"What?"

"I can read minds," he said, giving her a broad smile.

"Oh, wouldn't that be wonderful?"

"You don't take these walks of yours at night, do you?"

"Only sometimes. It depends."

"Aren't you a little afraid?"

"I'm a big girl now," she said. "I'm not afraid of the dark."

"I don't mean that. I mean—"

"The boogieman? No, I'm not afraid of him, either." She looked at him puzzled. "Why are you laughing?"

"I'm not, really. Just something that tickled me. Maybe I'll tell you sometime, but tell me, Sarah, do you take these walks for exercise, or to get away and think, or what?"

"All of that, I suppose," she said, giving him a smile that didn't seem to be a smile at all, but rather a kind of pathetic attempt to be courteous. She swayed a little, then, and his hand shot out.

"Are you all right?" he said, catching hold of her shoulder and feeling the frailness of it under her jacket.

"I'm fine, I'm fine," she said, embarrassed and moving away from his hand. "Sometimes I tend to overdo it; at least my mother says I do."

Again he looked at her closely, trying not to be obvious. "I think your mother may be right."

She sighed. "I hate to admit it but she usually is."

"Are you sure you're all right now?"

"Oh, yes. I get those little spells once in a while. They're nothing to worry about."

"Okay." He extended his hand toward the steps. "Going up?"

She went ahead of him, holding the railing and climbing slowly. Watching her made him forget his own pain. When she reached the porch landing she paused and stepped aside.

"Why don't you go on in," she said. "I think I'll just stay here a few minutes and get a little more fresh air."

"Sure,' he said, then remembering, asked, "Sarah, what time do the taverns close around here, do you know?"

She looked perplexed. "Three in the morning, I believe."

"Thanks," he said, going inside, wondering if he had given her the mistaken impression that he was going to ask her to go to a tavern with him. Or that he was a drunk.

Back in his room, his mind was on Sarah, seeing her again as he saw her moments before, standing on the porch, silhouetted against the dull afternoon light. He tried to visualize her face. As a whole it was a strangely elusive face, as remote as it was appealing, as if designed to defy apprehension. Or was it the quality, the wistful, melancholy essence of it that refused to be captured. He could see individual aspects of her face, though, the darkish semi-circles under her eyes, eyes that could still glisten in the light— the pale, dry lips and the dead white of her skin under her rosy cheeks.

Sometimes I tend to overdo it, she had said.

What did that mean? he wondered, patting the bed and stretching his body out carefully on it. And those spells she mentioned. What could she be overdoing, lifting a basket of wash? Making a bed? Scrubbing the floor? None of those things should pose a problem for a girl about twenty years old. And her mother, he hadn't yet seen her. Most likely she was an invalid? Well, sooner or later he'd get his answers.

He'd find out about that weirdo upstairs, too, with or without the landlady's help. He had a feeling he'd caught a glimpse of him from the corner of his eye a couple times, not counting the time he'd surprised him coming out of the bathroom, but every time he looked around, he saw nothing. It was like a mouse that flits by in a room; you don't really see anything but a fleeting shadow, yet you know something's there.

Slipping his watch from his pocket, he checked the time, and laid it on the pillow next to his head. He needed a rest, a nap, but he didn't want to sleep too long. He considered asking Mrs. Harmon to knock on his door at about 9:30, but memory of her explosive temper blew away that idea in a hurry. He wouldn't doubt she had murdered her husband. She seemed plenty capable of it. Maybe the guy upstairs was her lover and helped. Maybe—

There you go again, he could hear Shelley saying, *letting your imagination carry you away.*

Relaxed, drowsy, he felt the tension flow from his body. The week ahead would be crucial and he needed to think. Right now he needed to rest.

Chapter 18

It was the dead quiet of the house that woke Gary up. He tried focusing on his watch: a blurry eleven o'clock. A hell of a long nap. Too long. Now he probably wouldn't be able to sleep the rest of the night!

At the sink he splashed water on his face and combed his hair. Checking his pockets for his money, his comb, his knife, he slipped on his jacket, snapped off the overhead light and headed out the front door to the street, as quiet and dead as the house itself, except for the tapping of his shoes on the pavement.

Walking at an easy pace, he felt no sense of danger or fear of being mugged, even though he already had an encounter minutes after he'd arrived here. That seemed an aberration, somehow. And Sarah herself seemed to reinforce that feeling of safety, when she totally misunderstood his concern about her walking after dark.

You didn't even have to lock your doors in those days, he heard his Grandpa say again.

Maybe not, he said to himself, but he still stayed alert as he trod along, feeling better than he had all day. Even his ribs didn't hurt as much.

* * * * *

"Hey, hey, whataya say," Sam said in greeting, and reached a hairy arm across the bar to press a strong hand into Gary's. "Pull up a stool, my friend."

Half a dozen heads lining the bar and several at the tables along the wall swiveled around to look to see the cause of

Sam's sudden burst of enthusiasm. For a few seconds the piano stopped playing, then started up again with *The Object of My Affection.*

"What'll it be, kid, Pabst... Iroquois...?"

Gary slid up on an open bar stool. "Same as last time, Sam, Iroquois."

"One Eree coming up," he said, pouring from the tap and pushing the beer in front of Gary. "Boys," he called out, "meet Gary. Gary, the boys: Sittin' down there on the far end, the ugly one with the gray hair, that's Leo; that bean pole standing near him is Stan the Polack; the weasel next to him with the hook nose and rat eyes is dago Sal."

All except Leo acknowledged Gary with a shake of the head, and Gary nodded back.

"Then there's Chippie the gimp. Fell in a grain hopper some years back and almost got turned into shredded wheat— he'll tell you all about it sometime."

"Yeah," Dago Sal said, "he'll tell it to you over and over till your ears turn to pretzels." He pulled his own ears out like wings and twisted them.

"Fah-kyu," Chippie shot back. "You wouldn't be yapping like that if it was your leg caught in them gears, you goddamned weasel, you. Took them nearly—"

"Yeah yeah yeah, we know, it took nearly three years— Lookit my fuckin' ears, bending like pretzels."

"Can it you guys," Sam broke in, "can it. Save it for later. What kinda impression ya wanna give the kid here?" He turned back to Gary. "Those other bozos you see playing cards at the table back there up against the wall, you'll get to know later. Next we got Dapper Delaney, our Irish duke, always with the shirt, green bow tie and fancy cuff links."

"Right you are, lad, and I'll be having me regular, Sam, if it wouldn't be inconveniencin' you none," he said, tapping his cigar ashes on the floor.

Sam reached behind for a bottle of *Four Roses* whiskey. "And that's three-finger Corky next to the duke. Was an automobile mechanic till an engine fan relieved him of half his hand. Show him, Corky."

Corky held up his arm and gave his wrist a wriggle. "Still got two."

"Now Corky runs a bicycle shop. And he didn't lose any more fingers since, did you, Corky?" he said, his arm swooping down to fill Delaney's shot glass.

"Not a goddamned one, no sir." Corky stepped back, took aim at the spittoon at his feet and spat a stream of tobacco juice that splashed off the brass rim onto the brass rail.

"And right there closest to you, Gary, is our very own local celebrity with the busted nose, Tommy Fisher. Used to fight welterweight."

"That's right," Tommy said, stomping his foot on the rail of Gary's stool, grabbing Gary's hand and slapping it down on his flexed thigh. "Feel that, go 'head, feel it. Squeeze. Harder… harder. Like a rock, right? Like a piece of steel, right?"

Gary was amazed. The man's thigh was actually hard as stone. "You aren't kidding," Gary said.

Tommy threw out a straight left, like a jab, pushed up his sleeve, clenched his fist and curled his arm and wrist. "Go 'head," he said, grinning a gap-toothed grin and flexing. "Go 'head, feel that bicep, squeeze. Harder. All your might… that's it."

"Like a rock," Gary said.

"Like a rock, right? Was I shittin' ya? Believe me now?"

Gary drew his hand back. "I never doubted you," he said, picking up his drink.

"Forty two professional fights. Got in the game when I was fifteen," he said, rolling his sleeve down. "Fought everybody and anybody. 'Tiger' Tommy Fisher they called me."

Dago Sal piped up. "How many did you lose, Tiger? Tell him how many you lost."

"G'wan, get laid, you goddamned weasel," Tommy fired back, his jaw clenched and neck stretched to see Sal, nearly hidden behind the staggered line of bodies at the bar. "If them goddamned hometown judges didn't rob me on all those decisions, I'd pit my record against the best of 'em— Barney Ross, even Henry Armstrong," he boasted, his jaw working furiously. "And I still got enough juice left over in me now to mop up the floor with you and that string bean next to you together if I want to."

Chippie the gimp leaned back and winked at Sal. "Tell us, come on now, Tiger, come clean, tell the boys— how many times did you go into the tank?"

Inflamed with the leg-slapping laughter as much as with the words, Tommy sputtered. "You... you shit, you! Step outside, come on, crippled or not I'm gonna teach you a lesson you ain't gonna forget in a hurry. I'll show you who went in the tank."

Hoots and howls rolled over their heads.

Balling his fist, Tommy jerked away from the bar, when Sam's hand flashed across and grabbed him by the sleeve. "Easy, Tommy, take it easy. The boys are only having a little fun."

"Not by telling me I went into the tank, they ain't," he complained, trying to wrench his arm free.

"Chippie didn't mean nothin' by it, did you, Chippie. Go on, tell him, tell Tommy you was only teasing him, that you didn't mean no harm by it, go 'head, Chippie, tell him."

Chippie waved him off. "Okay, go on, give 'im a beer. On me."

Sam let go of Tommy's arm. "See, Tommy? Chippie didn't mean nothin' by it. He's even making a peace offering."

"Goddamned gimp," he muttered, snapping his arm back and bellying up to the bar.

"Whatta think, Champ," Sam said, trying to soothe him and pouring his beer, "who you pickin' to win the fight Monday night, Louis or Roper?"

Gary's ears perked up. *Joe Louis, heavyweight champion of the world. Grandpa considered him the best of all time, better than Rocky Marciano or even Cassius Clay. (Grandpa refused to call him Muhammad Ali).* Gary remembered that Louis had been champion for twelve years, but when did his reign begin? He'd know soon enough, and with it his chance to make a few dollars.

"My money's on Louis," Tommy said, thumbing his nose and making a fist. "Got power in both hands. He's a stalker, too. He'll catch Roper. No doubt in my mind."

Leo craned his gray head around to look down the bar. "G'wan," he sneered. "Louis ain't nothin' but a flash in the pan. He won't last the fight."

Tommy came right back. "Yeah, he took the belt from Jimmy Braddock, didn't he? They ain't callin' him the Brown Bomber for nothin'."

"Bullshit. Are you forgettin' how Schmeling put him to sleep a couple of years ago? You telling me he can take a punch? G'wan, he's got a glass jaw if I ever seen one."

"Glass my ass. Besides, that happened before he took the title. Look what he did to that Kraut the second go 'round. Flattened him in the first round. What about that?"

Sam broke in. "Hang on you guys, hang on. How 'bout we end this with a little wager. If nobody wants to put their money where their big mouth is, then drop it."

They started arguing among themselves and went silent

when Gary spoke up. I'm willing to put up my money," Gary said. "Everything I have."

Sam's mouth dropped. "Easy there, kid, what the hell do you know about the fight game?" He looked down the line of faces. "Gary's a college boy. He only knows books. Gonna be a school teacher. Don't nobody take no bets from him."

"Who do you want?" Leo called down.

"Leo, I said—"

"It's okay, Sam," Gary cut in. "I can take care of myself, trust me."

"Listen, kid, I know you want to fit in, but these guys would skin you alive for a buffalo nickel."

"Hey, Sam, what're you, his big brother?" Stan the Polack said, blowing smoke away and crushing his cigarette butt in the ash tray on the bar. "If he wants to bet, let him bet. If he's gotta learn the hard way, let him learn."

"He's right," Gary said, finishing his beer and sliding it back for a refill. "That's what you call the School of Hard Knocks, isn't it, Sam?"

Sam took his glass. "Okay, kid, have it your way. But don't say I didn't warn you."

Gary leaned forward to see Leo. "I'll take Louis."

Leo scoffed. "What odds you layin'?"

"Odds?"

"See what I mean, kid?" Sam scolded. "He wants odds because Louis is the champ. Leo don't like him, yeah, true, but that don't mean he's a sucker." He pinged Gary's glass with a snap of a fingernail. "That's number two."

Gary tried to remember how much money he had. He might need some for tomorrow, Sunday, but maybe not. He'd already broken the ten. The bad twenty in his wallet he had to keep for a real emergency. Yet he wanted to maximize his profits. He knew Louis would win because he held the title well into the Forties, and that meant for at least a half dozen years or more.

"I'll tell you what," he said, "I won't lay you odds, but I'll bet even money Louis beats this Roper in two rounds or less." As soon as he said it he had regrets. Winning was a certainty, but having to lay odds meant less money in the payoff. Making his offer risked everything, all for a few extra dollars. Of course he didn't know how long this fight lasted, but since he'd never even heard of Roper, he probably wasn't very good. And if Gramps thought Louis to be the best ever champion, then he had to be. They didn't call him the 'Brown Bomber' for nothing. He could only hope Louis 'bombed' him early in the fight. Real early.

"Hey, kid," Sam interjected, his face long and sad, "now wait a minute."

"I'm ready to lay my money down," Gary said, reaching into his pocket and putting half a dozen bills on the bar."

A bobble of heads and a lot of murmuring.

"I'll take some of that easy dough," Sal the weasel said. "Sam, you write it down, keep track and hold the money."

Sam sighed, shook his head and took the weasel's dollar. He turned around and noted it on a pad next to the cash register.

"Put me down for a buck, too," Chippie the gimp said.

A few more dollars waved in the air and Sam plucked them from their hands like daisies.

Tommy, standing next to Gary, shook his head. "Sorry, kid, I like Louis, too. But under three rounds? He's gonna have to finish Roper by the end of two. That's a sucker bet, if I ever heard one. I don't want to take advantage, but you're calling the shots." He laid a dollar on the bar and Sam scooped it up.

Sam counted out six bills from Gary and folded it over with the rest of the money.

A lone, gruff voice from the end said, "I'll lay you an even ten you're dead wrong."

"Hey, Leo," Sam said, "let's not get carried away here."

"I don't have it," Gary said, briefly considering the new money in his wallet. "I'm out."

Leo scoffed. "Uh huh, yeah."

Gary looked at Sam, looked straight into his eyes. "Sam, will you back me on this? I promise, if I lose, I'll pay you back."

Sam looked away, shaking his head. He picked up the bar rag. "Aw, kid, how you gonna pay me back? You don't even have a job. And, I don't like to say it, but you just moved into the neighborhood. Get my drift?" he said, wiping circles on the bar.

"I'm pleading with you, Sam. I'm asking you to trust me."

Sam stood a moment, his eyes locked onto Gary's, concentrating, as if trying to see inside his mind. The whole place went silent, waiting. Even the piano stopped playing. Then he threw down the rag. "Two rounds or less? That's crazy, but maybe I'm just a chump. Okay," he said, striding down the bar to pick up Leo's ten dollar bill. "For some reason I got faith in this kid."

One of the card-playing bozos at a table by the wall sang out, "You'll be sorrr-ry."

Thick blankets of blue cigarette smoke undulating like a sea fog drifted across the room, shrouding their faces and dimming further the already dim lights on the ceiling and back bar. Nick sat at the piano with his back to the crowd, playing a medley of love ballads. Gary's eyes burned, and he took a long swallow of beer to soothe his raw throat.

Three-finger Corky spoke up. "Whatta ya say, Sam, you puttin' out some lunch, or are you trying to starve us to death?"

"A fine proposal, that," Dapper Delaney said, "for which I

second the motion."

"And I triple it," Weasel Sal joined in, thumping the bar with his fist.

Sam raised a hairy finger. "Gottcha," he said, going off to the kitchen.

Gary remembered Gramps saying that saloons at the time used to set up a free lunch for their patrons.

Moments later, Sam emerged, carrying a huge metal tray and set it down at the end of the bar, next to the rugged Leo. "Right outta the ice box. Help yourself, boys."

"Hey, Sam," one of the bozos called out, "hit us over here with a fresh round, will ya?"

Gary eased himself off his stool, went down the line and stood behind Stan the Polack, who was already loading ham, cheese and salami on a slice of rye bread.

"No good to drink on an empty stomach," Stan said, chuckling and covering his lunch meat with another slice of bread.

Gary made a sandwich for himself.

"Get it while the getting'good," Three-finger Corky said, reaching around him and picking up his bread. "Gary, right? That's your name?"

"Right," Gary said, "and you're...."

"Corky, the bicycle man." He held up the thumb and pinky of his left hand and smiled wide enough to show that he hadn't many more teeth than he had fingers.

Gary brightened. "Corky, you wouldn't happen to have a bike for sale, would you? A good used one? Cheap?" Gary stepped aside to let him in.

Corky laughed and moved up to the plate. "Gary, my boy, I'm not sure you're gonna have anything left to spend at all after the fight Monday night. If you think Leo's gonna let you off the hook any way, shape or form 'cause he feels sorry for you or somethin', you got a good case. What I'm sayin' is, how cheap is cheap? For sure it don't mean free. Whatta ya gonna have to spend?"

"Do you have a shop, an actual shop?" Gary persisted.

"Sure, I got a shop, nice shop, clean, right over on Michigan Avenue near Seneca. Been there close on to five years. You probably seen it, Corky's Bicycle Emporium."

Leo leaned over in his stool. "What does 'emporium' mean, Corky?" His laugh was as gruff as his manner.

Corky shot him a dirty look. "I don't know and I don't care. You know why I don't care? I don't care because I like the name. It's classy, not like you, you rag ass. And besides, nobody else knows what it means, neither, so what's the difference?"

"Are you open tomorrow?" Gary asked, turning to go.

"Monday, nine o'clock, not tomorrow."

Leo spoke over his shoulder. "That's because he's too lazy to work on Sundays."

Corky fumbled his sandwich and almost dropped it. "Lazy, my ass," he exploded. "It's because I honor the goddamned Sabbath, not like you, you fuckin' heathen."

For the next half hour or so, the razzing went back and forth with intermittent bursts of laughter, shouts and threats, all the more raucous by the added voices of stragglers who had wandered in off the street and squeezed in at the bar and the piano in the background.

"You got one more drink coming, kid," Sam said. "You want it now or you wanna save it for another time?"

Gary was beginning to feel relaxed. "I'll have it now."

Sam sighed, snatched up the glass and brought it back, still foaming over the sides.

"Sammy, hey, Sam, what happened to Leo's name on the Wall of Shame? Supposed to be there another couple of days, ain't it?"

"Naw, he served his time, Chippie. His week's up."

"How did it feel to be King of the Dummies, Leo," one of them cried out. "We noticed we didn't see hide nor hair of you recently." His harsh laugh cascaded into a thick, phlegmy rash of coughs that sounded as if he was choking to death.

"Go 'head and laugh, laugh all you want. I'm ready to take on anybody, right now, anytime," Leo called back. "It was a fluke and you know it, every goddamned one of you know it."

Stan fiddled across his arm with an imaginary bow. He sang: *Beautiful dreamer, dream unto me...*

A chorus of voices joined in: *Beautiful dreamer, dream....*

"G'wan, kiss my royal Hungarian ass," Leo came back, fighting his temper, "you lousy buncha bums. I'll go head to head with anybody and bury every goddamned one of you, too. Guaranteed!"

"You willing to try the kid down here, Leo?" Sam said.

Leo leaned forward to take a good look at Gary. "He don't look so smart to me."

"I can tell you he is, and that's fair warning. I already said he's Joe college. I'll tell ya, he cleaned my clock this afternoon. That's gotta mean something to you."

"He don't scare me, not one bit."

"What about it, Gary, are you willing to face off with our homegrown professor there? He's good, no doubt about it."

Gary set his drink down. Even with a full stomach, the beer was getting to his head, making him a little woozy. "How does it work?"

"Easy. We flip a coin and the winner gets to ask the first question. If the other guy gets the answer, the first guy buys a beer. Then the second guy asks a question. Back and forth like that till one misses. First one to miss gets his name up on the Wall of Shame. Stays there a whole week. Easy enough?"

"It doesn't sound fair, "Gary said. "It seems to favor whoever asks first."

"Oh, it's fair all right, because the loser gets a chance to ask first the next week. We call that 'Revenge.' No guarantee you get off the board, though. One sap who don't come in no more stayed up almost three months. And Leo here, he was s'posed to get a crack at Jinx Carlo tonight, but Jinx didn't show."

"Sonofabitch," Leo said. "Probably scared. I was ready for the cocky bastard, too."

"You still game, kid?"

"I'm game," Gary said, taking a long drink.

"Leo?"

Leo gave a curt nod.

"All set, then? Okay." Sam flipped a coin, caught it in mid-air and slapped it down on the bar. "Call it, one of you."

Leo nodded toward Gary and Gary called tails. Sam lifted his hand. "Heads it is. Okay, you go first, Leo, shoot when you're ready."

The bar room went silent and the piano stopped playing. They all puffed on their cigars and cigarettes, watching Leo's gray mustache twitch under his broad nose, while they waited for him to open his mouth.

Leo sniffed once, twice, then said, "Okay, what's the highest mountain in the USA?"

Gary didn't hesitate. "Mount McKinley."

"Wrong!" Leo barked, smacking a thick hand down on the bar. "Mount Whitney's the highest. In California." His neck stretched and his head pivoted triumphantly to the chorus of cheers. "I'll take that beer now, Sam," he shouted.

Sam leaned over the bar to Gary. "Jeez, kid, that didn't seem too hard to me. Shouldn't ya have known that?"

"Sorry, Sam," Gary said, his head sunk low on his chest. Gary knew his mistake the moment he'd spoken. McKinley is the highest mountain, but it's in Alaska, and Alaska wouldn't be a state for another twenty years.

"Lucky," Tommy said. "Pure luck. The kid answered too fast, didn't give hisself a chance to think."

"Lucky, hell!" Leo cried back.

Stan spoke up. "Never mind luck, Tommy. This ain't no prize fight where a lucky punch can do it. Leo's still the best around. I'd bet'm against anybody, any day, including the kid here, even if he is Joe college."

"Right," a few more voices piped up. "We're with you Leo, even if you did make a horse's ass out of yourself last week."

A chorus of laughs erupted and Leo flushed. "Where's my goddamned drink, Sam. I'm still waitin'."

"And don't forget the Wall of Shame," the weasel said. "The kid don't get no special privileges around here. His name goes up like anybody else."

Still standing close to Gary, Sam said, "Sorry, kid. I shouldn't've pushed it like I did."

"It's not your fault, Sam. I asked for it. Anyway, I get my chance next week, right?" he said, reaching into his pocket for money to pay for Leo's beer.

"This is on me," Sam said, moving toward the tap. "To make amends, more or less."

"Hey, kid, how do you spell your name?" Stan called over, standing by the far wall under the slate board, and brandishing a fat piece of chalk.

Gary spelled it out for him, his voice weak and his head hanging low.

Sam carried Leo's beer over to him. "Don't choke on it," he said, setting it down.

"There it is," Stan cried out, and there it was, indeed, on the Wall of Shame, in big, bold letters for all to see:

G - A - R – Y   T - Y - L - E - R

Sam came back and leaned over the bar, close to Gary. "Hey, kid, don't feel too bad. Could happen to anybody. You had an off night, that's all. By the way, you were dead on with Pluto. Can't argue with ya there. So why don'tcha pack it in now. It's gettin' late and you're gettin' a nob on."

Gary felt his stomach starting to churn, and his head began a slow whirl. "I think you're right, Sam," he said, sliding off the stool and steadying himself a moment.

"Sure, kid, it's almost one o'clock. Just watch yourself going home. Walk straight, not like you're plastered, and don't fall down. Cops see that and they'll haul you off to the clink."

"I understand. Thanks, Sam."

"You know, kid, maybe it wasn't such a good idea, me backing you for a sawbuck on the big fight comin' up Monday night. Two rounds, that's nuts."

"If I lose I'll make it up to you, Sam, somehow."

"Ah, go on, forget it, kid, forget it. Sorry I spoke. I'm a man of my word, and I'm stickin' with ya. Just remember, be here for the fight. Don't let me down. Probably starts about ten o'clock so you maybe wanna get here a little earlier."

Gary turned and gave a wave back. "Nice meeting you men," he said, his tongue more than a little thick in his mouth.

No one paid attention or heard him over Nick's honky-tonk piano playing accompaniment to the duke, who was conducting a bar room choir with an imaginary baton, his cuff links winking time as he waved his arms about:

> *My Wild Irish rose,*
> *The sweetest flow'r....*

Gary's feet hit the pavement like wet sand bags as he slogged his way through the deserted streets, lit only by an occasional street lamp that threw circles of watery light on the ground. Behind trimmed hedges and porch awnings, the houses he passed along the way lay veiled in darkness. Clouds obscured the night sky and the faint odor of sewer gas tainted the cool air. Silent except for the scrape and drag of his own footsteps, the city slept a deep and soundless sleep. He felt lost and lonely in an alien world whose ways he was only beginning to grasp, a world that could never conceive of the future world he had come from.

Across the street, almost invisible in the opaque shadows behind a tree, stood a lone figure, watching him.

*   *   *   *   *

Gary climbed the porch stairs slowly, holding the railing, although his ribs did not hurt as much as he might have expected. Quiet as his clumsy feet would allow, he went in the front door and through the dim hallway to his room. Fumbling for his key, he found it and, still fumbling, found the keyhole. Mrs. Harmon's door opened a sliver and closed at the same time his did.

Chapter 19

A thumping and shuffling of feet in the hallway outside his door woke Gary up. He had fallen asleep with his clothes on and dug into his pocket for his watch. Mickey's arms pointed to the eight and the nine. Quarter to eight or twenty to nine? He yawned and stretched. His mouth tasted dry as cardboard and he was thirsty. A throbbing beat time in his head and his chest cried a little as he pulled himself up too quickly. Before getting up and going over to the sink to splash cold water on his face, he sat on the edge of the bed, scratching his scalp, rubbing his eyes and waiting for it all to come back to him.

It did. And it explained his parched throat and headache. He deserved to be on that Wall of Shame, letting the old jerk catch him like that. Mount Whitney! If he hoped to survive in this land that time forgot, he'd have to be more alert and to think before opening his big mouth.

His face fresh and his hair combed, he moseyed over to the table to see what he could salvage for breakfast. He parted the curtain and lifted the shade to let some natural light in and saw strolling along the sidewalk, a couple and their child—a little girl in a frilly white dress and straw bonnet with a red bow. The tiny red purse hanging from her dainty hand seemed to skim the ground. The man wore a straw hat and dark suit, and the woman wore a blue, ankle-length coat over her dress. Her wide-brimmed hat cocked to the side lent her a saucy look.

Behind them walked another couple, all dressed up in their Sunday best— that was it, Sunday. No doubt, these people were on their way to church. He was about to let the curtain drop back in place, when he saw Sarah walking slowly beside a woman, presumably her mother, and holding her left arm. The woman wore a black head scarf, and a shawl around her shoulders. Using a wooden cane, she hobbled along dragging a foot. Sarah herself wore a yellow head scarf and a beige coat that didn't quite reach the hem of her dress. Gary stepped back to avoid being seen in case Sarah looked his way, but she seemed fully occupied guiding her mother. He watched until they passed beyond his view.

Sunday. He'd been there less than two full days, yet it seemed he'd been there forever, and that his own time was no more than a dream, a distant dream, both backward and forward in time. Would he ever get home? he wondered.

A hard knock on the door startled him out of his reverie.

"I brought these back last night like I said I would, but you wasn't in," Mrs. Harmon said, handing over his clothes when he opened the door. "Forty cents." She held out her hand.

"Oh, sure." He pulled out his money and handed her two quarters and took the empty bag. "You can keep the change."

She looked from the coins in her hand to his face, back to the coins and to his face again, as if deciding to say something, then clamped her hand over the quarters and dropped them in her pocket. She cocked her head. "What kind of material is that shirt anyway? 'Polyester,' the tag says. How come I never heard of it?"

"Oh, that?" He forced a laugh. "It's not a material, it's a… a company… in another town."

"What town?"

"It was a birthday present from my aunt out in Los Angeles."

"And who owns the company, Greg Norman? Or are you using an alias?"

"Do I look like Public Enemy Number One?" He laughed again. "Actually, it's the name of the store."

"Pretty fancy shirt. And pretty fancy pants, too, with a

zipper and all. Didn't feel like cotton or wool to me, either, and hardly took any pressing. Who makes this new stuff, anyway, the Eye-talians?"

"Another present. Very expensive pants. My aunt's wealthy. That's why."

She scoffed. "Well, I'da gave Greg Norman a kick in the ass if he sold me something like this. I hope she didn't pay too much, your aunt, 'cause she got robbed."

"Robbed?"

"Look for yourself, you blind? They forgot the damned cuffs."

"You're right, Mrs. Har—Elsie. You - are - right."

She sniffed. "I'm taking your sweater in tomorrow, but it probably won't be ready till Thursday or Friday," she said, trying to peek over his shoulder into his room. "These one-day cleaners that take a week slay me!" She turned on an angry heel and left.

"Thank you, Elsie," he said, balancing the folded clothes in one hand, holding the shopping bag handles with the other and closing the door with his foot. He dropped everything on the bed.

Outside, the steady bong, bong, bong of church bells reverberated in the streets.

He stood a moment, considering going to the warehouse on Division Street and trying the doors again, but, remembering the cop, Ed, saying they're lucky to be open at all these days, much less on weekends, he gave up the idea. Tomorrow, he'd wait until tomorrow before making another attempt. Sooner or later he'd get back inside that building to see what's going on. If he had to camp on the sidewalk until he caught someone going inside, he'd do it.

With the house quiet and apparently everyone gone, he decided to take a bath. He could use one, especially after all he'd been through. The tape binding him didn't seem all that crucial and he debated whether to try taking it off right there or wait until it was thoroughly wet. Wet seemed best, even though he didn't have all that much chest hair to tear out by the roots. He knew that could hurt more than he cared to know.

Taking everything he needed, he left his room, locking the door behind him, and went into the bathroom, a cramped cubicle with barely enough room to turn around in between the sink, toilet and tub. On the wall were an ancient gas jet and a porcelain toilet tank.

Delicately, he tested the tub water with his toe, then his foot— it was almost boiling— climbed over the side, and slowly slid in up to his neck, moaning with painful ecstasy all the way. He soaked. Maybe there was something to this bath thing after all, he thought, feeling the heat penetrate and relax his muscles and bones. He grew drowsy. This is what the womb must feel like to a baby. Maybe that's why they cry when it's time to be born; it's too nice a place to leave.

He snapped out of his torpor when he heard a voice and someone rattling the doorknob. "I'll be out in a minute," he called, and began picking at the ends of the tape. They loosened nicely, and he gave several quick yanks to pull it all free. Rushing through the rest of his ablutions, he dressed, grabbed up everything and opened the door a crack to peek out before leaving. All clear. He snapped off the light and scampered down the hallway, unlocked his door and let himself in.

Back on his bed, he lay gazing up at the ceiling, thinking. Nothing could be done to solve his problems today, so he had to bide his time until tomorrow. Maybe he'd go to the warehouse first thing in the morning, or maybe go to see Corky and try to talk him into giving him credit. He needed a bike to scout the area where Dolly was going to be murdered so he could actually see the location and try to figure a way to stop the killing. He closed his eyes and saw her face, innocent, sad and angelic, like the laminated photographs of children he'd once seen attached to their headstones in an old cemetery.

He threw his arm over his eyes, trying to forget what his conscience wouldn't let him forget: If he chickened out and returned to his own time tomorrow, Dolly would die Friday, five days away. True, he could fail to help her and she could die anyway. But what if he *could* stop the killer? What if he *could* save her and give her a chance to grow up, get married and have children of her own, what would that be worth? Besides, he could always go home later, if he could ever go back to the future at all. The warehouse would still be there. Sure, he could try next week. By then it wouldn't make any difference one way or another what happens Friday night. He'd just have to keep out of the limelight and stay out of trouble until then. If he won his bet on the fight Monday night, he'd have enough money to carry himself for a while. If. Big if.

Then again, wouldn't he be tampering with history? Didn't theory hold that even the slightest change in the past could change the future dramatically? It would be like measuring between two points. If the line digressed even a minute fraction of an inch at its start, in the course of a few miles it would make a staggering difference. But maybe that was comparing oranges to orangutans. Who could say with certainty that altering an event in time would change the future. One thing was certain, though: a little girl would die if he didn't do something to prevent it. Or try to prevent it. Again, he had no choice. He'd stay.

His mind made up, he relaxed. He dozed. He slept. He dreamed:

...of Shelley looking up at the Wall of Shame and laughing

at him, of Leo, Stan, Corky, all of them laughing at him, and he himself sitting on a bicycle at the bar and wheeling out the door past a truck spraying water over him, soaking him as he rode past to the warehouse, where he dropped his bike and walked in through an open door and saw a little girl duck into a darkened office. When he opened the door to call to her, to tell her he wanted to help her, a man with a bushy mustache stepped out of the shadows and shouted for him to get out, that he didn't belong there. He spun around and ran into the hallway, confused, not knowing how to escape, then, seeing a door, rushed for it, searching blindly for the doorknob and, unable to find it, began banging on the door with his fists, desperate to get out, banging and banging...

A banging on his door startled him awake.

"Coming," he called, rising groggy and almost tripping, trying to get his pants on before hopping to the door and opening it a crack. "Yes?"

"This must be yours?" Mrs. Harmon said, handing him a comb, and scowling her displeasure at having been put out.

Poking his head through the crack he reached for it. "It must have fallen out of my pocket in the bathroom."

"I've been to three other apartments, looking. I might've guessed."

"I'm sorry, Elsie. Thanks. I'll be more careful next time." He saw her looking at his bare arm and shoulder suspiciously.

"This was on the floor, too," she said, thrusting out his pocket knife.

Reaching around the door for it with his other hand, he feigned falling through the opening. "Oops, sorry, Elsie," he said, catching himself. "I was warm in bed and I'm naked here, totally and completely naked."

She flushed, almost swallowing her gum, and as nearly as she could bolt, bolted away, choking on strange sounds.

Awake and glad to be awake after his nightmare, Gary tried to shake off the ill effects of it as he removed his pants and laid them on the bed. He refreshed himself at the sink and checked himself in the mirror. Since he wasn't going out anywhere, he put on his same pants and sport shirt. He'd save his clean clothes for tomorrow. And if he heard one more person comment on Greg Norman, he'd punch him right in the head!

Parting the curtain again, he looked out his window to the street and saw no one walking. Apparently, Sundays were as dead in this time as they were in his time. Dragging a funeral parlor chair from against the wall, he opened it, set it next to the table, and sat down. It was still afternoon and he had quite a bit of time to kill before turning in for the night. At least if he had a radio to listen to, or even a newspaper to read, he could pass some time. He considered asking Mrs. Harmon for her newspaper, if she had one— or a deck of cards would be nice— but gave up that masochistic impulse instantly.

A walk. That's it. The notion cheered him. Anything to get out of that depressing room. A walk in the fresh air would tire him out, make him sleep hard and bring the morning faster. He spread his hands, touched his chest and pressed. Sore, but not bad. Soaking in the hot bath probably helped. He took a deeper breath. Much better than he could have hoped. Obviously no fractures, as the doctor feared, just badly bruise ribs.

Slipping his feet into his loafers, he checked himself out in the mirror again, and counted his money before putting it in his pocket. Fifty-eight cents. Not much left from what he'd already spent. He snapped off the light and stepped out into the hallway, where the smell of baking filled the air.

Treading softly past Mrs. Harmon's apartment, he went out the front door and down the porch steps. Standing on the sidewalk, in the same place he had seen her before, was Sarah, the blue scarf around her neck covering part of her face, and her hands tucked into the side pockets of the same pathetic jacket she wore last time he was with her.

"Hi Sarah," he said, smiling and oddly excited to see her.

From the upstairs window of the house, a shadowed face behind curtains peered down on them.

Chapter 20

She turned toward him, slowly, gazing up to him with eyes almost hidden behind the scarf, high up on her nose. "Hello, Gary," she said, pushing her scarf down under her chin, revealing a pretty smile.

"Getting some fresh air?" he said, trying to resist the hypnotic effect of her eyes.

"I just came out," she said. "It was such a nice day today, I wanted to get a little more of it before it gets dark."

"It is pretty warm for this time of the year."

"Yes, it is."

"It cools off pretty fast after the sun goes down, though."

"Yes, it does."

"Pretty soon it'll be too warm."

"I don't like it when it gets too hot."

"Neither do I."

"At least when it's cold you can put more clothes on."

"I agree."

They stood there for an awkward moment, saying nothing, as if neither quite knew where to go from there, looking around nonchalantly, both watching the few cars that passed down the street as if they were the first they'd ever seen.

"Well," he said, finally, taking his hands out of his pockets, "I suppose—"

"Are you going to a tavern or any place special?" she asked.

"No, no, actually, I was just going to take a short walk around the neighborhood to kill a little time. I don't have a newspaper or a radio yet, so...."

"I guess we both had the same idea."

"Well, then, why don't we walk together." He extended his hand. "This way all right?" he said, moving around her to the outside.

Her steps were short, almost mincing, and he slowed his pace to match hers.

"You said you take walks when your mother's napping?"

"Usually. She's resting now. Any kind of activity wears her out. Just walking to church this morning took a lot out of her."

He wanted to say, 'Then why does she do it?' but thought better of it. "I don't mean to pry, but is she very sick?"

"She has just about every medical problem you can name. Sugar is the worst, I think, but she takes it all pretty well because she has a lot of faith. She had a stroke about a year ago. Most people would give up on God, but it made her faith stronger. I think it's amazing." She looked up at him.

"Faith, it's wonderful to have," he said, mildly amused by the simplicity of her mind.

"Slow but sure she's recovering."

"I'm glad to hear that."

"She says God is helping her overcome her burden."

"I hope so," he said, nodding. "And your father, is he okay?"

"Who, Dad? Oh, he was killed in an industrial accident when I was a little girl."

"I'm sorry, Sarah. I shouldn't have brought it up."

"You couldn't know, that's all right. It doesn't hurt much anymore. It happened out of a clear blue sky. My brother Donny was taking a nap, right after supper and—I don't want to bore you," she said, a nervous little laugh breaking between her words. "You don't really want to hear the sad story of my life, do you?"

"If you don't mind, I'd like to."

"Well, it was Christmas Day and we were putting our presents under the tree to open when Dad came home from work. Then we heard someone knocking. It wasn't loud, just tap tap tap, tap tap tap. Of course we thought it was him fooling around because he was always fooling around, which sometimes used to drive my mother crazy, and I ran to greet him like I usually did, but when my mother opened the door, we both almost fainted. At first I thought it was the boogieman, the way the eyes were so white and his face so black and I hid behind my mother's dress." She stifled a small laugh. "But it was a worker from the plant, Doug Hentley, all sooty and still in his baggy old work clothes, turning his cap in his hand round and round. He's the one who broke the news. It wasn't easy for him because he was Dad's best friend. That's why he was elected to come. He said Dad was hurt, hurt bad, and they took him to the hospital, that's all, not that he was killed or anything like that. Later they said he was crushed by a piece of machinery that broke loose from a…a cradle, they called it." She stopped to catch her breath.

"That's terrible, Sarah."

"My mother still blames herself because she made him go in. We were pretty poor and needed the money, and the overtime pay helped a lot. Besides, he would've been home early enough before us kids went to bed, so he went in even though he didn't have to. I think he really wanted to stay home and spend the whole day with the three of us."

"Three?"

"Yes, me, my mother and my brother Donny. He's a year younger than me. He left home about three years ago. My mother didn't want him to go because he was so young and still going to school, but ever since Dad died, Donny was different. No one could tell him anything, just always looking for excitement and getting in trouble. He was so mischievious, especially in school. But he was a happy kid, too. He liked to tease me, like Dad used to do. One day he was gone and left a note on the table saying he was going to California to look for work. The last we heard, he was up in the state of Washington cutting trees or building a dam or something. That's funny, isn't it? She made Dad go, and he didn't come back. And she didn't want Donny to go, and *he* didn't come back."

"You must miss him quite a bit."

"Late at night, sometimes I hear my mother crying, and I know it's over him. I think she thinks he's in jail or dead. He was the apple of her eye, and he knew it." She smiled up to him. "But I was the apple of my father's eye. I remember sitting on his lap and he would read the Sunday comics to me. The Katzenjammer Kids were my favorite. Alley Oop, too. Do you like them? Or don't you read the comics?"

"When I get time."

"I still do. They remind me of Dad...how he used to act out the parts. And he always smelled of pipe tobacco. Even now...whenever I read the comics I think I...can smell the pipe tobacco...cherry flavor...."

Gary noticed her voice weakening and her breath coming short. "Are you all right, Sarah?"

She stopped and put her hand on her chest. "If I exert myself too much I get this silly shortness of breath. It's just annoying, that's all," she said, walking again. "I'm fine."

For a moment Gary lost his bearings, then, reaching down deep in his pocket and feeling two quarters, said, "We're not too far from the drug store here. It's closer than the house. Would you like to stop for a Coke?"

"Yes," she said, her voice cheery, "I'd love that."

A few minutes later they approached Sid's Pharmacy and Gary guided her up the steps by the arm. "Don't catch your foot in one of those cracks," he warned.

Inside, he cupped her elbow as she slid up on one of the high wire-back stools at the soda fountain, and he sat down next to her. The druggist scurried out from his cubicle and around the end of counter.

"What can I get you, folks?" he said, looking cartoon-ish with his shiny bald head, his wide grin and big ears.

Gary pointed to the menu on the wall behind the counter. "How does a soda sound to you, Sarah?" he asked.

"Oh, thank you, no," she said. "That would be much too much."

"Are you sure? I think I'm going to try a soda, a chocolate soda."

"My favorite, too," the druggist said, picking a soda glass off the shelf and plunging a shot of syrup from a container into the narrow bottom of the glass.

"I'll have a Coke, a small one," Sarah said, plucking a straw from a box on the counter.

"Are you sure you don't want a soda?" Gary coaxed, watching the old man squirt seltzer water into the glass and plop in two big scoops of vanilla ice cream.

"A Coke is all I want," she said, "thanks."

Stretching his neck to watch the procedure, Gary said, "Don't you use chocolate ice cream to make a chocolate soda?"

The druggist stuck in a long spoon and slid the soda across the marble counter top to Gary. "Nope. 'Tain't done that way, son. The syrup is chocolate and that's all. Unless you want a real chocolatey chocolatey soda."

"I guess you know your business," Gary said, maneuvering the spoon down to the bottom and stirring it up a little.

"After forty years I guess I should," he said. "And don't forget, it was a druggist— or a chemist, as they more properly called themselves in those days, who invented Coca Cola.... And this is for you, young lady," he said, placing a Coke before

Sarah and pointing to her hand. "Not engaged yet, I see."

Sarah flushed. Gary himself was momentarily flustered.

"That's all right," the old man said. "Don't rush it. Never rush it. If it's true love it will wait. Take it from an old geezer who knows." He grinned. "Will there be anything else?" he said, his bony fingers playing lightly on the edge of the counter.

"How much do I owe you?" Gary said, taking the hint and digging into his pocket for the money.

"Fifteen cents, young man," he said, taking the quarter Gary handed him and finding a dime in his pocket. "If I can get you young people something else, just call. I'll be in the back."

"This is really good," Gary said, bringing up a lump of ice cream. "I wish you'd have ordered it, too. We still can, you know."

"Maybe next time," she said, nipping the paper off the end of her straw.

'Next time.' Her words both pleased and troubled him. "Sarah," he said, intentionally blunt, "is Dexter your boyfriend?"

"Dexter? Goodness no. Dexter's a very good friend, but he's not my boyfriend."

"When I met him yesterday, he seemed to give me the impression that he is. He's about the same age, and being there with you, I thought—"

"Dexter's twenty-two. For years him and his mother and two sisters used to be our upstairs neighbors when we rented our own flat. He did all kinds of favors for us after Dad died. Of course Donny helped, but he couldn't compare to Dexter. Dexter did everything, like shoveling the coal off the sidewalk where the truck used to dump it, and wheelbarrowing it around the side of the house and emptying it through the basement window into the coal bin—and I don't even think he was ten yet when he started. But he was strong. I guess he felt sorry for us. He shoveled the snow, ran errands on his bicycle and even painted our kitchen once."

"He sounds like a pretty decent guy."

"'Decent.' That's a good way to put it. Yes, and he would never even take a penny for anything. I think of him more as a brother than anything else."

Gary looked at her doubtfully. "I'm not so sure he thinks of himself that way, Sarah. I've seen the way he looks at you."

She pulled herself up tight and her nose lifted a little indignantly. "Well I can't help what he thinks. There's nothing I can do about it."

"Didn't he ever ask you to be his girl?"

She paused. "I suppose he was working up to it a few times, but he knows how I feel. I've even introduced him as my big brother sometimes."

Gary scooped up the last of his soda. "And how did he take that?"

She shrugged her narrow shoulders. "I don't know."

"But he still comes around, doesn't he?"

"Oh, yes, he does. He still runs errands for us sometimes, to the drug store or the grocery store if we need anything. Things like that."

"Why did you move out of the flat, if I'm not being too personal?"

"I guess I've already told you an awful lot," she said, sucking the bottom of the glass.

"I'm prying too much."

"No, no, it's all right," she said, reaching over and touching his hand. "I don't mind. You see, when Dad was killed the insurance company— or the steel company where he worked, I don't know which— they gave my mother a settlement of twenty-five hundred dollars. That took us quite a ways, but naturally it couldn't last forever. When the money ran out, we had to move because we couldn't afford the rent anymore, so here we are, living in Mrs. Harmon's palace."

"That's a pretty sad story," he said.

"Oh, it's not so bad. Some people are a lot worse off than we are. You know the song *Happy Days Are Here Again.* Well, some people are still waiting and some already have them. It all depends on how you look at it. What's a father worth?"

He looked at her, looked directly into the moist, brown eyes gazing back into his own. "Sarah," he said, "however you see it, know this, better days *are* coming. Worse ones will come first, then the better ones will follow. Believe me, it will happen much sooner than you think."

Looking intently, her eyes darted nervously. "I don't understand, Gary."

"Don't try. Trust me."

"The way you're talking…."

"Just trust me. Or borrow some of your mother's faith," he said, easing up. "Ready?"

He helped her get to her feet and led the way over the squeaky floor out the door.

"Good night, young people," the old man called from the back. "Come again."

Together, they walked the quiet streets, the sky above them dull in the dying light, saying little to each other, as if lost in secret thoughts, the shawl high up on Sarah's nose, her hands tucked in her side pockets. Beside her, Gary kept a slow pace, seeing in his mind's eye the both of them sitting at the soda fountain, a tableau— two sweethearts in a Norman Rockwell cover.

'*Not engaged yet, I see.*'

126

But he already was engaged. To Shelley!

Overall, the moment gave him a warm feeling inside, despite the chill nipping his nose and seeking his bones. "Maybe I should have suggested a cup of hot coffee instead of the cold stuff we had," he said, breaking the silence.

She smiled but said nothing, then took his arm and stopped. She began to cough, quiet, suppressed coughs that went on long enough to alarm Gary, and her breathing sounded erratic.

"Are you all right, Sarah?" he said, patting her back ever so gently.

Gradually, her breathing leveled out and they moved on again. "I'm sorry," she said, speaking haltingly, a few words at a time.

"That breathlessness doesn't sound so good. Have you had it long?" he asked, his brows knitted with concern.

"Not too. It only seems to happen when I overexert myself. My mother says I have a weak constitution and should drink more milk, but I hate milk."

"Have you seen a doctor?"

"We only go for my mother. Doctors are expensive. Besides, I'm sure it's something that will pass in time, maybe when we get settled in a more permanent place and she can do more for herself."

"Sarah, can I make a suggestion?"

"You mean 'may I,' not 'can I,'" she said, laughing. "My sixth grade teacher, Miss Wagner, told me it's 'may' if you're asking permission, and 'can' if you're asking if you're able to."

"Good for Miss Wagner," he said peevishly, and recalling her mispronunciation of 'mischievous.'

"I'm sorry, Gary. I guess I wasn't being very funny."

"Sarah, I know it's none of my business, and I barely know you, and you can tell me to shut up, but I do know a few things. And one of them is when a visit to the doctor is in order. That shortness of breath... could mean anything."

"Gary—"

"Listen to me, Sarah. You need to see a doctor. Not that you have anything seriously wrong with you, but because you want to make sure nothing's wrong. Something, anything, could be starting, like pneumonia, that you can catch early, before it gets worse."

"Gary, I appreciate—"

"I insist, okay? See a doctor. Don't worry about what it costs; I'll take care of it. You can try one not far from here, Doctor Goldman. He's good and he can put your mind at ease. It could just be a deep congestion in your lungs. I heard you cough, too."

"I can't take advantage of you like that, Gary. As you said, we've only just met."

"I'll worry about what's right. Just promise me you'll see him."

She looked embarrassed. "I don't know what my mother will say about this."

"Don't tell her."

"Oh, Gary, I couldn't do that."

"Why not?"

"I just couldn't do anything like that behind her back."

"Then let me talk to her. I think I can convince her."

"No, it's all right. I'll talk to her and let you know what she says."

"Sarah—"

"Please, Gary. I appreciate your concern, but leave it up to me, all right?"

He sighed. "Okay, Sarah. Just let me know and I'll make the appointment for you if it's necessary. Heck, I'll go with you to see him, personally."

She didn't need to stop again as they walked slowly along,

moving one behind the other to make room on the sidewalk whenever they passed others coming toward them.

He felt warmer now, with the walking, and was pleased that his chest hardly seemed to hurt at all. Secretly he took pride in his healing powers, and was smiling inwardly when a lightning bolt of pain shot out, making him wince. Well, he wasn't cured yet, but he was getting there, anyway.

"Gary," she said in a voice softly apologetic, "Gary, I've been selfish, doing all the talking while you've been listening to me ramble on and on without giving you a chance to tell me about yourself."

"Compared to your life, Sarah, mine's been pretty humdrum. Except for my grandfather. I'll tell you about him sometime if you like."

"I'd love to hear."

"When we get more time, all right?"

"If that's what you want," she said.

He asked how she was feeling, and after a few minutes, he said, "Sarah, do you know the man that lives upstairs? Not too tall... has a mustache?"

She looked up to him. "Oh, I know who you mean. He's like a shadow, up the stairs, down the stairs, in the door and out the door, and always with his head buried like he's afraid to let you see his face. All he ever says is 'hello.' That's all. No 'How are you?' or 'nice day' or anything, just 'hello.'"

"What's his name?"

"I don't know. Mrs. Harmon never mentioned it and I've only noticed him lately. I don't think he's been here a whole week yet, only, I'd say, a few days before you came, but I can't be positive. Why, is something wrong?"

"No real reason. It's kind of funny, the way he just seems to slink around."

"I never thought of it that way, 'slinking around,' but I

think you're right. Of course, Mrs. Harmon is happy to have anybody, as long as they pay their rent and don't bother her."

"I don't like to be overly suspicious, Sarah, but if he suddenly becomes friendly, I'd be on my guard."

As they approached their corner, neither Gary nor Sarah noticed the man standing in the recessed doorway of a building across the street, watching them.

Chapter 21

A rattling sound, the soft clink of metal on metal may have awakened Gary from a sound sleep. Or perhaps it was instinct, the alertness that manifests itself when the fear is aroused and danger seems to lurk in the dark. Gary listened, homing in on the scratching, scraping noises that started. Stopped. Started again. The water pipes? Steam rattling the radiator?

Gradually, his attention came round to the door. Someone was tinkering with the lock. He sat up, his heart tripping. "Who's there?" he called, throwing off the blanket and blindly ransacking his clothes on the chair next to the bed to get his knife. "Who is it!" he cried again, rushing across the room and fumbling for the light switch on the wall.

A muffled drumming of feet in the hallway, then nothing.

Throwing open the door, Gary lunged out into the hall, crouching, pivoting this way and that, his knife poised to slash. No one, nothing but still shadows and the musty smell of worn carpeting. He stood a moment, held his breath, listening. No sound except the ticking of wood framing tightening in the chill night air. Nothing but that and the dreadful dimness that strained his eyes. Slowly, he let his breath go out, his hand monitoring his ribs for surprises. Suddenly aware of his near nakedness, he ducked back inside.

As he had earlier, he locked the door and turned the key fully so that it couldn't be poked out. Setting the open knife within easy reach on the chair beside the bed, he lay down again. Who, he wondered, who would want to do him harm? He had no money. No one knew who he was or what he intended to do. The only person he could think of was Dexter. He might have spotted him with Sarah and had a jealous fit.

But no doors had slammed, neither front nor back, and anyone trying to avoid getting caught is not likely at that point to worry about making noise.

No, everything pointed to the intruder being someone in the house. But who? Mrs. Harmon? She couldn't have run more quietly than a hippo. On the other hand, why didn't she come rushing out to investigate the ruckus?

And it certainly wasn't Sarah. Who else lived in the house, with its multiple rooms and apartments? Though he'd seen no one else, he was certain of their presence, judging by the evidence they'd left behind after using the bathroom and by the footsteps he often heard tramping overhead.

The only suspect, the only logical suspect, had to be the mysterious stranger he'd caught skulking around. He couldn't imagine any motive the man could possibly have for wanting to hurt him, but from now on, he'd be extremely alert.

Just what the hell is going on!

Lying there with the light still burning, wide awake, his mind gradually turned to home, to Shelley, to Sarah and that cough he suspected might be tuberculosis, a common illness in this age, if he remembered his history correctly. Would she be sent to a sanatorium? Would she even live? He shuddered at the thought. Eventually, his thoughts turned jumbled and confused, his eyes closed and he drifted off to sleep.

* * * * *

"Ice," someone called, rapping at the door. "Ice."

"Coming," Gary called, snapping awake.

Slipping into his pants, he went to the door and opened it. "Come on in," he said, running his hand through his hair and smoothing down his face.

"How much does that weigh?" Gary asked, watching the

ice man, or, rather, the ice boy, lugging at his side a block of ice clamped between the serpent fang ends of the tongs.

"Twenty-five pounds," he answered, carrying his head low as he dripped a water trail over to the icebox.

"No school today?"

"I quit," the boy said, lifting the icebox lid with one hand, holding the ice above the opening and lowering it in with the other. Then he released the tongs and closed the lid.

"Quitting school. That's not the smartest thing you can do."

The boy's dark eyes flashed up at him, fiery and concentrated in their focus. "Fuck you," he said, holding the tongs at his side in a way that made it look like one of those fearsome baling hooks Gary had seen in the movie *On the Waterfront*.

Stung, Gary fell back a step. "Sorry about that," he said. "I didn't mean to offend you. I just—"

But the boy was already gone.

Gary shook his head. Touchy bastard. But with that kind of independence, the kid had the makings of a great CEO. Or a killer. He hoped it wouldn't turn out to be the latter.

Fishing his Mickey Mouse watch out of his pocket, Gary saw that it was just past ten, exactly when Elsie said the iceman would come. Hearing water run outside, he decided to shave and wash at the sink in his room, and beat it out of the house. Things had to be done today, and he was already tired with lack of sleep. He considered once more making a trip to the warehouse to see if he could get back in, but abandoned the thought. He could wait another what... five days? He *had* to wait.

Another clear morning, bright but still chilly that early in the day. Gary didn't mind; the fresh air helped work the sleep out of his eyes and invigorated him as he walked toward

Michigan Street, a half dozen or so blocks north. Despite the vintage cars going by, he still couldn't believe he had traveled back in time. It was so…so bizarre! If he ever did get back home, how could he expect Shelley to believe his story? How could anyone? They'd probably institutionalize him.

Ahead, just past a small boarded up theater, he saw the sign: **CORKY"S BICYCLE EMPORIUM**. Gary crossed the street over to it and stopped out front to look over a few bikes standing in racks in front of the windows on the sidewalk, then went inside. The place was dreary and smelled of rubber. Bending over the counter, chewing the thumb nail of his bad hand, was Corky, concentrating on some invoices next to a huge ledger with a cloth cover.

"Excuse me, can I get some service here?" Gary said, smiling.

Corky pushed himself back, squinted one eye and said, "Hey, kid. Just like you said you would, you showed up."

"I'm a man of my word."

"You wanted a bike, you said. A used one." He came around the counter.

"I said a good used one."

"Sure. Whatta ya think, I sell junk? Take a gander around for yourself and see."

The floor was crowded with bicycles, handlebar to handlebar, and from the age-blistered ceiling hung a crammed array of wheels, rims, chains and old tubes bandaged with orange patches. Greasy parts lay scattered everywhere.

"No doubt about it, Corky, this really is a bicycle emporium."

Corky winked, nodded and made a clicking sound with his mouth. "I'll hold my own with the best of 'em," he said, "yessiree." With the thumb and pinky of his bad hand he stroked the bristles of his bony jaw. "Seems to me, if I remember right, you had a little problem with moolah. A little tight for money. Broke."

"That's what I wanted to talk to you about, Corky. If you could see your way clear to give me credit until—"

"Credit! Come on, kid, whatta ya think I am, the Bank of America?"

"Only until tonight, Corky. I promise I'll pay you back. With interest if I have to."

"Can it, kid. You're makin' promises based on what?" He squinted an eye. "Oh, I get it, you're countin' on winning that bet on the fight tonight. But you're only hopin'. You didn't even have enough to cover Leo's bet, for chrissake. Sammy put the money up for ya. And if Louis loses tonight, you're out your dough. And Sammy's dough. And you're still gonna have to pay Sammy back." He hiked up his baggy pants. "Uh uh, kid, no go. Don't try to wheedle nothin' outta me."

"Corky, listen to me. I know Louis is going to win. Don't ask me how, I just know it. All I'm asking you to do is to trust me."

"Trust you, sure, that he takes him in under three rounds. With my dough."

From a rear room a voice called. "Hey, Corky, you want I should fill them tires now or wait?"

"That's my helper," Corky said, leaning over to see him through the doorway. "What's the matter, Jackie, can't you figger it out yourself?" He winked at Gary.

Jackie emerged from the back and stood in the doorway, his feet spread and planted, and a wrench in his hand. "Figger it for myself? Every time I try it one way, you say I should've done it the other way. Now make up my mind, Corky."

"Oh, suddenly you got a mind?" he shouted back. "Feisty little twerp," Corky whispered from the side of his mouth.

"Goddammit, Corky, I'm warning ya, someday I'm gonna

walk out that door and you ain't never gonna see my ass again."

"Don't do me no favors," Corky said, watching Jackie turn and stomp away, cursing.

Gary frowned. "If he's such a bad worker, why don't you fire him?"

"Who says he's bad? He's good; they don't come no better. Does his best work when he's mad, I found out, so I just like to pull his leg once in a while. Keep him on his toes. If you see the connection—pull his leg to keep him on his toes?" Corky chortled, and Gary realized he'd never heard anybody chortle before.

"Aren't you afraid he'll quit, riding him like that?"

"Quit? Jackie? Hell no, that goddamned half-pint ain't goin' no place. Where could he go in this lousy day and age, with no work anyplace? And he's trying to save enough money to open hisself a restaurant."

Jackie reappeared in the doorway again. "I'm still waiting for an answer, Corky. I told you before, I ain't making a move till you say so, that way, somethin's wrong, you got nobody but yourself to blame. I'm tired of gettin' shit on."

"Then fill the goddamned things up now!" he yelled, making a fist with his good hand.

"See?" Jackie whined. "What'd I say, mad again. My fault, always my fault."

"Well you're gettin' on my friggin nerves. Go on, get back to work. I ain't payin' you for nothing. And no doughnuts today. I ain't paying for no goddamned doughnuts so you can sit on your ass and waste time asking me questions." He poked a cigarette in his mouth. "Damn runt."

"Someday, Corky, I hope to God, if I ever get my own place you come in, 'cause if you do, I swear to God I'll spike your fuckin' coffee with rat poison and watch you croak on the floor!" He stormed off.

"Yeah, if you cook like you work here, you'll probably poison half the city."

Gary and Corky stood there a few moments listening to Jackie slam and bang things around in the back room.

"Now, where were we?" Corky said. "Oh, yeah, you wanna buy a used bike. Oops, excuse me, a *good* used bike, but you're short of cash and want me to give you credit."

"I promised I'd pay you."

"Yeah, kid, I know, and I appreciate your good intentions, but the truth is you can't even wipe your ass with good intentions. Only money talks." He raised his hand. "I know, I know, you promise, but promises are made to be broken. Look how many people get divorced, for chrissake. And, yeah, Sammy said you're a good kid, but Sammy didn't say if I get stiffed by you he'll pick up the bill. No sir, Sammy ain't that dumb, not by a long shot."

"All right," Gary said. "Just how much would a *good* used bike cost?"

Again Corky stroked his bristly jaw with his thumb and pinky. "Well, if you was buying and actually had the cash, I s'pose I could let one go for six bucks."

"Show me one."

"What for, kid? I toldja I ain't changin' my mind."

"Curiosity. Let's see."

Corky sighed and led Gary around behind a rack of new bicycles. "Here you go. A good selection, better than you could find anyplace else."

"How about this one?" Gary said, pulling a bike from the rack.

"That Schwinn? She's a beauty that one. Look at her. New balonies, and the pedals show just about no wear. Like new. Handle grips the same."

"How does it ride?"

"Like a dream. Jackie did all the work on it, so I know it's perfect. Got a new chain, too."

"What if somebody offered you five for it? Would you take it?"

"Five? Maybe. If some guy come in that door there waving a fin, I guess I'd take it. Hard to turn down Honest Abe when he's looking you square in the eye."

Gary reached into his pocket and pulled out his wallet. "I'll take it. Here you go," he said thrusting out the twenty. "You *do* have change?"

Corky's eyes bugged out. "Well for chrissake, kid, why all the fuckin' rigormortis about credit when you got that kind of loot?"

"The truth? You want the truth?"

"Yeah, I'm kinda partial to it."

"The truth is, I was saving it for my mother's operation," he said, keeping a poker face. "She'll have to wait a little longer for it, but that's all right. She should live till then."

A couple of brown teeth bit down on Corky's lower lip. "Whatsa matter with her?"

"I'd rather not say," Gary said, a quiver in his voice. "All I can tell you is that it's life-threatening."

"Goddammit all to hell, kid, you coulda told me instead of beating around the fuckin' bush like that and puttin' me on the spot." He shoved the twenty back at Gary. "Makin' me feel like a shit-heel. Here. Keep the fuckin' money and take the fuckin' bike." He waggled his thumb and pinky. "But I swear, if you stiff me—"

"Thanks, Corky, and don't worry, you'll be paid tonight," he said, taking the bike and jockeying it through the store to the door. "I'm a man of my word."

"Okay, okay, I heard ya. I'll be waiting to hear that fight

tonight, too." He swung around and yelled, "Jackie, ain't you done yet, for crissakes... pain in the ass."

Crashing sounds from the back room echoed in the store.

"One thing, kid," he said, turning back to Gary. "A favor. Being you're college and all."

"What is it?" Gary asked, straddling the seat.

"Just what the hell *does* 'emporium' mean?"

Gary laughed. "Emporium? It's no more than a classy name for a store that sells merchandise of all kinds. In your case, it's bicycles."

"Well, sure, that's right," he said, straightening up and puffing his chest. "Sure, because this *is* a highfalutin store. I knew it all the time."

"See you tonight," Gary said, pushing off.

The bicycle wobbled beneath him for a few yards, then steadied itself as he cruised down the street.

"God, please, Joe Louis, please knock that guy out by the third round."

Chapter 22

For ten minutes Gary wheeled across town toward the old First Ward, the overarching branches of budding trees— elm? lining the street, forming a tunnel, a time tunnel, as he thought it, although in his own time, these trees would be gone, a victim of some foreign blight. He bounced over several cobblestone streets and crossed one with streetcar tracks through neighborhoods that hadn't changed much. The houses, old even then, were painted and clean. Tidy lawns, hedges and flower beds fronted the properties. He saw people raking up winter debris, sweeping porches and cleaning windows, and he realized, to his own surprise, that poverty and squalor did not necessarily go hand in hand.

He felt a strange intimacy with this bygone world, this world his grandpa had so longed to return to. He could understand that longing, that nostalgic yearning. All around him life seemed so much simpler than it did in his own time. No doubt, this was a quieter time, a more peaceful time. Still, he had his misgivings. These people seemed to lack drive, energy, a will to rise above their circumstances and succeed. Didn't they realize how important money is, what a difference it could make in their lives? Maybe they just had no hope.

Ahead he saw a mailman come off a porch onto the sidewalk, carrying a pouch over his shoulder and shuffling mail in his hands as he came toward him. Gary slid over to the curb: "Excuse me, but could you tell me how I can get to the First Ward playground? I was told it's around here somewhere."

"No lie about that," the mailman said, looking up without stopping and jabbing the air with a handful of letters. "Go over a block and up one. You can't miss it."

Gary pushed off again, feeling a slight strain on his chest as he rose from the seat to put his weight on the pedal. *Not bad,* he thought, banking around the corner, *not bad at all.* Within moments he saw it, the playground before him, and an old building just beyond. This had to be the place, he assured himself, dismounting and walking his bike alongside the chain link fence enclosing the playground. Inside, ropes curled down from the top of a maypole standing in the center like a gray finger pointing skyward. A few teeter-totters, like creatures with flat heads gazing up, squatted around the yard, and a bank of swings hung near the fence closest to the house. Aside from a woman gently pushing and singing to a little boy on one of the swings, no one else was in sight.

The house stood two stories high, its steep, tarpaper and tin roof peeling away, while pieces of rusted gutters dangled dangerously overhead. The color of the flaked clapboard siding, where it still existed, couldn't be guessed at, and only one cracked attic window in front escaped the full effect of vandals' stones. Gary's bike leaned and bounced softly beside him as he walked the crumbled strip of concrete between the house and the playground fence. Where the side entrance had once been stood a fractured wood door nailed over with a couple of rotting boards. In place of the disintegrated steps lay a heap of broken cinder blocks. *No wonder the neighbors petitioned to have the place torn down,* Gary thought, as he walked the length of the house around to the empty lot in back.

Setting the bike against the house next to the back door, hanging loose on rusted hinges, Gary's eyes scanned the ground, rising and falling everywhere with mounds of dirt and rubble, glass shards, chunks of wood and tin cans. He would need something to stop the killer, but what? He had considered using his knife, but that could backfire if things didn't work out exactly right. What was he going to say, 'Okay, let's walk to the police station or I'll stab you'? Unless he killed him, how could he stop him? No, something else…. He hunted around, kicking aside debris until he saw the metal end sticking out of a pile of rubbish. Jacking it back and forth and up and down, he finally tugged it free.

Perfect! A beautiful length of galvanized pipe, three to four feet long that fit his hands like an ax handle. Or a baseball bat. He hefted it to his shoulder and swung it easily, testing it, testing his own body and wondering if it would betray him at the last minute. But right now he felt fine and he swung again, harder. *Whoosh.* Satisfied, he searched for a spot where he could hide it and grab it when he needed it. A hollow against the ruptured stone foundation next to the nearly collapsed steps to the door looked ideal. Leaving enough of the end to see, he kicked some dirt and old rags over the top to hide it.

Pushing his bike along, he wandered to the opposite side of the house, bordered by an empty lot. A lamppost stood by the curb and no door opened to that side of the house. Out front the porch sagged precariously with its broken pillars, and the spindle-less railing lay on its warped side. At some point the steps leading up to the porch had vanished, perhaps to be used as kindling in a wood stove. Painted in red on the boards nailed across the entry door was the warning **KEEP OUT**.

Gary looked down the street one way, then the other. While he surveyed the area, a few cars drove by, and a taxi cab stopped diagonally across the street from where he stood. In black lettering on the yellow door was the name *City Taxi* and below that the telephone number: *CL 4000.* This was a time before the three-digit prefix to telephone numbers, he remembered. 'CL.' That would stand for…'Cleveland.' Musing over the thought, he paid no attention to the man climbing out the door on the opposite side of the cab.

CLeveland, WAshington, GArfield, MAdison—all telephone exchanges. It really was a much simpler time, he thought, his attention coming back to the business at hand: *The little girl would have been safer walking the opposite side of the street, where, apparently, all the houses were occupied, but how could she have known the fate that awaited her?*

He didn't know which direction she would be coming from, not that it made any difference. Nor did it make any difference that her body was found in the lot behind the house. He could have killed her inside the house and then carried her outside to bury her. So he could have murdered her in either place. Possibly it could have taken place on the other side of the house, but that seemed doubtful. The risk of being seen there in an open lot with a street light so close was much greater.

No, the killer would have caught her out on the sidewalk and dragged her through the walkway between the house and the playground fence. And whether he would do his dirty work inside or outside, he, Gary, would have to wait inside. Outside, he had no place to conceal himself and he didn't want to merely scare off the maniac, he wanted to capture him and get him into the hands of the police so they could beat the living hell out of him and lock him up forever. Even if the attack took place outside, he would hear it and could be on top of him within seconds.

Straddling his bike, Gary looked the street over one last time to get a good mental picture of it. Slowly he rolled along the sidewalk, past the woman in the playground, still singing to her child as she gently pushed on the swing. Diagonally across the street near the corner, a man sat on the concrete stoop of an empty poolroom. Head bowed, he didn't look up when Gary looked across to him as he jumped his front tire from the curb to the street. Only after Gary had gone a distance did the man lift his head, staring after him and casually stroking his mustache.

Didn't that jerk know that sitting on cold concrete can give you hemorrhoids? Gary thought, picking up speed and sailing along.

Chapter 23

Sarah leaned forward in her seat and stretched to see over the railing when Gary rode up to the front of the house. "Hi Gary," she said, tilting her chin up to see him better.

"Hello Sarah. Hello Dexter," he said, holding a small bag in one hand and using the other to tip the bike way down to swing his leg over.

Dexter lifted a lazy arm and let it drop back, then looked off in another direction.

"Sarah, do you think Mrs. Harmon would mind if I parked the bike behind the house?" he asked, walking the bike closer to the steps.

"Whose bike is it, Gary?" she asked, pulling a plain white scarf down around her neck.

He smiled. "Mine, of course."

"My goodness, you don't waste any time, do you?"

Dexter stiffened and his jaw hardened.

"Or should I go right in and ask her?"

"I've seen others park there," she said, "but I'd tell her about it so she knows."

"Thanks," he said, "that's a good idea. If it's already there she's not so likely to refuse me." He started around the house. "So long, Dexter."

Gary leaned the bike against the garbage bin behind the house and carried the package in his arm. No one was about when he came in the back door and down the hallway to Mrs. Harmon's apartment. He knocked.

The door swung open and Mrs. Harmon stood there in a maroon housecoat and with a cigarette burning in her hand. "Yes?" she said, laying her whole hand against her face as she brought the cigarette to her mouth and sucked in a mouthful of smoke.

"Elsie, I bought a bicycle this morning and I wonder if it's all right if I park it behind the house."

Exhaling a thick plume of blue smoke, she dragged again, sucking in her cheeks with the effort, then blew that out off to the side. "Where's it now, this bicycle?"

"It's...a...well, it's out back."

She nodded. "Why didn't you ask first?"

"I...I—"

"I, I, my eye. Okay, go 'head. Just keep it out of the way of the garbage men for when they come. And if it gets stole or somebody trips over it and breaks their neck, remember, it's your responsibility, not mine." She started to shut the door.

"One more thing, if you please, Elsie..."

"What now?" she said, the door poised to slam shut.

"Do you have a telephone?"

"I do and it'll cost you a nickel if you wanna use it."

"Well, could I bother you to use your phone book first, if you have one?"

"Come on in," she said, lumbering over to the far side of her couch and bending down beside it to get the book. "Here."

Crossing over he took it from her hand and began riffling through the pages. *Tyler, Ambros; Tyler, Anthony...*He skipped to the G's. No *Tyler, Granville.* He might have guessed. Not many people owned telephones in these bleak times. He handed the book back.

"That's it?" she said, yanking it from his hands. "Just looking, no phone call?"

"Thanks a lot, Elsie," he said, backing out, smiling. "Sorry to trouble you." He grasped the doorknob. "Shut it?"

"Of course shut it. You think this is a damned barn?"

Gary stopped in his room to drop off his grocery bag,

hurried out through the back door, mounted his bike and slipped out the yard onto the street, heading north. Knowing his grandparents had lived in the house at 182 Compton for fifty years or more, he was eager to see if they'd lived there even longer. It was possible.

The thought had been on his mind almost since he realized he'd been transported back in time, nagging at him, haunting him— an opportunity to see his grandparents. Gramps first, then find Gram. To see them as they were then! He couldn't even imagine them as young people like himself. The very idea of it sent shivers up his back.

Weaving along between the heavier traffic on Boswell Avenue, he calculated: *Grandpa, he was more than sure, was born in 1919 or 1920, and that would make him about twenty now, and Grandma, eighteen. Strange to think that his own parents weren't even born yet, wouldn't be for another fifteen years or so in the 1950s. And here he was, ahead of them in time. How that could make any sense at all he didn't know, yet he couldn't argue with reality. He knew he was back in time! Now he had a chance to live the moment his grandpa would gleefully have given ten years of his life for, maybe more. The moment had arrived for him, though, Gary Tyler, to actually see them, especially Gramps—Granville Eugene Tyler, Jr., dead so long that he, Gary, much to his shame, sometimes had a hard time visualizing his face.*

Up ahead, in the middle of the block on Compton Street, his house— the same house he had left some sixty years ago last week, standing proud. Like the houses around it, all of the same design and vintage, it looked sturdier now and somehow taller. Pulling over to the curb, he dismounted, hiked the bike onto the sidewalk and began walking it past the row of houses, the same houses he had walked and run past a thousand times in his life. So familiar yet unfamiliar.

His knees weakened as he approached his house. The impulse to turn and run seized him, but he held firm. His steps slowed. He felt light-headed. Stopping, he looked up at the number, 182, checking it against the number of the house next door. The clapboard siding, painted a sickly yellow was probably still there beneath the brown aluminum siding his grandpa installed, or would install, some forty years hence. In front of the house a wire fence with a scallop design and no more than two feet high surrounded a patch of dead vegetation. Same house, different house; same year, different year. Hadn't he just run out that front door a few days ago? Where the hell was he!

The front door opened and a dust mop with two meaty hands around its neck poked its head through and shook vigorously. Behind it a red-headed woman appeared. "Looking for something?" she asked.

"This is number 182?"

She pointed to the numbers. "That's what it says."

"Does the Tyler family live here? Mr. Granville Tyler?"

"Nobody by that name here," she said, throttling the mop for another good shake. "A Taylor lives a few doors down, though. Jerry Taylor. And his wife Isabelle."

"Have you lived here long, Ma'm, if I may ask?"

"You can ask and I don't mind telling it's a little too long. The kids in this neighborhood get on my nerves with their screaming all the time. My husband, he's not in the best of health, either. Parents don't watch their kids the way they used to. Rest assured we'll be moving soon ourselves."

"So, you've been here awhile?"

"Eight years or so. That's 'awhile' enough, don't you think?"

"And no Tylers that you know of or can think of live around here?"

"I wish I could—wait a minute," she said, sticking her head back inside. "Louie," she called, "Louie, do you know anybody around here named Tyler?" She turned back to Gary. "What's the first name?"

"Granville."

"Granville Tyler," she called back into the house.

She popped her head back out. "No, he don't know that name neither. Wish I coulda helped you out, sorry."

Gary thanked her, got on his bike and pedaled off. What a disappointment! His heart was really set on seeing him, Gramps, more so than he had led himself to believe. There had to be another way, though. Maybe he could check through the electric company. Somehow he'd find it. Now that he'd started on this quest, he couldn't give it up. But first a quick trip.

The sky clouded over suddenly and sun showers fell out of the blue. Undeterred by, and unmindful of the rain wetting him down, he splashed through white clouds in silver puddles as he pedaled down the streets and swung a final corner.

And there it was before him, just as his grandparents had described it, in all its pristine and primitive glory, the buildings and shops and streets gleaming in the rain. He got off his bike and walked it along, his eyes drinking in the sights: the Bijou theater; Mason's Haberdashery; the Kit Kat Klub, where Gramps said he used to go to hear the latest Dixieland and jazz groups. And farther down the street, Jack's Groceries, its windows festooned with hanging cheeses and sausages; Heinrich's tailor shop, too dark inside to see Hammy himself; the soda shop, its delicious scent of syrupy ice cream surpassed only by the cruel, mind-altering fragrance of Franz's baked goods wafting out in torturous ecstasy. And him virtually penniless! He walked along, taking in the sights until satisfied, at least for the time being. The rain let up and he set off back home.

* * * * *

Back inside his room, Gary stripped off his wet clothes and laid them over the radiator to dry. From his pants pockets he took his wallet, knife and change and put them on top of the dresser next to his car keys. Half-turned to go to the table, he stopped, suddenly remembering. The newspaper article he'd cut out of the paper now lay on the opposite side of the dresser top. Or did it? He paused, concentrating. He could swear it wasn't where he'd left it. Or did he move it at some time or other without realizing it? Could a breeze have lifted it and drifted it over when he'd walked past?

He looked back to the door, to the lock that just about any skeleton key would open. Mrs. Harmon? She certainly was nosy enough to sneak in and snoop around. Or was he wrong altogether about the paper being moved? He'd had a lot on his mind, hadn't had much sleep, especially after that incident with someone trying to pick his lock during the night, not to mention all the riding around town. He shrugged and gave up. Well, if an intruder did get in, he didn't find much.

Back at the table, Gary opened the bag and dug out two bottles of Coke and the hamburger he bought on the way back from the First Ward. That left him with exactly ten cents to spend at the tavern later in the evening, enough for two beers.

Dressing up, he made a quick trip to the community john and had just stepped out to return to his room, when Sarah came in through the front door.

"Oh, I'm glad I caught you, Gary. I was afraid you might be taking a nap and I didn't want to disturb you."

"I probably would have been, but I had to go out and take care of some business," he said.

"Go out? I didn't see you leave."

"That's because I left through the back, up toward Boswell Avenue. Have you been on the porch all that while?" he asked, glancing over her shoulder.

"Mostly to keep Dexter company. My mother's been sleeping quite a bit today."

"Is Dexter gone?"

"Yes, he just left. He had to work. This week he's working mixed hours. He's not happy about that, but he should be grateful to have a job at all, I think."

"I guess anybody's lucky to have any kind of job these days," he said, noticing the whiteness of the scarf neatly tucked under the collar of her corduroy jacket.

"I wanted to ask you, Gary, seeing that you're alone and not really set up for cooking, well, would you like to have supper with my mother and me tomorrow?"

Gary felt a little shaky. He hadn't expected anything so nice as that. "Sarah, I, uh…what does your mother think of that idea?"

"Actually, the idea was hers. I told her about the other night and our walk to the drug store and she thought that was very nice of you. So did I," she added, her cheeks turning rosy with her words, and lowering her head.

"You really don't have to go to that trouble, Sarah. I'm doing fine, honest. I have… all kinds of stuff."

"My mother will be disappointed if you don't come. Honestly, it's no trouble for us. I have to cook for the two of us anyway. One more can't hurt."

"Sarah—"

"Unless you have other plans."

"No. It's just…"

"I'm making spaghetti. With meat balls."

"I'm sure it will be delicious."

Again she blushed. "You'll come, then?"

"If your mother doesn't mind and you really want me to...."

"I do," she said, a peculiar mixture of shyness and determination. "Come about four o'clock? Apartment three?"

"Four o'clock it is."

Back in his room, Gary locked himself in, stripped out of his clothes and stretched out on the bed. He felt strangely euphoric. Talking to Sarah had a soothing effect on him, as if she were nourishing some forgotten region of his soul. Something else about her, too, an indefinable essence, a vague reflection of something ethereal. On the surface she seemed like any other girl— pretty, sweet, polite. Yet, she had depth, a depth that he felt sure could never be plumbed, a murkiness of personality below the bright surface, like a current that runs so deep its source can never be traced. But maybe that was the nature of all women, when you really looked closely at them, he thought. He gave up, sighed and closed his eyes.

For a change, nothing hurt. He felt good, better than expected, given his injured ribs and the bike ride. He thought about tomorrow, Tuesday, and his spaghetti dinner; and Friday, just four days away, and what he would have to do to prevent little Dolly Czarnowski from being murdered.

But first things first. Tonight he had to win his bet, he just had to, otherwise he was in big trouble. Ah, but not necessarily, he thought, remembering the twenty dollar bill safely stashed away in his wallet. The thought comforted him and he dozed off.

Chapter 24

Later that evening, sometime after nine o'clock, when Gary opened the front door to Windy's tavern, he felt he was entering the anteroom to Hell, with its cacophony of sounds battling Nick's honky-tonk piano, and an acrid, eye-burning quilt of smoke hovering like a cloud of poison gas over the heads of men crowded up to the bar and hunched over the tables. Raised voices competed for attention:

"…Who, Weston? You call that ballet dancer a basketball player? Go on, I'll put my dough on Clark any day of the week. He can jump higher, shoot straighter and run faster than him and any other three of them sonsabitches put together, even.…"

"…What the hell ya talking about, Morey had that slut in the sack before Johnny ever got in the picture.…"

"…You kidding me? Louis? Shit, Dempsey woulda come out bobbing and weaving and busted him up like a box of crackers before.…"

Gary found a narrow spot at the bar and squeezed in.

"Heads up, everybody, look who's here," one of the bozos shouted, "the kid on the Wall O' Shame."

"Take a look-see up there—Gary Tyler. Shay monya, boy, shay monya." The emphasis was on the 'mon.'

Hoots and hollers and whistles and catcalls careened and ricocheted around the room and off the walls.

"Hey, kid, how's it feel to be dummy of the week?"

"Yeah, kid, what did they teach you in school, how to make valentines?"

They razzed him mercilessly.

"Hey, kid, tell your ol' man to get his money back from the school. He was robbed."

"You tell him, Gimp, tell him."

"My grandbabies won't be goin' to *your* school. You can make book on it."

They hammered the bar and whooped themselves hoarse. A few fell into choking fits.

"Never mind, you seedy bunch of bums," Sam yelled over the crowd. "What did I tell you? Gary's here, just like I said, so you better order a lot of beer and get ready to cry in it 'cause he's cleanin' you out tonight, everybody who bet against him."

"He's still chump of the week. Two rounds, hah!"

"We'll see who's chump after tonight, right, Gary? You ready to take their dough?"

"I hope so," Gary said, smiling a little wanly.

"Hey, I'm bettin' with you, don't worry...same?" he said, holding up a glass.

Gary nodded, digging for a nickel.

"You had me a scared there for a bit," Corky said, coming over and muscling in next to Gary and holding his drink out so as not to spill it. "Did you ride over on the bike?"

"I walked. I didn't want to chance having it stolen."

"Aw, go on, don't shit me. You were scared I'd grab it back if you lose tonight."

"I didn't think that."

"Yeah, don't try to shit a shitter, kid. Ha ha, you didn't think! ...So how is it anyway? Everything I said it was, right?"

"How's what?"

"The bike! What the fuck we talkin' about!"

"Oh, that, the bike. It's all right," Gary said, picking up his drink.

"All right! That's all you can say? That sonofabitch is a beautiful piece of work. It's a work of art. Jackie put his heart and soul into it, made it like brand new."

"He should. I paid enough for it," Gary said, licking the foam from his lips.

"Paid enough? Whatta ya talkin', whatta ya talkin' about? You ain't paid shit yet!"

Gary smiled and patted Corky's arm. "Only kidding, Corky. I'm only kidding. It's a great bike. It's better than I ever expected. Thanks."

"Fight's almost on, kid," Sam said, clicking on the radio on a shelf behind the bar.

One of the men sitting at a table called out, "Hey, Sam, set us up here. This time you better bring us a couple of pitchers."

Watching Sam fill the pitchers from the tap and carry them over to the table, Gary caught sight of a man sitting alone at a small table in the corner, a man he hadn't noticed before. The man's eyes met Gary's and held till Gary turned away. When Sam came back around the counter, Gary signaled him over. Sam leaned toward him, his ear close.

"Who's the guy in the corner by himself?" Gary asked, his voice low. "The baldy."

Sam's brows arched. "Tell the truth, don't know him from Adam. Came in right after you. Don't look familiar neither."

Gary shrugged and glanced back over his shoulder. The man was staring at him. Or was he?

From the far end of the bar: "Hey, punk!"

Half a dozen heads swung around, including Gary's. "Yeah, you, punk, with your name on the Wall O' Shame," Leo said, shaking his chin at Gary.

"You talking to *me*?" Gary said, giving his best Robert De

Niro impression.

"Yeah, college boy, punk...I'm talking to you, all right."

Sam jumped in. "Cut the shit, Leo, or I'll cut you off. I think you had enough tonight anyway."

"Bullshit. You put my name up on that fuckin' board last week and it shouldn't of oughta never been there."

"I ain't rehashing the issue, Leo, so drop it, drop it."

"I'm talking to the punk, anyway, not you. Hey, punk, you got any more dough you wanna blow?"

Gary told himself the man was drunk and tried to ignore him.

"What'sa matter, punk, scared? No tongue? No guts?"

That did it! Gary reached in for his wallet, plucked out the twenty dollar bill and slapped it on the bar.

Talking stopped and a bunch of curious grayheads goose-necked to see better.

Sam's eyes flared. "Hey, kid, was you holdin' out on me before?"

"Sorry, Sam, no. I just came into this. I'll explain later."

Half-standing to see, Leo himself looked surprised. "Twenty bucks? Where'd *you* get twenty bucks? You better check to see it ain't counterfeit, Sam."

Gary held his breath as Sam snatched up the bill, held it up to the light and snapped it a couple of times. "He called your bluff, Leo, so you can stop the stalling around. You covering this bet or do you just like to shoot your mouth off?"

"Okay, okay. You're on. Same terms, right?"

"Terms?" the weasel piped up. "Terms? What the fuck you doin', buying a car?"

Leo turned on him. "There ain't no odds, are there? So I can't say 'odds,' can I? And this ain't exactly an even bet. So mind your own fuckin' business unless you got some money to lose, too."

156

"Come on, come on," Sam said, snapping his fingers, "the money, Leo, the money."

Leo dragged out four fives and handed them over. "Same bet, right, Louis in under three rounds, you say?"

"Even money says he does it," Gary said, swallowing hard, worried he had gone too far.

"Sam, you hang on to that dough," Leo said, "and be ready to fork it over here."

"Anybody else wants to lay any bets," Sam said, "I'll cover. Only I'm taking odds, not like Gary." He looked around. "Nobody? Okay, Nick, cut the piano for awhile. You guys back there making your side bets, too, shut up," he hollered, going over to the radio and turning up the volume.

Gary glanced over his shoulder to the stranger sitting erect, his hand wrapped around his glass. It was hard to tell in that shadowed space whether he actually had a smile on his face or was just plain goofy.

The fight came on:

And in this corner, weighing in at...

The bell rang and excitement built in the room as the announcer, firing words like tracer bullets, delivered a nasally blow by blow description of the fight:

...and a left to the head, and Louis throws a left to the body, another left to the head, a...Now Roper, jabbing jabbing, and Louis comes back, throws a hook to the body and another to the body...

Shouts shook the bar room, died and rose again. They punched the air around them. Tiger Tommy Fisher, chin tucked, was throwing quick, stiff jabs.

"…Come on, Louis, flatten the bum…."
"…Kill him, kill that nigger…."
The cheers, the groans, then…

…and Roper is down, Roper's down…
One…two…three…four…

Over. Stunned, dazed, they turned to each other. First-round knockout! Leo's face flamed. Curses flew and an incendiary burst of tempers hop-scotched around the room like brush fires.

"That's it, you guys," Sam said, going into the cash register and scooping up a bundle of bills. He picked up a slip of paper. "I got the names right here and it's time to pay off."

"…It's a goddamned fix, that's what it is, a fix!…"

"…Roper took a dive, I tell ya. Two minutes twenty seconds! Shit…"

"…I don't give a goddamn what anybody says, the whole fuckin' game is crooked!…."

More heated words singed the air and set faces nose to nose over mouths spraying spit with their words. Angry hands tossed and grabbed money between them.

"Now now, boys, settle down. We want to be good sports here, don't we? Here you go," Sam said, counting out the bills in front of Gary: "Your six and six more. That's twelve." Raising his voice so everyone could hear, he said, "And here's the first ten from *Leeeeo* that I covered for you, that's twenty-two, and the double sawbuck you just put up and *Leeeeo* covered, is another forty. So for you, kid, that comes to sixty-two smackers, on the nose."

At the far end of the bar several hands slapping condolences on Leo's back did nothing to suppress the fire raging in his eyes.

"Sam," Gary said, "can you break this twenty for me?"

"Sure, kid, no trouble. It's a lot harder to lose a bunch of bills than just one, I know. How do you want it?"

"Fives and singles will be fine."

Sam counted and fanned the bills on the bar. "There you go, kid."

Gary picked up his money, folded it neatly and held it up in the air. "Thanks a lot, Leo," he called, slipping the money into his pocket. "This means more to me than you know."

The hands on his back held Leo back. "Go on, get laid, you goddamned punk-piss pot-bastard, you. I can take you apart any day of the week, even if you got me by thirty years."

"Ease up there, Leo, ease up," Sam said. "It ain't the kid's fault he won, and it ain't his fault he bet. You're the one egged him on and everybody knows it." He turned his attention back to Gary. "How 'bout it, kid, another one to celebrate?" he asked, already holding up the glass in his hand.

"And you have one, too, Sam, on me."

"How about me?" Corky said, sidling up to him, his tongue sucking the brown gaps in his teeth. "And don't put that loot too deep in your pocket, least not till you pay me the fin you owe me." One end of his cigarette was slimy with saliva.

"Corky, too, Sam," he said, digging out a five and handing it over. "And here's a dollar for Jackie. For his good work."

"Hey, kid, you're all right," Corky said, taking the money and stuffing it with his thumb and pinky into his shirt pocket. Smoke leaked out the gaps in his smile.

"He's was all right long before he met you, Corky," Sam said, setting up the beers. "He ain't been waitin' all his life for *you* to tell him he's all right."

About that time somebody cried out for the food, seconded by the Irish duke. Sam disappeared into the kitchen and came back minutes later lugging a heaping platter of lunch meat and bread and putting it in its usual spot at the end of the bar. No one wasted much time lining up and digging in. All except Gary. Although he'd hardly eaten anything all day, he didn't feel hungry.

His eyes wandered over the place, from the end of the bar where the men were bunched up, to the tables along the wall, to the doorway of the darkened dining room beyond. Apparently Sam had no family business, just the local yokels. His eyes drifted over to the stranger, sitting with a beer in front of him, apparently enjoying his own company. From where Gary sat, he couldn't tell much about him except that he was wearing a dark suit, blue or maybe brown, and an open-collar shirt. Completely bald and clean shaven, from the neck up he looked like an undressed shop window mannequin.

The arguing turned sporadic, the beer flowed freely and laughter broke out here and there like little bursts of sunshine. Gary wasn't sure if he was on his fifth or his sixth beer. He'd been light-headed for a while, but the thrill of his win buoyed his spirits and he didn't want to give up the night and go back to his empty room. Amused, he listened to the arguments:

"…Wall Street? Who cares. Let them rich bastards feel the pinch like us working stiffs…."

"…Hoover? You kidding me? You never heard of Hoovervilles, hah? Things was good before he…."

"…you maybe, but I don't believe none o' them conniving thieves. Gimme what they got in Russia, everybody equal, free schools, free hospitals…."

"…for all it means to me. I don't care what's goin' on in France or none of them other Godforsaken countries…."

"…They want to fight, let 'em. Let 'em bleed through their asses and kill theirselves. It ain't our business…."

Gary sat hunched over his beer now, hearing the arguments and insults being launched like missiles across the room. They were beginning to irritate him. *Uneducated ignoramuses, talking about things they knew nothing about.* He swallowed more beer. He brooded.

"… and two of my best buddies got gassed over there. Piss on 'em, I say. We saved their ass once and now they can bail…."

"…paid how much? Two million? Stewart's Folly, they called it then, and that's what it still is. Two million! For what, nothin' but ice and snow and more ice and snow. You know how many people you can feed with two…."

"…that's right, president for life, I'd make him. Who gave you the WPA? Who gave you Social Security, hah? Tell me that, and tell me…."

Gary's nostrils flared over the glass tipped to his mouth. *Fools! These absolute fools!* He felt like God, sitting there, looking into the foamy bubbles in his glass, as if they were miniature crystal balls breaking into pieces. They knew nothing, this gallery of living dead men, and he knew everything. He knew what tomorrow was going to bring, and the next year and the year after that. He could lay out the whole coming decade before them in detail. He knew Roosevelt would die in six short years, and that the world would explode into a new age with the devastation of Hiroshima and Nagasaki. He knew that in less than twenty-five years a president would be assassinated in Texas and in half a dozen years after that, Americans would walk on the moon. By then most of these guys would be history. Yes, he felt like God, and the more he drank, the more godlike he felt.

A few stragglers wandered in and, before long, joined in the verbal fray.

"…any amount of money you want to bet, we don't get in that mess. Roosevelt's too shrewd for that. Another war? The people would never stand for it, not after—"

"You'd lose, too," Gary said, lifting his head.

A hush fell over them. Even the piano playing stopped. "What the hell do you know?" Chippie said, leaning over the bar to see him better. "A kid like you, still wet behind the ears."

"Tell him, Gimp, you tell him."

"I know you'd lose that bet, just like you lost the fight bet to me."

The Irish duke set his glass down. "Now I wouldn't be gettin' up on me high horse if I were standin' in your shoes, lad."

"Well, you're not," Gary straightening up and turning in the stool he grabbed earlier. "Any of you ever hear of Pearl Harbor?"

They exchanged glances. "Nothing like that around here."

"Not around here, no," Gary said, casting a look of disgust. "Anybody ever hear of Hawaii?"

"Of course we have. Think we're ignorant? Down around Mexico, someplace. In the ocean."

"In the ocean, right. Someplace. Well, that's where it's going to start."

"What the hell's he saying?"

"Ah, he's talkin' through his hat. Don't listen to him, he's drunker'n a skunk."

"That's where your next war is going to start."

"Oh, yeah, who we fightin'?"

Gary emptied his glass and pushed it toward Sam. He rose, holding onto the stool.

"Hey, kid, maybe you had enough, huh?"

"Fill it, Sam." He skipped from one face to another. "Japan, that's who."

"Japan!" Stan broke in. "That bunch of midgets? Why, they live a million miles away. What reason we ever gonna have to fight them? Even if we did, we'd wipe 'em out, which should take all of about... three or four hours," he crowed, thrusting out his chest and basking in the warmth of laughter and friendly hands rubbing approval into his shoulders.

Gary bristled with their guffaws and their stupid heckling.

"And who we gonna have to fight after that," the weasel said, "King Kong from Hong Kong?"

The place rocked with laughter.

"Laugh, go ahead, laugh," Gary said, facing them down. "But you won't see the end of this Depression until the war starts."

"And when might that be," the duke asked, "if you wouldn't mind imparting that privileged information?"

"When? I'll tell you when." He raised his glass, took a long swallow, and ran his wrist over his mouth. "December 7, 1941, that's when."

"1941, is it? Well, then," the duke said, whipping out his pocket watch and moving it back and forth to bring it into focus, "a year and half or thereabouts goes mighty fast. Shouldn't we be rushin' home to load our guns?"

They howled.

"Maybe get our fly swatters ready, too, for them yeller mosquiters."

They howled louder.

"Hey, kid," Sam said, motioning him to sit down, "that's enough, huh?"

"Let him go, Sam," Leo called down the bar. "It ain't often we get a college boy drop in and make an ass out of hisself. He ain't got his name up on the Wall O' Shame for nothin', you know."

"You, Leo, you—you're the biggest fool of all," Gary shot back. "You're the biggest fool because you think you know the most and you know the least. You got a big mouth and you don't know when to shut it and you don't understand anything, anything at all. Nothing, nil, zilch."

"Why you lousy punk—"

Half a dozen hands checked Leo's clumsy struggle to get at Gary.

"Easy down there, Leo," Sam said, "easy." He turned back to Gary. "Don't press it, kid. We don't want things goin' haywire here."

"And I'll tell you something else. Did *Gone with the Wind*, the movie— did it come out yet?"

A confused mumbling of opinions.

"When it does it will be your next Academy Award winner."

"I might have told you that myself, lad," the duke said.

"Sure, like you might have told that dummy down there that it was *Seward's* Folly, not *Stewart's* Folly, but you didn't."

"I thought he did say that."

"You thought, uh huh. Like you thought he said seven million, not two. And maybe you could have told me that Roosevelt's going to run for another term and that Truman's going to be your next president after Roosevelt dies in office?" He nodded, godlike in his presence, lording it over them. "That's right, Harry S. Truman."

"Truman? Who the hell's Truman?"

A smoke-heavy silence fell over the room.

"Go on, go ahead and stare at me like I'm crazy, but— what's that your Al Jolson likes to say, 'You ain't seen nothin' yet'? Well you ain't, because a bomb is coming along, a bomb so great, so powerful, it won't only blow away a hundred thousand people in a blinding flash, but your past, too, and your complacence and all your goddamned cynical innocence with it. Yes, I said 'cynical innocence.' You figure it out." Tears flooded his eyes. "And I pity you, I really do, every last one of you for the pain you and your wives and your families are doomed to suffer when Western Union comes knocking to *regretfully inform* you that your precious Johnny or Joey or Jerry died on the bloody beaches of Wake or Midway, Iwo Jima or Anzio or Normandy. Their young lives snuffed out, and all for what? So that those they saved the country and the world for can spend the next forty years trembling under the threat of nuclear—"

"Hey, kid, kid, come on, come on...."

"And you back there in the corner, yes, you, Sardonicus, with the dumb grin on your face, you think it's funny? You another one who thinks I don't know what I'm talking about?"

His eyes piercing the smoky gloom, Sardonicus raised his glass in salute and said nothing.

"Okay, kid," Sam said, "enough's enough. Sit down. Sit down now, I'm telling ya! I'm cutting ya off. This's gone far as I'm lettin' it go. Bangin' heads with the boys is one thing, but new customers are hard to come by...Sorry, buddy, he called." He slung a wet rag under the bar. "What the hell, is everybody gone nuts around here tonight?" He walked to the end of the bar and waved Tommy Fisher over from where he was sitting at a table with a few others.

Tommy glanced around, pointing *me?* to himself, then getting up and springing over on bandy legs, like a boxer coming out of his corner at the sound of the bell.

"What, Sam, you want me for somethin'?"

"Yeah, Tommy, you in pretty good shape?"

"You mean am I sober? Sober enough to walk a pretty straight line. Sure, why?"

"I want you to take the kid home."

"Me? Sam, I don't even know where he lives. Maybe it's out of my way."

"I'm askin' ya, Tommy. As a special favor to me. I think the drinks affected the kid's brain. You heard how's he's talkin' out of his head, like a nut. Hell, he could fall down and kill hisself goin' home. Or could even get rolled, the condition he's in."

"Aw, hell, Sam...."

Sam laid a hairy hand on his shoulder. "Tommy, remember when you needed the bail money to—"

"Okay, okay, Sam, you made your point, but s'pose he don't wanna go, then what?"

"He'll go. Go on, go stand by him." He nudged him. "Go 'head."

Gary sagged in his seat. His rheumy eyes had lost their focus and he fumbled for his glass on the bar, but Sam snatched it away.

"That's it, kid, time to pack it in."

Gary started to protest. "I'm...I'm okay, Sam, I'm okay."

"Sure you are. Nothin' wrong with you a good night's sleep won't fix. Go 'head now. Tommy here's gonna walk ya. He'll tell you some good fight stories. Got a million of 'em. Come on now, come on. Help him up, Tommy. That's it. Now go 'head with Tommy, kid. You're in good hands with him."

"That's right, kid. Just if you're gonna throw up, give me fair warnin' so I can get outta the way."

"Make sure he gets inside, Tommy. Don't leave him

standin' out on the street where the cops can nab him and toss him in the cooler."

Tommy threw Sam a salute and helped Gary through the door.

"Thass right, Tommy," Gary slurred, wobbling on his feet. "Save me...so Dolly...li'l Dolly...one good turn... "

A few minutes later, the baldheaded stranger Gary called Sardonicus stepped out of the bar, surveyed both ends of the street, turned up his collar and walked off into the dark.

Chapter 25

Gary's head hurt when he tried to lift it from the pillow and he dropped back moaning. Arm flung over his eyes, he tried to think. Last night at Windy's, yes, but how did he get home? He couldn't even remember.

Gradually, his memory reasserted itself with pieces missing, like an un-restored strip of old movie film. *The bar... Corky, on one side of him, smiling, smoke filtering out between his gapped teeth... On the other side, Tommy, his baby-blue eyes with his nose punched flat between them... Sam ordering him to sit down.* He groaned and rolled to his side.

What a fool! He had talked, talked too much about...about what? In his mind he saw images of Pearl Harbor, just the way Gramps had painted them in his mind on their Hawaiian vacation:

...the screams of hungry gulls now the screams of Japanese Zeros swarming out of the sun, peeling off and swooping in, machine-gun fire stitching bombing paths before them as they skimmed the harbor and released their deadly payloads of treachery, raising flaming bouquets of water like bloody remnants of unrealized dreams, and pocking a trail home to ships rocking with explosions— thunder wrapped in black smoke coiling wraith-like over burning water and foundering ships, their steel bows fighting for the surface, and the Arizona, still leaking oil like blood from a tomb....

Too much! He had shot his mouth off about Pearl Harbor. What else, what other information had spilled from his saturated brain? His head swam with broken images of presidents and bombs and war. *Gone with the Wind... The*

*stranger grinning in the corner, Sardonicus, like a demon...
and Joe Louis... Joe Louis—*

The bet! He'd won the bet, thank you, Lord. He slid his hand into his pocket and pulled out a wad of bills. Squinting, and still unable to see, much less focus, he dropped the money at his side. One consolation, he had money, anyway, though he couldn't remember how much. Like sandpaper, his tongue was so dry he could light a match on it. Time, what time could it be? In the dark he couldn't tell. Slowly, holding his head so it wouldn't fall off, he eased himself up through sheer force of will, and sat on the edge of the bed. How was it that alcohol could turn a perfectly healthy mind and body into mush and waste?

Water, that's what he needed, water to re-hydrate his dehydrated organs.

Oh, hell! What time is it? Reaching for his watch, he half-lunged to the window to lift the shade. It was... straining his eyes to see Mickey's pointing mitts... yes, ten past two. He relaxed. "Thank you, God, thank you again," he said aloud and going for the sink, where he gulped cold water out of his hand and doused his face before putting his whole head under the tap. The shock sent a shiver through his body. He still had time to freshen up with a bath and a clean shave. Maybe rest a little more. He needed the time to recover, and he wanted to look his best when he went in to meet Sarah's mother. And Sarah. He wished he had bought some after shave lotion.

Waiting behind his door, Gary checked the time: two minutes to. He made a last minute dash to the mirror, smoothed his hair with his hand because he'd misplaced his comb, and smoothed down his clothes. Just like a damn woman, he thought. Well, at least he didn't lick his palms to keep his hair in place, the way he'd seen women do. And cats.

Taking a deep breath to relax himself, he opened the door,

stepped into the hallway, where he could smell the spicy sauce, locked his door, dropped his key in his pocket and, hiding his excitement, strolled casually down to apartment three.

Chapter 26

Standing in front of Sarah's apartment, straightening his collar and tie and tucking in his white shirt, Gary glanced around at the sound of footsteps thumping his way.

A tall redhead about his own age came bearing down on him. "Good afternoon, sir," he said, a beaming smile lighting his way. He had the mellow, resonant voice of a radio announcer.

"Hi," Gary said, taken aback by the sudden intrusion.

"My name's Joe Berty," he said, stopping and reaching over to shake hands.

"Gary Tyler," he said, leaning back, instinctively on guard.

"I just moved in this morning. Hope I didn't disturb you with my racket."

"Hardly," Gary said, "no, not at all."

"Your apartment?"

"No, no, I'm down the hall there."

"Well," he said, breaking off as abruptly as he'd broken in, "I'm off. Can't waste time, you know. Time's money and life's too short." He laughed a hearty laugh. "Pleasure meeting you, Gary."

"Same here, Joe," Gary said, watching him stride away, his shoulders squared, long arms swinging.

Gary rapped and the door opened a crack, then all the way. "Hi, Gary." She poked her head out a titch. "I thought I heard voices out here."

"Some guy—"

"Come in, come in."

The rich smell of pasta sauce poured out, almost rocking him back on his heels. "Thanks," he said, hesitating.

"Come on, it's all right. We won't bite you," she said, touching his arm and coaxing him inside. She closed the door. Her warm smile encouraged him.

The apartment was neat, but shoe-box small. He could see it all: the cramped living room, where he stood, and beyond, the kitchen with a doorway at the far end, presumably leading to a bedroom.

"Gary, this is my mother," she said, extending her hand to the woman sunk deep in a sofa on the opposite side of the room.

"How do you do, Mrs...Mon..."

"Montera," Sarah finished for him.

"Mrs. Montera," he repeated, nodding politely.

"So you're Gary," she said, appraising him with a sharp, dark eye.

"We went for a soda together the other day, Mama, Gary and me."

"I know I know, you told me all about it," she said, waving her off and leaning forward to arrange her shawl around her shoulder. "I don't know why, I'm always cold, always cold, even on the warm days I'm always cold, especially my feet. Maybe it's the dampness I can't take." She looked up again. "Sit, sit," she said, "over there, that's the best chair."

"Thank you," Gary said, glancing at Sarah and going over to a blue, wing chair. He sat down, adjusting one of the doilies on the arm. "Very cozy apartment you have here," he said, looking at the old lady and back to Sarah. "Very cozy."

"We try to make it that way, don't we, Mama?" Sarah said, seeming to come out of some momentary confusion.

She shrugged. "Sarah, get him something to drink. You forget your manners?"

"No, Mama, I was just—Gary, what would you like? We have some whiskey, or red wine, or—"

"Wine would be fine," he said, holding his hand out. "About this much." He held his thumb and forefinger about two inches apart.

"How about you, Mama?"

"Maybe the anisette. Soothe my throat. Warm my old bones a little, too. I think maybe I'm coming down with something. God forbid, I don't need anything else."

Sarah spoke from the kitchen. "Gary, I hope you saved your appetite. I made a lot."

"I did."

Sarah came in carrying the drinks. "I'll put it on the table next to you here, Mama. I hope your hand's not shaking too much."

"Don't worry about my hand, my hand can take care of itself."

"Gary...?" she said, a lovely vision smiling down at him, handing him his wine.

Gary watched her pull a straight back chair into position. "How about you, Sarah, aren't you having anything?" he asked, hoping her mother didn't notice him trying not to notice how lovely Sarah looked with her long, dark brown hair and pink sweater.

"Not right now for me."

"Drinks don't agree with her," her mother said, tapping her breast. "Her constitution, it's not so strong like it should be."

"Mama, please." The light caught the sheen of her dark hair as she fluffed it over her shoulder and folded her hands on her lap. Her legs, pressed close, leaned to the side and were crossed at the ankles. "You can use the table next to you for your drink, Gary."

Mrs. Montera made phlegmy hacking sounds in her throat after sipping her anisette. "So tell me again, your name. Gary, Gary what?"

"Tyler," he said, setting his drink aside.

She looked to Sarah and back to him. She scratched her cheek lightly. "What kind of name is that? What country?"

"Mama, don't—"

"What? I can't ask a simple question?"

"That's all right, Sarah," he said, looking back to the dark eyes that seemed to harbor an atavistic cunning. "Actually, Mrs. Montera, I'm a mixture." He smiled. "A mongrel, I guess you'd say."

"But what?" she pressed. "What's in it, this…" she rolled her hand, "this mixture?"

He picked up his drink. "Mostly English, I think, some French, some German."

"No Italian?"

"Mama!" Sarah buried her face in her hands.

"What? I said something wrong? I'm only asking if this mixture has some Italian in it." She turned back to Gary. "Maybe just a little bit?"

"I think somewhere down the line, I think I may have some, yes."

"Siciliano?"

"Sicilian? That I can't say for sure."

She leaned back, satisfied. "See?" she said to Sarah. "So bad? Now you know."

As they talked, Gary stole furtive glances around the room. The sofa looked like a shoddy mate to Mrs. Harmon's, and the same sad, colorless carpet lay over the floor. Tucked here and there were little tables, nicked and scarred but polished to a high finish. The personalities of the Monteras showed in the details: Doilies covered almost everything— sofa, big chair, table tops. On the wall behind him hung a framed picture of Jesus in the Garden of Gethsemane, and in the middle of the adjoining wall, a picture of the Madonna and Child hanging close to a wooden crucifix with a pitiful Jesus gazing down on Mrs. Montera. A knickknack shelf in the corner held shiny glass figurines: an elephant with an upraised trunk, a duck, a squirrel sitting on his haunches, a cluster of purple grapes. On a table at the opposite end of the sofa sat a wicker basket bulging with balls of yarn and knitting needles pushing up the lid.

"Those are very pretty," Gary said, pointing to the vase sprouting yellow flowers.

"Yes, aren't they?" Sarah said. "Mums. They last awhile if you take care of them. I love them."

The old lady snuffled into a handkerchief. "Dexter— you don't know him yet— he brought them. He's so good. Always thinking of us, eh, Sarah? Ever since he was little."

Gary wasn't sure if it was the mention of Dexter or the sweater coloring Sarah's face pink.

"I think the water's boiling," she said, smoothing her dress behind as she rose. "Time to throw the spaghetti in. Do you need more wine, Gary?"

He held up his glass. "I'm fine," he said, "thanks."

"Sarah, put the radio on," her mother said, brushing a graying hank of hair behind her ear. "Some nice music, eh?" She sipped her anisette. "And remind me tomorrow, you do my hair. I can't stand it the way it is." She smiled across to Gary. "The curse of old age," she said. "Look." She held out her hand. "Arthur-itis. My fingers, they don't want to close or I could do my own hair. Look, my skin." She touched her face. "Wrinkles, that's one thing, but this, already like a prune? My feet," she pointed—

"Ma, please," Sarah pleaded from the kitchen, "Gary doesn't want to hear all about your aches and pains."

"What, I can't talk now? I have to keep my mouth shut in my own house?"

"Then pick a different subject, can't you?"

"Did you turn on the radio like I said?"

Music spilled from the kitchen.

"This is pretty, no?" the woman said, raising her finger like an aerial bringing the music in.

Gary cocked an ear. "It's familiar but…what's the name of it?"

"You don't know it?" She raised her voice. "Sarah, what's the name of this song?"

"*Harbor Lights.*"

"*Harbor Lights*, that's it."

Sarah came back into the room and sat down again on the edge of her seat. "We'll be eating soon," she said, lowering her head shyly. She looked over to her mother. "You okay, Ma? Do you want anything?" She had taken off her sweater.

"I'm fine, fine, don't worry about me."

They were at a loss for words for a few moments, then Sarah, imitating her mother's actions of a few minutes earlier, raised a finger and said, "This is a beautiful number, don't you think so?" she asked, looking at Gary.

"It's too sad, for my money," her mother interjected.

"Oh, Ma…."

"'Oh, Ma,' nothing. It's about somebody who lost somebody they love, no? So the world is blue. My world is blue enough. I don't need any more blue in it."

"Do you like it, Gary?" Sarah asked, turning to him again.

"It is sad, true, but beautiful, too," he said.

"*Blue World*," Sarah's mother said. "That's the name of it. How come I can remember everything I don't want to, but can't remember anything I do want to?"

"*It's a Blue World*," Gary repeated. "I know the song."

Mrs. Montera's shaky hand set the anisette on the end table beside her. "Gary, Sarah tells me you are a teacher. No, no, not Sarah. Elsie told me, told us— the landlady."

"Not quite yet, Mrs. Montera. I'm applying now to one of the schools."

"What kind of school?"

"High school."

She nodded as if hearing something remarkable. "That's good. A teacher. That's very good. You can make a good living. Respectable. And that way you don't have to work for somebody in a factory so they can kill you and forget about you like a dog."

"Mama," Sarah said, "please don't start that again." She got up. "Come on, I'll help you into the kitchen. I'm putting it on the table now."

"Can I give you a hand?" Gary asked.

"If you'll get her cane off the floor for me..." Sarah said, pulling her mother forward.

Gary held the cane, watching Sarah help her mother inch up to the edge of the couch.

"I'll take it now," Sarah said, bracing the cane for her mother.

Her mother grasped the handle, "Okay, I got it." She made several attempts to get up, bouncing a little higher each time, with Sarah's hand under her elbow giving her some lift. "Ah, she said, steadying herself on her feet, "the curse of old age."

Gary wondered just how old she could be. If Sarah was nineteen... maybe somewhere between fifty and fifty-five? No doubt she looked a lot older than that.

Gary lagged behind, watching Sarah guide her mother as the old lady hobbled into the kitchen and plopped herself with an "oomph" into the closest chair.

"Gary, you can sit there," Sarah said, indicating the head of the table.

A white table cloth was neatly laid with three large plates, wooden salad bowls, knives, forks and spoons. In the center were a jar of red pepper, an open bowl of grated cheese and salt and pepper shakers. Three water glasses, with chipped ice, were already filled and stood in their places. On the chairs lay folded cloths.

Gary sat and laid the cloth, actually a dish towel, over his lap. The kitchen was claustrophobic, so tight that Gary could reach out and touch almost everything in the room. At the sink behind him, Sarah poured the spaghetti out of a metal strainer and dumped it into a pot, ready to serve.

"…That was Sarah's dream, too, when she was a little girl, to go to college," Mrs. Montera said, recovering her lost train of thought, "but things didn't work out so good. First her father, he dies—" she clasped her hands and looked up, shaking them, "Oh, Deo! Then *my* troubles start. Thank God we have the church, that's all I can say, thank God for the church.

"We say grace first, eh?" Sarah's mother said, her eyes, hidden under the brows of her bowed head, fixed on him.

The prayer was brief and they ate their meal, leisurely, making small talk as the salad and the meat went around the table.

"This is delicious Sarah," Gary said, "the best I've ever had."

Sarah thanked him, blushing, and her mother's smug expression said 'Of course!'

They talked about their favorite radio programs, like *Search for Tomorrow* and the *Jack Benny Show,* and after a while Gary asked, "Tell me, do you know who else lives in these apartments?"

Sarah set her fork aside. "Well, there's Mrs. Harmon, of course," she said, "and that strange man you mentioned before."

"Who, Sarah, who?"

"I don't think you saw him yet, Mama. I think he only moved in a few days ago."

"Oh. And don't forget my friend Mamie, upstairs."

"Mamie, yes, Mrs. Lutz," Sarah said. "She's a widow. Very dignified, and she always asks after my mother, doesn't she, Ma?"

"Sometimes she brings cookies or fruit. She's like me, a widow."

"Also, there's Mr. Danner. He's upstairs, too, across from Mrs. Lutz."

"He's a big, you know what," the old lady said, making a cup of her hand and bringing it to her mouth as if to drink. "And what about the Orsinis, Sarah, the 'mice'?"

"Them too. They're very quiet and you hardly ever see them. They stay to themselves."

"The night owl, don't forget," her mother said. "His name, Sarah, it's a funny name. What is it again?"

"Nathaniel, Mama. He's the one you always see going to the post office with packages under his arm. Mrs. Harmon says those are books he's mailing, and that someday we're going to hear about him."

"And that man we saw once the other day, so sneaky, remember, Sarah?"

"Brrrr," she said. "We saw him passing by your room, like a... like a wolf. But we haven't seen him since, thank God.... I think that's all right now, Gary."

"Not quite," Gary said. "Someone else just introduced himself to me in the hall."

"Oh, is that who you were talking to," Sarah said. "I thought I heard voices."

"He said his name is Joe, Joe...I didn't catch his last name. A very friendly guy...."

They ate, gabbing about the weather and how warm it was for April, and about the times and how hard they were.

From a shelf on the wall, the radio played soft music.

"Isn't this a pretty song?" Sarah said, "*Blue Moon.*"

Now that, that's a nice one," Mrs. Montera said, keeping time with her fork and singing along:

> *Blue moon,*
> *Da da de da da de da da,*
> *Without a da da de da da,*
> *Da da de da da,de da.*
> *Blue moon...*

She continued humming the melody.

"Very pretty," Gary said, looking across to Sarah, who dipped her head when their eyes met.

"My Sarah, she likes everything with blue in it, blue moons, blue worlds, blue skies. Even the dress she's wearing is blue. You see? Under the apron?"

Gary nodded, his blue eyes taking in the lovely creature across from him who seemed blue even when she was smiling. He noticed that she hadn't eaten much.

Before they finished, Sarah had gone to the stove and turned on the gas under the coffee pot. "You will have coffee, won't you, Gary?"

"I'd like that," he said.

"Guess what came today, Gary?" Sarah said, brightening.

"I don't think I can."

"My son," her mother interrupted, "Donny. He sent us a post card. Get it, Sarah, go get it. On the dresser I put it, by the mirror, next to the hair brush."

Sarah dabbed her mouth with the napkin, and left the table.

"I don't see where—oh, here it is," she said, coming back

and handing the card to Gary. "Excuse his writing," she said. "Donny wasn't exactly an honor student in school."

"Nice picture," he said, taking it from her and turning toward the light. "Napa Valley. That's California grape country."

"Napa Valley," Sarah repeated. "I wonder if it's anywhere near Mount Whitney. I believe that's highest mountain in the country."

"The highest mountain, yes," Gary said wryly. "I thought it was in Alaska."

"Oh, no, Mount Whitney is in California. I distinctly remember that from school."

"See, Sarah's smart. She can be a teacher, too. Maybe yet she will. She's cut out for it. Go ahead, Sarah," the old woman urged impatiently, "read it, it's okay to read it. Read it out loud, real loud so I can hear good."

Gary flipped it over and squinted out the words: "'Hi mom and Toots...'"

"Toots, that's his nickname for Sarah. Go on, read read."

"'This is like on a farm where I work its hot and it aint easy but it pays ok. Im working my way down to L.A. because Im gonna give the movies a try. Ill writ you later wen I get time, your movie star son Donny.' PS I dont ever want to see or eat anouther garpe.'"

"My son, a movie star." She dabbed her eyes. "I can't believe it."

Sarah took the card back. "Don't count on it, Mama. It's not as easy as the movie magazines make it look to become a movie star like James Cagney or Clark Gable."

She yipped. "Are you kidding? My son's better looking any day than that Clark Gable with the elephant ears. Bring his picture, Sarah. Let Gary see."

"Not now, Mama. Another time. At least we heard from

him, even if he can't spell and doesn't like 'garpes.' He's well, that's all that counts. You know how worried you've been about him."

"Of course I worry. A mother who don't worry about her children is not a mother, in my book. Mothers are supposed to worry about their children. That's their job."

Gary's eyes followed Sarah into the bedroom, apparently the only one in the apartment, which meant the two had to sleep together. All he could see of it was the foot of the bed and the near end of the dresser where a figure of the Madonna stood with an unlit candle before it. He thought he could hear Sarah stifling a cough.

"How about you, Gary, your mother. She's not worried about you?"

"I'm sorry, Mrs. Montera, but my mother's dead. My father, too."

She laid her hands over her heart. "Oh, what a shame. That's too bad, too bad."

"Mama!"

"No, Sarah, it's all right," he said, facing her coming out of the bedroom. "It happened a long time ago. I was raised by my grandparents." It felt good for a change not to lie.

"Maybe we can talk about that another time," Sarah said, picking the cups and saucers out of the cupboard and setting them on the table. "I hope you saved room for dessert, Gary."

"How did it happen, your parents?" the old lady pressed.

"I was told they died in a car accident. I was just a boy."

"Mama! I said another time." She turned to Gary. "Do you like lemon pie?"

"Lemon pie. It's my favorite."

They made more small talk while they finished their dessert. Sarah left for a few moments to take off her apron and put her sweater on again. When she came back, Gary noticed that she'd also put on a light coat of lipstick.

"Shall we sit where it's more comfortable?" she said, moving around to help her mother up and into the living room.

They sat for a while, chatting back and forth, until Gary noticed the old woman showing the strain. "Can I give you a hand with the dishes before I leave?" he asked.

"Absolutely not," Sarah said. "I'll take care of everything."

"Well," he said rising from his chair, "then I think it's time to move along."

"We're not chasing you, Gary," Sarah said, rising with him.

"Thanks, but it's late enough."

She turned to her mother. "I'm going to walk Gary into the hall, Mama. Only for a minute."

"Leave the door open."

"Very nice meeting you Mrs. Montera," he said, still with the best manners he could muster, "and thank you both for a great dinner." He laughed. "An old bachelor like me really appreciates a home-cooked meal."

Sarah escorted Gary into the hall, leaving the door open a few inches. "Sarah, thanks for inviting me. I really enjoyed the evening." Even in the dim hall, he could see the bright pinpoints of light in her eyes.

"I'm glad you could come, Gary. It was nice. And seeing someone new really gave my mother a lift. I haven't seen her in such good spirits in I don't know how long." Her voice dropped to a near whisper. "She likes you, too, I can tell." She turned away when she said it.

"Sarah," he began, hesitating, "I couldn't help hearing you cough in the bedroom. Did you mention to your mother what we talked about, you know, about seeing a doctor?"

"I did, yes, last night. She seemed all right with the idea. She didn't object."

"Look, Sarah, I'm free tomorrow morning. If you can get away for an hour or so, I can go over with you. Doctor Goldman's office isn't far, so it shouldn't take long."

"How far is it?"

He understood her concern. "Not far, but we'll take a cab anyway."

"Gary, I don't want to put you out. You have things to—"

"Sarah," her mother called.

"I have to go inside now."

"Fine. Meet me right here, say, about ten. Is that okay?"

"Gary…"

"No arguments. Ten o'clock sharp."

She looked into his eyes. "All right. I'll be here." Their hands reached out, touched, clasped and squeezed.

* * * * *

Gary lay a long time without sleeping, reliving the evening, thinking of everything they'd talked about. He thought of Sarah's mother, a much tougher woman than he had expected to meet. She may be old, he thought, but she knows what's going on. In his own day she'd be called a survivor. But, he supposed, in their own way, they were all survivors— her brother Donny, Corky, Mrs. Hartman, everybody. Now he could include himself, as well.

And Sarah. What could he make of her? Why did there seem to be a dimension of her that he sensed lay beyond his understanding? She was lovely, so lovely with her pale complexion and dark hair, the fullness of her lips and the sparkling smile that seemed to reflect an inner peace, an acceptance of an imperfect world for what it was. And her eyes, shining, as if able to see beauty in that imperfection. When she stood close to him he could smell her freshness, like the freshness of flowers after a rain. In a strange way, it seemed that he had known her all of his life and, at the same time, that he didn't know her at all, that he could never know her.

He fell asleep with her face before him, and still feeling the warm touch of her hand squeezing his when they said goodnight.

Chapter 27

Tossing and turning, Gary slept fitfully, dreaming:

... Sarah, and Sarah's mother with dark eyes skinning him alive, and him, trapped and sweating, reaching out to Sarah but unable to touch her, and Sarah, unaware, stirring a pot of sauce and singing It's a Blue World, and suddenly he is riding his bike past his old house. He's happy and feels free as a bird, his spirits soaring, when he sees Shelley up ahead, standing in the street, her hand out to stop him, but he can't stop the bike and runs into her, runs over her, and keeps going, hearing her keening cry behind him—

He woke up sweating. And relieved. He reached over for his watch on the funeral parlor chair beside his bed and checked the time: 8:10. Good. He had worried he might oversleep. He dressed and, screwing up his courage, went down the hall to Mrs. Harmon's apartment. She answered on the first knock, looked at him and said nothing.

"Elsie, I wonder," he began, "could you possibly call a cab for me— of course I'll gladly pay for the call— and have it here by ten o'clock?"

Her mouth made a dry, smacking sound. "It'll cost you a dime."

"I thought you said—"

"A dime. I have to look up the number, don't I?"

"I believe it's President...Cleveland 4000."

"What the hell are you talking about?"

"I mean, the 'CL' stands for 'Cleveland,' I believe."

"It's still a dime," she said, holding out her hand, "for the trouble you put me through last time and didn't make a call."

"Thanks, Elsie," he said, picking a dime from his change.

"Would you be sure to tell them to make it ten sharp?"

The door slammed shut.

Dashing around, Gary straightened up his room and cleaned some crumbs off the table. He ran to and from the bathroom, put on his own good pants and golf shirt and checked himself out in the little mirror beside the sink. A few minutes before ten, he hovered around the front door, watching for the taxicab. When it pulled up to the curb, he stuck his head outside and gave the driver a 'wait-a-minute' signal. At precisely ten o'clock he was standing in front of her door. He could hear voices inside.

"Good morning, Sarah," he said, before she was out the door. "The cab's waiting."

"I'm leaving, Mama," she called back, "I'll be home soon." She closed the door.

"Good morning, Gary."

He touched her arm, leading her out. "Right on time," he said. "Looks like a decent day."

He guided her down the stairs to the taxi, where the driver stood holding the door open and smoking a cigarette. Once inside, he set the meter. "Where to, folks?"

"I'll have to show you the way," Gary said. "I'm not sure of the street name."

Sarah looked small in the back seat with him, small and frightened, with her chin sunk into her red corduroy jacket. "Are you feeling all right, Sarah?" he asked.

"My mother had a bad night, so neither of us got much rest. She's still in bed, but she seems better this morning."

When they arrived, the driver said, "Heck, it's not that far. You could've walked here and saved yourself two-bits."

"That's all right," Gary said, helping Sarah out of the car.

"How much?" he asked, ducking down to look in the window.

"Like I said, two-bits. A quarter."

Gary handed him a fifty-cent piece. "Keep the change. Now, can I ask you to pick us up in about an hour and a half?"

"Sure, sport. It's not a long trip but sure, I'll be here," he said, moving away.

Although they walked slowly she was out of breath before they reached the door. "Sarah, are you sure you're feeling okay? Here, hang on to my arm."

"It's the stairs. They seem to take a lot out of me, but I'm fine, honest."

The waiting room was deserted when they walked in, and they took a seat just inside the door. "You probably have a touch of something," Gary said. "I wouldn't doubt it. Having to keep the apartment so warm for your mother, well, when you go outside in the cold air you're bound to pick up something."

She smiled and said nothing.

"I really enjoyed myself last night," he said.

"We're glad you came. My mother said it was so nice to have company."

"For me, too," he said.

The murmur of voices grew louder, clearer, and an elderly man hobbling on a crutch came through the door from the back room.

"Three weeks," the doctor said, standing behind him. "It's all on the card."

The man slapped on his cap and limped past them out the front door.

Doctor Goldman raised his freckled arm and pointed. "Greg, right? Greg...."

"Gary, Doctor, remember? Gary Tyler." He stood up. "With 'Greg Norman' on the shirt?"

"Oh, yes, with the fractured ribs. Still giving you trouble? I warned you it—"

"Not me, Doc, not this time. I'm all right. It's her," he said, looking down to Sarah.

"I see. Well, then, won't you step back this way, please?"

Gary gave her a hand up. "She might have caught a bug or something like—"

"I'll do the diagnosis if you don't mind, Mr. Tyler," he said, extending a speckled hand to her as she approached him. "You can wait here. If Miss…."

"Montera," she said.

"…Montera wants you after the examination, we'll call you. Please, this way."

Gary settled in the hard chair and stretched his legs out, prepared to wait. Because he didn't know how long the visit would take, he told the cab driver to come back when he did, figuring it was cheaper to wait for the taxi than it would be for the taxi to wait for them. Besides, it gave him more time with Sarah.

He shifted on his haunches, one side to the other, crossed his legs this way, then that way. His butt and legs were going dead and he got up to walk a little to get back his circulation. He grew fidgety. It seemed she'd been in there an awful long time. He checked his watch. Almost forty minutes. He was beginning to worry. Of course, by the time he asked all his questions—and if he gave her a thorough his exam, it would take about that long. He relaxed.

But only temporarily. He bounced up and paced again. Almost an hour had passed and she still hadn't come out. He felt as if he was in a maternity ward waiting room. Drifting over to the door leading to the back, he debated whether to step inside and ask if they had a problem, when the doctor appeared and beckoned him in.

Stepping inside the little office, he saw Sarah sitting in the same chair he had sat in just a few days earlier. The faces of both her and the doctor appeared disturbingly sober.

"Mr. Tyler, Miss Montera…Sarah tells me you're a close friend and wanted you to hear what I have to say. Please, pull up a chair."

Gary lifted over a chair from the corner.

"I'm not a specialist, understand," he began, swiveling around to face them both. "As I told Sarah here, I don't particularly like what I'm hearing through these," he tapped the stethoscope hanging around his neck, "and, along with other symptoms I won't go into detail about, I am a little concerned." He rattled the papers in his hand.

Gary nodded, afraid of something like this.

"What I am recommending is that Sarah see a specialist. I know an excellent cardiologist right here in the city and I'm sure he can put your mind at ease after he runs a few more tests. If you would like, I can make an appointment for you now."

Sarah raised her eyes to Gary, a helpless expression in them that hurt him to see. "If I see him," she said, "and he wants to put me in the hospital…."

"That's anticipating more than is necessary at this time," Doctor Goldman said.

"I think the doctor's right, Sarah. Why don't you let him make an appointment?"

"Doctor, my mother's recovering from a stroke. She needs me."

"Sarah," the doctor said in a gentle voice, "you said you've had these symptoms for almost a year. If you don't look after yourself, in my professional opinion, you may not be in any condition to take care of your mother anyway."

"Sarah, just see the doctor," Gary said. "Hear what he has to say. You don't have to do anything beyond that, but at least you'll know where you stand."

She looked from one to the other, her pale face drawn and worried. "All right, doctor, if you think it's best."

"Fine. In the meantime, here's a prescription for that cough," he said, scribbling it out and handing it to her. "Now…" he said, running his finger down a list of numbers.

They sat quietly, Gary trying to look normal and relaxed to comfort her while the doctor made the phone call.

"All set," he said, writing on a yellow card like the one he gave to the old man who'd just left. "You have an appointment for next Thursday, the 27th."

Sarah's lip trembled when she spoke. "That soon?"

"Yes," he said, turning and handing the card over. "I want this done as soon as possible. Doctor Webster is the best, and therefore extremely busy. He's working you in as a favor to me."

"If he's that important…."

Gary anticipated her concern. "Don't worry about the cost, Sarah. I'll take care of it." He looked back to the doctor. "I'm paying for her visit, Doc, and the money I owe you from last week. I didn't forget," he said, digging into his pocket. "How much for Sarah."

"Make it the same," he said.

"She was in with you a lot longer than I was, Doc."

"Yes, well, she's a lot prettier, too," he said, smiling a boyish grin.

Gary stood up, handed over six dollars, and reached to help Sarah to her feet.

"Good," the doctor said, folding the bills and sliding them into his pocket. "I think you'll be very pleased with Doctor Webster. He's a fine man with an excellent reputation and has a great deal of experience in his field." He glanced up at the wall clock. "I have a hospital appointment now," he said, rising from his chair and escorting them out. "If you're going downtown and don't have a ride, I'll be happy to take you along. You were my last patient of the day."

"Thanks, Doctor Goldman," Gary said, leaving him at the door, "but I have a taxi coming to pick us up."

They descended the stairs slowly, Sarah holding the rail, with Gary at her side holding her elbow. "We were in there awhile," he said, taking out his watch. "The cab should be here any minute now."

"Gary, your watch." She laughed. A Mickey Mouse watch?"

He held it up facing her and, doing his best as a ventriloquist said, "You want to tell Sarah what time it is, Mick?"

Sarah laughed again. "That is *so* cute. But why aren't you wearing it, Gary?"

"For the simple reason, dear lady, that the band is too tight for my wrist."

"Then why did you buy it?"

"That, Sarah, is another story I may tell you some day."

"I hope it's soon," she said. "I'd love to hear it."

"Don't bet on it," he said, looking over her shoulder at someone coming toward them, walking fast, with his hands in his pants pockets and leaning forward as if bucking a head wind. Gary watched him come, moving fast, his head sunk between thick shoulders and covered with his jacket hood. When he had almost reached them, he turned abruptly up the walkway to the doctor's office, mounted the steps and disappeared inside.

"Another character," Gary said, looking both ways for the taxi.

"Who?"

"You didn't see him. Some creep. It seems you can find one of them any time, any place. He came from behind you and went up to the doctor's office."

"I thought he said I was his last patient of the day."

"Maybe he thought so, but when you have walk-ins, you better lock the door or you can get stuck." He took out his watch. "Cab's almost five minutes late. But he'll be here, don't worry," he said, seeing the frown on her face.

"Gary, do you hear something?"

He listened. "I don't think..."

She looked around. "Calling. Someone's calling." She turned to him. "Gary, it's coming from the office. Somebody's screaming!"

The words had hardly passed her lips and Gary, forgetting his still tender ribs, was bounding up the walk onto the steps and inside the door. Hearing cries and the crash of breaking furniture coming from the back, he dashed inside to the office and saw them on the floor, the 'creep,' with his back to the door, straddling the doctor's chest, his bloody fists driving down— and the doctor writhing beneath him, crying for help, his arms useless against the punishing blows.

Momentarily frozen, Gary coiled to leap, but instead, reached for the brass bust on the shelf, stood up and slammed it against the hooded skull. The woody crack of fracturing bone and the solid feel of a bat connecting for a home run ran the full, satisfying length of his arm. The fractured head toppled sideways with the body, and Gary kicked it free of the doctor. Bending down, he cradled the doctor behind the neck and eased him up.

"I'll call an ambulance for you," he said, dropping the bust and pushing the blood-splattered shirt up to the doctor's nose to stanch the bleeding.

Dazed, his eyes glassy, the doctor nodded.

"The number, Doc," he said, stretching over to the desk for the phone, "can you tell me? The hospital number?"

Cut and swollen lips parted. "Opera...or."

Gary picked up the phone, dialed 'O' for the operator and reported the emergency.

"Help is on the way, Doc," he said, hanging up. They'll be here any a minute now. Doc, can I move you? Is it okay if I help you up into a chair?"

The doctor nodded, holding his shirt to his nose. Gary had just lifted him into the chair when Sarah appeared in the doorway, the cab driver behind her.

"Oh, Gary," she said, clasping her mouth.

"It's okay, Sarah. Why don't you go out to the waiting room. The ambulance will be here and they can take care of things."

"Holy cripes," the driver said, tipping his hat back and looking around in amazement. "What tornado hit this joint?"

Gary pointed to the body crumpled on the floor. "That's what happened, him, that slime ball."

The driver peered in, gaping. "Cheez, is he dead?"

"He's breathing," Gary said, turning his attention back to the doctor. "Doc, is there anything we can do for you in the meantime?"

"I think he needs these," Sarah said, rushing over to pick up a stack of cloths and carrying them to him. She peeled one from the pile, dampened it under tap in a corner sink, and hurried back. She pressed it to his nose, wiping and turning it every few seconds.

Gary turned to the driver. "As soon as the ambulance gets here, we'll go. You have your meter running, don't you?"

"Yeah, buddy, but I didn't expect—"

"The police will probably be right behind them, and you know what they're like— questions questions questions. They might even take us down to the station house, and you know how much time that can eat up."

"Yeah, yeah, I know what you mean. And I can't afford to lose the time, I got a fambly to feed."

"They have their man, anyway, so they don't need us. The doctor can tell them everything they want to know."

"Yeah, you're right, but you did that to him, didn't you?" he said, indicating the blood pooling around his head. "What if he dies?"

"I'm more concerned with him," Gary said, looking back to the doctor, sitting with his head tilted forward and Sarah cleaning blood off his face. "Doc, Sarah has to get back to take care of her mother. You understand?"

Slightly recovered and more alert, he managed a weak "yes."

Moments later an ambulance screamed up to the curb outside the office.

Gary took Sarah's arm. "Sounds like they're here, Doc, so we'll be going." He patted his shoulder.

"Goodbye, Doctor Goldman," Sarah said, handing him the damp cloth.

"Thank you," he muttered, dabbing the cloth and examining it. "Thank you so much... I hope... hope no one thought it was one... of my patients making the fuss." He smiled through bloody teeth.

They had to step aside when the ambulance team dressed in white uniforms burst through the front door, one of them carrying a stretcher. "Straight back," Gary said, "the doctor, and some guy who tried to mug him. You'd better call the police."

"They're already on their way," one of them said. "They ain't never beat us to a scene yet."

The driver was already in the taxi by the time Gary escorted Sarah down the walkway to it. Hearing a siren in the distance, he tried to hurry her along.

"I hope he'll be all right," Sarah said. "I think his nose is broken."

"I wouldn't doubt it," Gary said, helping her into the taxi and climbing in after her.

"Back to the same place?" the driver said, adjusting his cap and resetting the meter.

"You don't have to do that and lose your time," Gary said, seeing the approaching police car through the rear window. "It wasn't your fault that this happened."

"You let me worry about that, buddy, okay?" he said, watching them through his rearview mirror. "And since we're all witnesses to a crime, I think we should get better acquainted." He smiled into the mirror. "I'm Tony. My friends call me Tony Baloney, not so much because I'm full of baloney, like in a sangwich, a baloney sangwich, but because my last name is pronounced that way." He spelled it out for them: "b-o-l-o-g-n-e."

"Nice to meet you, Tony. I'm Gary and she's Sarah."

"Very nice to meet you, Tony," Sarah said.

They sat listening to Tony ramble on about his six kids and having his 'very own cab one of these days,' and Gary made the necessary 'I see's' and 'really's.' But his mind was on Sarah and next week's visit to the cardiologist and how he would get the money to pay for an operation, if one was necessary. He knew Sarah was thinking along the same lines and was scared for more reasons than that.

"Here we are Gary and Sarah," he said, turning in his seat and flashing a broad smile. "I got that right, didn't I—Gary and Sarah, Sarah and Gary? SarahandGary. Sounds like some kinda desert I read in *National Geographic.*"

"Tony, I'd say you have a very dry sense of humor," Gary said, sliding out after Sarah. "Nice meeting you. I hope you get your own taxicab some day."

"Thanks," he said, "and thank you, Gary, I—hey, you don't gotta pay me no buck. What're you doin'? Two bits do it fine."

"That's all right, Tony. Good luck to you, now."

They stood together on the sidewalk a moment before going inside. "Do you want me to get that prescription filled for you now, Sarah? It's probably just codeine or something like it."

"Gary, isn't that dope? I don't want to turn into a dope addict."

He laughed. "Sarah, you're not going to turn into an addict."

"Let's wait anyway, all right? I'm feeling fine now. If my cough gets worse, then I can get it…. Gosh, we were gone longer than I thought. Good thing I asked Mrs. Lutz to look in on my mother."

"I'm sure she's in good hands," he said, noticing two men crossing the street from a parked car. Both were dressed in dark-blue suits and gray fedoras. Gary could even see the shine on their black shoes.

"Mr. Tyler?" the taller of the two asked, stepping up to them and flashing his wallet.

Was it a real badge? Or any kind of a badge at all? Gary thought, letting go of Sarah's arm. "Yes," he said, apprehensively, "why?"

"Step here, please," he said, moving up to him and running his hands over Gary's body. He pushed him toward the car.

"Can you tell me what this is all about?" Gary asked, digging in his heels.

"Keep moving," they ordered, prodding him along. "Just keep moving."

"Gary," Sarah cried, "what is it? Why are these men…."

"In, inside, inside!"

"Don't worry, Sarah," he said, ducking his head into the back seat. "It's all a mistake. I'll be—"

The tall one, clean-shaven to his blue roots, placed his hat on his lap and put his hand inside his breast pocket. Gary understood the gesture.

"Now can you tell me what you want and who you are?" Gary asked, looking back at Sarah, still standing on the sidewalk, wide-eyed, with her hands over her mouth, watching him go.

Chapter 28

For a frozen moment, Sarah stood watching the car fade from sight, her mind reeling from the sudden intrusion. One minute, they were standing there talking, and the next, two strangers were mauling and searching him and shoving him into a car. Worried, confused, she climbed the stairs to the porch. Pausing to catch her breath, she was surprised to see Mrs. Harmon standing in the front door.

"Who was that?" Mrs. Harmon demanded, snapping the door wide open.

Sarah touched her breast. "Oh, you scared me. I didn't see you there."

"Who were those men?"

"I don't know, they didn't say."

"Then what *did* they say?" she pressed, taking a deep drag on her cigarette and flipping it out onto the sidewalk.

"They just wanted to know his name," she said, trying to squeeze around her. "Please, Mrs. Harmon...."

"What for?"

"I don't know."

"I'll bet they were cops," she said, squinting suspiciously.

"If you'll let me pass, please...."

"Yeah, I'll bet, even though they were dressed too good for cops. Maybe FBI, yeah, maybe them, all spruced up like that. Listen, you better not get mixed up with that guy. I'm warnin' ya, he's trouble. I can smell it a mile off." She moved aside and Sarah squeezed by. "Something fishy about him, I tell ya, mighty fishy. So fishy it stinks to high heaven." She snorted. "Maybe they're gonna lock him up!" she called after Sarah, already far down the hall. "Yeah," she muttered to herself, "and if he thinks he'll get one miserable cent of his rent back, he's got another think coming."

Upstairs, the boarder with the bushy mustache listened to the conversation through his open window.

* * * * *

"Well," Gary said, reminding himself of Shelley, "do I have to play twenty questions here to get an answer?"

"I'm Riley, Treasury Department. He's Special Agent Smith," he said, indicating the driver. "We want to have a talk with you downtown."

"About what?" Gary asked, nearly overwhelmed by the powerful scent of shaving lotion.

Riley pursed his lips. "In due time, in due time."

Privately, Gary worried. *What if they lock me up. Will I ever get back to my own time? If they find out who I really am, where I'm from, could they ever afford to let me go? Would they squeeze all the information out of me like juice from a lemon, then dispose of me? 'Dispose—' nice word for 'kill.' Who would know if they did kill me? I could disappear off the face of the earth and no one would even notice. Oh, yes, Sarah, of course, but she'd forget in a while. She'd probably think I drifted off somewhere, just as I had drifted in from nowhere. If she didn't think of it herself, someone would eventually convince her of it.*

If he hoped to survive, he'd have to stay very alert.

Bracing him like bookends, they led him into a concrete building from a side door, their feet echoing in the stairwell as they climbed to the second floor, walked a long corridor and stepped inside a room, barren except for a desk, a few chairs scattered around, and a picture of President Franklin D. Roosevelt on the wall. And two men, one tall, one short.

"That's him, he's the one," the little man cried, jumping up from his chair and furiously stabbing the air. "He's the one."

The man beside him—obviously another agent— made him sit down as they led Gary into the room and sat him in a chair in front of a desk and across from the little man he recognized as the owner of the second-hand clothing store.

"I'll ask you to say not a word, do you understand me, Mr. Gorman?" Riley said to the man.

"I understand, I understand," he said, twisting the brim of his hat, his ragged mustache quivering beneath his nose.

Tipped back in his chair behind the desk, legs propped, Riley looked over his steepled hands from one face to the other and said, "Now we can begin." He turned to Gary. "Ever see this before?" he asked, nodding to Smith, his partner. Smith stepped over and held a bill up to Gary's face.

"A twenty dollar bill? Of course. I've seen lots of them."

"Not like this one. Look close."

Gary studied it. "Why, is the wrong picture on it?"

Riley's feet dropped to the floor and he hunched over his desk. "Don't get smart. This isn't the place to do it. Savvy? Gabeesh? Understand?"

Gary reflected. He wasn't intimidated the way the people of that time were intimidated by anyone in authority. He wasn't scared, but he decided it would be in his own best interest to play along and get the hell out of there as soon as possible.

"Sorry about that," he said. "Okay, let me see it again."

Smith held the bill up again.

"Mr. Riley—Agent Riley—I don't know what I'm supposed to be looking for. If you'll give me a hint, maybe I can be more helpful."

"Don't you recognize it?"

"It looks like any other twenty dollar bill to me, although I have to admit, I don't see them all that often, much to my regret. Am I supposed to recognize it?"

"You don't see anything unusual about it?"

"As I said, it looks like any other twenty. Isn't it?"

Mr. Gorman jumped to his feet. "You lie! You know what it is! You gave me it! Here you put it," he cried, slapping his palm, "right here, in my hand like it is out now!"

Riley rose to his full six feet plus. "Mr. Gorman, do you want me to put you in handcuffs?"

"No, oh, no, please, no handcuffs, I won't do it again, I promise, my hand to God above in heaven, I swear it, I promise I won't say anything until you tell me it's okay to open my mouth."

"Then sit down!" He looked back to Gary. "This bill," he said, taking it from Smith, "this…is a counterfeit twenty dollar bill."

"I see," Gary said, "counterfeit. It would've fooled me, I can tell you. Then again, I've never seen a counterfeit bill, that I know of. Until now, of course."

"Yes, it could fool almost everybody except a hawk-eyed bank teller who noticed it when Mr. Gorman made his daily deposit."

"What did this teller see that I couldn't see?" he asked.

"First of all, the numbers are way out of line with anything on the other bills."

Gary looked amazed. "You mean a teller knew *that*?"

"Actually, no, not that." He handed the bill back to Smith to show it. "Notice near the bottom what it says?"

"You mean 'series'?"

"That's right. Look close. 'Series' what?"

"1996."

"That's right. And what year is this?"

"1939."

"That's right. So how do we come up with a bill showing the year as 1996?"

"Maybe it's not supposed to represent the year. Maybe it's just another kind of serial number, one-nine-nine-six, for a different index or accounting process, like the long one on top." Gary looked from Riley to Smith and back to Riley. "That's possible, isn't it?"

The agents looked at each other, their expressions mixed.

"Where did you get this bill?" Riley asked.

"Where did *I* get it?"

"You heard the question right. Where did you get the bill from?"

"As far as I know, I never had it. And until now, I doubt I've ever even laid eyes on it before."

Riley sighed. "Mr. Gorman, what do you have to say about this?"

Mr. Gorman sprang to his feet, twisting the brim off his hat. Tics shivered his cheeks. "He, him, he gave it to me, that I know. Nobody else that day gave me a twenty dollar bill, only him. He bought pants, shirts, tie, I remember like ten minutes ago, and he turned down a suit." He clasped his hands. "A suit," he rhapsodized, "such a beautiful suit you have never seen one like the one I offer him for a price I can't believe myself, and he, him, that— he just the same as spit in my face. Ptuii." He spit to the side again. "Ptuii."

"All right, Mr. Gorman, sit down! And if you ever dare do that again, I swear I'll lock you up for the rest of your natural life! Do you understand?"

Mr. Gorman crumbled back into his chair. "Yessir, I'm sorry, sir," he said, dabbing sweat off his brow, "I'm sorry."

Riley glared a long minute, then turned back to Gary. "Mr. Tyler, would you please let us see your wallet?"

"You want to check my money, is that it?"

"That's the general idea, yes."

"Is it legal to do that? Without a warrant or a court order, I mean. Or at least without my attorney present."

Riley's blue roots darkened. "Are you a wise guy?"

"Wise, I don't know. But I do know that as an American citizen I do have certain inalienable rights."

Riley reached for the phone on his desk. "We'll just see—"

"But," Gary said, interrupting him, "I'm willing to waive those rights if it will mean helping you put this matter to rest." He reached into his pocket, pulled out his wallet, and began removing the bills, when Riley reached across his desk and snatched the wallet from him.

"I'll do that," he said, parting the folds.

Gary smiled. "Afraid I might try a little legerdemain?"

The agents exchanged glances. "Legerdemain." His eyebrows went up. "Apparently you have more than a little education, Mr. Tyler."

"I'm a college grad. I'll be teaching at Lafayette High in the fall."

"Is that so?" Riley said, setting the wallet aside and leaning forward on his elbows.

"History. My specialty is American Government."

Riley leaned back, folding his arms. "I'm impressed. Very impressed," he said, looking over at his partner. "Aren't you impressed, Smitty?"

"Very impressed, more than impressed."

"Thank you very much," Gary said, choosing to ignore the sarcasm.

"One thing we've found in this business is that counterfeiters are an intelligent bunch. Not necessarily highly educated, but intelligent, nevertheless."

Mr. Gorman started to leap up but Riley's icy glare froze him half way and he slowly sank back.

"So, where were we?" he said, picking up the wallet. "Oh, yes, the money. Any secret compartments here?" He squinted into the pockets his fingers forced open. "I guess that's it." He spread the bills on the desk and picked them up one by one.

"This is okay," he said, studying it, then holding it to the light. "And this one...." After going through them all, he handed them back with the wallet, then turned to Gorman. "I'm sorry, Mr. Gorman, but we can find no evidence that this man is a counterfeiter. If we could, we might perhaps force him to make restitution before we locked him up. Unfortunately, without evidence...." He shrugged. "And unless you can offer proof of some kind—"

Mr. Gorman pleaded, his tragic eyes watering. "But this *is* the man, I swear it. I even give change for the twenty dollar bill." He turned to Gary. "You remember, don't you? The truth, admit it, tell him, tell him how I almost make a mistake giving you change and you—"

"If you made a simple mistake like that," Gary said, "how can you remember everybody who came into your store that day? Of course I remember buying clothes from you, but—a twenty dollar bill! And I don't recall getting the wrong change."

The little man's eyes bugged in disbelief, then he exploded. "You don't recall! How can you not recall only a few days ago, in my store, you put the twenty dollar bill in my hand, this very hand, and I counted you out one dollar, two dollars—"

Riley broke in. "That's enough, Mr. Gorman, that's quite enough!"

Tears started down his cheeks. "You mean, you take my twenty dollars, tell me it's no good and you don't give me another one in its place!"

"I'm sorry, Mr. Gorman. That's the way it works." He signaled with his eyes for the third agent to take the old man out.

"You can't do this to me," he protested. "That man, that... that thief, he—"

"Be careful of what you say in front of witnesses, Mr. Gorman. He can sue you for slander and you'll be out a lot more than twenty dollars."

"Sue me? *Me?* He steals *my* money and he sues *me?* This is justice? This is the United States of America? First he takes *my* clothes, then steals *my* money and then sue *me!*"

The third agent carried him out, shrieking all the way.

"Riley stood up, extending his hand. "Sorry to put you through all this trouble, Mr. Tyler, but, you understand, we were obligated to investigate this matter. Counterfeiting is a serious business and more widespread than you can imagine. We'll track this culprit down, yet. The Treasury Department always gets its man. Agent Smith here will take you back home. But let us make this inconvenience up to you with a dinner. On the government, of course." He nodded to Smith. "Take him to Montgomery's." He smiled to Gary. "Best steaks in town."

"Thanks," Gary said, glad to escape the interrogation and the cloying smell of his shaving lotion. "I don't want you to put yourself out," he said, lying his heart out.

"That's all right. Agent Smith doesn't mind, do you Smitty? He gets in on the free meal, too."

* * * * *

Gary enjoyed his steak dinner and without much trouble managed to parry and ward off Smith's questions with questions of his own. When they had finished, Smith paid the bill, as Riley had promised, and dropped Gary off back home.

Gary came in through the front door and was going down

through the hall to his room, when Mrs. Harmon popped out the door behind him.

"Hold on there, mister. It's time you got it in your head I run a decent establishment here. It's bad enough you come rolling in in the middle of the night pie-eyed, but when the cops start hangin' around and—"

"Sorry about the other night, Elsie, but those men I left with earlier…?" He covered his mouth. "Undercover agents," he whispered. "The same ones who chauffeured me home, or didn't you notice that? Anyway, Mrs. Harmon, Mrs. Elsie Harmon, since you witnessed what you witnessed, I have to advise you to say nothing to anyone. This is all very confidential and I can't discuss my role in this investigation, but believe me, it will be all over in a few days and if anything or anyone interferes with it— well, let's just drop it there."

She chewed a wad of gum, scowling. "Go on, I seen how they man-handled and frisked you out there in the street in plain sight of everybody. What am I, a moron? Criminals and crooks, they get that treatment, not law-abiding citizens, so don't try to gaff me, Buster, I been around."

"Of course. They have to do that—in plain sight—as you say, to make it look good. We never know who may be watching. Now, Elsie, I don't want to play hardball with you, you understand? I could have you shut down here for any number of reasons, like the lack of facilities for the number of people here and all that exposed wiring and— well, you get the idea, health and fire violations. I've tried being courteous to you and in return you've given me a lot of unnecessary grief. Frankly, that rubs me the wrong way even though I'm trained to be tolerant and polite. In fact, the gentlemen you saw me with asked if you were being cooperative. You're a widow and all alone, so, out of sympathy, I covered for you and held my tongue, which, to be perfectly honest, wasn't exactly easy."

"Well, crissakes, you coulda shown me a badge or somethin'."

"I wish I could have, but this operation is so secret, I'm not even allowed to do that."

Her face sagged in contrition, but not without some residual defiance. "Hell, I had no way of knowin'. If you'd of given me some kind of a hint...."

"Now, that tenant you have upstairs, for instance, the one with the mustache I asked you about? That would have been a big help in our investigation."

"Him? I couldn't tell you much about him, even if I wanted to. Mr. Bocker or Bockler, or somethin'. Just one of them strange ducks that come along. Saw him stagger out with one of my other boarders the other night, drunker'n a skunk, both of them looked. Another strange duck that other one— Mr. Lundow, Loondow, on that order. And crazy as a loon, too, the way he popped in and out of here at all hours, wild-eyed, like he was hiding from somebody. Come to think of it, I ain't seen him since."

"Do you know where this Mr. Bocker and the other guy works or anything about them?"

"I don't ask no questions and don't want to know anything except they follow house rules and pay their rent on time."

"All right, Elsie, thanks. You've been a help. And I won't forget it."

"Well, of course, you can't blame me for holding back. As I said, I run a respectable house here and try to keep everything I see confidential and on the up and up."

"I respect that, Elsie; no need to apologize. You're a fine woman, that's obvious to anyone who knows you, but remember, not a word of this to anyone, not anyone. Everything you've seen and everything we've just spoken about, forget. Forget it all. It never happened."

Chewing her gum furiously, she stood looking down the hallway long after Gary disappeared into his room.

Chapter 29

Dropping back on the bed, Gary threw his arm over his eyes. He felt as if he were caught up in some crazy dream that grew ever more complicated. He had to think! No doubt about it— somehow he'd slipped into a time swamp, almost seven decades deep, and 1939 didn't look quite as appealing now as it once did. But he was here, indisputably here, and that was fact. Sooner or later he'd find a way home. Of that he was certain.

In the meantime, despite the drawbacks, being here also presented him with an opportunity to do what countless others throughout history had dreamed of doing: he could fix things! The information he carried in his head was beyond value to the government, to any government, and to business. And being so valuable meant that others would kill for it. Kill *him!* Which in turn meant he could do only so much and say so much, limit his exposure and get the hell out of there. Fast!

First things first, though. Dolly had to be saved. No matter what, come Friday night, he had to save her. Next he had to get Sarah to the doctor and arrange a way to pay for the operation she most likely needed. That would be next Thursday, a week away. After that, he could contact the FBI. Of all the future events he could warn them of, the most important of all would have to be the coming sneak attack on Pearl Harbor. If they listen, the country could not only prevent the attack, but probably avoid war altogether, a horrendous war destined to claim hundreds of thousands of casualties, including the thousand entombed in the *Arizona.*

A rapping, so soft he almost didn't hear it, interrupted his thoughts. He listened, heard it again and went to the door.

Standing there, looking small and worried, was Sarah. "I saw the light on under your door."

"Step inside," he said, noticing her nervousness. "Come on, it's all right."

She hesitated, then came in. He closed the door. "I was worried, Gary. Those men... Mrs. Harmon said they were police. That they came to arrest you."

Gary laughed. "Here, sit down."

She glanced around, skeptically. "No, thank you. I can't stay."

"Sarah, don't listen to that old busybody out there because she doesn't know what the hell she's talking about." He spread his arms. "Am I here? Or am I locked up someplace else?"

She relaxed. "I'm glad but...then what was that all about? I don't understand."

He reached over and took her hands. "They took me down to Montgomery's for a nice steak dinner, that much I can tell you. I'll take you there sometime." He gazed into her eyes, soft and warm, looking deep into his own, as if seeking something. "We had a little discussion, one of the two Treasury agents you saw outside, and they dropped me off home."

"A discussion? Treasury agents? But why?"

"Sarah, no more questions now, all right? I'll answer all your questions, but not now, not at this time. I can't." He drew her a little closer. "Do you understand?"

She didn't resist. "Gary...."

He pulled her in close and slipped his arms around her. "I don't want you to be scared."

She turned her face up to his. "I'm not," she said, her eyes shining.

He touched his lips to hers, lightly, and she slid her arms around his neck. They closed their eyes, lost in a kiss that seemed to go on forever, yet not nearly long enough. The ocean-sweet scent of her skin and hair made him giddy, and filled him with the sensation of falling in space. He could feel the softness of her breasts against his chest, and the warmth of her breath on his face like an aura enveloping him, wrapping him in a silken web of desire, enfolding him in skeins of pleasure beyond pleasure that seemed to absorb him, melding them in a mysterious embrace of two worlds. He pulled her in tight, his hands firm in the small of her back, his rushing blood pounding in his temples.

She broke suddenly. "I have to go, Gary. I have to go now."

"Wait," he said, still holding one of her hands tight. "Not yet, Sarah."

"Please, Gary, please, let go. Please."

Her eyes reflected pain. Or shame. He couldn't tell. Maybe both. "All right, Sarah. All right. I'll talk to you tomorrow." He let her hand slide off his.

"I'm sorry, Gary," she said, opening the door. "I'm really sorry."

"Sarah—"

He closed the door and went back to his bed, still heady with the moment that seemed to have come and gone like a dream, a beautiful dream he couldn't hold. He replayed the scene again in his mind, trying to recapture the magic of the embrace, when he saw the flush on her cheeks, the trembling fullness of her pale lips, the fluttering of her lids closing off the shining light from her eyes and cloaking the mystery of her soul. He could still feel her hands on his neck, her sweet breath on his face. He dozed off thinking of her, trying not to think of anything else but her. She drifted in and out of his consciousness.

Again, a rapping on the door roused him from a deepening

sleep. Rubbing the dopiness out of his face, he opened the door. "Sarah—"

In Sarah's place stood a man in a dark-blue suit. "Mr. Tyler? Mr. Gary Tyler?" the man said, bringing a shiny badge up to eye level. The dark shadow beneath the brim of his fedora hid his eyes, but couldn't hide the square jaw with a deep cleft.

Gary smiled. "Agent Riley already beat you to it. I've been downtown and—"

"Bradshawe, Federal Bureau of Investigation," he said, tucking his ID away in his hip pocket. "Get your coat and step out here, please. And keep your hands where I can see them."

The man was all business. Gary did as he was told and stepped out into the hall where a second agent stood off to the side. "Is it okay to get the key out of my pocket?" he asked. "To lock up?"

The second agent stepped up, patted him down, drew out the pocket knife and handed it over to Bradshawe. He pulled up the Mickey Mouse watch, stared at it a moment, shaking his head sadly, and handed it back.

After he locked the door, they arm-locked him, shoulder-vised him, and escorted him down the hall.

The door to Mrs. Harmon's room opened and she poked her head out.

"Friends," Gary said over his shoulder as they marched him wooden-legged outside and into a waiting sedan.

Chapter 30

"So, where to?" Gary asked Bradshawe, sitting beside him in the back seat.

Bradshawe put his finger to his lips without bothering to say 'Shhh.'

Gary asked no more questions as they drove toward the downtown area. He had thought of contacting the FBI, but not until next week, after he'd taken care of business, and on his own terms. Instead they got to him first. The big question was 'Why?' If he had an idea, he could prepare himself with a story. He couldn't afford to be held in jail. He had things to do and timing was crucial.

Within minutes, he found himself inside a building, a different building, where a similar scenario played itself out: a square-jawed agent behind the desk, his partner sitting in a chair along the wall. No Mr. Gorman this time.

Bradshawe leaned forward and spoke for the first time since introducing himself. "Would you pass your wallet here, Mr. Tyler?"

Gary sighed and reached into his pocket. "The money's already been checked," he said, handing it over.

Bradshawe took it, turned over a few times and tapped it on his hand. "Where did you get this wallet?"

"I…I don't remember. It might have been a gift. I've had it a long time."

"What's it made of, can you tell me?"

Gary racked his brain trying to think of what materials were available in 1939. "I think leather," he said, unable to come up with anything else.

"Leather, you say. It's not like any leather I've ever seen, although I suppose it could be some fancy, new process. So I'm asking you again, where did you get it?"

"A gift," Gary said, "I'm sure it was a gift, a birthday gift, last year."

Bradshawe pursed his lips, tapping the wallet against his palm. "Who from?"

"Who from? I think…I can't really say. Probably from a relative."

"I see. And you live…where?"

"You know where. You just picked me up there."

"Your home, I mean, where your parents live."

"My parents are deceased. I lived with my grandparents, but I figured I put a burden on them for so many years, it was high time I got out on my own and make it for myself in the world, now that I'm graduating."

Bradshawe lowered his head. "Graduating." He looked up. "From…?"

"The university. Over in Amherst. I'll be teaching in the fall. History. My major is American Government."

"That's interesting," he said, leaning back, still tapping the wallet on his palm, his eyes fixed on Gary like prey. "Where will you be teaching?"

"Lafayette High School," he said, feeling the pressure of the cat and mouse game. "But later I hope to teach in a college."

"And your parents live where?"

"My grandparents. My parents are deceased."

"You said that, yes. Sorry. Your grandparents live where?"

"Not far from downtown here, on Compton Street."

"The same name you carry—Tyler?"

Gary felt the noose tightening. "Yes. Granville E. Tyler."

Bradshawe removed the money and handed it back to Gary. 'We're going to keep this for a while," he said, tapping the wallet and slipping it into his vest pocket.

Gary nodded.

"No objections?" Bradshawe asked, eyebrows lifted.

"You're the FBI. Who am I to argue with one of Hoover's men."

Bradshawe tightened, his jaw hard. "All right, Mr. Tyler. Let's get down to brass tacks. Storytelling time is over."

Now it's coming, Gary thought, tense, but secretly relieved to end the charade.

"First let me tell you what we know. We know that you have no job at Lafayette High School and that there is no record of a Gary Tyler who is or who has ever been enrolled at any college in the area. We know that the only family by the name of Tyler living within striking distance of Compton Street is—at least you're right about the name— Granville Tyler, who has a wife and three children, Junior being the oldest... living over on..." he drew out a piece of paper "...Let's see here, yes, 495 High Street." He looked up again. "We interviewed that family an hour ago and no one has ever heard of a relative named Gary Tyler. Further, for your information, we happen to believe Mr. Gorman's story, not yours? Ahh, you look surprised, Mr. Tyler, genuinely surprised."

"Well, since you seem to know everything, Mr. Bradshawe, suppose *you* tell me who I am?"

"That, Mr. Tyler, or whoever you are, is what I was hoping you would do."

"And if I don't?"

"We take care of business, Mr. Tyler. One way or another we take care of business."

"You mean you'd kill me?"

Bradshawe looked across to his partner. "Oh, we won't necessarily make a Dillinger of you, but we can be persuasive."

"Can I go?"

He chuckled. "No, Mr. Tyler, I'm afraid I can't let you go. The only reason Treasury released you is to give us a chance to investigate. No, Mr. Tyler, you can't go. In fact, you won't be going anywhere for a very long time."

"I have my rights," Gary said. "As an American citizen I know my rights, and I know you can't just lock me up someplace and keep me there without a trial."

Bradshawe smiled, his Cary Grant cleft exposing hairs his razor missed. "I love innocence, Mr. Tyler. It is such a…such an endearing quality." He turned deadly serious and gave a curt nod to his partner.

"Wait a minute," Gary said, knowing he had no chance but to gamble on the truth. "Suppose I have information crucial to the national interest, would you let me go?"

Bradshawe waved the other man back. "Say again?"

"National interest," Gary said. "Believe me, it is of supreme interest."

"Another lie to stall for time, Mr. Tyler?"

"Lies, yes, I've been telling lies. I've been lying through my teeth. But before you just cast me aside and lock me up as some kind of a sneak thief or counterfeiter or something, think about this: You saw my wallet. Send it to any lab and see what they tell you about it."

Bradshawe slipped it out of his pocket again, and ran his fingertips over it.

"Then think of the twenty dollar bill I gave to Mr. Gorman. Who would be stupid enough to make a 'series' mistake like that, 1996. And the name of the Treasury Secretary, Rubin, do you recognize it?"

"Treasury spotted that instantly."

"Of course. So why would any counterfeiter who is capable of making such an authentic-looking bill make up a name instead of copying the one you have?"

"We wondered the same thing."

"Lastly, who am I? Where did I come from? What am I doing here? Did you check City Hall birth records to try to identify me?"

"We did."

"You work very fast, but I could have saved you time and told you that you won't find me there, nor in the church records nor in the telephone book." He beckoned Bradshawe forward. "Do you know why?"

Bradshawe, leaning forward, shook his head no.

"You don't because," he hesitated for a dramatic pause, "because I haven't been born yet."

Bradshawe fell back, slack jawed. "What in hell are you talking about?"

"I'm talking about the future. My home. Do you understand, finally? Do all the pieces now fall into place for you? I'm from the future. I know the future. I know what is going to happen to this country and to the world for the next half century and more."

Bradshawe shook his head, his expression, like his partner's, stony and dumb.

"Yes," Gary persisted. "You wanted to know. Now you know but you don't want to believe. Well, believe me, because what I say is irrefutable. You have physical proof and all the facts, and the facts all fit. You have a logical mind. You can't deny the evidence."

Bradshawe opened his mouth to speak, but Gary cut him off. "Look, I know you've been keeping track of me ever since I arrived. Or was it the Treasury Department? I don't know what tipped you off— the money, I suppose— but when I saw that baldheaded Sardonicus in Windy's tavern, I suspected something. Was that bit of reverse psychology designed to throw me off, by making him so obvious? I guess I was too drunk or too stupid to care; I still shot my mouth off, didn't I? Well," he said, folding his arms, "now you know the story. So what's the next move? You call it."

Neither of the agents stirred, then, as if snapping out of a reverie, Bradshawe screeched his chair back and bounded around the desk. "Stay with him," he said to his partner. "Keep him here. I'll be right back."

Gary watched him bolt out of the room. "Where's he going?"

The agent pressed his finger to his pursed lips. "Shhh," he said.

Gary worried. Had he spoken too much, revealed too much? Was Bradshawe sending for an ambulance to have him committed? Were they going to lock him up?

After what seemed an hour, Bradshawe returned. "Okay, let's go."

"Are you taking me back home?" Gary asked, instantly knowing from the steely jut of that Charlton Heston movie star chin that he'd asked a stupid question.

Scrunched down in the back seat, Gary looked out the side window at the houses gliding by as the car wheeled off into the night. "Where are we going," he said, "if it's not too much to ask?"

Bradshawe, settling himself in, turned to Gary and studied him for a long moment, the way one studies a magician's act to discover his trick. "We're going for a ride, a long ride, so make yourself comfortable."

"How long?" Gary asked, seeing the city limit sign flare in the headlights, then fall dark as they passed it.

"Long enough," Bradshawe said.

"Too bad you don't have freeways yet." Gary said, "It'd be much faster."

"The road is free. There's no toll on it."

"Most freeways aren't free, either."

Bradshawe gave Gary a funny look, then said, "You might as well get yourself some shuteye. I will, too. And don't get any sudden notions about getting away. We have another car following us. Even with my gun you don't stand a chance." He smiled and winked. "Just remember Dillinger."

Gary twisted around to see the headlights following them. "Are we heading for Washington? Is that where we're going? Will I see J. Edgar, personally?"

Bradshawe pressed his finger to his pursed lips.

"What's that, part of the training program for you guys?" Gary asked, peeved.

"What's what?"

Pressing his finger to his pursed lips, Gary whispered, "I'll tell you later."

* * * * *

Gary didn't know how long he had slept. It seemed no more than a couple of hours. All he knew for sure was that his legs felt cramped, his neck hurt and his almost-healed ribs ached. The harsh light of the rising sun stung his eyes, but it let him know they were heading east. New York City? He would have expected Hoover to be in D.C.

On the seat beside him, Bradshawe snored softly, his square chin sunk into his chest. From the back window, Gary saw a black sedan following close behind, no doubt filled with agents. He settled back, wishing for more room, and watching the driver's head dance with every bump in the road. Every now and then he caught his eyes watching him through the rearview mirror.

Now they were crossing the Hudson River and heading south. New York City, for sure. The sun climbed higher, the car jounced on some rough pavement and Bradshawe stirred. His eyes opened and he blinked, apparently forgetting for the moment where he was.

"Good morning, Mr. Bradshawe," Gary sang out. "Did you sleep well?"

Bradshawe ignored him, hiked up his cuff to see his wristwatch, then reached forward and tapped the driver's shoulder. "First place you see to eat, stop." He eased back, yawning. "We can pick up some sandwiches."

"Sandwiches?" Gary protested. "Why not breakfast?"

"We're on a tight schedule."

"I'm sure Hoover's anxious to hear my story," Gary said. "He can wait."

Bradshawe looked at Gary and smiled. "He can, can he? You may know the future, my friend, but I know the present— and my boss— better than you do." He slid down and rested his head against the cushioned seat. "So be quiet and don't talk. My head hurts when I don't get my proper rest. If it wasn't for you, I could be home sleeping in my own bed. As you might guess, I'm not happy making your acquaintance." He closed his eyes.

The sun rose higher, warming Gary's face as they traveled along. "No air conditioning in this jalopy?" he said to no one in particular just as the car suddenly lurched and pulled off the road, kicking up stones rat tat tatting in the wheel wells on a gravel drive in front of a ramshackle restaurant boasting the name *Gert's*.

The second car followed them in, spraying a dusty cloud of stones, and veered off to the side.

Bradshawe opened his eyes and looked around. "Okay" he said to the driver, "go in and bring us sandwiches, any kind. Tell him who you are so you get fast service. We can't be late. And don't forget coffee," he called after him, "black."

Gary rolled down the window and yelled. "Cream and sugar for me."

Bradshawe turned his attention back to Gary. "You know, I'm beginning to believe your story. Tell me, is everybody as screwy as you are in a...you know, where ever you say you come from?"

"FBI agent Bradshawe, trust me, you can't begin to imagine what lies ahead."

"If everybody's like you there, I'm glad I'm here."

Gary laughed. "You think I'm screwy? Wait till the Sixties. That would be about twenty-five years from now. You should still be around for that. Then you'll really see what 'screwy' is. I hope you survive it."

A few minutes later the driver returned, carrying a flimsy cardboard box in his arms. Struggling not to lose it, he contorted his body trying to open the door, finally did it, and slid the box over on the front seat. "Hamburgers," he said, getting inside and passing them to the back. "Relish and mustard."

Bradshawe took one, peeled the wax paper wrapping back and parted the roll, his face sour. "Relish and mustard? Who puts relish and mustard on a hamburger?"

"I wasn't trained to be a cook," the driver said, unperturbed by the complaint. He passed the coffee back.

Gary held the coffee cup between his knees. "Someday you're going to see a restaurant, a whole chain of them, in fact, and they'll be serving hamburgers strictly with mustard, ketchup and pickle. The same for everybody." He bit into his sandwich.

Bradshawe looked over at him. "Mustard and ketchup and pickle. On a hamburger? And everybody's got to eat them that way?" He scoffed. "They'll be out of business in a month."

Gary laughed. "Agent Bradshawe, Mr. Bradshawe— what

can I call you?"

"You can call me Bradshawe, just as long as you say it with respect."

"Okay, Bradshawe, let me give you the best tip you'll ever get in your life. When this restaurant comes into being— probably not for another twenty years, I'd say— when it does, buy a franchise if you can afford it. It'll make you a millionaire. Or buy stock when it goes public and hold on to it. If you don't live long enough to become rich working, you can still leave your family well off."

"Is that so? Tell me then," he said, biting into his hamburger, "what's the name of this wonder company that's going to put me on Easy Street?"

"McDonalds."

"I get it, like the song, 'Ol' McDonald had a farm,' like that? In this case a restaurant or, as you say, a what? A chain of them?"

"That's a good way to remember it. Pay heed to what I say. Someday you'll thank me."

Another agent emerged from the restaurant carrying a similar box to the black sedan parked a little distance away.

"This coffee tastes like mud," Bradshawe complained, taking another gulp.

"I didn't make it," the driver said, drinking his coffee and looking straight ahead.

When they had finished, they tossed the cups and wrappings into the box on the front seat. The driver balled up his trash, dropped it in the box, opened the passenger side door and threw it out on the ground.

Bradshawe kept checking the time and looking over to the other car. "Okay," he said, finally getting a signal, "let's get rolling."

No one spoke as they followed the winding road along the

Hudson River, the other car following close behind. The sun lifted itself higher in the sky and brightened the morning. Gary relaxed again, his eyes getting heavy and beginning to close, when he saw the sign ahead. Coming fully alert, he turned to Bradshawe.

"Hyde Park? If I'm not mistaken, and I'm sure I'm not, this is where President Roosevelt's home is, isn't it?"

Bradshawe turned to look out the back window and gave a hand signal.

Gary sat up straight. "Are we going to be stopping here first for something?"

Bradshawe scanned the road ahead and to the side.

"Are we going to see the president himself?"

Bradshawe leaned forward and whispered into the driver's ear.

"Is this where we're meeting Hoover?" Gary asked.

"Maybe Hoover's meeting with the president," Gary said to Gary.

"Do you really think so?" Gary asked Gary.

"A strong possibility," Gary said to Gary.

"Maybe Hoover can deliver the message right there, directly to the president," Gary said to Gary.

"That's a very—"

Bradshawe glared at him. "Shut up."

The car braked hard and threw Gary against the door as it swerved into a long narrow driveway. A short way in they stopped and the driver rolled down his window. A guard peered in, then stuck his head inside, exchanging whispers with the driver as he checked his ID. He grunted something as he reached over, took Bradshawe's ID, studied it a moment and handed it back. "Okay, sir," he said, withdrawing, signaling them in and beckoning the black sedan idling behind them.

The car rolled on into the property, swung left and stopped

close to a large outbuilding that resembled a barn. They waited for the sedan to catch up and park behind them.

"Bradshawe, can I ask a favor of you?" Gary said, rushing on without waiting for an answer. "Would you snip off a piece of my shirt?"

Bradshawe stared at him. "Are you a mental case?"

"Seriously, it can't do any harm. Just that, a tiny square off the bottom."

"I don't get it."

"Nothing devious, believe me. Please, as a personal favor."

"You're asking me to cut your shirt? Am I hearing right?"

"Yes, please, I'm asking you to do it," he pleaded. "I'll explain later. Please."

Bradshawe's lips twisted. "Maybe I'm whacky, too," he said, reaching inside his pocket. "All right, put your hands behind your back and keep them there." He thumbnailed the blade open. "You sure you want to do this? This is a pretty snappy shirt."

"Off the bottom. A piece about an inch."

Bradshawe made the cuts. "You ruined a perfectly good shirt, you know, and for what?" He pressed the blade back and put the knife away. "Okay, here, take it."

"Thanks," Gary said, snatching it and shoving it in his pocket.

The sedan rolled up behind them. "All right, Mr. Tyler," Bradshawe said, "out this way, please."

Gary scooted over and slid out, shaking the stiffness from his legs. Four agents spilled out of the car behind and surrounded him.

"This way, Mr. Tyler," said one of two men stepping beside him and leading him along. Bradshawe tapped the brim of his hat when Gary glanced back to him.

A quick turn on the path and the mansion came into view,

stately with its broad steps, white portico, railings and columns. It had a quiet majesty about it, a strength and durability suggestive of the man who lived there and who would one day lead the nation in its coming time of crisis. *Unless I can help avert it,* Gary thought, as they walked him up onto the north end of the veranda.

One of the men stepped up to a door, one that seemed little used. It opened and a man with flat, black hair and a pendulous nose cocked his head, beckoning Gary inside. The two men beside him repeated the motion and Gary stepped into a small room.

"Sit there," the man ordered, his nose dipping almost to his upper lip.

He's obviously not Hoover, Gary thought, seating himself in a wooden captain's chair, and observing the room—a cubicle, really—one not much bigger than an oversized closet, while the man backed away and stood against the wall near a second door that apparently opened to the inside of the house. Standing rigid, his vacant eyes focused on nothing specific, he looked as neutered as a suit of armor guarding the hall of a castle.

Unimpressive in every aspect, the room held nothing much more than a couple of chairs, a telephone, and a desk with what looked like an old-fashioned microphone perched on one side of it. Gary twiddled his fingers, waiting. Knowing Hoover's reputation for being tough, and for seeing things one way and only one way— his way, Gary determined to be straightforward and stay on the good side of him— if he had one. He also knew that in big-time politics, assassinations occur and people mysteriously disappear. It worried him that he himself could be considered dangerous in ways he couldn't even imagine, and that to some people he could be much more desirable dead than alive. Of course, if Hoover gave any hint of wanting to dispose of him, he would yell out to everyone within earshot that Hoover wore dresses.

Moments later, a side door opened. Gary's breath stuck in his throat as President Roosevelt appeared, sitting in his wheelchair and pushed from behind by a male attendant. Speechless, Gary watched the man position him behind the desk, pull a blanket up higher on his chest and depart. Roosevelt nodded to the suit of armor, who also stepped outside the room to the inner hall.

"President Roosevelt," Gary stammered, starting to rise. "I didn't expect to...."

The president raised his hand with an unlit cigarette in a cigarette holder between his fingers. "Be seated, Mr. Tyler. Now..." he said, adjusting the blanket and turning his full attention to Gary, "I've been informed of all that has transpired since yesterday. I'm not certain of the truth of everything, and I have but a short time to determine if these statements you made have any validity, preposterous as you know they must sound to me."

But apparently not preposterous enough to be ignored, Gary thought. "I understand, Mr. President, so I'll come right to the point," he said, absorbed in the wonder of that dramatically high-pitched voice that seemed to carry every sublime quality of humanity within it, and trying to keep his knees from trembling. "Mr. President, this country will be attacked by the Empire of Japan on December 7th, 1941."

The president showed no expression on his face, as he repeated the date. "1941. That's some time off, more than a year. And this, you say, is a fact?"

"Yes, sir," Gary said, riveted by the blue eyes riveted on him, eyes not yet weighted by black crescents beneath them. "It's already part of history."

"Where will it take place, this hypothetical attack?"

"With all due respect, sir, it is not hypothetical. It will be a surprise attack that will occur at Pearl Harbor, Hawaii."

The president's hand wandered to his chin. "Hawaii. That is many thousands of miles from Japan. Any attack, particularly a surprise attack, would be difficult if not impossible from that distance."

"Nevertheless, sir, it will come, and it will come at a time when negotiations are taking place in Washington between our people and the Japanese. Two carriers will be out to sea when it happens, but virtually our whole Pacific fleet will be destroyed and so many American lives with it. An Admiral Yamamoto, educated here in this country, will lead the attack. You can check him out."

Gary watched the president bow his head, a magnificent patriarchal head, as if in deep thought, and couldn't help feeling overwhelmed in the presence of the man. In manner, intellect and appearance, he was a giant of a man who seemed to epitomize the aristocracy in all its splendor and, at the same time, to convey that aristocratic bearing as a panoply of virtues belonging to the common man, and himself as a symbolic embodiment and reflection of those virtues.

When the president raised his head, he said, "This is a scenario anyone with imagination can write."

"That's true, Mr. President, but surely you've been given other evidence by the Treasury Department and the FBI. Please, sir, indulge me a moment and listen to me further. The Japanese are presently engaged in dominating Asia, isn't that true?"

The president nodded.

"And you have been pressuring Japan to give up its expansionist policies in Asia, isn't that true?"

The president made no response.

"Then I will tell you. You are contemplating holding back

valuable raw materials the Japanese require for their war effort. Particularly, oil."

The president seemed jarred by the comment, but said nothing.

"I'm telling you this, Mr. President, because if the attack comes to pass, hundreds of thousands of casualties will result from the war that follows, a world war, the second of this century."

The president steadied his eyes on Gary. "Another world war?"

"Yes, and we will have to fight it in Europe as well as in the Pacific."

"In Europe. Against...?"

"Germany and Italy. In fact, Germany will invade Poland this coming September."

"I see," he said, brooding over Gary's words. "And will we win it this time, too, this second world war?"

Gary hesitated. If he kept the president in doubt, he had a better chance of swaying him. "It's not for me to say, sir, but if it does come to pass, you will refer to the sneak attack as 'a date which will live in infamy,' and you will open the door to a war that will engulf the world."

The president repeated the words, "A date...which will live... in infamy."

"Yes, Mr. President. And please understand that my primary reason for telling you this is to avoid all the bloodletting on foreign soil and on islands foreign to the minds of most people today. The only positive thing to come of it is that it will end the Great Depression. As you know, your own economic policies have achieved little so far."

Bristling, the president studied Gary long and hard enough to make him very uncomfortable. "You seem to know certain things, Mr. Tyler, that most citizens are not privy to. That is somewhat unsettling to me."

"I'll tell you this, too, Mr. President. It will be rumored that you knew an attack on Pearl Harbor was imminent, that you had broken the Japanese Purple Code, and that you actually wanted the attack so that we would be forced into a war against Japan."

The President leaned forward. "You *dare* to—"

"I'm only telling you, sir, so that you can protect yourself against—"

"Enough! I will tell you now in language you must not misunderstand: You must never repeat the words you have spoken here to anyone ever again. This conversation never took place, do you understand? You have never met me, you have never been here. Am I understood!"

Gary felt his blood chill down to the marrow of his bones. The conviction in that voice was unmistakable, a voice that carried no hint of warmth or kindness, no note of friendliness or familiarity. It was as cold as the steely blue eyes boring into his own misty blue eyes.

As if by magic, the door to the veranda opened.

"You may leave now, Mr. Tyler."

"Wait, sir, please listen," he said, delving into his pocket and bringing up the swatch of material. He stretched forward and placed it on the desk. "I ask only that you turn this over to any scientific lab in the country for analysis. They will find, as you will learn, that no such material exists in the world today. It is from this," he said, plucking his shirt.

The president looked at the piece but didn't touch it. "Most everything you've said, Mr. Tyler, can be explained away, including that," he said, regaining control. And now I'm instructing you to remain living where you now reside. You may be contacted later."

Gary rose to his feet. "Thank you, Mr. President."

The president called just as he reached the door. "Mr. Tyler, as a matter of idle curiosity, tell me, if you can, will I run for office again?"

"Yes, you will."

"Against whom, if you care to say?"

"Wendell Willkie."

"Ah, Wendell. I see. And will I win?"

"You will have your third term, Mr. President. Just one word of warning, sir, if I may…?"

The president waited.

"Don't trust Stalin."

* * * * *

Back in the car, traveling north along the Hudson, Gary sat gazing out his window, unable to believe what had just transpired. The microphone on the desk made sense now, of course; it was used by the president for his radio fireside chats that entranced millions of citizens. Transmitted from that very room. And he had been there to actually see it.

It boggled his mind to know that he had just talked to— talked with— the 32nd president of the United States of America! It would be an experience he could never share because no one would ever believe him. It might as well have been a dream. But it wasn't.

He wondered, would Mr. Roosevelt believe him and take steps to prevent the war or to at least prevent the carnage at Pearl Harbor? And were his inquires regarding his coming election merely a way to test the reliability of his prophesy of war? Time would tell all, either when he got back to the future, or even if he didn't. The question most crucial, the one he tried to ignore, was that if he proved successful in altering history, history as he knew it, would it benefit the country, or lead to something worse?

He felt uneasy. At first the president seemed receptive to his predictions, but then apparently had a change of mind and dismissed him as no more than a crackpot who perhaps made a couple of good guesses. But if that were true, then why did he warn him to keep his mouth shut and to stay close to home? Did that piece of cloth put him in doubt?

Bradshawe broke into his thoughts. "Not many people get a private interview with the Big Man himself," he said, huffing his breath on his handgun and polishing it with a large white handkerchief. "It must have been quite interesting."

Gary looked at Bradshawe, at the gun, at him again, then turned to look outside.

"Not everybody gets an opportunity like that."

Gary put his head back and closed his eyes, ignoring him.

"Tired, aren't you?" Bradshawe said. "Well, I don't blame you, it's been a long night. You can rest up when we get back. You won't be making any plans for a while."

Gary opened his eyes. "Plans?"

"Sure. It's my understanding you'll be hanging around where we can get in touch, if necessary."

"Are you trying to tell me something, Bradshawe?"

Bradshawe eyed the gun barrel, blew into it, and poked the end of the handkerchief inside with a pencil. "I did, Mr. Tyler." He turned, a thin smile drawing a line across his square jaw. "I already did." His smile faded.

Something ominous lurked in that false smile and in those words. The threat was subtle but real: stick around, or else! They'd be watching him now to make sure he didn't try to leave town. But what did it all mean?

Gary neither spoke nor slept much on the way home. His mind raced to no place in particular and every place in general. He knew only that a subtle fear had taken hold of him.

* * * * *

They let him out at the curb in front of the boarding house and Gary bent down to look inside the car. "I can't say it's been a pleasure," he said, directing his attention to Bradshawe, "but you can bet your shoes, socks and shiny blue suits I hope I never meet you fellows again."

"You can always hope," Bradshawe said. "Which reminds me, what was that deal with the shirt I cut up?"

"Which reminds me," Gary countered, "where's my knife?"

Bradshawe pondered the question, swiping a hand across his square jaw before bringing up the knife and handing it out through the window. "Another quarter inch on that blade and I'd have confiscated it."

"I guess size does count, after all," Gary said, backing off.

"Hey, what about the shirt?"

"I ate it."

"Uh huh," he said, tapping the driver on the shoulder. "We'll be seeing you, wise guy."

Gary watched them go, then went inside.

Chapter 31

No more than five minutes had passed after Gary had entered his room, when the sharp crack of knuckles on wood startled him. What now, he thought, going to answer the door, the Internal Revenue Service?

Standing in the doorway, the fingers of one hand drumming the door frame and chewing her gum like cud, was Mrs. Harmon, the fingers of her other hand hooked around a wire hanger on her shoulder.

"Elsie," he said, feigning surprise.

"Your sweater," she said, handing it over. "Thursday, just like I said, today. I came this mornin', but you weren't here."

"I wasn't, was I?"

"I thought you were sleepin'. Almost busted my damn hand, knocking."

"Business, Elsie." He winked. "You understand."

She narrowed her eyes on him. "Thirty-five cents."

"Thirty-five cents," he repeated, digging into his pocket. "Say, didn't I pay you for this already?"

"You most certainly did not! I told you I'd collect when I delivered it. It was the ice I made you pay for up front."

He smiled. "Elsie, you're right, you - are - so - right. I guess we all make mistakes sometime or other, don't we?" He handed her a dollar bill. "You keep the change."

Stunned, she stared at him.

He winked again. "Government expense account," he said, closing the door. From the other side he heard her raspy 'Thank you.'

Dead tired from the long ride and lack of sleep, he hooked the hanger over a chair and flopped on the bed. He couldn't afford to sleep yet, but he could lie there and rest while he thought about his next moves. He wondered if Sarah had stopped by to check in on him. It might not be a bad idea to knock on her door and ask her out, if she could manage it. A movie. She probably hadn't been to one in a long while. Maybe stop in one the restaurants along the way for a bite to eat. It would help him stay awake and keep his days and nights straight.

A quick shave and freshened up, and minutes later he was standing in front of her door, where he could smell cooking. He knocked before his courage completely faded.

"Gary," Sarah said, her voice full of surprise when she opened the door. "Come in, come in."

"I hope I'm not interrupting your meal or anything," he said, gingerly stepping inside and seeing her mother sitting on the couch and another woman sitting across from her in the chair Sarah had occupied the last time he was there.

"Hello, Mrs. Montera. How are you today?"

She had a black shawl over her shoulders and a black rosary wound between her fingers. "For an old bag, what can you expect. Come in. Sit. Over there," she said, the beads rattling in the shaky hand she pointed with.

"Gary," Sarah said, "this is Mrs. Lutz. You remember we mentioned her when you were here?"

"I certainly do," he said, "coming around and looking into the friendly face of the woman smiling up to him and graciously extending her hand.

"Mamie's our good friend," Mrs. Montera said. "She lives upstairs here."

"And you're Gary," she said in a pleasantly dignified voice. "I've heard about you, too." She touched her crown of tidy white hair. "All good, I assure you. It's so nice to meet you."

"We just finished our meal," Sarah said, "but there's plenty left over if—"

"No, thank you." he said, taking the same chair he sat in last time.

"Or something to drink?"

"No, thanks, Sarah, I'm fine."

They talked and Gary did most of the listening as the older women reminisced over what they called 'better times,' when the children were small, their husbands alive, and the aches and pains few and far between.

Rising suddenly, Sarah went into the bedroom and returned with a Brownie box camera. "I hope there's enough light," she said, surprising the three with a quick shot.

As she turned to go, Mrs. Lutz said, "Just a minute, Sarah, you're not in the picture. Here, give it to me. Let me take one."

"Not with me," Mrs. Montera piped up, blocking her face, "no picture for me."

"Then you, Sarah, and your new friend together. Come here next to Gary. That's it," she said, bringing the camera to her eye. "Closer," she said, waving a dainty hand, "a little closer, that's it. Now smile. Good," she said, handing the camera back. "I do hope it comes out."

When they had reached a rare lull in the conversation, Mrs. Lutz looked up as if with a sudden inspiration. "Sarah, if you and Gary here would like to go for a stroll, I'd be very happy to stay and chat with your mother until you get back. I have nothing pressing."

"Oh, Mrs. Lutz—"

"Maria, is that all right with you…if they go and I stay?"

Sarah's mother looked up sharply. "Well…."

"To be frank, Mrs. Montera," Gary said, "I came over to ask your permission to take Sarah to a movie this evening. If she could get away, of course."

"Why, I think that's a splendid idea, Maria," Mrs. Lutz said, sitting straight up with her little fists on the arms of her chair. "Sarah, I'll bet you haven't been to a movie in ages, I'll just bet that." She was as excited as if she herself were going.

"I promise to have her home in less than three hours, Mrs. Montera." He waited expectantly, and Sarah seemed to be holding her breath.

"Well," she said finally, "okay. It's enough for Mamie to sit here and keep me company."

"Thank you, Mama," Sarah said. "I'll do the dishes and put some coffee on before we leave."

"I'll give you a hand," Gary said, following her into the kitchen.

Mrs. Lutz folded her hands on her lap and smiled sweetly over to Mrs. Montera. "How wonderful to be young, isn't it, Maria?"

"That young is too long back for me to remember," she answered, adjusting her shawl.

"Ah, Maria, now think back to when you and your husband Angelo first met. Oh, I've seen your eyes when you talk about him. That's love, Maria, love that never dies. And it begins when we're young... like that," she said, tipping her head toward the kitchen. "I know what you're thinking, Maria, and what you're afraid of, but Sarah has to have her chance, too. We had ours. In the end," she looked heavenward, "He takes care of us."

"So what are you saying?" Mrs. Montera said, "push her out? With just anybody?"

"Of course not, Maria. I'm only saying don't be afraid to let go a little. Try to remember what it's like to be young, when the world is brand new and full of wonder and exciting places to go and so full of things to see and do in it. Let her feel the joy that we once felt. And Maria, when you see that in her, you will live it all over again, through her, through your daughter and the grandchildren she will give you one day."

Sarah came out of the kitchen, Gary close behind her. "The coffee's on the stove, Mrs. Lutz," she said, "whenever you want it. Cups are on the table."

Gary helped her into her red, corduroy jacket. "Mrs. Lutz," he said, "it was a great pleasure meeting you and talking with you."

"Thank you, young man," she said, sitting primly in her chair. "The sentiment is mutual, I'm sure."

"I'll leave my purse, Mama," Sarah said. "I don't think I'll need it."

"And don't worry about Sarah, Mrs. Montera, she's in safe hands with me."

Sarah's mother nodded this way and that, making little faces he could only guess the meaning of.

Chapter 32

Gary stopped in his room for his jacket and went out the front door with Sarah holding his arm. "I forgot about transportation," he said. "How far is the show?"

She smiled at him. "The closest one is about a mile," she said. "The Regency."

"We don't even know what's playing, do we? And I don't have a newspaper."

"Does it make a difference?" she said.

He looked into her eyes. "Not to me."

"Me, neither."

"Okay," he said, breaking eye contact, "that's a little far to walk, so how do we get there? Should I go back inside and ask the Monster Lady to use her phone to call a cab?"

"I have an idea," she said, "why don't we ride there on your bike?"

"On my bike?"

"Does it have a carrier on the back?"

"Yes, but it will be better if you sit on the bar in front of me, that is, if it won't be too uncomfortable for you."

"I don't mind if you don't mind," she said, taking his arm and walking around to the back of the house.

"Sarah, are you sure about this?"

"Promise you won't let me fall?"

"You won't fall," he said.

"I wouldn't be so certain," she said, uncertainly.

Sarah rode side saddle on the bar in front of him as they got off to a shaky start, but they soon had the feel of it and breezed down the street toward downtown.

"This is fun," she said. "I can't remember the last time I

was on a bike."

"Enjoy the ride," he said, smelling the freshness blow out of her flying hair into his face.

"Gary!" she cried as he swooped around the back side of a car that shot out of a side street across their path.

"Scare you?" he asked, bringing the bike up from a dramatic dip and slowing down.

"Not at all," she said. "I knew you wouldn't let anything happen to me."

Oh, wouldn't I? he thought, remembering the events of the past twenty-four hours and the not-so-subtle threats that were beginning to sink in. Danger seemed to be closing in, and he didn't know from which direction or how to protect against it. He knew only that he had to find a way back to his time, and that feeling guilty over her, over Sarah, was not going to help either of them. She was no more than a date, anyway, a date with a relative stranger he'd known only a few days, and they were going to see a movie. That was it. That was all!

So why the hell did he feel tormented? Could he help it if she was sickly and had to take care of a sick mother? None of that was his fault or his responsibility. These things, sad as they were, tragic as they could be, were not of his making. He just happened along, a freakish accident in time that brought him here to carry out a wish, a desire, a dream. His basic intent, his primary purpose, was to save a little girl from being murdered. That was personal, something he could control. Sparing the country the grief and agony of war, however, was far beyond his power, and something he could only hope to indirectly influence.

"There it is," she said, "on the right."

"I see it," he said. It was just a little theater that no longer existed in his time, its marquee lit up with rows of yellow bulbs surrounding the white panels securing the black letters, a few cockeyed in their track: *Swing Time.* A banner hanging below said, *Bingo Every Sat Nite.*

Pulling alongside the curb, he put his foot down and helped her slide off the bar.

"Look," she said, "it's with Fred Astaire and Ginger Rogers. Oh, I love them, I just love them."

He lifted the bike onto the sidewalk. "That's an excellent musical."

"Have you seen it?" she asked, brimming with excitement.

Only about a dozen times. "No, but I heard about it. And a Hopalong Cassidy Western co-feature, too."

She wrinkled her nose.

He set the bike against the building, and she stopped him to look at the stills displayed on the walls around the entrance: A debonair Astaire thrusting out a pair of gloved hands, and a swirling Ginger Rogers frozen in mid-step, her fur-trimmed gown flared.

"Let's go in," he said, slapping a dollar down at the ticket window.

They found seats in the center, near the middle of the theater, but not before he bought a Hershey bar for himself, and two boxes of popcorn, half of which he spilled while walking down the aisle and squeezing into the narrow rows. The darkness was already tugging at his eyes and he had to struggle to stay awake.

Entranced, Sarah watched, absently dipping into her popcorn box and smiling dreamily as if she herself were up there dancing with Astaire. "Isn't it just wonderful?" she whispered over to him after every musical number.

"Great, just great," he said, fighting sleep and polishing off his popcorn. He dropped the empty box and kicked it under the seat ahead of him.

Almost without thinking, without being consciously aware,

her hand touched his and he took it and held it, feeling a warm, mystical, magical energy flowing between them straight to his heart and mind. At the same time Ginger Rogers filled the screen, her blond hair bringing to mind Shelley, his Shelley, trusting Shelley. He felt horrible, yet he couldn't let go of the hand holding his hand. It reminded him of a record his Grampa used to play, with a line that went: *...when I'm not fondling the hand that I'm fond of, I fondle the hand at hand...* He closed his eyes, trying not to think. He drifted....

"Gary?" she said, jostling his shoulder, "Gary?"

"Sorry," he said, pulling himself up and blinking hard.

"It's over," she said. "Do you want to see the second feature?"

"No," he said, trying to look awake. "Not if you don't want to."

"Then we can go," she said, getting up. "I don't care for Westerns."

Outside, the fresh air flushed the sleep out of him. "I was only resting my eyes, you know, but I was listening," he said, turning the bike around and walking beside it, and her beside him.

"Oh, I know that," she said.

"I wasn't actually sleeping."

"I didn't think you were."

"Honest, I was concentrating on the music."

"Of course."

"Sometimes I give that impression, but that's because I'm so relaxed."

"I believe that."

"I don't want you to think I'm just a stick-in-the-mud kind of guy."

"That thought never entered my mind, Gary."

"You want to get on now?"

"Why don't we keep walking for a while," she said.

"We can," he said, taking in the street, the advertising signs, the little shop windows— lit up now. How bleak, he thought. It wasn't only the movies that were black and white, the world itself was black and white— the people, the houses, even morality was essentially black and white. It seemed a two-dimensional world of rich and poor, old and young, today and yesterday because no one believed in a tomorrow where one could expect more or newer or better. They were innocents in a day when innocence ruled. Life was hard, the movies were their opiate, a place where they could weep, laugh and forget with the Gishes and Chaplins, the Arbuckles and Gables, the Colberts and Lloyds. Movies were the stuff of dreams, and dreams were all they had. He wondered if nostalgia was ever anything more than self-delusion.

He remembered Sarah's face watching Rogers and Astaire singing and dancing, opening a world to her she could never have, but which she could borrow, if only for an hour or so. For a while she was Ginger Rogers, dancing, twirling, singing, and for a short time she was elevated from her drab and hopeless existence. It seemed a dark and dusty world, with little to show—

"I don't think we were gone too long, Gary, do you?"

"Not bad," he said, "especially with skipping the second feature. That saved about an hour. Do you want to— wait, there's a hardware store. Let's stop in for a minute."

Inside, it was dark and cluttered so badly that it would take a miracle for anyone to find anything in it.

"What can I do for you?" the old man said, shuffling stiff-legged to them. He looked older than the store itself.

"I'd like a chisel, one that will crack open a steel door, and a good hammer, please."

Sarah looked at him quizzically.

"I'd also like a flashlight. With batteries," he called to the man, now burrowing somewhere among ten thousand gauges, pails, boxes of nails and screws, stove pipes and tools.

"Gary, you're not going to rob a bank, are you?" Sarah asked, with just enough seriousness to make him believe she really was serious.

"Anything else?" the old man asked, emerging like a stooped creature from a metal jungle.

"That will be it," Gary said, paying the man and carefully guiding Sarah out as if through a mine field.

Sarah held the package as they bicycled home. "Gary, can I ask you, if it's not too personal, why you need these things?"

"Let's see now…'can' means 'able to,' and 'may' means permission…or is it the other way—?"

"Gary, stop it, please, stop making fun of me."

He laughed. "Either way you say it, Sarah, I can't answer, not yet."

"Gary, I don't understand you. Why are you so mysterious? Are you hiding something? Are you wanted by the police?"

"Sarah," he said, moving his head around to keep her hair out of his eyes so he could see, "Sarah, I hope I can explain all this to you, I really do. It's a little complicated and more than a little unbelievable, but bear with me, okay? Just a while longer? But no, to put your mind at ease, I am not a criminal?" He broke off suddenly. "Would you like to stop for a soda, like last time?"

"I don't think so. I think I should be getting back. Besides, the wind is giving me a chill."

"Sorry, Sarah. I didn't think about that when we started. We're almost home," he said, swinging the corner toward the house. No one was around when he rode up around the back of the house. Dropping the bike in the yard, he took the package and held her hand as they walked over to the back steps, where they stopped.

She turned to him, still holding his hand. "Thank you so much, Gary," she said, gazing up to him. "I can't remember the last time I had such a good time."

Going to a cheap movie is a good time? "I had a good time, too," he said, seeing her lustrous eyes, even in that dark place. "I hope we can do it again. Or maybe visit the zoo or something...." He pulled her close. "Sarah, I can't promise—"

She put a finger to his lips. "Don't say anything, Gary. It's all right. I understand."

"No, Sarah, I don't think you do," he said, his face hovering close to hers.

"You won't be staying, Gary. I can feel it. And that's fine. We can't always have everything we want, the world isn't made that way. But just being with you this short time has meant a lot to me, more than you know." She looked up. "It's sort of like a bright star in a dark sky. Isn't it better to have seen it even for a minute, than never to have seen it at all?"

"Sarah, listen to me. I promise to clear everything up. Soon, I promise."

"Words are unnecessary. Don't say anymore, Gary," she said, bringing her lips close to his. "Don't say—"

He dropped the package and his mouth was on hers before he could stop himself, his arms crushing her close, her arms encircling him, her hands on his neck, pulling him tight, drawing from him his strength and his will. How long they held that kiss, he could never remember. He could only remember it transporting him across time and space to a moment in a paradise he knew he could never inhabit. The kiss was a dream, as Sarah was a dream, no more than a dream that must of its very nature recede and fade— destined never to be fulfilled.

They pulled apart, embarrassed, saying nothing, merely holding hands there in the darkness, trying to find an equilibrium and perhaps a decorum suited to the moment.

"Are you ready to go in?" he asked, picking up the package from the ground.

She brushed her hair back over her shoulders. "Yes," she said, letting him guide her up the steps by the hand.

Before they'd reached her apartment, Gary said, "Don't go in yet, Sarah." He squeezed her hand, urging her along, "Come on."

"Gary...please..." she whispered, trying to hold herself back, resisting and looking around helplessly, fearfully.

"It's all right, Sarah," he said, taking his key from his pocket and opening the door to his room. "Come on, it's all right, nothing's going to happen, come on."

She let herself be pulled inside and stood blinking in the light. "Gary, this isn't right. If Mrs. Harmon—"

"Forget the old battle-axe," he said, tossing the package on the chair and leading her over to the bed. "Sit a couple of minutes, warm up. What can I get you? I have—"

"Nothing, Gary, thank you. My mother... Mrs. Lutz, they'll be wondering—"

"It's all right, Sarah, it's early, we have time. We can talk here, just for a while, in private, without anybody spying on us. Don't worry, no one saw us come in. Give me your jacket. Here, sit. It's more comfortable than these old wooden chairs she must have stolen from a funeral parlor." He stood in front of her and eased her down on the bed and sat beside her.

She sat with her knees tight together, her hands on her lap. "Gary—"

"Not much of a room, is it?" he said. "It could use a woman's touch, I suppose."

"Gary, I think I'd better go. I'm afraid."

He put one arm around her, and with the other he turned her face to his. "Don't be afraid, Sarah. I just want to talk. There's so much to say, so much I want to say...."

"Don't, Gary," she said, her eyes pleading. "I told you words aren't necessary."

"Somehow they are, Sarah. I can't even pretend to understand all this. All I know is that a few days ago, for the first time, I saw you. You were on the porch, remember? All wrapped up in your shawl, right up to your beautiful chin."

"Gary, please. This isn't helping. You're going away; you as much as said so."

"Sarah, look at me. Look at me," he said, holding her face. "Something I can't explain is happening to me. I don't know what it is; we hardly know each other."

"You already know a lot about me, Gary, but I know so little about you."

"Look in my eyes, Sarah. They can tell you more than my words can."

She tried to pull away, but he held her tight. "Let me go now, Gary, please."

He firmed her in his arms, his eyes blazing into hers, then passed his lips lightly across hers. She pushed her fists against his chest, but he held her locked in his embrace.

She squirmed against him, twisting her face away from his. "No...Gary, no."

"It's all right, Sarah, it's all right," he said, catching her mouth again and savoring the sweetness of her warm breath as he brushed his lips back and forth across her lips, finally taking them firmly and feeling the moist fullness of them.

She struggled to free herself, more weakly now, with tiny whimpers leaking from her throat. Gradually, by degrees, she relaxed and let her arms slip around him as he eased her back and lay beside her, his mouth tasting the freshness of hers, and her own mouth clinging to his with a growing hunger that seemed to come from some lost place deep within her.

In the midst of their heated passion, he rose swiftly, turned off the light, and hurried back to her.

"Gary," she whispered, rising to her elbows, but he eased her back with his mouth on hers, and once more her arms enveloped him. Enraptured, calling his name over and over, she clung to him, her face flushed, the last futile shreds of resistance melting away, all her fears and doubts and worries and cares evaporating with the heat of a consuming love that flamed within her. She succumbed to him....

* * * * *

Stillness marked the moment. Together they lay there quietly in the dark, breathing the mystery of intimate knowledge, their bodies damp, their thoughts and emotions beyond expression— forgetting time, forgetting themselves, knowing only that, despite themselves, they had become one, eternally joined in mind, heart and flesh....

"There's my comb if you need it," he said, throwing on his shirt.

She stood in front of the mirror, smoothing her hair and her face, looking at herself as if into the face of a stranger. She arranged herself, and he helped her into her jacket.

"What time is it?" she asked, worry lines spoiling her forehead.

He dragged out his watch. "It's early enough."

"Do I look all right?" she asked.

"Angel eyes," he said, "you look beautiful. You're glowing." She dipped her head self-consciously. "Ready?"

"I'm scared, Gary," she said, taking his arm.

"Don't be. Just be natural. Make yourself believe nothing happened."

She looked up at him. "Can you do that, make believe nothing happened?"

"We have to try, don't we?" he said, bending to her and kissing her lightly.

He cracked open the door and listened before poking his head out. "All clear," he whispered, taking her by the arm and leading her out and down the hall.

Before they reached the apartment door he stopped, turned her and held her at arm's length. "Sarah, there's one thing I want you to know: I did *not* fall asleep in that theater."

"Gary," she said, trying hard to smile, "I never for a moment thought you did."

"I'm back," she said, opening the door and urging him in with her.

"That's nice," her mother said. "But not so early like I thought."

"Well, did you two have a good time?" Mrs. Lutz said, setting aside her cup, and half-turning in her chair to face them, still standing near the door.

"Wonderful," Sarah said, trying to be cheerful. "We saw *Swing Time*, with Fred Astaire and Ginger Rogers. Oh, it was so beautiful, the music, the dancing, her beautiful costumes...wasn't it, Gary?"

"To tell the truth, I didn't pay much attention to the costumes."

"Just like a man," Mrs. Lutz said, beaming. "Maybe you can tell us about it tomorrow. I'm sure your mother would love to hear it."

"Well, why are you standing there?" Sarah's mother said. "Take off your coats."

"I'll be going, myself," Gary said, helping Sarah off with

her jacket. "It's about my bedtime, too."

"Maybe you'd like some coffee before," Sarah's mother said. "We had ours, right, Mamie?"

"If I may take some liberties, here," Mrs. Lutz said, looking up at Gary, "since we're old friends now, may I ask you a personal question?"

Gary held his breath, afraid of what may be coming, but she said, "First let me say you're wearing a beautiful shirt. I don't believe I've ever seen one quite like it before."

Gary shrugged. "It's just something I picked up along the way on my travels."

"But it is a shame," she said. "I noticed it at supper."

"What, Mamie, what?" Mrs. Montera butted in.

"Would you step around here a moment, please?"

Gary did as she asked, and stood in front of her.

"The first thing I noticed were the names stitched on it, Greg and Norman."

"Those aren't two first names, Mrs. Lutz," Gary said, "That's the whole name."

"Oh, I see, 'Greg Norman.' Did the seamstress make a mistake with your name, 'Gary Norman'?"

He smiled. "No, my last name's Tyler. Greg Norman is a... a friend."

"Oh, I see. It's Greg's shirt, then."

"What, Mamie," Mrs. Montera interrupted again, "what's the shame, you said?"

"This," she said, pointing to the cut.

Mrs. Montera stretched to see. "Looks like a bite somebody took out of it."

"May I?" Mrs. Lutz asked, lifting her hand.

"Sure, go ahead," Gary said, moving a little closer to her.

Delicately, her fingers slid along the hem, caressing the material in little circles. "It has a marvelous feel to it. Very much like silk, but not silk."

"I don't know what it is," Gary said.

"Mamie knows," Mrs. Montera said, nodding wisely. "She's a seamstress, the best."

"Retired, Maria," she said. "I don't know if I can do anything with this. I have a variety of threads that I can look at and—"

"Mamie, look. You see. A whole full basket of them you can use."

"Yes, Maria, if I have to look further, perhaps."

"I don't want to put you out, Mrs. Lutz," Gary said. "It's really not a big deal."

"Oh, my. Such a beautiful shirt, it would be a shame. Why don't you give it to me tomorrow morning? Or give it to Sarah and I'll pick it up later. I can't promise to make it original, but I surely can promise to make it presentable."

A few more words passed between them, and Gary bowed out as gracefully as he could.

Sarah saw him out into the hall again. "Gary," she whispered, taking his hand, "I hope this doesn't change anything." Her eyes glistened. "I mean, I hope you don't think—"

"Stop it, Sarah. What could possibly change? If anything, we're closer than we've ever been."

She stood on tiptoe and kissed him lightly. "Goodnight, Gary."

"Goodnight, Sarah," he said, watching the door close behind her.

Back in his room, in bed, the light out again, gusts of shame blew over him, shame and a guilt he couldn't hide from. Twisting over on his stomach, he buried his head in his pillow, trying to forget the tremble in her voice and the fright he had seen in her tearful eyes afterward, her nervous, agitated movements when she was dressing. He reached over and touched the spot she had lain in only minutes ago. What kind of an injustice had he inflicted upon her? What damage had he done? And the question he didn't want to face: Was he falling in love with her?

He forced himself to stop thinking of Sarah, and to turn his thoughts to Dolly, to the little girl destined to die tomorrow unless he could reverse history. Thoughts askew, he fell into a troubled sleep.

Chapter 33

Friday morning, April 21st. Gary woke up miserable. The big day, the day he'd come back to 1939 for, had waited all week for, had come at last. But his first thoughts were not of the little girl doomed to die tonight, but of Sarah. Again he caressed the spot where she had lain, and picked a long dark hair off the pillow. He ran it between his fingers, remembering how he had grasped fistfuls of it, pulling her face toward him as he kissed her, and kissed her again, and again, and again, a perfumed and misty sweat sucking air between them.

"Stop it," he said aloud, and throwing off the covers. He had to think of Dolly, to concentrate on that, and that alone. Exactly when her murder would take place, he didn't know, but he guessed it would be around dusk. But not if *he* could help it.

Out of bed, into the tub for a fast bath, shaved and dressed, and he was ready to take on the day. Picking up his Greg Norman shirt, and afraid to sniff it, he carried it out to Sarah's apartment. He rapped, waited, and rapped again. 10:15, by Mickey's reckoning. They should be up. Then again— The door opened.

"Sarah's not so good," Mrs. Montera said, leaning on her cane, her neck curving out of the buzzard hump on her back. "I think maybe she caught cold."

"I'm sorry to hear that, Mrs. Montera."

"Eh, there are worse things," she said. "And that's the shirt for Mamie, no?"

"Yes," he said, handing it to her. "Thank you. Will you tell Sarah I said hello, and, if it's all right, I'd like to check in with you later to see how she is. Maybe I can get something at the drug store if you need it."

"That'sa nice," she said. "I'll tell her."

Gary stood outside the door for a moment. Was she really sick, or just too embarrassed to see him. Either way, he should have known better than to take her out on his bicycle, jerk that he was. She couldn't afford to be sick. Doctor Goldman didn't say it outright, but no doubt she had a serious problem. This cold she had, if it was a cold, didn't help. He remembered now hearing her cough several times last night, little suppressed coughs she'd buried in her hand.

Over at the table Gary stood a moment, thinking, then removed the flashlight, took the package holding the hammer and chisel, left his room and went out through the back door.

Finding some twine on the ground near the garbage shed, Gary tied the package tight to the handlebars of his bike and started off. He had no intention of going through with this trip through time, not for another week, anyway. Why he was bringing these tools with him now, he didn't know. Maybe just to see if it would work when he did decide to go back.

Spotting a black car squatting across the street as he left the backyard and skirted the building, Gary swung by and waved to the two shadowy figures propped stiff as dummies in the front seat. He wondered if they had followed him to the theater last night. The surveillance was something he'd almost forgotten about and he promised himself to be more attentive. If they found out what he was up to, they could easily mess things up for him.

Maybe, he thought, if he could get inside the warehouse, maybe he could go back to his own time, just to make sure it's possible. Why not? It would put his mind at ease to know that he wouldn't be stuck here forever. The idea was tempting, so tempting, especially with all the grief he had to put up with since he'd arrived.

The idea sounded rational and appealing, but how could he be sure he'd return in time, in fact, by this very afternoon? Too much depended on accuracy, and he had no way of knowing just how precise his timing would be. He had no control over that. A miscalculation of a few hours would doom Dolly. And who could say how much time Sarah would have to live without medical help? Of course, he couldn't do anything more about the coming war; that was out of his hands now, but there was Dolly. And Sarah. He didn't want her to think he had run out on her. But what else could she think if he didn't come back?

He made up his mind: no more than a dry run to check the situation over and be ready for it when the moment was right.

Looking over his shoulder he saw the black sedan following in the distance. Cutting sharply and crossing a few neighborhood backyards, he lost them and sailed down the street, feeling much lighter and more optimistic than he did when he'd left the house earlier. The sun warmed the morning air, and the traffic was light and grew lighter yet as he approached the warehouse district. The row of houses, drab and drearily alike, fell behind as he swept past.

From a block away Gary could see not only the North Division side of the warehouse ahead, but also some activity around it. Pedaling up to the corner of the intersection, he pulled over, got off his bike and walked it across the street. A manhole cover lay on the pavement and a city work crew milled around, setting up wooden barricades and equipment. Near the curb, alongside the building, heaps of earth lay piled next to open holes.

Gary sidled up to one of the workers. "Problems?" he asked.

"Okay," the man growled to one of the men behind him, slouching over his shovel, "start that generator." Stroking his face with a dirty gloved hand, he peered down into the hole.

"Problems?" Gary asked again.

The man shot him an impatient look with a face as gruff-looking as his voice sounded. "If it ain't one goddamned thing it's another."

Gary leaned forward and peered down the hole where a couple of voices argued back and forth.

"And those guys are something else," he said, spitting an amber stream of tobacco juice into the hole."

"Hey, godammit!" one of them yelled up.

"Is this job going to take long?" Gary asked, judging the proximity to the door of the building to be no more than twelve feet away.

"Hell, who knows. We get a job, we do it, if it takes a day, a week or a month."

"You think you'll be done today?"

"I just said I didn't know, didn't I? It depends on what those birds find down there, but I doubt it'll be today. Nobody's in a rush to kill the job, anyway," he said, spitting another long stream of juice into the hole. "If you know what I mean."

"I know what you mean," Gary said, hearing the curses below and watching for a minute before turning his bike and walking it around to the other side of the building.

The front wheel was just clearing the south corner, when he spotted a police car parked almost directly in front of the door and jerked the bike back out of sight. *Dammit! Probably John and Ed, the same two doughnut-eaters who grabbed me before. Didn't they ever go anyplace else, or was this their permanent beat, so to speak. Now what?*

Maybe he could come back later in the day to check the situation over, he thought, but how much later? Time was picking up speed already, and he had to allow himself enough leeway to get to the First Ward before the killer did. Taking a last peek around the corner of the building and seeing the car still parked there, he swung the bike around and headed out of the district.

No question about it now, he'd be stuck here for at least another week. But in some odd way he couldn't explain to himself, he felt relieved. Fate had intervened to make sure he didn't give in to temptation and leave before taking care of business here. And if fate were that kind, he thought, it would make sure he'd eventually get home.

A surge of optimism and confidence coursed through him as he breezed along, thinking of Sarah and wondering how she was feeling. About half way home, he caught sight of the black sedan cutting out from a side street he'd just passed. "Well, here we go again," he said, deciding to take them on a merry ride and give them something to think about.

* * * * *

Minutes later Gary wheeled up in front of Windy's tavern and dropped the bike on the sidewalk out front, while half a block away, the sedan pulled up to the curb and stopped.

"Hey, kid," Sam said, stretching a hairy arm across the bar to shake hands. "Long time no see. Good to see ya." Against the far wall Nick was at the piano, playing quietly.

"All of what, Sam, four days?" he said, shaking hands. "Are you open yet?"

"Not officially, but if you want something, you got it."

"No beer, Sam," Gary said, hauling himself up on the bar stool.

"What, then, juice? I got orange juice I can give you, or Coke, birch beer..."

"The birch beer sounds good, Sam."

"Man, you really cleaned those guys out the other night. I ain't heard the end of it yet," he said, setting the glass in front of Gary. "A couple of them think you were on the inside of a fix, and a couple of others think you got a crystal ball. Imagine that?"

"Imagine that," Gary repeated, sipping his drink.

"So you got home all right, then. Boy you were pretty much under the weather, but I knew the pug would getcha back okay."

"Pug?"

"Yeah, Tommy, you know," he said, running his thumb alongside his nose and raising his fists in a fighting stance.

"Ah, Tommy Fisher, so that's who it was."

"That's the guy," he said, grabbing a towel and polishing bottles on the back bar. "So what are you doing around here so early in the day, kid?"

Gary looked up to him, smiling. "Mainly I came to see you wipe my name off the Wall Of Shame. The week's up today, right?"

"Right, kid, right, but your time ain't quite up yet. That's the way we been doin' it, and you know how the guys get when somebody breaks a rule."

Gary stayed awhile, carrying on small talk, mostly about the economy. He had a second glass of birch beer.

"Hey, Stan, set me up again, will you?" Nick called over from the piano. His voice was raspy.

Gary looked around. "Did he call you Stan?"

"That's my name," Sam said, pouring a beer from the tap. "Nick's the only one who calls me by my real name, him and my mother. Stan— Stanley Henry Wiater. Harder to say than it is to spell—w-i-a-t-e-r. In Polish it means 'wind.' And since my old man was a non-stop talker, too, naturally the joint gets called Windy's." He carried the beer over to Nick and came back.

"My uncle labeled me when I was a kid because even then I was so hairy. Said I was adopted and I was really an Italian." He tossed aside the towel and rolled down his sleeves. "It stuck. So I showed 'em all. Now I talk like an Italian and I act like one."

"Interesting, Sam. Well, I guess I'll be shoving off," he said, pushing his glass back. "I'll try to get back tonight. If not, tomorrow night for sure. I want my revenge." He motioned him close, jabbing his thumb over his shoulder. "What's that song Nick keeps playing over and over?" he whispered.

"*Alice Blue Gown,* I think is the name."

* * * * *

Gary pedaled away, humming the tune and fully aware of the sedan tailing him from a comfortable distance. He took pleasure imagining them back there wondering what he was up to. In fact, he wasn't up to anything yet, but they didn't know that. He led them along, sometimes slowing almost to a crawl, sometimes suddenly racing around a corner, then swinging back in the opposite direction and circling the same block several times. He hoped he was driving them as nuts as they had driven him on his long ride to Hyde Park.

Twenty minutes later he pulled up in front of **CORKEY**"S **BICYCLE EMPORIUM**, parked his bike and went inside, where he saw Corky pulling a bicycle wheel down from a ceiling hook.

"Hi, Corky," he said, coming in and leaning on the counter. "I was in the neighborhood and thought I'd drop by to say hello."

"Howya doin', kid?" he said, pulling a cigarette out of his

shirt pocket with his thumb and pinky and lighting up. "Goin'
down to Windy's tonight?"

"I expect to, but probably a little later."

"Well, you better watch it, Leo's gunnin' for ya."

Just then Jackie appeared in the doorway in the back of the
shop. "Who is it, Cork? Need any help up there?"

Corky's eyes twitched. "Naw, nobody, go on back to
work."

"Isn't that Jackie, your helper?"

"Yeah, who else?" he said, dragging hard on his cigarette.

"The one who did such a good job on my bike."

"That's him, that's the pain in the ass."

"Well, I'd just like to go back a minute and compliment
him."

"Well, hell's bells, don't do that," Corky said, getting over
and blocking his way.

"Why not, Corky? He deserves a little credit, doesn't he?"

"For chrissake, do that and he's gonna be throwin' it up in
my face and askin' for a fuckin' raise every time I turn around.
Forget it, okay? I'll tell him for you my own way."

Jackie planted himself in the doorway again. "What's
wrong, Cork? Somethin' wrong?"

"Naw, go on, get back there and mind your own business."

Gary called back, "Jackie, I just dropped in to let you know
that I like the bike. You did a great job with it."

"You hear that, Cork?" Jackie hollered, "Goddammit, Cork,
did you hear it?"

Corky dropped his cigarette butt and stomped on it. "See
that?" he said, glaring so hard that his eyes threatened to pop
out of their sockets. "Upset the whole goddamned apple cart.
Why the hell'd you have to stop and stir up—"

"By the way, Corky, after the bets last Monday when I paid
you off, I also gave—"

"Well, for chrissake, will ya shut up," he said, looking around, his hands dancing a jig at his sides. "Sure, I remember now that you remind me, but I forgot. You think I'd chisel my help for a measly goddamned buck? I forgot. Here," he said, plucking bills out of his side pocket, "it's right here."

"Why don't you call him up here, then. Make like I just gave it to you so he won't think you were holding out on him. I believe you forgot, but he might not. Or I can—"

"Okay, okay," he said, stretching his neck to see better. "Jackie, come here, come on up here, I got somethin' for you."

Gary moved around Corky toward the door. "I'll see you later, Corky," he said, tiptoeing over bicycle parts and careful not to slip on ball bearings scattered around the floor.

"What's up, Cork?" Jackie said, picking his way down the aisle.

Gary lingered in the doorway just long enough to hear Corky tell him, "...lost a bet to me on a fight so outta the goodness of my heart...but you gotta buy the doughnuts and promise...."

Gary hopped on his bike and pushed off. He considered going over on High Street to see his grampa, if possible, but thought better of it. It didn't seem wise right now, not with the blue-suits watching his every move. Tomorrow, he'd go tomorrow, when he had a better chance of losing them. Just thinking of it excited him. The thought of seeing the old man at an age younger than he himself was now, boggled his mind. 495 High Street, that's what Bradshawe said, 495. That number had burned itself into his brain as soon as he'd heard it, and he wouldn't forget it.

Horns beeped and cars cut in and out as he toured the streets looking for a shop he knew must be there someplace. A streetcar hurtled toward him, rocking and swaying to a ponderous rhythm, and he moved to the side as it rolled past him, its bell jangling, its iron wheels squealing over the track. Then he spotted it, tucked between a music store and a novelty shop. Crossing over, he parked his bike outside and went in.

"...a lovely gift," the woman said. "Obviously a very sensitive lady, one with a fine sense of appreciation for the more... beautiful and delicate things in life."

"Obviously," he said. "Do you have something I can use temporarily, just until I get home? And a cover for it?"

"I think we can manage that, certainly."

Paid up, he carried his purchase out, mounted his bike with one hand and carefully pushed off. Behind him, he saw one of the agents dash inside the store. "Let's keep them guessing, hey, Toby?" he said, breaking into a fast clip down a side street and zigzagging across several others. He laughed. "By the time they realize I'm home, they'll have cruised and probably cursed every street in town looking for me."

Swooping into the back yard, he jammed the tools in his belt, hid the bike behind the garbage shed and went inside and down the hall to Mrs. Harmon's apartment. He knocked and he could feel the floor creaking with her coming.

"Yes?" she said, suspicious.

"Elsie, this is for you," he said, handing it over to her. "I hope you like it."

Her brow furrowed. "What the—" She pulled the cover off.

"When I saw that over there," he said, pointing, "well, I thought this might bring a little cheeriness into your apartment. And into your life. God knows, you deserve it, Elsie."

She looked back at the empty bird cage. "A canary," she said, wiping a corner of her eye, "a yellow canary. Things just ain't been the same since... since—"

"I hope you like it," he said. "The woman told me he sings all the time."

"That bird cage has been empty for a year. I just couldn't bring myself...."

"I understand your sadness, Elsie. Well, gotta get moving now."

Her face sagged like melting wax. "Thank you... thank you so much."

"Don't mention it. Oh, by the way, you know how your brother's always whistling?"

"Always whistling, yes. He's a whistler all right. Since he was a kid."

"That's the reason I named the bird 'Toby,' but feel free to change it."

Gary went down the hall and knocked at Sarah's door, waiting a long time for it to open. When it finally did, it opened only a crack and freed a strong smell of Vicks. Sarah's face, half hidden behind the door, peeked out. Her hair hung loose to the side and her eyes looked lifeless, with dark circles beneath them.

"Gary, I'm sorry, I'm not feeling very good."

"A cold, Sarah? Did you catch a cold?"

"I don't think so. I didn't sleep very well, and I feel a little weak."

"Maybe you have a touch of the flu."

"Maybe. I've been in bed all day."

"Well, you stay there, Sarah. Is your mother all right?"

"She's fine."

"Do you need anything from the drug store?"

"No, we have everything we need for now."

"Okay, then, Sarah. If you do think of something, I'll be in my room, at least for a while. I'll check on you later."

"You won't have to, Gary. I'll be fine. I just need rest...Gary?"

"Yes?"

"Mrs. Lutz took your shirt this morning."

"Good." He turned to go.

"Gary…?" she put her hand out the door.

"Yes?" he said, taking it and squeezing it.

She smiled a wan, sad smile. "Nothing."

Chapter 34

Back in his room, Gary picked up the flashlight from the table and clicked it on and off a few times to check it out before setting it down again. He felt his pocket for his knife, secure in the knowledge that it was there in case he needed it. The time was drawing close and he couldn't help feeling nervous. If everything went as planned, it would be fine. But if it didn't, what then? If he ended up dead, no one would ever know who he was. He'd be buried as an anonymous John Doe. And in his own time he would have simply vanished off the face of the earth. His grandma would be telling the police he received a letter and went running out of the house. Shelley would tell the police his story and the police, agreeing to its absurdity, would interpret that as an alibi to run away and start a new life someplace. Eventually they would find his car at the warehouse and think it to be no more than a ruse to mislead everyone. In both eras, he would remain forever an unsolvable mystery.

Physically tired but mentally alert, he stripped off his old jacket, lay back on his bed and tried to relax. Gazing up at the ceiling, he remembered the whole crazy chain of events that had led him to this spot: His love of the past, rummaging in the attic and finding the old newspaper with Dolly's face on it, the ad, the order he went to pick up at the warehouse, and all the crazy events since then.

What was left to do before getting back to his own time? First, save Dolly. Then get medical care for Sarah. But what of Sarah after that, Sarah and him? The question haunted him.

He considered leaving her a note explaining everything should he end up dead, but felt superstitious about doing it and let the idea go. Checking his watch, he got up, put on his jacket and forced the flashlight into the side pocket. By the time he got to the First Ward and looked things over again his timing should be just about right.

* * * * *

Pausing by Sarah's door, he debated whether to knock, just to ask after her, but changed his mind. Outside in the backyard, he pulled his bike up from behind the garbage shed and turned, turned around to face Dexter, standing in front of him, his sinewy arms hanging at his sides, his legs spread and anchored to the ground.

Gary looked at him, surprised. "Dexter."

"That's right, Dexter."

"I have to go someplace important, so if you'll—"

"Think you're some kind of a slickster, don't you?"

"Dexter, I don't know what the hell you're talking about, so if you'll move—"

"Move? Like you been moving in on Sarah?"

"Dexter, you have nothing to say to me about Sarah, so let me by. I don't want any trouble," he said, looking around him for the blue-suits who were supposed to be watching him.

"I got everything to say about her, and you got nothing to say about her."

"Well, isn't that for her to decide, anyway? I told you I don't want any trouble, so—"

Dexter lunged, caught him by the lapels and hauled him up so close Gary could feel his hot breath in his face. "No trouble? That why you been sniffing around her like a hound dog, talking so nice like you're better than me?"

"Let go of me, Dexter," Gary said, feeling the raw strength behind his grip.

"I saw you. You think I'm blind. I been on to you since the first. Think I don't know you went out with her? Think I wouldn't find out? Think you could get away with it?"

"What business is it of yours anyway if I do talk to her," Gary said, trying to pry his fingers away, "or if I do take her to a show? You're not going with her. She's not your girl."

"She's not?" he said, his nostrils flaring. "She's not?" He threw Gary back, stepped forward, grabbed him the same way and threw him back again, up against the fence.

"Hey—" A punch Gary didn't see coming caught him across the temple, staggering him.

"She's not my girl?" Dexter said, unleashing another hard punch.

Gary covered his face and gasped as a solid punch to the ribs sent a searing pain to his brain. He groaned and sagged.

"Who says she ain't?" Dexter sneered, his fist burying itself in Gary's stomach and two more punches in quick succession driving new agony into his body.

Gary buckled, his arms embracing his chest, the wracking pain renewing itself. He sank to the ground, slowly, choked for air, with Dexter standing over him, his knotty fists doubled, his face scowling with hate.

"Guys like you cutting into somebody else's territory got to be taught a lesson. Didn't like you then, and I don't like you now," he said, one hand jerking Gary up by the hair, the other cocked to fire, when somebody caught his hand in midair.

"That's enough!" a voice barked.

"Who the fuck are you?" Dexter said, ripping his hand free and swinging around. "What business is this of yours?"

Gary recognized the voice, recognized him—Joe, the new boarder who had introduced himself in the hall outside Sarah's apartment.

"You're hitting a man that's down. Can't you see he's had

enough?"

"Not as far as I'm concerned," Dexter said, starting back for Gary.

Joe grabbed him again and shoved him back. "I said that's enough. You want to kill him?"

"Maybe I do, so what?" Dexter said, his defiance waning.

"So you're going to have to go through me first," Joe said, bringing a fist shoulder high. "Come on, tough guy, let's see how tough you really are. Come on."

Gary saw Dexter blink and he knew it was all over.

"Come on," Joe taunted, "let's see how you do against somebody your own size. Let's go, what are you waiting for?"

Dexter sidled away. "You shouldn't be butting into other people's business," he said, getting braver the further he moved off. "I'll be running into you later, buddy!"

"So you can jump me from behind, too? Is that how you operate?"

"Fuck you!" Dexter said, his hand on the doorknob, "and you, slickster, if I catch you near her again I'll bust you up a hundred different ways." He disappeared inside.

Joe reached down to him. "How bad are you hurt?" he asked, helping him to his feet.

"Not too bad," Gary said, grimacing and hugging himself.

"Is there something I can do...?"

"Gary."

"Gary... right. Some way I can give you a hand, Gary? Just say the word."

"You've done more than enough, Joe, thanks. You saved my life, I think. I'll be all right," he gasped, feeling the pain rip through him as he tried to straighten up. "Hurt my ribs a little."

"Looks like more than a little. Sure I can't help?"

"If you'd pick my bike up for me...."

"Sure," he said, taking the handlebar and righting the bike. "But you're not going to ride that thing now, are you? Come on, let me help you inside."

Gary pointed. "My flashlight…try it."

Joe picked it up and tried it. "It works," he said, handing it over.

Gary pocketed it, helped his leg over the seat, and pushed off.

Joe watched Gary go, hunched over the handlebars, the bike trembling so badly under his weak grip that it looked as if it would topple.

Chapter 35

Gary kept glancing around to see if he was being followed as he threaded his way painfully through the streets over to the First Ward. *Well, they weren't there when I needed them, either.* It seemed much farther this time than it did last time, and his ribs shot arrows of pain to his brain every time he took a deep breath. He worried, and for a brief moment considered turning around and heading home. What good would it do if they were both murdered? he thought. Then again, the article didn't mention anything about a second body. Of course, it was possible they just didn't find it. He saw Dolly's face before him again, the smile of perfect innocence, and he knew his mission, regardless of the outcome. He girded himself for what he had to try to do, for what he *had* to do.

Like the last time, the street was quiet when he pulled up to the curb in front of the playground and eased himself off the bike. A few cars passed as he stood there looking around for anything out of the ordinary, but he saw nothing to arouse his suspicions. No black sedan or any other car parked nearby. If any of the agents had been following him he'd have spotted them by now, of that he was certain.

Cautiously treading the crumbled walkway, he wheeled the bike to the back of the house, where he stopped to rest and listen. Nothing but the sound of a distant train whistle and his own labored breathing. Pushing the bike well to the rear of the yard where the lengthening shadow of the house had already swallowed the dusky light, he laid it behind a large mound of rubble, and walked gingerly back over the treacherous ground, holding his ribs tight. He rested again, cursing Dexter for putting him at such a disadvantage. Dexter wanted to kill him, he could see it in his burning eyes, but he didn't have to; someone could do him the favor tonight.

Lowering himself slowly, he squatted beside the foundation, dug his fingers under his rag marker and pulled up the length of pipe he'd buried there. It felt cold and hard and deadly in his hand, but could he swing it? Would his body betray him at the last minute? He dared not try now. He had to save his strength, what little he could muster, for when it counted most.

Holding the corner frame and stepping on the rotted steps, Gary put his shoulder against the door and leaned into it. It scraped back slowly, its warped wood catching the remnants of a torn up floor and finally binding, but giving him enough room to squeeze through. Pushing the door closed, he took out his flashlight and flicked it on, the bright beam slicing a tunnel of light in that smelly cave of darkness.

Trash everywhere—boards, hunks of plaster and lath, cans, newspapers, beer bottles, cigarettes and not a few shriveled condoms littered the place. Standing walls punched through with holes separated rooms which had once been filled with furniture and people. From where he stood just inside the back door, he could see through an archway leading to the next room a sliver of daylight in the side door on the walkway side of the house. He let the beam play over the area. It didn't seem likely the killer would bring Dolly in that way because the debris piled behind it would make it very difficult, if not impossible, to get inside. The boards nailed across the door on the outside were another deterrent. And the fact that he could still be spotted from the street cinched it. He flashed the beam around. No, he had to bring the girl in through the back door, if he brought her inside at all.

Casting the light about for something to sit on while he waited, he spotted a wooden nail keg just inside another doorway leading to an adjoining room. Nimbly he stepped over debris and retrieved the keg by moving it with his foot a little at a time, until he had it about where he wanted it. The best place to sit, he decided, was a few feet behind the back door. It would put him in perfect range. All he had to do was stand up, raise the pipe over his head, and drive it down into that sick skull as soon as it appeared inside the room. He knew he'd probably get no more than one shot and he vowed to make it good.

Scraping out a level place on the floor with his foot, he set the keg upright on the spot, found solid footing for himself and sat down, laying the pipe across his lap. If all went as planned, Dolly would be safe and he'd be getting the hell out of there soon, very soon. The sooner the better. He bounced the light around one last time to get a fixed picture of his surroundings, then clicked the light off and mentally rehearsed for the decisive moment, the moment he had traveled back into time for.

Squatting there in the blackness, the noble and heroic gesture he had initially envisioned for himself didn't look quite so noble and heroic now. If he had ever been more scared in his life, he couldn't remember when, especially at the very instant he turned off the light and suddenly realized that he might not be able to see at all when the time came to strike. He had to be ready for an alternative: perhaps wait till the killer drags her inside, snap on the light for an instant to see him and nail him before he has a chance to react. As added insurance, he reached into his pocket, took out his knife, thumbed-nailed the blade open and carefully slid the knife back into his pocket, point facing down.

Just as the sour smell of garbage and rotting wood grew less noticeable with the passing minutes, so too did the solid blackness gradually dissolve to a deep, greenish gloom, creating a kind of dancing near-light that plays tricks on the eyes, creates living shadows and detects motion where none exists. Gripping the pipe to still his shaking hands, he waited, waited and listened for any foreign noises outside the ticking and creaking of wood shrinking in the cooling evening. He took shallow breaths to prevent being heard and to ease the wicked pressure on his ribs. *That goddamned Dexter!*

The minutes crawled and it was too dark to see the time. After awhile he wondered if this was a wild-goose chase, the same as he'd led the blue-suits on earlier that afternoon. Could be that the article itself may have mistaken the date. The newspaper was famous for getting things wrong, wasn't it? This could all be in vain—

Something! Had he heard something? A stifled cry? An animal? A cat? Holding his breath, he cocked his head, trying to determine the direction of the sound. Yes, a mingling of whimpers and harsh whispers. Scuffling. But from where? He stood up, his grip firm on the pipe beginning to sweat in his hands. If only he could see!

The sharp snap of wood cracking, the crush of plaster and glass grating under pressure. From the side. The side door. The sonofabitch was breaking down the side door!

Breath held, Gary took a tentative step, then another toward the archway, feeling for firm footing in the debris. Bringing the pipe shoulder high, he peered into the next room. Silhouetted against the dying outside light, a pair of burly shoulders wedged their way sideways into the opening, splintering wood, and jacking the door back inch by grinding inch.

Gary braced himself, watching the man, a bear of a man, twist and slam his back against the door until it gave, gave with such a mournful rending that it seemed the door itself was crying for the child. The man stumbled in, turning, the little girl, waist-high, caught in his bear hug, only a dim reflection of her terrified eyes showing above the hand smothering her face. Looming over her, his shaggy head hidden in the shadows, and unaware of Gary standing motionless in the dark of the archway, the man muffled her screams as he frantically tore at her clothing.

Gary remembered little of the ensuing moments, only that his tortured body cried in pain as he lunged, howling, swinging the pipe and losing it as it caught the top of the archway instead; then stumbling forward, trying to free his snagged feet, hands scrambling in search of the lost pipe, when a whirlwind clamped his throat in a vise, suffocating him; hearing screams, fading; punching at the exploding force lifting his body into the air and hurling him backwards onto the floor.

Sharp objects gouged his flesh as he lay pinned, unable to reach his knife or to escape the dark visage of death hulking over him and shifting its massive weight through its arms surging with strength down to hands gripping like iron shackles, choking off his windpipe, crushing his throat. Struggling, unable to breathe, Gary felt his eyes bulging, his face filled to bursting. A banshee out of Hell had seized him, was strangling the life from his body… a nightmare consuming him… darkening the world….

Dead. Or thought he was dead. For a while he felt no pain, no pressure in his head. Then his windpipe suddenly opened and sucked in screaming air, his eyes fluttered and his chest heaved despite the rekindled agony wracking his body. He stirred, gasping, his breathing gradually leveling off. Straining, he pushed the dead weight crushing him off his body and raised his head. He held his hand up to shield his eyes against the beam of light shining in his face.

"Who are you?" he cried, straining to hunch up on an elbow and trying to see around the blinding light. "Who are you!"

The light went out.   When it went on again, the disembodied head of a man hovered in the dark, his shadowed face grotesquely illuminated from below the chin to the top of his head.

"Who are you!" Gary cried again, a new fear taking hold.

The man smiled out of the gruesome light.   "Don't you know?"

Chapter 36

"You!"

"Me," he said, reaching down. "Give me your hand."

"I don't get it," Gary said, his words stifled by the pain as he came slowly off the floor.

"You will." He circled his arm around Gary, helping him out the back door and down the steps. When they were on solid ground outside, he took Gary's arm and guided him along the driveway to the street. Standing in the pool of watery light under the lamppost Gary saw his face clearly: the mysterious stranger upstairs, the boarder with the mustache. Standing there beside him, Block, or whatever Elsie said his name was, obviously wasn't the stooped, ineffectual character he had pretended to be.

"The girl," Gary said, "Is she…is she okay?"

"No need to worry, Mr. Tyler, she flew home like a little bird. Scared, no doubt, but safe… ah, good, very good," he said, signaling the taxicab parked near the corner. "We'll go someplace where we can talk." He studied Gary, his stare peculiar in some way Gary couldn't quite tell. "Are you all right, Mr. Tyler?"

Gary held the post to steady himself as the cab wheeled up to the curb and the driver hopped out to open the door.

"Dependable," Block said, giving Gary a hand in, "I like that."

"Overtime is worth it for the kind of dough you—hey! Gary, right? SarahandGary, like the desert. 'Xactly what I said when I picked up this gentleman earlier at the same place. Ain't *that* a coincidence?"

"Hi, Tony," Gary said, gingerly sliding over on the seat.

"What's the matter? You hurt or somethin'?"

"No questions now," Block said, "if you don't mind. He's all right. Just take us downtown to that quiet little restaurant you mentioned earlier?"

"Oh, sure. You mean Ferara's Italian Kitchen. Nice atmosphere, terrific food. The old man took off to Florida a couple of years ago, said he couldn't take the weather no more, so his wife Carmie runs the joint alone. Does it all herself, too, from 'A' to Z-ti." He laughed. "Get it? 'A' to ziti, the macaroni."

"You said it's private?"

"Oh yeah. It's a cozy place with all kinds of nooks and corners."

Neon lights advertising Beck's beer blinked a warm welcome from the window when they pulled up in front of the restaurant. Gary helped himself out and Block slid out behind him. Tony came around to the passenger side.

"I won't be on duty no more when you get out, so—Cheez," he said, taking the bill Block handed him, "a twenty. I don't know if I can break—"

"Keep it," Block said, taking Gary's arm and leading him inside. "You earned it."

They left him standing there staring at the bill, goggle-eyed.

A waitress showed them to a small booth they requested in a dark corner, away from several other patrons scattered at tables about the room. They sat opposite each other and ordered coffee to start.

"Anything in particular you care for, Mr. Tyler?" Block asked, opening the menu and casually scanning it.

Gary looked across to him, to the mustache, the thicket eyebrows, translucent skin and unruly black hair. "You can start by telling me who you are," Gary said, observing the suit, vest, shirt and sporty tie.

"Wouldn't it be more appropriate to start by thanking me for saving your foolish life?"

"I guess," Gary began sheepishly, "I guess I do owe you that. Thanks."

"Just a guess? Well! ...Does the antipasto sound good to you, Mr. Tyler?"

"I'm not really up to eating, but sure, anything."

"You can call me Blocker," he said, reaching across the table to shake hands. "Just plain 'Blocker' will do. Now I suppose you'd like some answers."

Gary nodded, releasing the hand and shrinking before the reptilian eyes fixed on him.

The waitress returned with their coffee, took the antipasto order, and left.

"I thought you would." He lifted the cup to his lips and took a sip. "Ah, this is such a nuisance, especially when I drink," he said, lifting the corner of his mustache and peeling it off. "Surprised, Mr. Tyler?"

Gary just stared.

"This might as well go, too," he said, stripping off his toupee and his eyebrows and stuffing them in his pocket.

"You're...."

"Yes, Sardonicus. I can't say I appreciated the allusion much."

"You're one and the same person, the boarder and—"

"Yes, the mysterious man in the bar. Bravo, Mr. Tyler, bravo." His glittering eyes seemed to smile.

Gary tried to collect himself. "But why? Why are you following me, watching me?"

"Aren't you glad I did? Otherwise, to put it in the modern idiom, you'd be dead meat."

"I still don't understand," Gary said, uneasy and unable to

tear his eyes away.

Blocker set his cup down and sat back. "My looks unsettle you, I see. It's a common reaction, Mr. Tyler, but if you look closely you'll see that I am not merely bald, I am totally hairless. An historic condition not yet conquered called alopecia. Affords me a rather demonic presence, don't you think so? Especially the eyes. If I don't blink, I can cast a most frightening spell over people, the way a snake does. And it comes in so handy in my line of work."

"I'm not interested in your missing eyebrows or eyelashes or the effect your appearance has on others," Gary said, his growing irritability sparking his courage. "I want to know what your game is and how you knew I would be in that house tonight. No way you could have followed me or I'd have spotted you."

"I was there before you arrived."

"Before? How is that possible?"

Blocker leaned forward on the table, his snake eyes locked onto Gary's. "Mr. Tyler, do not release your bowels here and now, but...I am from the future."

Stunned, Gary fell back in his seat. "You mean...like me?"

"Like you, yes, but not exactly like you. I am in fact from *your* future, some two hundred years beyond your backward age."

"Wait a minute now, just hold on there," Gary said, incredulous. "Do you expect me to believe that?"

"Would anybody believe you now, that you are from their future?"

Gary pondered his words. "Okay," he said, trying to pull himself together, "let's get this straight. You say you came from the future, my future."

"Correct."

"To help me save the girl, is that right?"

"You couldn't be more wrong, Mr. Tyler. In the first place, don't flatter yourself; I'm not here on your behalf. As the saying goes, you are 'small potatoes.' In the second place I came not to help you save the girl, but to make sure you *didn't* save the girl."

"*Didn't* save?"

"Did not. Exactly. Unfortunately, I blew it, as you say."

"But why try to stop me?"

"Why? Why? Don't you understand that you have tampered with history? Do you not understand the possible ramifications of that?"

"A little girl...."

"A little girl, yes, nine years old, so insignificant, one of millions, how could saving her life possibly hurt the future? Is that what you're thinking, Mr. Tyler?"

"Yes, that's what I'm thinking, that's right."

"Mr. Tyler, you were but a child then, I suppose, but do you remember the rocket that exploded over Florida in the 1980s, the one that took the lives of seven or eight astronauts? Do you remember reading about that?"

"Well, sure. It was a national tragedy."

"Indeed it was. Do you remember the cause of the disaster?"

"I think a part malfunctioned, froze or something."

"An 'O' ring, Mr. Tyler, a miserable, apparently inconsequential little piece of rubber worth mere pennies, one minuscule part among millions of parts, and look at the effect it had on the people, on the whole American space program."

"Well, if the girl is so important why didn't you let that maniac kill her?"

"Because, Mr. Tyler, you'd be dead, too, and I couldn't have that because... well, your life is more valuable for... reasons I'm not at liberty to divulge."

The waitress arrived with the antipasto and paused, looking around, confused.

"This is the right place," Blocker said, pointing to his head. "I was warm."

Rattled, she set up the dishes, asked if they wanted more coffee and scurried away.

"How did you know I'd be coming here tonight," Gary asked, wincing as he raised his arm to pull from the large bowl.

"Simple logic. That newspaper article you left on your dresser? I was sure then of your high-minded and honorable motive and intention to carry out a plan when I read it."

"So you're the one I heard trying to sneak in my room that night."

Blocker laughed. "No, Mr. Tyler, it was not I. That was Lundow, the other boarder. A scoundrel, an escapee, a renegade from another era who tried to get in. He would have killed you, too, if you hadn't awakened. And he would have killed you twice before: once with a car when you were on your way to the mail-order house, and once minutes after you left it. Getting beat up by that gang was unfortunate, but infinitely better than if they hadn't happened upon you."

"So he was the man I saw standing off in the distance. But wouldn't you have stopped him?"

"I wasn't in a position to. It wasn't until you first went into the diner that I reviewed events and picked up your trail again."

"But why? Why would he want to kill me?"

"I'm sorry, but that has to do with your future, and not for you to know. Take my word for it, though, he would have found a way to kill you by now if I hadn't taken care of him. With this," he said, taking a small packet of needles from his vest pocket. "It's similar to one of your tranquilizer drugs, but far more effective. Works instantly."

Gary remembered. "So he's the one Mrs. Harmon thought you took out drunk the other night."

"Dispatched, and never to return. Bravo again, Mr. Tyler. Which reminds me..." he said, tucking the packet away and setting his napkin aside. "...If you'll excuse me, I have to make a phone call."

After he left the table, Gary mulled over everything Blocker had said, and wondered if all of this was some kind of elaborate ruse by the government agents who had interrogated him. But to what end? He tried to think of everything that had happened to him over the past week to see if he could discover a connection.

Blocker returned and sat down, flapping his napkin over his lap. "All taken care of."

Gary waited for an explanation.

"The beast, the would-be rapist-murderer? The police will have him shortly."

Gary sized Blocker up. "How did you stop him? I mean, he —"

Blocker patted his vest. The same way I subdued the renegade, only with a stronger dose. He'll sleep until the police arrive, and for some time after that."

"So what will they get him for," Gary said bitterly, "trespassing? Vagrancy?"

"No, no. I reported the little girl's name. They'll get the whole story. He won't be enjoying the psychological pity-party given criminals in your day." He leaned forward baring his teeth: "They'll hang his ass!"

Gary smiled. "I wouldn't think you'd know what swearing is, coming from two hundred years in the future?"

"What, you think your generation invented swearing? It was going on two hundred years before you were born."

"The fuck it was."

"The fuck it wasn't."

Gary eased his aching body back. "So, it was that renegade, Lundow? He was the one who tried to run me off the road just before I got here?"

"That's right. You were on your own, then, and lucky to survive."

"Then it wasn't Shelley who left that message on my computer that said if I want to live I'd better forget the past. I thought Shelley put it there to scare me. Instead, it was the renegade, only he meant business."

"No, not him. That was me."

"You? But how did you get access to Shelley's—"

"Your Shelley uses the computer at the university. I waited for her to leave it for a few moments and—you see?"

"I don't get it. Why go to all the trouble? Or rigormortis, as one of my new buddies at Windy's says."

"Just trying to save myself a headache and to keep you out of trouble. Don't try to figure out the paradox." He pulled more antipasto onto his plate. "It was interesting watching you case the place, though. Not that it would have done you much good."

"The one sitting on the stoop, the guy with the hemorr— That was you."

"Of course, watching you. That's when I was certain of what you were up to."

"A cab came along around that time, distracted me. But I was trying to figure out how that little girl, Dolly Czarn—"

Blocker raised his hand. "No no no. No names, please. I do not personalize anyone in my line of work. I can't afford to."

"You know my name."

"It's necessary now. I'll soon forget it, I assure you."

"This is crazy."

"Isn't it, though. Now, I want you to tell me what has transpired since you arrived here. Everything you can remember."

"First you tell me why you want to know," Gary said, emboldened with the realization that he might gain some leverage with him. "What is it to you? Who are you, really?"

Blocker paused, as if deciding, then spoke. "As I said, I'm from two hundred years in your future. My job is to travel the Time spectrum and pick up anyone attempting to tamper with history, particularly at the pivotal points. I told you before that you flatter yourself if you think I'm here because of you. You, my young interloper, are incidental. I'm here on other business, the renegade being but another minor aspect of it."

"You mean there are others floating around like me?"

"Not like you. You are an accident. A fluke. You have accidentally found a rip in the Time continuum, a split, a rent, a tear. You have found a doorway to the past that should not exist, but occasionally does."

"You mean like a portal? A portal in time?"

"A portal in time, precisely."

"Is that how you got here?"

He scoffed. "Of course not. I have my own entry point, one far more reliable than what you've discovered. I can pinpoint my coming and going. You cannot. You may be off by a day, a week, or even a month. Possibly longer. That would cause complications in my work. I am one of many performing this job."

Gary marveled at what he was hearing. "It must be fascinating to travel back in time. Can you go anywhere, to any time period? Colonial times, for instance?"

"If my assignment calls for it."

"Have you met people like Washington and Lincoln?"

"And Napolean, that stunted megalomaniac, and

Michelangelo, whose nose I broke when I stopped him from killing Pope Julius, and even Alexander the Great, the historical brat with a genius for war. I've had to insinuate myself into the lives of many powerful people, and not always with alacrity, I assure you. One misstep and I could have been dead a dozen times over. But I'm careful. It's my job."

"My God," Gary said, full of wonder, "the stories you could tell!"

"They all go into the archives, secure and unobtainable. There is the public record of historical events, and then there is the true record of historical events, the stuff that does not find its way into the history books. My job, and that of the others like me, Mr.Tyler, is not simply to apprehend villains and to prevent the corruption of the Time line, but also to 'set the record straight,' if I may use that cliché."

"That is absolutely incredible," Gary said. "What a wonderful job to have."

"Frankly, I hate it. I have a home beyond your imagining, and a family I love but rarely see. And am I there with them? No. I'm here on assignment, back in this dismal time period, living in relative squalor, and associating with primitives."

"Then why do it? Why not quit and go into something you enjoy?"

"Where I'm from, one doesn't have a choice. We're given occupations based on our psychological profiles. I am a blocker, and it means exactly that. I block anyone who attempts to interfere, modify, change, alter or in any way influence the course of history. It's an unending task. Had I not been busy with other matters, I might have kept a closer watch on you and found a way to prevent your meddling."

"Now that I have meddled, what will happen?"

"A good question, a very good question, one that I can't answer yet. Life is not perfect and this is not a perfect operation. We have our glitches."

"It's possible, then, that I've changed history?"

"Possible, but I don't think likely. Of course you could have shifted us to a parallel time track, several of which are so closely related to this one that you would be hard put to see the difference. As that celebrity from your time, Yogi Berra, once said, 'The future ain't what it used to be.' He was speaking more truth than he realized. But, in this case, we can only hope the little girl is not the 'O' ring in this scenario. If we're wrong, we may not be here to carry on this conversation." To Gary's questioning look, he said, "We may be eliminated from existence." His eyes glittered with his smile. "But let's be optimistic, Mr. Tyler, we may merely end up on a different time track rather than in oblivion."

He drained the last of his coffee and signaled the waitress for a refill. "Now, to you. Every detail. Leave nothing out."

Except for his private moments with Sarah, Gary told him everything he could remember, from the time of his arrival to Hyde Park to his bungled rescue attempt.

Blocker slapped his fork down. "You fool, you utter and absolute fool! Are you so naïve that you don't understand the nature of men? Their lust for power? Don't you realize that as soon as they get the laboratory results of your shirt and wallet, they will have you in custody so fast you won't have time to blink. They'll grill you and wring you out like a dishrag, suck your brain dry, and when you are no longer of use, they will either kill you or bury you, not in a mental institution, but in an insane asylum, where they make no distinction between the criminally insane and the normally insane, if I may use that oxymoron. They are probably combing the streets for you at this very minute."

The waitress approached, poured their coffee and asked if they wanted anything else. Blocker waved her off.

He continued. "If Roosevelt decides to avoid war, don't you see the repercussions? Hitler is already consolidating his power in Europe and he has a team of brilliant scientists working for him on a rocket program. If America stays out of the war, Germany will have time to develop the atomic bomb, then where will this country be? True, it will eventually be drawn into the war, but at a much later date and a much greater cost, too late to stop the devastation that will visit these shores. Losing a couple of thousand men at Pearl Harbor, tragic as that sacrifice will be, it will be as nothing compared to the losses that will come later in Europe, here at home, and in the Far East where the Japanese will have even more time to entrench themselves." He knocked his plate away and picked up his coffee. "Well, at least you didn't tell the old man the outcome of the war."

"I guess I wasn't thinking," Gary said.

Blocker rocked back, his varnished head glowing in the soft light, his eyes glittering. "Ho ho, Mr. Tyler, *that* is the understatement of the century."

Gary digested what he'd heard, trying to distinguish fact from fantasy, and truth from lies. In the end, he had no choice but to trust Blocker and hope for the best.

"You certainly can't go back to your room tonight," Blocker said, signaling for the bill. "We'll get you some lodging nearby. We passed a little hotel just down the street." He popped a black olive in his mouth. "Are you able to walk?" he mumbled.

Gary held the table, grimacing as he got up. "I can pay the bill."

"No, let me," Blocker said, rising with him. He pointed to Gary's leg. "That blood on your pants looks as if you fell on something sharp. You'd better clean it up right away before it gets infected. No miracle antibiotics yet, you know."

Gary reached into his pocket, pulled out his knife and folded the blade back. "This was supposed to help me," he said ruefully.

Blocker paid and Gary limped out the door behind him. He had a bad feeling in his gut of what was coming next.

Chapter 37

Disheveled and sleepy behind the counter, the clerk greeted them with a grumpy 'good evening.' "For two?" he asked, adjusting his spectacles.

"One," Blocker said, "for Mr. Jones here."

Gary looked around at the dingy lobby, with its artificial potted plant, couch, a couple of misshapen armchairs, and pictures of the American desert hanging cock-eyed on the wall. The proverbial flea bag, he thought, maybe a step or so up.

"Two dollars," the clerk said, turning the book to be signed.

"Do you have a room on the first floor?" Gary asked, scribbling 'Jack Jones,' and peeling off two singles.

The clerk scratched his head and picked a key off the board behind him. "Number seven."

Blocker spoke. "You get a good night's rest," he said. "I'll pick you up in the morning. Can you be ready by, say, ten o'clock?"

"I guess so. But where are we going?"

"Leave that to me," Blocker said, laying a five dollar bill on the counter. "Can you get Mr. Jones some breakfast in his room by nine in the morning?"

"Why, sure, mister, but—"

"And keep the change."

"Why, thank you, sir, thank you much," he said, deftly pocketing the bill.

Gary hobbled down the corridor to his room, went in, sponged the blood from his leg at the sink, reeled off to the bed and passed out almost instantly.

* * * * *

At ten sharp Blocker was standing at the door, nattily dressed, and wearing his mustache and toupee, neatly combed. "Here's a fresh pair of pants for you," he said, stepping inside and looking around. "Did you get your breakfast?"

Gary nodded toward the empty dish on a small round table. "Where to, Blocker? What do you have in mind?"

"All in good time, my dear fellow, all in good time."

"You must know by now that I don't like mysteries?"

Blocker mocked him: *Ah, sweet mystery of life at last..."*

"No joke, Blocker. I ache all over, my head hurts like hell and I'm having a hard time just putting these pants on. So if you don't mind...."

"Just having a little fun, Mr. Tyler. Today all problems will be solved. I have a cab waiting outside. I'll tell you everything once we're out of here. Ready?"

"Tony driving?"

"Somebody else."

Gary felt a little more limber walking out to the street, but not by much. They climbed into the waiting cab and took off. Gary noticed that the driver hadn't asked their destination.

"Shouldn't you tell him where we're going?"

"He knows."

"Nice. Then how about telling me."

Blocker turned to him. "Gary, didn't we talk about you-know-who keeping an eye on you-know-who and what will happen to you-know-who if they get their hands on you-know-who? Sure you do. They've been crawling all over the house last night and this morning and it looks as if they're getting pretty desperate. So leave everything to me, okay?" He reached into his pocket and handed him a slip of paper.

"What's this?" Gary said.

"It's the article. On top of your dresser?"

"No it's not." He squinted at the words. "This talks about a department store burglary."

"Of course. That's because the you-know-what never took place."

"You mean Dol—you mean it's a done deal?"

"For better or for worse it's, as you say, a done deal. So feel good, Mr. Tyler, you've accomplished your mission."

"You broke into my room again."

"'Broke in' is rather strong. I couldn't let you walk around in those bloody pants you left behind, could I?"

Recognizing the ragged edge where he'd torn the article out of the newspaper, Gary felt a surge of satisfaction lift his spirits. He'd done it, he'd actually done it. *I saved Dolly Czarnowski's life.* Sure, with a little help, he thought, wadding the paper and tossing it out the window. *Still, if not for me—* "Hey," he said, looking around, "this looks like we're down by Division Street."

"Bravo." Blocker drew a letter from his inside pocket. "Here, Mr. Tyler, look at this."

Gary saw that it was addressed to him. "This is a confirmation letter," he said, looking puzzled, "instructing me to pick up my order for…a package of brassieres?"

"Sorry. It was the first thing I saw and, as you can imagine, I was very pressed for time when I placed the order, especially after witnessing all your boasting down at Windy's. It's your passport out of here. I'm surprised you didn't think of it yourself."

"And you expect me to walk into the warehouse now and leave?"

"That is precisely what I expect you to do." He checked his watch. "And we're right on time." He tapped the letter. "I'll give you this before you go in." Leaning forward, he handed a bill over the driver's shoulder. "You can let us out here. Keep the change."

The cab pulled over to the curb and Blocker got out. Gary folded his arms. "I'm not getting out," he said. "Not here, no way."

"Driver," Blocker said, "this man has no money and refuses to leave your taxicab."

The driver swung around, laying his arm across the front seat, his fist clenched. "Best you have some dough, buddy, or be ready to lose a couple of teeth," he said, showing his own square little teeth, like a row of Chiclets with dark spaces between them.

Gary dug into his pocket. "I have money. Right..." He felt his watch, his knife, but no money, tried the other pocket, and no money there, either. He looked over to Blocker, bending down and peering in through the window, his reptilian eyes glittering.

Blocker smiled. "When I helped you in...."

"Pretty rotten trick, Blocker, pretty damn rotten."

"Driver," he said, pulling out a wad of money, "it might be better if you take him directly to police headquarters downtown. Tell them to notify—"

"I'm coming, Blocker, you win," he said, inching painfully across the seat and sliding out.

Blocker slammed the door and the taxi pulled away. They stood on the sidewalk facing each other. "I'm not walking with you, Blocker. I can't go, don't you understand? Not yet and you can't make me. I have to look after Sarah, at least until next Thursday when she has her medical appointment."

"No, Mr. Tyler, I'm sorry, not even an hour. She'll have to accept her fate, such as it is, and you wouldn't stand a chance anyway, not with half the federal government out looking for you. I'm surprised they haven't already notified the local authorities."

"I'll take that chance, Blocker. It's my life."

"It's far more than that, Mr. Tyler. The whole future may be at stake and I can't have you— to quote a saying from your time— 'running around like a loose cannon.'"

"I don't care. I'm not going."

Blocker removed his jacket and laid it over his arm. "Do you see the snub nose of this gun peeking out from under my jacket, Mr. Tyler? You're going home where you belong, unless you prefer dying here on the sidewalk."

Gary smiled. "You can't bluff me, Blocker. You already told me you couldn't afford to let me die. That's why you saved me from that maniac. You won't shoot."

"True, Mr. Tyler. But that was then. Circumstances are somewhat different now. To be sure, killing you would be taking a risk, but it's one I must take. Considering all you've told me, I have no choice, don't you see? If you doubt that I would pull this trigger, I give you one example to ponder: Another shot was fired by an unknown assailant that fateful day in Dallas in the 1960s. Can you guess who fired it?"

"You mean you killed—but why?"

"Why? Because another renegade had manipulated the Time line. That election was a major distortion that would have created a dynasty. What had already begun as a cult, would have progressed to dictatorship. We needed a fall guy, a dupe, before we could correct the situation. The inept Oswald gave me my chance. You see, Mr. Tyler, the battle between the good guys and the bad guys never ends. At this very moment renegades are traversing the Time line, attempting to alter history to benefit themselves or their organizations. And it's my job to stop them. Instead, I'm here, wasting my valuable time with a do-gooder. So, just know that I will kill you if I have to. I'd rather not, and I don't think you want to die, either. So walk. Walk ahead of me, just a step." He handed Gary his car keys. "Here, I brought these, too. Take them, you'll need them, I'm sure."

Gary knew Blocker wasn't bluffing. Assassinations were apparently as necessary a part of his job as preventing assassinations. He had the future to protect, and the future of everyone was more important than the insignificant problems of an insignificant individual. He probably had a heart, but he couldn't allow it to interfere with his duty.

"I'm walking, Blocker, I'm walking," he said, shoving the keys in his pocket.

"Good. We're only a block away. Can you manage all right?"

"Would it make any difference?"

"I'm glad you understand."

"Blocker, do me a favor, will you?"

"I don't do favors."

"Just one. Will you see that Sarah gets to the doctor. If she needs an operation, she'll need money. You obviously have resources. Can you do that, help her?"

"No, Mr. Tyler. That would be interfering with the natural flow of things. You're having difficulty because you've allowed yourself to become emotionally involved. Do you see why I refuse to establish ties with anyone or remember their names? I can't even sympathize with *you*, don't you see? But perhaps you can sympathize with me for the lonely life I live ten months out of the year."

"Can you at least tell her that I didn't just run out on her, that I care for her deeply, in fact, that I—"

"No. In the first place, there is no way to explain what has happened here. She would think me a liar or a lunatic. No, Mr. Tyler, let her believe that you are a scoundrel who ran out on her. It will make it easier for her to forget. Your way would only create a fantasy that would leave her pining forever. Don't you see, she would romanticize your relationship beyond anyone's power to compete. No other man could ever hope to win her over. You'd relegate her to spinsterhood. Is that what you really want?"

The warehouse, gray and oppressive, loomed before them, and Gary slogged painfully and reluctantly along. His brain raced to find some chink in Blocker's emotional armor, some compelling argument he might present, when a police car swung around the corner into view.

"Keep walking," Blocker warned. "Be natural."

When the car was close enough, Gary jumped aside, pointing and yelling, "He has a gun! He has a gun!"

The car screeched to a stop in the middle of the street and two cops tumbled out, guns drawn.

Blocker stood, confused, turning his gun on Gary.

"Shoot me, Blocker," Gary said, "and you'll have to kill two cops, too. Or they'll kill you. How will that affect the future?"

"Drop it," the cops cried, shielded by their car. "Drop the gun and put your hands in the air!"

"You son of a bitch," Blocker said, dropping the gun. "You son of a bitch."

The cops rushed over, collaring Blocker, throwing him face forward against a brick wall, wrenching his arms behind his back and clamping on a pair of handcuffs.

"Thank God you got here in time," Gary said. "He beat me up, tried to strangle me and stole my money." He pulled his collar back. "Look, look at the choke marks on my neck. Can you see them? He said he was going to kill me."

"We didn't expect to see you around here anymore," Ed said, picking the gun up off the sidewalk, "not after the talking-to we gave you last time."

Huffing, John jerked Blocker away from the wall and hauled him to the police car.

"And you wouldn't have seen me, either," Gary said, "believe me. The guy said he was taking me to quiet place to 'rub me out,'—is the way he put it."

"Well, you're going to have to press charges."

"Certainly, officer. But please, my money, he has it in his pocket."

"Hold it, John," Ed called. "Come on," he said, tapping Gary's elbow and walking him over to the car. "Dig out his money, John, and see what he's got."

Gary could see the wad coming out of Blocker's pocket in John's hand.

"How much did he take?" John asked, wetting his thumb and starting to count.

"At least a couple of hundred," Gary said, "probably more."

John peeled the bills back, one by one. He gave out a low whistle. "Looks like maybe even three hundred dollars here." He turned to Gary. "Say, where'd you get this kind of money?"

Gary lowered his head. "Funeral money."

"Funeral—" John stammered. "I...I guess she didn't make it, huh, your mother?"

"Right on her birthday, too," Gary said, touching his eye.

"Sorry, but I still gotta ask, how do we really know it's your money and not his?"

"He took a letter from me, too. It's in his pocket. Look, you'll see. It has my name on it, Gary Tyler."

John held the letter up. "I guess he's right, Ed. Here it is, some kind of order sheet," he said, shoving Blocker in the car.

"Okay," Ed said, "take it."

Gary took the letter and the money. "Thank you, officers. And to show my deep appreciation, let me give you a tip." He peeled off a twenty.

John held his hands up. "Oh, no, we couldn't do that."

"Buy lunch. It's the least I can do to thank you both. If not for you, I'd be dead."

"Well…what do you think, Ed?"

"Okay. We'll donate it to the police association….All right," he said to Gary, "get in."

"No, not in the car," Gary said, clutching the money and backing away, "not with him in it, no, please." He trembled visibly. "I can't do it, look at his face, look at his eyes, his killer eyes. I can't do it."

"Go on, get in," Ed said. "For chrissake, what are you getting all panicky about? He can't do anything to you. We'll protect you."

"Please, no, don't make me," Gary pleaded. "He'll find a way, he'll find a way to hurt me, I know he will. He's crazy."

Ed and John exchanged disgusted looks. "Okay," Ed said, "we'll take him downtown and be back in an hour or so to pick you up for your statement. You," he said, poking his finger, "be sure you're there. Give us your address again…and don't forget the twenty."

Gary gave him his Compton Street address and scampered out of the area as quickly as his lame body could manage it. He had to get back to the house, but how? Walking would take a lot out of him, but the real danger lay in being spotted and picked up by the federal agents. Blocker had told him what to expect, death or an asylum. And he believed him.

Ahead, a blue, metal telephone logo jutting from the side of a candy store caught his eye and he knew what he had to do if he hoped to survive.

Chapter 38

"The telephone is on the wall," the elderly lady said, handing Gary a Hershey bar with his change.

"Do you have a phone book?" he asked, glancing around.

"Gracious me, is it gone again?" she said, flitting over and rummaging through a pile of confectionery boxes stacked near the telephone. "Anymore, they just never think to bring things back. But you can dial Information."

"Thanks," he said, hearing the clang of the nickel drop and dial tone before dialing, getting his number and dialing again. "Yes," he said, "is Tony on duty now...? Tony Baloney, right... like he says, a baloney sangwich. I'll wait, thank you....

"Tony? Gary, here, from last night, remember, Gary and Sarah?... Fine, thanks... Tony, listen, I want you to pick me up— no one but you, can you do it?... Yes, corner of..." he looked out the window, "...corner of Cedar and Eagle streets, the candy store. And Tony? ...it's an emergency, so make it fast."

Again he called Information, got his number and dialed again. "Come on come on," he said, "pick it up."

At last. "Hello, Mrs. Harmon, this is Gary, Gary Tyler, your boarder?"

"Good morning, Gary," she said, her voice almost musical, "I was just changing the paper in Toby's—"

"Mrs. Harmon, can I ask you to—"

"—cage. Oh, you were so right, he sings so byoootiful and he really fills the room with sunlight, just like his feathers, just yellow sunlight everywhere and I can't thank you enough, Gary. Is it all right if I call you Gary? And why I didn't think of—"

Gary bopped his head several times with the receiver. "Yes, yes, you're welcome, Mrs. Harmon, I'm glad it makes your heart sing, too, I'm very glad... yes, like he's welcoming springtime, I know, but please, listen, Mrs. Harmon... yes, I mean Elsie, can you call Mrs. Lutz to the phone so that I can talk to her for a minute?...Yes, I know my rent was due yesterday, Mrs. Harmon— I mean Elsie— thank you for reminding me, no I won't forget, yes, I'll wait....

"Mrs. Lutz? No, never mind the shirt. Listen to me carefully, please, and please trust me, it's very important...."

Hanging up, Gary stood just inside the door, munching on his Hershey bar and tapping his foot. *Let's go, Tony, let's go!* It wouldn't be long before police cars would be crawling through the streets like lice, looking for him. Blocker had said he was surprised they weren't already notified.

The instant Tony pulled up, Gary bounded outside as fast as his lame body would allow and dove inside the taxi. "Go to my place, Tony, don't speed, and I'll tell you what I'd like you to do."

"What's the big mystery about, Gary," Tony said, "somebody get killed?"

"Not if you can help, Tony."

"Me?"

"You. Now listen. I want you to put this money in your pocket and take it to Sarah's apartment, straight down the hall, number three. A lady, Mrs. Lutz, will meet you at the door. Give it to her, all of it except fifty dollars. You keep that."

"Gary, do you know what you're doing?" he said, looking at the roll and stuffing it in his jacket pocket."

"Next, you get Sarah, walk her out and help her into the cab."

"Why don't you get her, Gary, something wrong?"

"Very wrong. I can't explain now, but the place will probably be staked out by FBI agents planted in cars around the house, so be nonchalant, like you're picking up a normal fare. As soon as Sarah gets in, drive to 270 Division Street. Can you remember that?"

"270, yeah, 270 Division Street. I guess I'll remember, all right. But you can remind me in case I don't."

"You have to remember. I won't be in the car."

"You getting out?"

"Yes, pull up here and let me get in the trunk."

"You kidding? And did you really mean it about the FBI?"

"Don't worry, you're not breaking any law so you won't get in trouble. Swing over now, Tony, before we get any closer."

Tony pulled up, climbed out and unlocked the trunk. "I don't know about this, Gary, and I don't think I want to know," he said, helping him into the trunk.

Gary tucked himself in, grimacing. "Don't forget 270 Division Street. The south side of the building. Got it? South side."

"I got it, Gary, and, hey, you don't have to give me no fifty bucks, cheez. A fin will be plenty, including for the trip, too."

"Fifty, Tony. Save it toward your new taxi," he said, folding his legs. "Okay, shut it. And don't dilly-dally in the house. Get Sarah out as soon as you can. Time is crucial. If anybody asks, you haven't seen me since you took us to the doctor on Wednesday."

Gary smelled gasoline as the taxi cruised toward the house. He regretted not telling Tony to turn off the engine when he gets there. The danger of being asphyxiated was very real, and he didn't want to die yet, not after all he'd been through.

The taxi slowed and stopped and he heard the door shut. The engine was still running. If he felt himself getting at all sleepy, he determined to kick the back seat out for air. Better to die in a hail of bullets than to die like a euthanized dog.

Inside the house, Tony stood inside the doorway of apartment three. "Gary said to give this to Mrs. Luz."

"Lutz," she corrected him. "I am she," she said, taking the money and calling back. "Sarah, hurry."

"Taking my daughter where?" Mrs. Montera said, twisting her rosary between her fingers, "I pray to God everything is all right."

"It will be fine, Maria, don't you worry," she cooed, "nothing bad is going to happen. Sarah," she called in a hushed voice.

"He said we shouldn't waste any time," Tony said.

Sarah emerged from the bedroom, wearing a plaid head scarf and her red jacket. Her lips were lightly painted and her cheeks highlighted with rouge. She carried her purse against her breast. "Mama," she said, bending over to kiss her, "don't worry. I'll be back soon. Gary has something important to show me. It's a surprise."

"Quick," Mrs. Montera said, "Mamie, you bring me some garlic from the kitchen, and some salt to get rid of the curse, in case anybody put the evil eye on us."

"I'm going, Mama," Sarah said, kissing her mother on the cheek.

Tony tipped his cap and led Sarah by the arm down the hall. Before they reached the door, Mrs. Harmon stepped out in front of them, blocking the way.

"Sarah, have you seen your friend today?" She cocked her head toward Gary's room.

"No, I haven't, Mrs. Harmon."

"Well, I don't usually make no apologies, because as far as I'm concerned most people don't deserve them. Besides, it makes me feel like I'm putting myself on a lower level, if you know what I mean. What I mean to say is that I take back what I said about him," she cocked her head again, "and maybe I jumped the gun too soon. He seems like he's an okay guy. I want to show you what he gave me."

"Excuse us, please, Mrs. Harmon, but can you show me later? I'm really in a hurry."

"This is only going to take a minute. Come on in. You'll be surprised, but not half as surprised as I was when he brought Toby for me."

"Look, Missus," Tony said, "this lady is in a hurry, so would you please let us pass."

Mrs. Harmon glowered under knitted brows. "What's eatin' you, Buster?"

"Time is my bread and butter. I got a fambly to support."

"Well, aren't you the odd one?" she said smiling, then scowling. "Who doesn't!"

Sarah coughed softly into her hand.

"Can't you see the lady's sick?" Tony said. "I got to get her to the doctor."

Sarah coughed again, and Mrs. Harmon stepped back, as if to escape a plague. "For God's sake, why didn't you say so?" She stepped aside. "Go ahead, then."

Tony led Sarah down the steps to the taxi. On the opposite side of the cab, a man in a dark overcoat was hunkered down looking inside, his hands cupped against the window.

"Lose something, mister?" Tony asked, opening the back door and helping Sarah in.

The man stood up, tall and imposing, his complexion dark, his expression bored. Saying nothing, he sauntered to the back of the car, stood there a moment, chewing his gum slowly and rapping lightly on the trunk lid with a knuckle, as if considering some weighty question, then turned, crossed the street, climbed into a dark sedan and shut the door.

Getting into the driver's seat, Tony noticed several cars parked around, all black except a tan one nearest the corner.

Sweating in the tight space, Gary felt enormously relieved when the cab pulled away and started to move again. After they'd gone what Gary estimated to be a safe distance, he banged on the wheel well with his fist. Tony pulled over, got out and unlocked the trunk. Gary shielded his eyes from the light as he contorted himself trying to get out.

"Do you hear that?" Gary said. "Sirens, let's move." He hauled himself out all the way with a helping hand from Tony and dragged his stiffened body around the car to the back door. His eyes lit up when he saw her sitting against the far door.

"Hi, Sarah. Are you feeling all right?"

She brightened. "Gary, what in the world—"

"No questions," he said, sliding in next to her and giving her a peck on the lips. "Not yet."

"That was 270, right?" Tony asked over his shoulder.

"Right. Don't speed, but don't waste any time," he said, looking out the back window and ducking down as a police car raced toward them. Tony pulled to the side until it passed, its siren wailing.

"Almost there," Tony said. "You sure you want the south side. I have to go around the block if you do."

"Yes," Gary said. "You can step on it now; those sirens behind us are getting louder."

Sarah reached for his hand and held it. She said nothing her worried eyes didn't already say better.

"Okay," Tony said, swerving over to the curb. "I don't see anything here, Gary, just this old warehouse that looks empty."

"Pull up near that door," Gary said, sliding over and pulling Sarah with him. "Right here, that's good."

He opened the door and helped Sarah out. If that letter didn't work, he was dead, and he knew it. Blocker seemed to think it would, and he prayed he was right as he led her up the walkway toward the door. He ignored the pains tracing fiery paths across his body.

"You're all set, right, Tony?"

Tony was standing on the sidewalk. "I'm fine," he said, lifting his hat and scratching his head with the fingers of the same hand, "but can you tell me what the heck you expect to do here?"

A tan car screeched up to the curb behind the taxi.

Sarah stopped. "Dexter," she cried, looking at Gary. "What's he doing here?"

Dexter sprang out of his car, pivoting and advancing like a dark and dangerous storm.

"Come on, Sarah," Gary said, jerking her roughly, "come on!"

"But it's Dexter," she said, watching him stride like a man possessed.

Wailing sirens died as two police cars, one behind the other, screeched to a stop, the doors instantly flying open. A black sedan rolled up immediately behind them.

Sweat had already soaked Gary's shirt by the time he reached for the door handle. *Please, God, one break, that's all I ask, just this one.*

Four police officers rushed up the sidewalk, a dozen steps behind Dexter, who stopped, looking around in confusion.

Gary pressed the lever but it refused to retract the bolt. "Come on, dammit, come on!" he said, furiously bearing down on it. It gave. The bolt retracted and the door swung open. Adrenalin pumping, he caught Sarah by the waist, lifted and dropped her inside, pressing in behind her just as the door slammed shut mere seconds before he heard furious fists banging and hammering against it. He could hear the shouting outside.

Breathing hard, he leaned against the wall, holding his chest. "Are you all right, Sarah? Did I hurt you?"

"Gary, where are we? What is this place?"

"Let's hope it's what I think it is."

"It's so spooky. Is it some kind of a warehouse?"

"No, Sarah, for us it's a doorway to tomorrow," he said, taking her hand and following the arrows tacked to the wall along the passageway.

Gary remembered the secretary who ran the office saying people occasionally get lost and end up on the wrong side of her office. It seemed best to go through the procedure in reverse, rather than try to find his way around in the dark.

"Good morning," he said, ushering Sarah in ahead of himself and closing the door.

As before, the woman sat behind her desk pecking away at her typewriter, her glasses perched on her nose. "Good morning, sir," she said, "and ma'm."

"I have this order to pick up," he said, taking the letter from his pocket and handing it to her as she rose from her desk and came around to them.

"Most certainly, Mr…Tyler," she said, reading the name. She adjusted her glasses and looked up at him. "Oh, yes, I recognize you now. You're the gentleman who entered from the other door last week. You've noticed, I'm sure, that the situation has been rectified…

"Now let me see," she said, running her arm out along the shelving, "TA, TE, TH…yes, TY…Tyler, here it is," she said, grasping the package and bringing it down. "One package of—" she flushed.

"Brassieres, isn't that right?" he said, getting a perverse kick out of her obvious discomfort.

"If you'll sign here," the woman said, averting her eyes.

"Certainly," he said, "it isn't every day a man picks up an

order for a package of brassieres. I wonder though, are you sure those are the proper size? What are they, a double-D cup?"

"Oh, my, sir," she said, turning scarlet and fumbling for the fountain pen, "you can read that for yourself, sir. On the shipping order."

Gary smiled and turned to Sarah, who was blushing, as well.

"Thank you," he said, taking the package in his arm and Sarah by the hand. "I think we'll leave by that door there."

"But, sir," she protested, pulling at her collar, flustered. "Sir," she called, running after them, "you can't get out that way." She poked her head out the door. "Sir. Sir...?" But they had already faded into the murky depths of the corridor.

"Do you know where we're going, Gary?" Sarah said, walking timidly beside him.

"I hope so."

"Almost there," he said as they passed the offices of *Danglos; Castro; Clark; Coster & Son.* Ahead, barely discernible in the light, Gary saw the exit. *One last door, please, God, one last Open, Sesame!* As if before an altar, they stood facing the door, unmoving.

Sarah looked up to him. "The lady said we can't get out this way."

"Cross your fingers she's wrong, Sarah. And pray," he said, placing his hands against the door and girding himself against the wincing body pain. He pushed.

It opened. Light flooded in, hurting their eyes. "Come on, Sarah," he cried, elated, "let's go." They stepped outside, squinting into the brightness.

Standing on the sidewalk beside a huge pile of soil, he saw no change. The street crew was still milking the job. Same buildings, same world. No difference. His spirits plummeted.

The joy of moments earlier went out of his heart like the body's final breath in a death rattle. Instinctively he looked up the street for police cars.

"We have to get out of here, Sarah," he said. "They'll pick us up any minute."

"But where are we going, Gary?"

"Anywhere, anywhere it's safe. You're okay. I'm the one they're after. There's a candy store not far from here. Maybe I can contact Tony again."

Tentatively, hand in hand, they walked past the dirt pile to the curb. "Sarah," he cried, "look, look, we did it, we did it!"

"What, Gary, what did we do?"

"Don't you see? It's a *new* pile of top soil. They were just dumping it when I first came through. Open your eyes, Sarah, open those big, brown, beautiful eyes and look," he said, pointing to his car standing at the curb, right where he'd left it a week ago. He had feared that it would have been towed away by now. Then again, how long had he been gone?

The keys jingled in his hand. "Want to go for a ride, sweetie? A real ride?" he said, forgetting his aching ribs as he took her hand and almost jacked her off her feet.

Sarah eased into the bucket seat beside him, her eyes wide with wonder as she ran her fingers over the dashboard.

"That's a cell phone you see in front of you, Sarah. A telephone."

"In a car? A telephone?" she said, looking for wires. She turned sideways, touched the velour seat covers, looked up and around. "Gary," she said, "I'm scared."

"And this is my stereo system," he said, turning the volume up full blast.

She put her hands over her ears.

"Welcome, Sarah, welcome to my world," he cried, pinning them to their seats as he tromped on the gas and peeled away,

laying a black rubber trail behind.
   "Yeeeeehaaa!"

Chapter 39

"Gary, can you tell me what's going on? Where are we? What's happening?"

"Brace yourself, Sarah, because you are going to be as shocked now as I was last week." He turned down the volume and looked over to her. "Are you braced?"

"You're not kidnapping me, are you?" she said, leaning toward him as he swerved around a corner.

"Sarah, get ready for this because I can't think of a way to soften the message. Sarah, this is the year 2007." He smiled. "You heard right, 2007 A.D."

"I don't see the point of the joke," she said.

He reached over and rubbed her hand. "It's not a joke, Sarah. I'm serious. That's why I couldn't explain things before, because I didn't belong in 1939."

Trouble lines spoiled her brow. "What do you mean 'didn't,' Gary?"

"See for yourself, Sarah. Sure, the buildings look pretty much the same because we're basically in the same old neighborhood. But wait till you see the suburbs. And did you ever lay eyes on a car like this one? Or these others around us?" A light rain began and he flicked on the wipers.

"She stared out the side window."

"Sarah, I asked you to trust me before, and I'm asking you to trust me again. I don't want this to be traumatic. I had to face a strange world alone, but you don't have to worry, you have me. Remember that."

"I don't think I'm following what you're saying, Gary, but I'm getting a funny feeling about this."

"Classic rock," he said, turning the volume up and hitting

the gas. "From the Sixties."

They drove along, Sarah's head turning to see one thing or another, and Gary thinking of the consequences of this sudden turn of events. He thought of his grandma and hoped he hadn't been gone long enough to worry her. And how would she take his bringing a strange girl home? And Shelley, what of Shelley, who suddenly seemed a very real person again.

"Gary, where are we going?" she asked.

"You mean, where are we?" He pointed. "We're there," he said. "That's where I live."

She sat up straight to see. "If you live here, why were you staying at Mrs. Harmon's?"

"Still don't get it, do you?" he said, his tires squishing up to the curb. "Today they call it 'living in denial.' Sounds more sophisticated, I guess." He cut the engine and opened his door. "Wait and I'll help you out," he said, hunching his shoulders against the rain and hurrying around the car.

She covered her head with her purse as they huddled together scurrying up to the house. "Now don't worry about a thing," he said, flinging open the front door and pulling her in behind him. He slipped off his wet shoes and Sarah did the same.

"Gary? Gary, is that you?"

"It's me, Gram," he called back from the kitchen.

"Make sure you take your shoes off," she said, emerging from the utility room, carrying a basket of wash. "The darn dryer's starting to sound—"

"Gram," he said, bringing Sarah around to the front and placing his hands on her shoulders, "this is Sarah. Sarah... my grandmother."

Sarah blushed lightly. "How do you do—"

"Call her 'Grandma,'" Gary cut in.

"'Grandma' is fine. It's a pleasure, Sarah," his grandma

310

said, her keen eye making an instant appraisal of the pale, young lady standing before her with a childlike fright in her eyes. She set the clothes basket on the floor.

Gary helped Sarah out of her jacket.

"Give it to me," his grandma said, taking her jacket from him and handing over a towel from a rack by the stove. "Here, wipe yourselves good before you catch your death of pneumonia. Now, what was so important— Gary, what happened to your neck?" she said, pulling his collar back to see better.

"Nothing, Gram," he said, shrinking back. "I fell, that's all. Hurt my leg a little, too, but I'm okay."

"You'd better put some Neosporin on those bruises. They look nasty. And now tell me what was so important in that letter this morning that it sent you flying out of here like the house was on fire?"

Gary looked at Sarah, then back to his grandma. "Gram, I hope your ready for this, because I'm going to tell you a story, one so incredible and fantastic that both you and Sarah are going to think I'm crazy. Sarah doesn't realize it yet, but she's living proof of it. Gram, what day is today?"

"Why, it's Monday. You know that, Gary. You took your exam this morning. And it's my wash day."

He turned to Sarah. "Sarah, what day is today?"

"Today? Today is Saturday...isn't it?"

He took Sarah by the hand and walked her across the kitchen. "What is that?" he said, pointing to the television set in the living room.

She studied it a moment. "It looks like a fancy icebox."

"With a glass door, right." He took her back across the kitchen and extended his hand. "What's that?" he asked, looking over to his Grandma, whose puzzled expression reflected Sarah's.

"I...I'm not sure."

"Does this help?" he said, swinging open the door.

She gasped. "An icebox?"

A refrigerator, much different from the few antiques you might have seen, with that screwy-looking motor on the top."

Sarah seemed to sag and he put his arm around her. "Gram, let's go in there where we can talk. And I hope you're in a listening mood, because what you're going to hear is going to boggle your mind. And yours, Sarah," he said, guiding her into the living room and sitting on the couch beside her.

Grandma hung Sarah's jacket in the closet.

"Would you like something to drink before you get into this mystery?" she asked, coming into the room. "A snack? I don't want you to have too much or it will spoil your supper."

"Good idea, Gram."

When they had settled down, Gary began: "Gram, you know how much I'm like Gramps, his love for the past...."

They picked away at the crackers and cheese, and sipped their drinks as Gary related a radically truncated review of the past week. He left out all the major events, including any mention of Blocker, and simply told how he'd found himself back in 1939, took a room in a boarding house, met Sarah, and found his way back with her.

Sarah listened, apparently guessing he'd left out the gory details to spare her any pain, while his grandma never took her eyes off him as he spoke.

"So that's it, Gram." He raised his hand. "God's honest truth," he said, waiting for her reaction.

"Just don't get those crumbs on the floor," she said, starting to get up.

"One last very important thing, Gram, that I have to ask."

"You're going to ask if Sarah can stay. Well, we have the spare room."

"I always knew you were a mind reader." He turned to Sarah. "My grandma's a mind reader."

"That's not all, Gram. Sarah is going to have to see a doctor. The one she saw there said she needs a specialist, so, I'm going to try to set up an appointment for her."

"Well, I make very good chicken soup. It cures everything," she said, smiling down to Sarah. "In the meantime I'll put some towels and a new toothbrush out for you. I'm going to do a little ironing now, then I'd better get started with supper if we're going to eat sometime today."

Gary reached over and picked up the television remote. "Here, Sarah," he said, putting it in her hand. "Aim this at that icebox with the window and press the button in the corner."

"Like this?"

"Good. Now wait a second and…voila."

"My God, Gary, my God…."

"It's called television, Sarah. Light years away from the one they demonstrated at the 1939 World's Fair."

"Gary, look, it's Fred Astaire and Ginger Rogers, just what we saw." She turned to him. "Gary, what's going on?"

"I'll explain later. Hit that button there, that's it. Now look." The channel jumped to a scene of an airplane skimming the shoreline of Miami beach. "Go on, keep going," he said, watching with pleasure the expressions on her face changing with the changing channels, from disbelief to wonder to delight.

"And all in color!" she said.

"Right," he said, getting up and taking her hand. "Come on, let me show you the miracle of the Computer Age."

Chapter 40

"That's quite a sad story," Grandma said, running the soapy dish under the hot water and handing it to Sarah.

"Life isn't easy for anybody," Sarah said, drying the dishes and stacking them in piles. "My mother always says the only people who don't have troubles are the dead, so we should be happy with whatever troubles we have because they could be worse."

"Be happy? That's a pretty tall order."

"My mother says that's why we have Faith. If we didn't have it, she said, we might just as well dig a hole and jump in." She stifled her laugh. "Those are her words, 'dig a hole and jump in,' not mine."

"Gary, will you turn down that music, please?" Grandma called. "We can hardly hear ourselves talk."

Behind his closed door, Gary reached over from his desk, lowered the volume and went back to flipping pages in the telephone book. "Mrs. Harmon," he said aloud to himself, "would you mind if I looked up a number in your telephone book? ... *You're goddamned right, I'd mind....* "Only for a minute. It's very important."... *Yeah, well, it'll cost you—*

"Cardiologists," he said, running his finger down the column, "cardiologists...cardiologists. This one looks okay, not too far from here," he said, talking to himself and jotting down the phone number. He was just about to close the book, when his eye fell on the name Goldman, Warren E. Goldman. *Is it possible?* he wondered. He jotted that number down, too, got up and called out the door.

"I'm on the extension in here, Gram, so don't use the phone." Pushing the book aside, he pulled up his chair, punched in the numbers and waited, hoping the doctor's office was still open. Sarah couldn't fool him by coughing in her hand and pretending she was only clearing her throat, not after the first couple of times, anyway. When the secretary finally answered he explained as forcefully as he could the urgency of the situation.

"I'm sorry, sir, but not without seeing a primary doctor first," she said. And how could he tell her she had already seen a doctor.

"Isn't there any way Doctor Goldman can take a look at her?"

"I'm sorry. Even with a referral, the doctor has no openings for a month, at the earliest."

"Does the doctor have office hours there, in your building?"

"Yes, Monday and Wednesday mornings, and Tuesday and Thursday afternoons. But it won't do any good—"

He hung up, dialed again and tried a second doctor. And a third and a fourth. All with the same story, and not one of them available in less than a month. He worried. How sick was Sarah, really? He remembered the expression on Doctor Goldman's face when he said she needed to see a specialist. He looked grim when he said it, a little too grim. He punched his fist into his palm. Think, he told himself, think, dammit!

When he left his room, Sarah and Grandma were sitting in the living room talking. "Darn," he said, "you did all the dishes and didn't call me to help?" He sat in his same place next to Sarah.

"Go on, you rascal," his grandma said, "you're just a little conniver like your father was, God rest his soul."

"Would you like to see more television, Sarah?" Gary said, picking up the remote.

She nodded, her eyes dancing with excitement.

315

"I think I'll finish up my ironing," Grandma said, rising from her chair. "And I'll get the spare room ready for you, Sarah."

"Thank you very much...Grandma," she said, embarrassed. "And thank you so much for supper. It was really delicious."

"If you like that barbecue flavor, I'll give you the recipe before you leave here."

Gary wondered when that would be and how it would be. Back in 1939 her presence wasn't a problem, but now it was a major problem. He'd have to call Shelley pretty soon and tell her... tell her what? Tell her that he brought a girl back with him from the past? That she was there at that very moment sleeping in a bedroom next to his?

"What is that, Gary?" Sarah said, touching his arm to stop the channels from flipping by.

He backed up. "That's the Travel Channel. They take you all over the world to exotic places. That's Hawaii there. And that mountain, actually a dead volcano, is Diamond Head, near Waikiki Beach."

Balanced on the edge of her seat, Sarah shook her head, oooing and aaahing every five seconds, enthralled by the images flashing across the screen.

When Grandma came back into the room, she was holding clothes in her hands. "I didn't see you bring in any luggage, Sarah. Did you leave any in Gary's car?"

She shook her head. "We left in such a hurry, and I never expected—"

"No problem, that is, if you don't mind wearing a pair of Gary's old pajamas. My nightgowns would never fit you. I'm afraid you're a little too slender."

"My grandma never throws anything away," Gary said. "And she talks about my grandpa being a collector of old stuff."

"Thank you," Sarah said, "I don't mind at all."

"Never mind him," his grandma said, wrinkling her nose at him, "what I save is useful." She lifted her chin and strutted out.

Gary handed Sarah the remote and watched her as she channel-surfed, totally absorbed in the endless array of programs skipping by. How lovely she looked, with her dark hair contrasting with the whiteness of her skin, her liquid brown eyes capturing and reflecting light. The brown dress she wore might have been slightly frayed around the collar and looked too thin for the season. A quick jolt of sympathy hit him. Poor as she was, she seemed to accept that poverty with dignity, as if that was her station in life, her destiny. As if that was all she deserved or was worthy of.

"Sarah."

"Yes?" she said, her head turning, but her eyes still fixed on the set.

"Sarah, you don't have any clothes with you, and there's nothing here for you to wear, so how about we go shopping tomorrow and pick up whatever you need."

He had her attention. "Gary, I don't even have enough money with me to buy a penny post card."

"I told you before not to worry, didn't I?" he said, looking so deep into her eyes he could hardly tear himself away. "We'll go tomorrow. That is, if you feel all right." He got up. "Right now I'm going to surf the Internet and you can go right on doing what you're doing. Just one word of advice," he said, picking up the programming card, "stay away from these two channels. They show nudity, and the language is probably worse than anything you've ever heard." He remembered reading of the shock Clark Gable brought to the movie-going public in 1939 when he told Scarlett, 'Frankly, my dear, I don't give a damn.'

Gary's warning left her speechless.

"I'll be back after while," he said. "We can watch something together. Maybe Gram will join us. We can even throw a tape in." He smiled. "I'll explain that later, too."

After an hour Gary returned and saw his grandma and Sarah talking on the couch. Though he wasn't quite sure why, it pleased him to see that they were obviously taking a liking to each other. "Gram, I think I'm going to run a movie that Sarah might enjoy. Do you want to make some popcorn and stay, or do you want to make some popcorn and not stay?"

Grandma shook her head. "Isn't he something?" she said to Sarah. "Did you ever see the likes of him before?" She pushed herself up. "I think I'm going to clean up and watch my program in my bedroom."

"She tapes her soap operas," Gary said, raising his brows.

"Well, it's better than your old History channel. At least I'm up to date."

"How about the popcorn?"

"In my own good time," she said, leaving.

"With butter," he called. "A couple of Hershey bars, too."

Sarah asked so many questions as they sat there in the near dark that he was almost sorry he had suggested watching a movie. When it was over he rewound the tape and showed it to her. Even after his explanation of the tape and the VCR, she was mystified.

"That's all right, Sarah. I know it's a lot to digest at once." He slipped his arm around her shoulder and she turned to him, her face, her eyes, her lips soft and inviting. Their lips met.

"Sarah," he said, breaking away, a thin sweat filming his brow, "Sarah, wait."

She buried her head in his shoulder, clinging to him.

"Sarah, we can't...not now...Sarah."

"Gary," she said, her eyes seeming to swallow him, "I love

you."

"Sarah, no, don't say it, not yet. Everything's so upside down right now—"

Her lips were on his again, pulling him under her spell, making his head spin so that he could hardly think. He tried to pull away from the arms coiling his neck, holding him, draining him of his strength, his will.

He turned his head to the side and her lips and hot breath found his ear, sending chills down his spine. He felt strangled. He couldn't stand it. "Sarah," he whispered, his breathing short and tight, "Sarah, my grandma could walk in."

Instantly she jerked back, tugged at her dress and swept her hair up and over her shoulders. "I'm sorry, Gary," she said, sitting back, her hands in her lap.

"No, don't say that. There's nothing to be sorry about. It's just…just circumstances."

She looked at him. "Oh, Gary, what have I gotten into?"

"I told you not to worry," he said, tucking in his shirt. "Leave everything to me." He took her hand. "Why don't we turn in now? You've had quite a day. So have I, and my bones are begging for rest."

"I think that's a good idea," she said, letting him help her up and smoothing her dress."

They walked out through the kitchen, lit only by a small light over the kitchen stove. "Would you like a snack before going in?" he asked.

"The popcorn filled me more than I needed," she said, "but if you don't mind, I'd like to look inside the refrigerator. Just to see?"

"Sure," he said, opening the door and watching her face as the light flooded over it.

"My God, Gary, the food!"

He shut the door. "Yeah, that's why everybody's so fat

today. Wait'll you see."

"Well, at least you still have a good old-fashioned bread box," she said, pointing to the countertop.

"That's no bread box, Sarah, it's a microwave oven. I'll explain that tomorrow, too. You have a world out there you're not going to believe," he said, walking her to her room. "I'll have Gram rap on your door when it's time to get up."

"Gary?" She held him back and stood on her toes to kiss him. "Goodnight, my love," she whispered.

Chapter 41

"Sarah's still in the shower," Grandma said, preparing breakfast.

"I'm glad it's not raining," Gary said, letting the curtain go, and coming from the parlor into the kitchen.

He lowered his voice. "Gram, thanks for letting her stay."

She stood there with the dishes in her hand. "Gary, that story you told yesterday...."

"I know what you're going to say, Gram, but every word is true, I swear it."

"Don't tell me any more. True or not, I don't care. I don't want to know. I don't even want to know where Sarah comes from. All I want to know is what are you going to do about Shel—"

The bathroom door opened and Sarah padded into the kitchen in a floppy pair of Gary's slippers. Her freshly-scrubbed face had a rosy hue, and her glossy near-black hair fell smooth, flat and damp down the sides of her face from each side a white, razor-straight part. "Good morning," she said, her voice soft and cheerful.

"Good morning," Gary said, smelling her freshness.

"Eggs, Sarah?"

"Oh, please, don't go to any trouble."

"Now now now, Sarah, you have to eat to keep your strength up. Would you like fried or scrambled?"

"Scrambled, then, thank you."

"Sit, Gary. Pour yourselves some juice."

"Anything you say, Gram," he said, pouring for Sarah.

Sarah slid the carton close, studying it.

"By the way," his grandma said, "Aunt Shirley called

earlier and wanted to know why you dashed out of the house yesterday when I was on the phone with her."

"And what did you say?"

"What could I say? I told her you had to take a long trip to another world."

"And what did she say?"

"She said you're quite a card."

"And what did you say?"

"I said isn't he, though?"

"And what did she say?"

"She said yeah, just like her brother."

"And what did you say?"

"And I said right, just like his father, God rest his soul, and that's enough of your nonsense. Eat!"

They ate.

"Ready to go shopping, Sarah?" Gary said, pushing his plate aside. "Gram gave me the name of a couple of stores to go to. We can pick up whatever you think you need."

"Gary, what I have is—"

"Not enough. So no arguments, all right? I'll help Gram and you get yourself ready."

* * * * *

"Is the seat belt too tight, Sarah?"

"I feel like I'm in a straight jacket."

"It's the law, but you'll get used to it."

"You mean it's against the law not to wear the seat belt, but not against the law to have nudity and bad language on television?"

"That's the way it is these days," he said, glancing over his shoulder and pulling away from the curb. "Did you sleep all right last night?" he asked.

"Truthfully, I didn't know where I was when I woke up" she said. "This is all like a dream, Gary. It still seems like a dream."

He reached over and patted her hand. "I know. And it's not over yet," he said, showing off a little as he turned up the radio and zoomed across a number of secondary streets to an 'on' ramp, where he gunned it and merged with the oncoming traffic.

"I've never seen such a big road," she said, tilting her chin up to see better.

"Three lanes on each side," he said, weaving between traffic and whipping over to the far lane. "It makes commuting much faster."

"If we live," she said. "Just how fast are you going now?" she asked.

"The speed limit's sixty-five, but everybody does at least seventy."

"Gary, these cars are awfully close."

The car banked as he wheeled onto an 'off' ramp and slowed down. "Dis is de place," he said. "The Galleria."

He came in through the south entrance, skirting the first buildings and swinging around the back.

"Oh my God," she said, "I've never seen so many cars in one place."

"And those buildings up ahead aren't buildings, they're parking ramps." He squeezed into a spot not far from the entrance. "Sometimes you get lucky," he said. "Come on."

They stopped to see a plane rising from the nearby airport, watched it approach and pivoted with it as it soared overhead, its screaming engines ripping the sky and leaving a thunderous vapor trail in its wake as it climbed, diminished and shrank from sight.

He gave her a gentle yank. "No propellers, see? A jet,

come on," he said, ushering her inside and leading her to the main concourse. His body hurt with the walk.

Walking hesitantly, looking down through the vast open space to the far end, thronged with people, she squeezed his arm. "My God, Gary, my God," she said, viewing the translucent dome above. "This is like… like the future."

"It is. It's your future, but think about now, Sarah. I hope you have an idea of what you need because I hate hanging around stores. Let's go. There's Kaufmann's right near here. Gram said you can get everything you need in one stop."

Dazzled, she seemed rooted to where she stood and he had to practically drag her along. Once inside the store, he had to coax her away from every mannequin and clothing rack and bin along the aisle.

"We don't have too much time, Sarah, so think of what you need." He saw a saleslady and waved her over.

"May I help you," she said, her blonde hair seeming to dance on her shoulders as she walked to them.

"Yes, my cousin here probably needs a little advice on styles. Can you help her out?"

"I'd be more than glad to," she said, her creamy complexion and blue eyes even more striking up close. "What, in particular, are you looking for?"

"She needs everything, from top to bottom— dress, shoes, blouses and stuff, including… unmentionables."

The saleslady had a soft, throaty laugh. "I understand," she said.

"But I think you're going to have to explain—" he blocked the side of his mouth so Sarah couldn't see, and mouthed, "pantyhose."

"Gary? Gary, what did you say to her?"

"And she'll need a coat, something casual. You can tell her what you like, can't you, Sarah?" He turned to the saleslady.

"I'll leave her in your hands and trust to your good taste."

"We won't disappoint you, I'm sure," she said. "Shall we start down here?"

"Oh, Miss, I don't know how good you are in math, but try to keep the numbers reasonable, okay?"

Her smile was fleeting, but dazzling. "I understand perfectly, sir."

"And I'll be running around someplace and come back in about an hour, Sarah. Just hang around and wait for me if you're done first."

After more than an hour of losing himself in a bookstore, Gary returned and found Sarah discussing a blouse the saleslady was holding against herself. The way Sarah was feeling the material reminded him of the way Mrs. Lutz's sensitive fingers had tried to read the material in his shirt, like a safecracker's fingers trying to read the numbers inside a tumbler. Catching their eye, he signaled his whereabouts, found a chair near a post and sat down to wait. He folded his arms and closed his eyes. He dozed.

"Gary," she said, shaking him, "I'm ready."

"Oh, so soon? Is the movie over already, Ginger?"

Sarah laughed, remembering. "Everything's on the counter."

"Then let's go get them," he said, rising.

"Gary, all this is costing a fortune. Do you have enough money?"

"Sarah, I have about ten bucks in my pocket."

She put her hand to her mouth. "Oh my God. Stop her, Gary, stop her. She's wrapping everything up."

"But I do have this," he said, holding up his credit card.

He handed it to the blonde and she processed it through. "Sign here, please." She handed his card back. "Sarah has wonderful taste. I know you'll be pleased with her selections."

"Thanks," he said, swallowing hard at the size of the bill. "Can we leave these here for a little while? Just until we get a bite to eat in the food court."

Gary led Sarah out of the store. "A sandwich will hold us until we get home later. Or as Tony would say, a sangwich." They laughed.

They wandered from one food stand to the next. "This is what is known as 'fast food,' and they started it all," he said, pointing to the McDonald sign.

They picked what they liked, ate, and when they were finished she asked if they could go into a few more stores. He told her she could go and he'd wait in the food court. When she finally came out of the last store, they went back to pick up the packages.

"Guide me so I don't run into anybody," Gary said, loaded like a pack mule and trying not to drop any of the boxes as he maneuvered through the crowd and around the cars outside. Seeing the joy in her face was worth every pain in every one of his bones.

"There," he said, after filling the trunk and dumping the last few into the back seat. "Let's go."

"Oh, Gary," she said, looking at him with an expression of mixed excitement and guilt. "I can't wait to put my new clothes on and show you, but...I can't believe what they cost. The shoes alone were seventy-five dollars! Why, for that much money, I could—"

"It's called inflation, Sarah. Don't worry about it."

She put her head back, smiling. "Are we going home now?" she asked, as he peeled away.

"No, Sarah, not yet. I'm shooting for a long shot, and I'm praying it pays off. But first I want you to look in your purse. I'll tell you why when we get there. "

Chapter 42

Holding her arm he walked her across the lot to the building.

"What's in a medical building, Gary, a hospital?"

"No. Just doctors' offices, labs, almost anything you can do to or for a person, short of operations. Different procedures and tests of all kinds."

Inside, he checked the directory next to the elevator. "There it is," he said, "under 'G,' Goldman, Warren E. Goldman. On the second floor, room 22."

She tugged at his arm. "Gary, that's the same name as...you don't think he could be related, do you?"

"As I said, Sarah, it's a long shot, but we can hope."

"What good will it do, even if he is?"

"That remains to be seen. In the last week I've learned to discount nothing. You just never know." He jabbed the elevator button a few times, as if that would hurry it.

She smiled up to him. "Whatever happens, however things turn out, Gary, I believe it's for the best. If it isn't, then, something good will come out of it. If you think about it, it always does."

"I'd rather fight things, Sarah. I'm not big on philosophical stuff."

"I know you're trying to help me, Gary, and I really do appreciate it." She put her head against his shoulder. "But what I'm trying to say is that if things don't work out, I don't want you to feel bad. I know Doctor Goldman was worried when he examined me, but that's all right. You can't control life, nobody can. All any of us can do is try our best, and if God says no to our plans, then we have to live with His decision."

They stepped inside the elevator, rode to the second floor and walked down the corridor. "This is it, room 22. He opened the door, saw an old man sitting in the waiting room and closed the door again.

"Aren't we going in?" she asked, bewildered.

"Looks like he has one patient to go, and...." He took out his watch "...it's a few minutes to four."

She laughed. "Gary, aren't you ever going to get rid of that silly Mickey Mouse watch?"

"Never," he said, "it's become my good luck piece. *Our* good luck piece. Come on." He took her hand. "We'll sit here in the hall in one of these beautiful, futuristic, plastic chairs it's impossible to fall asleep in."

She sat beside him. "It feels so good to sit, but what are we waiting for, Gary?"

"A break. One, big break."

Sarah paid close attention to the people leaving other offices and walking to the elevator. "Everyone looks so beautiful," she said, "these women, the way they're dressed and their hair styles."

"That one, too?" he asked, indicating a young woman with hair hanging in stringy curls down past her shoulders and wearing a short leather jacket over a black leather miniskirt. A tattoo showed above her open neck blouse.

"Oh my God!" Sarah whispered, turning her head and peeking through her fingers as the girl clopped past them on platform soles two inches thick. "Won't she get arrested?"

"It's one of the styles, I guess."

"And by her throat, Gary..."

"A tattoo. Pretty common these days."

Shocked and almost disbelieving, Sarah went on asking question after question on everything of possible interest to a woman, reminding him how truly ignorant he was of fashions and colors and materials, but he answered the best he could. He couldn't avoid thinking of Shelley; she could have told her everything she wanted to know, and more.

The clicking and clacking of heels on the tile floor quieted as the traffic slowed to a trickle and the offices emptied. The hallway had a hollow silence about it.

"It looks like everyone's gone," Sarah said.

"Not quite. A woman came out, but the man in the waiting room didn't. As soon as he does—"

The door opened just then and the old man slowly closed it behind him before shuffling past them in quick, short steps, almost sliding his feet along.

"Is that him?" she asked.

"He's the last one," Gary said, feeling himself tense up. "Now we wait. And hope."

His patience sorely tried, Gary was about to give up when the door finally opened again. A man stood in the doorway, only the long herringbone coat over his back visible to them. "...and the rest you can take care of tomorrow," he was saying to someone inside.

He turned and came toward them, slightly stooped, his worn face a mask of self-absorption. He passed without seeing them.

"Doctor Goldman?" Gary said, standing up. "Doctor Goldman?"

The doctor stopped and turned. "Yes?"

"Doctor, my name is Gary Tyler. Can I speak to you a moment, please?"

"Concerning...?"

"Sarah, here, has a medical condi—"

"Get an appointment," he said curtly, starting on his way again.

"Please, doctor," Gary said, following a few steps behind. "This is extremely urgent. Will you please listen to me?"

The doctor stopped again and turned to face Gary directly. His eyes glared from cold, watery pouches. "This is not only not the proper procedure," he said, "it is rude. Don't do this again."

"Gary," Sarah said, trembling in her chair, "please...?"

The doctor gave her a sharp look, turned and continued on his way as Gary watched him go, his heart sinking. He'd hoped the doctor would have been more receptive.

"Gary...?"

Gary looked to Sarah's pleading eyes, hesitated a moment, and turned back to the doctor, waiting for the elevator. "Doctor?" he called. "Doctor, is your middle name Emile?"

The doctor turned a deadpan face to him.

"Doctor, I knew your father."

The doctor ran a scathing eye over him. "Are you mad?"

"I can prove it."

The elevator doors whisked open with a musical 'bong.' The doctor hesitated, then walked back.

"I knew your father, Emile Goldman," Gary said.

The doctor appraised him closely, viewing him with a world-weary shrewdness. "How is it you know my middle name?"

"A guess. That was the name on your father's shingle."

"My father's been dead thirty years!"

"I'm sorry, doctor, but I did know him. We both did. I was hoping to avoid getting into all that."

"What did you say your name is?"

"Gary Tyler. And she's Sarah Montera."

The doctor looked from one to the other. "And you say her name is... Sarah?"

"Montera. Sarah Montera," Gary said.

The doctor shook his head slowly, drawing his lips back so that the lines framing his mouth carved deeper grooves. "No," he said, frowning, "not possible, not conceivable." He started away.

"Doctor, will this help?" Gary said, snapping his fingers and taking the paper Sarah had ready and handed him from her purse. Gary stepped up and gave it to him.

"What's this?" He reached inside his pocket for his eyeglasses, curled them over his ears, and read the paper in his hand. "Codeine," he murmured. Stunned, disbelieving, he looked several times at Gary and Sarah and the prescription with his father's signature. He folded his glasses and put them away with the prescription. "Come with me," he said, suddenly resolute.

They followed him through the waiting room past a secretary sitting behind the reception window. "I'll be here awhile, Sandy. Call my wife," he said, leading them back to his inner sanctum.

"Sit, please," he said.

"Now," he said, hanging up his coat and sitting behind his desk, "perhaps we can get to the bottom of all this quickly. First, why are you here?"

Gary looked to Sarah and back to the doctor. "Sarah needs to see a specialist. At least that's what your father said."

The doctor raised his hand. "Please, not that, not yet."

"She needs to see a cardiologist, and when I saw your name listed…."

The doctor scrutinized Sarah as she sat there with her hands in her lap, interested and alert, yet strangely unmoved by the seriousness of the conversation. Then he reached into his pocket and smoothed the prescription in front of him, read it again and set it aside. He folded his hands, his wrists and forearms flat on the desk, waiting for Gary to finish.

"I'm a man of logic," the doctor said, speaking softly, "consequently, there are things in this life that I shall never understand. Nor do I intend to try. Now let me read something to you," he said, swiveling around and drawing a book from a bookcase. "It's titled *Medical Mysteries,* my father's autobiography." He opened the book and thumbed through the pages. "Here we are. Would you like to hear?"

Both Gary and Sarah nodded.

"I'll translate the doctor language," he said, and began:

One of the strangest incidents of my life occurred in early spring of 1939, at which time a young man named Gary Tyler, somewhere in his mid-twenties, came to me with cuts and abrasions to his mouth and ribs, apparently resulting from a fight with a gang of hoodlums. He seemed confused and disoriented at the time and (what seemed most odd) simultaneously, quite alert and confident.

I remember him vividly for several reasons, the first being that he asked for penicillin, an antibiotic that would not be available until 1941, two years later!

Being neither a doctor nor one involved in medical research, Tyler explained that he had read about the antibiotic in a magazine but, to my knowledge, no literature at that time had made mention of such a discovery.

Of course, at the time, I made nothing of the comment and would perhaps have forgotten it completely if, several days later, Tyler had not saved me from being beaten to death by a young morphine-addicted thug who attacked me in my office.

Tyler had been there minutes earlier with a young lady, obviously of little or no means, whom I suspected—

"I'll skip a little bit here and there," the doctor said, then continued:

...rather unusual style of outerwear, and emblazoned on his shirt the name 'Greg Norman,' which I particularly remember because of my friendship with Jefferson Norman, of Lancaster, Pennsylvania, and, secondly, because I had never known a man to stitch another man's name on his clothing.

To my great regret I never saw Tyler again to adequately repay him or even to properly thank him for saving my life. The young lady, whose name I believe was Sadie, never kept the appointment I had scheduled for her with the late Doctor Webster, a prominent cardiologist and personal friend, and I have often wondered if...

Much later than I should perhaps have waited, I searched the city directory for a Gary Tyler, a Gary Taylor, and other possible variations of the name, and though a number of those surnames existed, no party I reached had ever heard of the young man in question.

...small mystery I take with me to my grave, as I take so many more regarding a number of my former patients who miraculously....

The doctor closed the book. "A small mystery to him, perhaps, but a great mystery to me," he said, picking up the prescription and tapping it lightly against his fingertips. "I don't pretend to understand what transpired then, Mr. Tyler; however, I will say this: whether you be the Tyler of 1939, and Sarah is the Sadie of 1939, I care not. For all I know, you may have acquired this prescription by fair means or foul, or somehow gained access to the information here—" he touched the book "—or you may indeed be the *son* of that Gary Tyler referenced here. Regardless, a debt is owed. And since my father could not discharge it himself, I take it upon myself to repay it for him, whether it be to the proper party or some other in need. Call it a kind of poetic justice working itself out in the

Grand Scheme of things, if you wish, but a debt is a debt and, even in this age of rampant irresponsibility, it cannot be ignored." He rose stiffly from behind his desk "Sarah, would you leave through that door and go into the first room on your left, please. I will be there shortly. Mr. Tyler, you may remain here."

Sarah did as he instructed.

"Doctor," Gary said, "Sarah has no money, and I have very little. Enough to pay for this examination, but far from enough for an operation, but I'll sign anything you want and take full responsibility for whatever it costs."

"Did you not hear me say a debt cannot go unpaid, Mr. Tyler? Assuming this incredible story is true— and I assume nothing— but assuming it *is* true, then my siblings would not be here today. Can I pit cold logic against the possibility of something existing beyond my comprehension? Put another way: dare I chance it? For the sake of my father, I think not. Therefore, repayment is not only on my father's behalf, but on that of my family, as well. Now, I ask you," he said, leaving the room, "isn't that worth a modicum of my time and skill?"

Gary sat awhile, then got up and occupied the time perusing the books lining the shelves. He picked up the doctor's book from the desk and reread all that Doctor Goldman had read, including the parts he'd skipped. As Gary had surmised, the senior doctor had recognized a serious heart condition, feared it to be inoperable, and limited Sarah's time to perhaps six months at best. Gary took his seat again, hoping to hear the doctor say that modern day miracle drugs alone could help her condition, whatever it was. A few minutes later he returned.

"Sarah is dressing," he said, sitting again behind his desk with his clipboard in front of him. "She's a very sick girl, Mr. Tyler— Gary, if I may."

"Of course."

"You've brought her to me none too soon." His fingers drummed his desk. "Gary, I want to run a series of tests on Sarah as soon as possible. Can you have her in the Suburban Hospital tomorrow morning by six o'clock?"

"Is it that serious, Doctor Goldman?"

"The tests will show the full extent of her condition," he said, scribbling on his pad.

"I'll have Sarah there by six sharp."

"Fine. Report directly to Admissions," he said, extending a handshake over the desk. "By the way, Gary, can you describe my father for me?"

Gary smiled. "Of course. I saw him only a week ago, remember. He is—I mean, he was about forty years old but very youthful, light blonde hair, rather thin on top, and pale skin with a lot of liver spots on his hands. He even joked after he was attacked, saying he hoped no one thought it was a patient doing the yelling."

The doctor showed a glimmer of a smile. "He mentions that in the book."

"He seemed to be a very easy-going man."

Doctor Goldman smirked. "Well, he didn't raise *you*, did he?"

Sarah came into the room, buttoning her jacket.

"So then, Sarah," the doctor said, "Gary will be bringing you in for tests in the morning, and here's a sheet of instructions. As I told you, it's nothing to be nervous about, so get a good night's rest."

They thanked the doctor and left through the waiting room. The secretary was no longer behind the glass window in the office.

"Well, Sarah," he said, pulling out of the lot, "tomorrow everything will be straightened out. We were lucky."

She smiled over to him. "We were blessed," she said, unfolding the instruction sheet.

Chapter 43

"It took a little longer than I thought, Gram," Gary said, toting in a second armload of boxes and dumping them on the living room couch.

"Well, it looks like you've been on quite a shopping spree, Sarah," Grandma said, warming potatoes on the stove.

"I really didn't need—"

"Never mind," Gary said, coming into the kitchen and washing his hands in the sink. "She needed all that stuff, every bit of it. Even the saleslady said so."

"Well, sit down now and eat," Grandma said, dropping slices of roast beef into a pan of gravy.

"I feel awful," Sarah said, "intruding like this. If I can make it up—"

"Never you mind, Sarah," Grandma said, "you can use a little meat on your bones."

Following Sarah's lead, they said grace together before eating. Sarah talked about her shopping experience at the mall and how exciting it was. Gary waited until they were finished before mentioning the doctor visit.

"Sarah has to go into the hospital tomorrow morning, Gram. They want her there by six, so we'll have to make sure we're up in time."

Grandma looked concerned. "Hospital?"

"For tests, yes, at Suburban Hospital," he said, talking as nonchalantly as possible. "The doctor wants a thorough checkup."

"Like a complete physical," Grandma said, showing relief.

"Right." He looked at Sarah. "Routine," he said. "Everybody has to go through it nowadays."

"Can I pour the coffee?" Sarah asked, "or is it may I?"

"Yes, you can and you may," Gary said, smiling up to her.

"That would be nice, Sarah," Grandma said, amused by the interplay between them.

When they had finished, Sarah pitched in clearing the table and doing the dishes, while Gary disappeared into his room, where he turned on his computer and read his messages, most of them urging him to key in on some sex-otic site guaranteed to satisfy his innermost desires. He dropped the cursor and clicked on the latest message:

Don't you ever read your e-mail? Call me, love, Shell.

He replied:

Hi Shelley, So busy cramming for my exam on Thursday that I haven't checked my messages. Sorry about that. I hope everything's on track for you. Keep in touch and maybe we can get together for a couple of hours this weekend, okay? Later. G.

He had purposely avoided the 'love' because of his conscience. He didn't want to think of love now. He couldn't think about love now; too many things were happening at once. He needed time.

Pulling his school books off the shelf, he tossed them on the bed, changed into his sweats to get more comfortable and went out to the living room where Sarah and Grandma were sorting out the boxes.

"I want Grandma to see what I picked out," Sarah said, her face as lit up as a kid's on Christmas morning.

"Sure, good idea," he said. "That's girl stuff anyway, so I'm going back in my room to do a little studying for my exams this week."

"I'm sorry," Sarah said. "I didn't know you have exams, Gary. I've been taking—"

"Never mind," his grandma interrupted. "He's too smart to fail. Come on, now, I'm anxious to see what's in all these boxes."

"Gram, Sarah's going to have to take a bunch of tests tomorrow, so maybe you can advise her on what to wear. Something in one of those boxes, maybe."

"That's no problem. It looks like half the store here. Just tell me what time so I can set my alarm and make breakfast."

"The sheet the doctor gave me said I have to fast for twelve hours."

"I'll get up anyway, Sarah. I'm telling you, these hospitals are crazy with those hours... Come on, Sarah, let's look at what you got...."

Chapter 44

The whole week blurred in Gary's mind like time-lapse photography: Hoping the early morning ride to Suburban Hospital through the gruesome dark of the morning wasn't symbolic of what lay ahead; Sarah's frightened eyes as he guided her from Admissions through the labyrinthine hospital corridors from one station and floor to the next; the battery of tests over the next two days that left her alternately pale or flushed; the dreaded angiogram and the doctor's somber prognosis that her heart required immediate repair for a congenital condition; the awful waiting during the operation; the good news and interview afterward with Doctor Goldman, looking so unlike a doctor and like a mere mortal with his wrinkled greens and cap; finally, the hectic back and forth hospital visits between studying and exams to see her, propped up in bed, her face a healthy pink, framed by her dark hair fanned out against her white pillow, and reading the women's magazines she'd requested; to the day of her release, with Gram along to help her dress and get ready to leave.

"...therapy and some time to recuperate," Doctor Goldman was saying, "but she's young and she'll do fine." He turned to Sarah. "I hope I was as good a doctor for you as you were a nurse to my father," he said, for the first time showing his teeth with his smile.

"Doctor, I don't know how to thank you enough," Sarah said.

"And I don't know how to thank you enough," he said.

To their questioning look, the doctor said, "For helping me find the human touch I had learned from my father and had lost somewhere along the way." He leaned over and kissed her on the cheek....

* * * * *

"Gary," Sarah said, sitting on the couch swaddled in a quilted housecoat and wearing a knitted pair of slipper socks, "Gary, it's been two weeks since I've been out of the hospital. Has the same amount of time passed since we left my time?"

"I don't know, Sarah, but we did leave Mrs. Lutz with enough money to take care of things until we get back."

"I'm worried that my mother's worried."

"I know," he said, clicking the remote. "Old movie or new?"

"Oh, new, of course. I still can't believe what I'm—Oh, look, Gary, Buck Rogers on Mars."

"Discovery channel. That's Neil Armstrong on the moon." He laughed. "You have a lot to catch up on... You know, Sarah, I never told you how pretty you looked in your new clothes, even when you were sick and on your way to the hospital."

"Even in sneakers? I never would have believed they could ever be fashionable," she said. "I know my mother wouldn't approve." She laughed. "Especially wearing them to church."

"And jeans, don't forget. How would she take that?"

"She'd be mortified...but Gary, how are you going to pay for everything? Everything is so expensive. You don't even have a job."

"Don't worry about it. I have a bank account. Remember, I didn't just go to school, I had jobs, part-time jobs and summer jobs. And I saved. Not to mention school loans, which helped pay for tuition."

"How much do those jobs pay, if you don't mind my asking?"

"Anywhere from five to six dollars."

"A day?"

He laughed. "No, an hour."

"An hour! Oh my God, no wonder you can afford to have everything."

They watched for a while together and Sarah reached over and put her hand on his. "Gary, it's wonderful here in your time, but I think it's time for me to go back home."

"You still have a lot more therapy coming," he said. "When it's finished, we can do it."

"But, Gary, how long can I stay here like this? Eating here, sleeping here, it's just not right. And how does it look to others? Gary, I really think I'd like to go back."

He turned to her. "Sarah, you have to complete your therapy first. Doctor's orders."

"All I'm doing is exercising and walking on that machine...that treadmill. I can do that just as well at home walking around the block, can't I?"

He pulled his hand away. "Why don't we wait, anyway, Sarah. By then we can decide if you stay here, or I go back with you."

"I can't stay here, Gary. I have my mother to think about."

"Right, but I can go back because I can come back here anytime. I was gone a week and we came back a few hours later, remember? I can do that forever."

"But where will you work? How will you make a living? There's no record of you going to college back then. Gary, you weren't even born yet." She counted on her fingers and put her hand to her mouth. "Gary, unless this is all a dream, do you realize I'm over eighty years old right now?" She counted on her fingers. "Eighty-six?"

"No kidding? You look great for your age, Granny."

"Gary...I wonder...is it possible that I can go out and

actually see myself, meet myself as I am now, and as an old woman?"

"Wow, that's something to contemplate, isn't it?"

"Yes, but…what if I find out I passed away, say, ten or twenty years ago? I wouldn't want to know that."

"I don't blame you, Sarah, neither would I. So let's give up the thought, okay?"

She took his hand. "Gary, I love you," she whispered. "I don't want to lose you."

"We'll find a way," he said, glancing over his shoulder for his grandma. "I'll think of something. Right now let's just enjoy the movie."

After supper Gary went into his room while Sarah and Grandma finished up the dishes and cleaning. He clicked on his computer and went on-line to read his mail, starting with the latest. A bad feeling had already lodged itself in his gut, when the message popped up on the screen:

Don't you believe in answering your mail? Where are you?

No 'love' tacked on. Shelley was really burned up and he knew it was time to explain the situation to her. With Sarah's recuperation and physical therapy trips, his studying and exams, plus all the incidental running around he'd been doing, he had no time. But that wasn't true, and he knew it. He'd avoided Shelley because he didn't know what to say or how to say it. Would she believe his incredible story? And how could he resolve the mixed feelings that had been torturing him since he'd returned? A little more time is all he needed. He opened his screen, and tapped out his message:

Up to my neck in work. Talk later…G

Closing it up, he sat back thinking. *Why not?* he thought. He had a little time before going out in the other room. What could he hurt? He slid the cursor to *Search*, and waited.

When Gary emerged from his den, his grandma and Sarah

were having coffee in the living room. Wrapped in her housecoat, her legs tucked under her, Sarah was in her spot on the couch.

"I was just telling Grandma that I'd like to go back, Gary, but maybe I should leave it up to you, for when you think the time is right."

"I think she should wait a little longer, don't you, Gram?"

Grandma set her cup on the coffee table. "That's for you two to decide, Sarah," she said, "you're welcome to stay as long as you need to or as long as you like."

The doorbell rang

"I'll get it," Grandma said, getting up. "I have to bring in more coffee anyway."

Gary sat down beside Sarah and took her hand. "I want you to wait, Sarah, wait until we think this out. You have a follow-up appointment with Doctor Goldman next week. Be patient till we hear what he has to say. Then we can—" Her eyes looked past him and she pulled her hand away. He turned.

"Gary, Shelley's here," his grandma said, standing behind her in the archway. "Didn't you hear her voice coming in?"

Shelley stood rigid as stone, her hands jammed in the pockets of her white leather jacket, open over her blue jeans and salmon-colored blouse. "No, Grandma, he apparently was too busy listening to another voice," she said. Her icy-blue glare frosted the room.

Gary popped up off the couch. "Shelley meet Sarah, a friend of mine. Sarah, Shelley."

Sarah put her feet on the floor. "I'm pleased to meet you," she said, obviously frightened and embarrassed by Shelley's palpable hostility.

"So this is the work you're 'up to your neck in.'"

"Shelley, give me a chance. I can explain everything, believe me."

"Cramming. Isn't that what you said? You were cramming?" Her words carried a vicious bite in them. "I see what you mean," she said, shrinking Sarah with her scathing words and cold eyes.

Sarah started to speak, but Shelley cut her off. "I wasn't talking to you," she said scornfully, "I was talking to *him.*" Tears welled in her eyes. "Well, I'll tell you Mr. Gary Tyler who's so busy studying and cramming he doesn't even have time to make a phone call to his fiancee to find out if she's dead or alive, I never want to see you again. Ever!" She twisted the ring off her finger, squeezed it in her fist, and tossed it at his feet. "Keep it."

"Shelley, give me a chance," he said, throwing himself down to grab the ring, rolling under the chair.

"A chance for what, for more of your incredible stories?" Tears traced paths around her mouth. "For more lies!" She spun on her heel and stormed away.

"Shelley," he called after her, holding the ring out, "Shelley."

He could hear his grandma's voice going with her to the front door. When he looked back to Sarah she was crying into her hands.

"Sarah...."

"No, Gary, don't say anything, please."

He dropped on the couch and put his arm around her. "Believe me, Sarah, I can explain."

She shrugged his arm off. "Please, Gary, no more. I can't take any more. Put the ad in now," she sobbed. "Put it in now. I want to leave. I want to go home."

Grandma came back, dabbing the corners of her eyes, and Gary waved her over. "Gram, will you sit with Sarah for a while. Lately, I don't seem to be doing anybody much good."

Back in his room, Gary took the newspaper off the dresser

345

and scanned the pages for something Sarah could use. A heater, that's it, he thought. Just like the picture in the ad, a nice little electric heater to help Mrs. Montera keep her feet warm. He made out his order, took a twenty dollar bill and put them together in an envelope, sealed it, stamped it and went through the kitchen out of the house.

On the way to the post office, he stopped at the library to follow up on his internet search, and the ATM, where he emptied his account. When he returned home he paused by the living room, debating whether to go in, but decided not to when he saw his grandma still sitting on the couch beside Sarah, her arm encircling her. Absorbed in their private talk, neither looked up.

Chapter 45

The next few days passed painfully slow and uneventful. Gary tried to get Sarah by herself, where he could talk to her, but she managed to stay out of reach by sticking close to Grandma. She helped with the cooking, the dishes and even the ironing.

"Sarah can iron wonderfully," his grandma said, holding up one of his shirts for him to see. Sarah blushed. "And she insisted on using my washer and dryer."

"It's all new to her, Gram," Gary said, trying in vain to catch Sarah's eye.

Grandma hung the shirt on a hanger. "Why don't you take the garbage out now, Gary, and check the mail. I think it came."

Gary performed his chore, collected the mail and brought it inside. "Looks like junk, Gram," he said, sorting through it. "Wait, here's one."

Sarah stiffened as she watched him tear open the envelope.

"It's here," he said, looking miserable. "We can pick it up anytime."

Sarah lowered her eyes.

"Well, not today," Grandma said. "I'm making barbeque ribs and it's just too much for two of us."

"Is tomorrow okay, Sarah?" Gary asked.

She tried to smile. "I couldn't miss out on Grandma's ribs," she said, her eyes moist.

They ate together, no one saying much. Grandma tried to get a conversation going, but her words died in the air, so she launched into a half hour monologue, talking about everything, from recipes to television to taxes. After they'd finished, Gary tried to help with the chores but they chased him into the other room.

"Go watch the news," his grandma said, slapping a dishtowel at him. "We'll come in after we're done."

They said little as they watched a few programs. Every time Gary thought he had a chance to talk to Sarah whenever his grandma left the room, Sarah found an excuse to leave, too. After a couple of strained hours, Grandma spoke up:

"Well, Sarah, if you're going tomorrow, shouldn't we start packing your things? You're leaving with a lot more than you came with, you know." She got up and turned to Gary. "And why don't you go upstairs and bring down one of the suitcases. A big one." She waggled a finger. "And don't get lost!"

"Don't worry about that, Gram. Don't *ever* worry about that. Not anymore."

Gary stayed in his room while they packed the suitcase with Sarah's new clothes, including sneakers and a new jacket. He wondered if she was wearing pantyhose now. When he came out, the suitcase was setting on the floor, all packed and ready to go.

"Sarah says she wants to turn in now," his grandma said, "and I think it's a good idea. That way she'll have a lot of rest."

"Sure," he said, looking toward her closed bedroom door. "Don't let me sleep past nine, Gram."

His grandma looked him over with sad eyes. "Sarah asked me to get her up by seven. You know girls," she said, trying to be cheerful, "by the time they wash and do their hair and…you know."

"I know," he said, going in and closing his door.

* * * * *

Morning came and he was awake well before his grandma knocked on his door. He didn't sleep well and had done a lot of thinking. And he knew what he had to do. His mind was made up.

Grabbing a sheet of paper, he wrote a note to his grandma explaining his intentions:

...but if everything goes as it should, Gram, you won't notice me gone for more than a couple of hours, maybe for a few days at most and this note won't mean a thing, so in any case, don't worry okay? If I didn't believe that with all my heart and mind I could never leave you, you know that. One more thing, Gram, if I'm gone for more than a day, have somebody pick up my car where I mentioned by the warehouse on Division Street so it doesn't get towed away and impounded. (the spare key is in my top drawer) If Shelley calls, and I don't think she will, tell her I'm truly sorry and that I always loved her. Love, Gary.

He placed the note on his pillow and went out into the kitchen where Grandma was pouring coffee. "I made up my bed, Gram," he said, sliding a chair over, "so you don't have to go in."

Sarah came out of her bedroom wearing the clothes she wore when she arrived, except that they had been cleaned and pressed. She herself looked fresh, with her skin glowing with health and her hair shining. "Good morning," she said.

When the time came Sarah put her arms around Gary's grandma and kissed her cheek and she hugged her back. "Thank you so much," Sarah said, her eyes watering. "You were just wonderful. Gary's so lucky to have you for his grandmother."

Gary left the suitcase by the door and came to give his grandma a kiss. "I won't be long, Gram, so whatever happens you can be sure I'll be back." He held her at arm's length. "Hey, do I sound like Arnold Schwarzenegger?... Ah'll be bach."

"Go on," she said, slapping at him and turning to Sarah. "I hope we see you again, Sarah. I'll miss you. Oh, and here's the barbecue sauce recipe," she said, picking it off the counter and tucking it in her purse.

"Don't worry, Gram," Gary said, "I'll even say hello to Mrs. Harmon for you." He picked up the suitcase. "I'll tell you about her sometime.... Ready?" he said to Sarah.

She slipped into her red jacket and held up a tote bag. "I think so."

* * * * *

"I'm going to loop the long way around so you can get a quick look at the suburbs first," he said, wheeling across town.

"This is too much to believe," she said, looking out the window in amazement. "Is everyone a millionaire?"

"The banks own most of them," he said, swinging around.

"I'm going back with you," he said, coming into city traffic again.

"No, Gary, it won't work. You have a life here."

"I'm not arguing. I'm going back with you, and that's final."

She looked over to him, softening. "Oh, Gary, this isn't right. You have someone, and you never told me about her. That wasn't fair. She loves you. I could see that, even as mad as she was."

"You need me, Sarah."

"Yes, I need you because I love you. But you never said you loved me, Gary, never once."

"I didn't think I had to," he said, an uneasiness in his voice.

"I know you mean well, Gary, but it's not meant to be.

350

We're from different worlds. These are your people, these are your times. You belong here."

"Don't you love me, Sarah?"

"Please, Gary, you know I do." Tears flooded her eyes.

"Then that settles it. We're going back together."

"Gary, what chance do you have there? Can you get a job? Can—"

"I'm resourceful," he said, his face stony.

"But you can't give up all this. You're used to too much. My world is empty and drab, by comparison."

"I'd have you."

"I wish I didn't love you so much," she said, gazing up to him. "If—oh, Gary, listen."

"The Four Freshmen," he said, turning up the volume.

My days and nights that once were filled with heaven,
With you away, how empty they have grown.
It's a blue world, from now on....

"Isn't it beautiful?" she said, laying her head back. "So beautifully sad?"

"Very," he said, but his mind was on his future in the past. The only real worry he had was that of being picked up by the police, but he'd already been working on that. He could get Tony or Sam to hide him while he scouted out an apartment elsewhere, better even if out of town. In the meantime, Sarah could go back to her apartment and get ready to move out with her mother. Hell, he might grow a beard and a mustache, too.

"Is that it up ahead?" she asked.

"That's the place," he said, crossing the intersection and pulling up to the curb. He looked at her. "Ready?"

"Gary, I love you so much, you know that," she said, taking his hand and holding it to her cheek. "I've loved you since the first moment I met you on the porch, remember? And the walks we took and how gently you held me in your arms when I almost fell, remember? And your silly Mickey Mouse watch—"

"I remember," he said. "But come on, now, we have to move."

She carried her tote bag out of the car with her and stood on the sidewalk as he lifted her suitcase out of the trunk. He slammed the lid.

"Okay," he said, moving her ahead of him and feeling the strain as he carried the suitcase up the walk behind her. Setting it next to the door, he rang the bell and looked around. They waited. He pressed the buzzer again. "If this doesn't work, Sarah, you're—"

The door popped open a crack and he pulled it farther back.

"Gary, is something ringing? I think it's coming from...."

He looked back. "My cell phone. Here, hold the door open," he said, running down to his car, unlocking door, and reaching inside.

Gary Tyler?

Speaking.

Gary, Rich Stegler, Rescue squad. Don't be alarmed, sir, but your grandmother has been seriously stricken. We're ministering to her right now, so—

Gary dropped the phone and ran up the sidewalk. "Something's happened to my grandma," he said, tearing his clothes apart searching for the letter.

Sarah's eyes were frantic. "What, Gary, what?"

"I don't know," he said, pulling the letter out. "Maybe—I don't know."

"Oh my God, Gary, oh my God."

"Look," he said, "take this letter and go inside and wait. If I can't get back in time, don't worry. Pick up the package, a foot warmer. I'll place another ad and join you as soon as I can. Go on now and make sure you go through the same office we came out through— Morgan Fisher Enterprises," he said, hefting the suitcase and sliding it inside. "It's heavy, so grab the handle and pull it up; it's got wheels."

"Gary," she said, clinging to him and gazing into his eyes, "I'm afraid."

"It'll be all right, Sarah. Don't worry."

"Whatever happens, Gary, remember, remember that I love you, I love you now and I'll love you always, across the years, across all the years, all the years of my life, forever and ever." Her tears wet his face as she clung to him, kissing him goodbye.

"I have to go now, Sarah," he said, breaking away and running down the walkway.

He jumped into his car, started it and tromped on the gas, his tires screaming on the pavement. In his rearview mirror, he saw her waving from the doorway.

Tearing his way across town through traffic, he roared down his street to his house. Heart pounding, he slid up to the curb and the car jerked and rocked as he jammed the gear into park and leaped out. *Where the hell's the ambulance? Did they have to rush her to the hospital?*

He bolted up the stairs and into the house, running through the kitchen and stopping dead in the living room archway. "Gram," he said, seeing her sitting on the couch watching television. "You're okay?"

"Of course I'm okay. What's the matter, Gary, you're pale as a ghost. And why are you out of breath?"

"And no rescue squad here?"

"What in heaven's name are you talking about?"

"What a rotten prank to—"

"Did you see Sarah off all right?"

He nodded dumbly. "Yes, yes, I did..."

She turned the volume up. "'Breaking News,' Gary, what you always make fun of. Let's see if a dog got hit on the corner of Main Street," she said, chuckling, "or is it a cat this time?"

"Gram, something funny—"

"Oh, my gosh, Gary, will you look at that? That warehouse on Division Street you were talking about, look, it's on fire!"

Gary stood riveted to the spot, watching the flames leap into the air. A sound tore from his throat as he pounded out through the house. The door slammed.

"Gary," she called after him, "Gary, what's wrong?" Getting up and parting the drapes, she saw him leap into his car and speed away down the street.

* * * * *

From a long distance off he could see the flames shooting high in the sky, and by the time he got there, the police had the area cordoned off, forcing him to park several blocks away. He ran as far as the corner, where a policeman stopped him.

"Hold it there, mister," he said, corralling him with his arm.

"Let me by," Gary said, trying to push his way around him. "I have to go in there, somebody's in there!"

"Nobody's in there, mister, it's an empty warehouse."

"I'm telling you—"

"You ain't telling me nothing, mister, now get back!" he ordered, grabbing his jacket.

"At least let me try," Gary yelled, struggling against him.

"Try and fry," the policeman said, brandishing his club. "Now unless you want to get bashed right here, get back and get back now!" He called over his shoulder to another policeman. "Hey, Mahaney, help me get this nut out of here!"

Mahaney rushed over, all two hundred fifty pounds of Irish

cop, and together they grabbed Gary and backed him up.

Gary knew it was hopeless. If Sarah was still in there he'd come back too late. He could only hope she'd made it through. He prayed she did.

The heat burned his face as sheets of fire battled tons of water streaming up and arcing like silver fountains over the rooftop. Fire trucks jammed the street and firemen scurried like black shadows between them. Sirens wailed in the distance. A fireman dragging one of a dozen hoses slithering like snakes on the wet pavement wandered close, and Gary, cupping his hands around his mouth, shouted to him over the throaty roar of the flames. "Did you find anybody? Was anybody trapped in there?"

The fireman waved him off with a motion that he couldn't hear him.

"Listen to me, mister," the policeman shouted, "and listen good. The building's been vacated at least six years now that I know of. So go on home. You got nothing to worry about."

No, nothing to worry about.

Gary watched the flames devour the building and send billowing clouds of black smoke swirling skyward, carrying with it a tower of golden sparks that mushroomed and showered down over the street. Bursts of hot gases and the crackling of burning timbers rent the air. A wall suddenly gave, crumbled, and exploded in a rolling thunderball of gray dust, grit and debris.

"Better back up, mister," the policeman shouted again. "Too dangerous here. Go on, now, move! Move before you get hurt."

Gary backpedaled slowly, watching the fire consume the carcass and bring down a second wall before a mighty blast collapsed what remained of the roof. The acrid stench of burning embers smoking through water drifted over the streets.

Chapter 46

Heartsick and full of regret for the things he should and shouldn't have done, Gary slouched into the house to the living room, where his grandma was still sitting and watching television.

"Look, Gary," she said, "they're showing the fire. It's not out yet."

"Gram—"

"They said it was the work of arsonists. Why do they say 'work'? I thought they did it because it's fun."

"Gram, don't you remember the story I told you?"

She looked at him, her face serious. "Gary, I hear things but I don't hear things. Do you understand? Let's leave it like that. Now," she said, pushing herself up, "anything special you want for supper tonight?"

"No, Gram," he said, dragging his feet to his room, "nothing."

"Don't worry, she's all right," she called after him. "Where ever she is, she's all right. I feel it in these old bones."

Gary closed his door, snatched the old newspaper off the dresser, crumpled it in his hands and threw it in his wastebasket. He flopped on the bed, his arm across his eyes. What could she be thinking now? he wondered. At her end, the building was still intact, would be for over another sixty years. Would she think he'd decided to break away from her? Would she believe, as Blocker once said, that he was a scoundrel not worth thinking about and forget him? Or had she forgotten him a long time ago because her time would have caught up to his by now? He was making himself dizzy and his head hurt with thinking.

For several days Gary remained in a funk, depressed, with little appetite. Sleep was difficult and he had a hard time concentrating. One night, waking after a particularly bad dream, he got up and sat at his computer to distract himself. His messages popped up and he clicked on the latest.

Gary, meet me at McDonald's across from the university. Ten tomorrow morning.

Again, no 'love' tacked onto the end, but at least Shelley was willing to talk, or maybe to blast him good. He had hurt her badly, and saw again the shock on her face when she first came into the living room, could still hear the awful cry in her throat when she said she never wanted to see him again. *Ever!* He reached over for the engagement ring and rolled it between his fingers.

No, Shelley deserved better than he'd given her. Up to now he'd been thinking only of himself. She deserved an explanation, an apology. A promise to make up for the pain he'd caused. But would she listen?

* * * * *

The next morning at ten sharp, Gary pulled into the McDonald's lot and parked. He was glad Shelley didn't pick noon time, when it would be so crowded the line would be half an hour long.

"Coffee," he ordered looking around for her.

He took his cup and walked along the side to one of the last tables where they could have privacy. No one in that section except an elderly couple, farther down, silently facing each other with their coffee cups in front of them, and, in a niche, a man with his back to him, hunched over a cup of coffee.

Gary took a sip and watched out the window for Shelley's car. Something inside his stomach quivered and he looked around, looked again at the man with his back to him, saw the black hair, shaggy over the collar, and he knew.

"Blocker!"

Blocker swung around, his eyes glittering with his smile. He picked up his coffee, walked over to Gary's table and sat opposite him. "Well, you did it, didn't you, Mr. Tyler?" he said, leaning back and folding his arms.

Gary stiffened, visibly shaken. "What choice did I have?" he said bitterly. "You weren't going to help, and for all you cared, Sarah could have died of heart trouble back there."

Blocker's eyes were steady and unblinking.

Gary leaned forward. "Just one thing, tell me, is she all right? Did Sarah make it back all right?"

Blocker's lips formed a pout. He nodded. "She ended up returning a month before you first arrived and, naturally, she was totally confused, but I fixed her proper time."

"And the operation? Was it a success?"

"Gave her a new lease on life."

Relieved, Gary fell back in his chair. "I would have been with her, but the building burned down, you know. That warehouse we came through? That portal? Of all times, right after she went—" The revelation hit him like a punch between the eyes. "Blocker. I should have known. Blocker, you did it! You did it, didn't you?"

"I had to cauterize that wound in the Time continuum sooner or later."

"And the rescue squad…the phone call….?

"Me, of course. You're a pretty persistent character. I couldn't think of any other way to keep you here, short of— you get the point."

"So that was your revenge for my getting you locked up."

"No, I'm not that petty, although I can't say I enjoyed being in the temporary embrace of those Neanderthals. Besides, your disappearance left them with no case whatsoever."

"But they caught you with a gun."

He held out his palms, his eyes flared with innocence. "It wasn't my gun. I told them it was your gun, but you disappeared. I don't know how it got on the ground. My word against— well you understand. No, I did what I did and do what I do because it's my job and because I don't wish to risk putting myself out of existence— Nobody fucks up the Time Line! Not if I can help it."

"Well, then, why are you here? Apparently my warnings to President Roosevelt did no good. As far as I could learn, I didn't influence history at all."

"On the contrary, Mr. Roosevelt took your words and the evidence you presented quite seriously and was prepared to choose a different course of action, at least to the extent he would protect his legacy and reputation. I saw to it that he didn't."

"So nothing changed."

"It's my job to see to it, Mr. Tyler, that crucial events are never altered!

You've caused a ripple or two, but did no serious damage…Gary. Do you mind if I call you Gary?"

"I thought you didn't believe in getting personal with any of us… Neanderthals."

Blocker smiled broadly. "Perhaps I'm getting soft. Seeing you, and a few others like you— that inexplicable sense of nobility… that, and being separated from my own family for so much of the time… In short, Gary, I'm retiring. I've lost my heart for the business— or should I say I've found my heart, what little may be left of it after all these years? I thought I might atone to some small degree for my rigid application of the law before I go back permanently to my own time. Insuring of course that I do not in any way distort the historical record."

"So what good deed do you intend to perform now?" Gary asked, looking skeptical.

"Not a good deed, perhaps, Gary, but a sad one that I'm sure will be of interest to you."

"And that is....?"

"Sarah's dead."

Blood drained from Gary's face and he thought he'd pass out. "Sarah—" He held his head.

"Buck up, my boy," Blocker said, reaching across and patting his arm. "Keep in mind, Sarah was no longer the young woman you remember. She was well up in her years and had a good, full life."

Gary drank some coffee and, after a few minutes, pulled himself together. "You know, Blocker, I looked in the phone book just yesterday and checked the Internet for the Montera name. I did call a few, but no one ever heard of Sarah."

"No, because she married."

"Dexter Ried?"

He shrugged.

"Then tell me, why didn't she ever try to get in touch with me? She knew my name and even where I live?"

"That she did, but remember, she had a good many years to wait for you to be born. Besides, I had a talk with her and told her it would mean your death should she ever contact you."

"And she believed you?"

"Of course she believed me! After what she'd been through, do you think she could doubt anything I told her, especially after I briefed her on the details of her life, and yours, details that no one else could possibly know?"

Gary paused and looked off in the distance. "You know, Blocker, I seem to remember... so strange... I was just a little kid playing in front of the house... I fell down and scraped my knees and was crying a little, and a lady got out of a long, black car... a very fancy lady with a furry collar and...and a wide hat with a veil in front.... She bent down to face me, almost kneeling, and I remember her voice, so soft, when she asked if my name was Gary... Funny, I always thought it was a dream... she had the prettiest smile behind the shadowy netting... and her breath smelled like flowers when she talked to me. What stuck in my mind most was that she gave me a candy bar, a Hershey bar, saying that she knew it was my favorite. I couldn't understand how she knew that... and all the while, she was shaking her head and looking deep into my eyes, and I wondered why she had tears in *her* eyes. She held me there a long time, just gazing at me with this odd, sad smile on her face, and before she left she lifted her veil and kissed me on the cheek and hugged me, hugged me real hard like she didn't want to let me go. I remember her cheeks were... wet...Oh, God, Blocker... wet just like they were the last time I kissed Sarah goodbye before she... Blocker... Blocker, do you suppose...?"

"Hard not to suppose, isn't it."

Gary snapped out of his reverie. "Blocker, if you know, tell me, did Sarah think I ditched her? Did she see me as a rat?"

"To set your mind at ease, no, she did not. She had doubts, of course, and worried that something serious might have happened you and to your grandmother."

"And you set her straight? Did you tell her what happened? About the fire?"

"That I did," he said, swirling his coffee around in his cup. "I told you I was getting soft, Gary."

"Thanks," Gary said, seeing in the shiny face and glittering eyes a human being, rather than a machine. "When did she die?" he asked, not truly able to believe that the beautiful girl he pictured in his mind and had kissed only days ago could be an elderly woman, much less a dead woman.

"She was buried the day before yesterday. I'll take you to the gravesite tomorrow morning, if you wish to go."

"I do," he said, "I very much want to go."

Blocker finished his coffee. "I have some business to clean up here, so—"

"Blocker, can I ask a favor of you? Maybe a couple?"

"I'm beginning to have regrets already," he said. "What are they?"

Gary took his pen from his pocket, and jotted a note on a napkin. "This is for Sam, at Windy's. Can you give it to him?"

Blocker took it and looked up at Gary from under his hairless brows. "What's it about?"

"I searched the Internet for the different people. Just out of curiosity, you see, and I found Sam's name listed."

"Go on."

"Well, having learned the date of his death as 1962, I stopped at the library and hunted up the old newspaper and found an article describing the details of how he died."

"Go on."

"It seems he took his wife, son and two grandchildren on a flight—"

"Commercial?"

"No, a small plane, a Cesna or something. Anyway, he was piloting and crashed in a fog somewhere in the Pennsylvania hills. They all died. I wrote it down here telling him to avoid flying that day. I really want to see him live, Blocker, him and his family. I really do."

"Deaths are tricky business," he said, snatching up the napkin and putting it in his pocket. "I'll see what I can do to help in case he ignores the warning. Now, what else?"

Gary pulled out a packet of money. "I've been carrying this around since the day I was supposed to go back with Sarah," he said. "Of course that didn't work out, so what I'd like to do is to help a couple of people."

"How much is there?"

"Almost seven hundred. I want some to go to Tony, the cab driver. He has his heart set on getting his own taxicab. This can help him and those six kids of his," he said, tapping the money.

"Who else?"

"Mr. Gorman, the clothing store man I cheated out of twenty dollars. I'd like him to have twenty, and five in interest."

"And?"

"The rest is for Sarah. She already has..." Gary tried to call his words back.

"I know. The money you got that day from me. *My* money," he said, and broke out in a hearty laugh.

"You'll do it, then?"

"Put your money away, my friend. It would likely get them in trouble, as you should well know. I'll see that your wishes are carried out."

"But the money..."

"Money is no problem for me. In fact, let me go you one better, and I'm surprised you didn't think of it yourself. I'll go back to right after the Crash of '29 and buy shares for them in a few promising companies that won't go belly up. Not enough stock to make them rich, but enough to give them security until times improve and they can make it on their own."

"You can do that?"

Blocker swelled a bit. "I can do anything!"

"I don't mean to look a gift horse in the mouth, but is that ethical? I mean, you knowing the future and all?"

Blocker smiled. "Was it ethical for you to take that Joe Louis bet?" He held his hand up. "Ah, but they were ready to clean you out as well, weren't they, with that two-round sucker bet they thought they had going? By the same token, why should only the big shots have the advantage of— shall we call it 'insider trading'? In the end it all evens out."

"Blocker, you amaze me. I wish I knew more about you, where you're from, what it's like two hundred years in the future."

"I can't impart anything like that, Gary. Just remember that nothing lasts forever, neither the good nor the bad. 'Change' is the only constant. Dickens had it right when he said it was the 'best of times and the worst of times.' It always is."

"You know, Blocker, this whole experience, everything that's happened, it's all been like a fantasy...a dream...an illusion."

Blocker smiled. "Isn't everything?"

"Well," Gary said, sitting back with a weary sigh, "I guess the only thing I have to worry about now is getting back into the good graces of Shelley. She caught me sitting on the couch holding Sarah's hand, and Sarah only had on her housecoat." He reached into his pocket. "She threw this back to me," he said, twirling the ring between his fingers. "I doubt there's any hope that she'll ever forgive me."

Blocker stood up. "Mount Calvary Cemetery's on the way from here, so why not meet me here outside in the lot tomorrow morning, say, at half past ten. We can take both cars because I'll be driving off in a different direction afterwards."

Gary stood up and shook hands with him. "Thanks, Blo— don't you at least have a first name I can call you by?"

"Theodore. My name's Theodore." His eyes glittered. "But you can call me Theo."

Chapter 47

A timeless wind swept white clouds from a timeless blue sky, letting the sun burst over the world and through a peaceful grove, where it scattered a mottled brilliance like diamonds on black velvet and turned polished headstones into gleaming mirrors. The loamy fragrance of rain-freshened earth, newly turned, larded the air, while overhead, robins flitted, singing hollow imitations of joy.

Gary stooped to lay a fistful of yellow chrysanthemums over a rainbow profusion of flowers blanketing the grave. He rose and for a long moment he stood there, remembering the girl with the liquid brown eyes, the wistful smile and the sweet breath that once whispered words of love in his ear. He remembered, too, the simple faith that had imbued her soul, and her eager embrace of life, despite its meager offerings and hardships.

Deep in thought, he neither saw the car stop on the path below, nor heard the woman's labored breathing as she ascended the incline. Lost in time— was it sixty-eight years ago, or was it only yesterday?

"Excuse me...

"Excuse me," the woman said, breathless, clutching her purse and watching her footing on the soft ground as she tread her way up to the gravesite.

Startled out of his reverie, Gary turned to face an attractive woman comfortably past middle age and slightly stout. She was wearing a green raincoat and a brown hat resembling a bird's nest. On her left hand, she sported a large diamond, and on her right hand, a red birthstone.

"Excuse me, young man," she said, "are you a

groundskeeper?"

"No, I'm not," he said, looking himself over and stepping back.

She glanced down at the flowers and back to Gary. "Do you represent one of those organizations like the one that puts flags on servicemen's graves?"

"No, I don't."

"Then you didn't bring these yellow mums? They weren't here yesterday."

He shuffled his feet. "No," he began, then, "yes, I did," he said.

"Well, is it yes or no?" she said, appraising him suspiciously.

"I did."

"May I ask, do I know you?"

"No, you don't," he said, his mind opening to a possibility he couldn't deny.

"I didn't think so. You knew my mother, then?"

"Yes," he said, looking around nervously and seeing her car down below with a man sitting inside. Across the road Blocker, or Theo, stood with his arms folded, leaning against his own car.

"Mother knew so many people in her line of work," she said.

"I suppose she had a lot of students who loved her," he said, guessing she had realized her dream of becoming a teacher.

"Students? Oh, goodness, no. Mother wasn't a teacher, she was a fashion designer. Have you never heard of the SaGar Blueline Clothing and Cosmetic Company?"

"I'm not really up on things like that," he stammered. "Somehow I thought—"

"Mother was the very best, simply miles ahead of

everyone. She seemed to have a sixth sense, an uncanny instinct for what fashions would work and what wouldn't. And we're having a wonderful monument put up for her, but it won't be ready for several months, they tell me. That's my grandmother and grandfather's stone over there to the left."

He could read the names from where he stood. "Angelo and Marie Montera."

"Yes," she said. "I'm named Marie, after my grandmother."

"I see. And, by any chance, is your last name Ried?"

She looked puzzled. "No, my name is Stevens."

"But that's your married name, isn't it?" he asked, glancing down at the diamond ring sparkling in the sun.

"It is, yes. Oh, you mean my maiden name. It's been so long, but I used to be Marie Jeffers. Dad is ailing badly and is in a nursing home now."

"I thought your mother might have married Dexter Ried."

"Oh, that Ried. Dexter Ried. Yes, occasionally Mother spoke of him, and Grandmother spoke of him all the time, about what a great help he was to them when they were down and out during the Depression. That was before Mother got that surprise windfall of airline stock that my grandfather apparently bought years earlier and forgot he had."

"That was a real break."

"Wasn't it, though? Mother used a lot of it to get her business started. Thank God it all worked out. It certainly saved them from poverty. The stories I've heard would curl your hair." She stopped abruptly and looked at Gary, her curious blue eyes fixed on him.

"But how do you know about Dexter?"

"Your mother mentioned him, I think. I'm not really sure how I know."

"It seems he left home suddenly, without explanation. It

saddened my grandmother, especially when she heard Dexter died in the war. Somewhere in the Pacific, I believe, and they say he was a hero. He joined the service, the marines, I think, shortly after—"

"After...?"

"Oh, it makes no difference," she said flustered. "I never knew him, anyway."

"So Mr. Jeffers is your father."

She flushed. "My step-father, but enough about me," she said, breaking off that line of thought. "Tell me, how do you happen to know my mother?"

"Well—"

"It's so very strange," she said, cutting in. "Mother left instructions that I should come to her grave every day for a week after she is buried." She put her fingertip to her cheek. "Every day from eleven to noon. But she never gave me a reason." She looked directly into his eyes again. "Don't you think that's an odd...? You ...you look so familiar to me, young man, I feel I know you. Your eyes... Are you sure we've never met?"

"I really don't think so," he said, changing the subject and looking for an escape route. "But, uh, tell me about your Uncle Donny? Did he ever become a movie star?"

"Uncle Donny? Would you believe I never met him? He went away out West one day and never came back. He broke my grandmother's heart. She never got over it. I think that's what really killed her."

"That's too bad."

"But I still can't imagine why Mother asked that I make this... this pilgrimage every day for a week. My husband won't let me come alone. That's him sitting in the car," she said, jiggling her purse his way. "And yet he is so grumpy and impatient coming with me. I told him, for goodness sake, Jack,

I don't need an escort, I'm a big girl and can still get around quite well, but he simply will not listen to me. Sometimes men can be so…so difficult.

"But I shouldn't be carrying on like this, chattering away. Mother always said I was a regular little chatterbox and she didn't know where I got it from, and I used to tell her, Mother, would you like it if I couldn't talk at all and you had to use sign language like an Indian? She thought that was so funny, my saying that, because I was only five or six at the time, and she used to hop around the kitchen whooping like an Indian with her finger making circles in the air and grunting, 'How, How,' and patting her mouth with her hand and chanting, 'woo woo woo woo,' like you've seen them do in the movies?"

She suddenly turned melancholy. "Mother was so much fun, and so good. She loved to cook, too, even though we had people to do that for us. And she had the most delicious secret recipe for barbeque sauce! I miss her so much already. She had her blue moments, but I think she had a good life, despite—"

Gary understood what she stopped herself from saying. And he was more than certain now of who she was.

"I think I've chewed your ear off enough, young man. Is it noon yet? Do you have the time?"

He reached into his pocket and pulled out his watch.

Her mouth dropped and her eyes opened in amazement. "A Mickey Mouse watch?"

"It's my good luck piece," he said.

"I thought…because Mother was in the final stages of cancer and largely incoherent…I thought— oh, but that is impossible, simply impossible!"

Gary felt his legs beginning to tremble. He shoved the watch back in his pocket.

"Of course I didn't take her seriously. She had been

rambling on for days about everything under the sun, and most of the time during her final weeks she was hallucinating. Yet... piecing it together, it made a crazy sort of sense and seemed to explain things that had no apparent explanation... a boy, a young man she said... the future... that she would have died of heart failure if... Over and over she'd say, 'Mickey Mouse watch, Mickey Mouse watch,' smiling at some warm memory lodged deep in her mind. And, yes... the photograph she asked for in a lucid moment, the one that's been in her jewelry box for ever so many years, so old it looked as if a spider had spun a web on it. The names were on the back, I remember." She opened her purse and began rummaging through it. "I took it with her things after— here, in here... someplace," she said, scrutinizing his face as her hands dug furiously into her purse.

Gary began backing away. "It was a pleasure meeting you, Mrs. Stevens."

"No, wait, young man, I have it here, I know it's here, I tucked it in with the papers—"

"Goodbye," he said, going down the shorter but steeper side of the slope.

"Wait, please," she called out, flustered. Then to her husband, "Jack! Jack!"

"Marie," he called back, laboring to get out of the car, "what's the matter, Marie?"

"Young man," she called, waving the photograph, "young man? Wait, please. Is your name... Gary? Gary... I can't read the last name...."

Gary waved goodbye from the road as Theo walked him to his car. "Did you set this up, Theo? Did you set this up with Sarah?"

Theo smiled his glitteriest. "Gary, you don't like mysteries, and I don't like loose ends," he said. "Now go on. I put Shelley in your car."

"Shelley? What's she doing here?"

"Never mind. You convinced me, and so did she, that she would never believe you so I took the liberty of taking her back for a brief trip, only an hour or so—blindfolded, of course, to avoid any future temptations, and not without a certain measure of, shall we say, coercion? I don't have to tell you how strong-willed she is. Nevertheless, I think it worked out fine."

"Then she knows?"

"She knows that compassion and infatuation combined with fantasy do not necessarily equate with love."

Gary ducked his head to look inside. "Are you all right with this, Shell?"

Her golden hair cascaded over her shoulder when she turned to him. "I'm ready to begin," she said, her demeanor pleasantly reserved.

Gary turned to Theo and shook his hand. "Thanks again, Theo, whoever you are and wherever you're from."

"Well, keep in mind that you don't have to save a life to be heroic. And you don't have to run off to some fantasy world to do it, either. If you can accept things as they are and muster the courage to face the day, every day, in your own time, that's heroic enough. That in itself would improve the human condition."

Gary nodded. "This is where I belong, Theo, I know it now. My grandma knew it a long time ago."

"You know the old saying, Gary, 'live and learn.'"

"Yeah, but why does it always have to be the hard way?" he said, reaching into the car and taking out a package. "Oh, and don't forget the special order you placed."

Taking it, Theo frowned, remembered, flashed a smile and straggled off to his car.

"Oh, Theo?"

He stopped and turned. "Yes?"

"Do everybody a favor and get yourself a decent toupee?"

Theo threw him a salute, got in his car and drove away.

Marie Stevens was clinging to her husband's arm as they descended the perilously slippery slope, desperately trying to reach Gary before he drove away. "Oh my God!" she was crying, "Oh my God!"

In his rearview mirror, Gary saw her standing in the roadway, could see her mouth working and her arm frantically waving the photograph, waving much the way her mother waved to him when he tore away from the warehouse so many years ago yesterday.

CHAPTER 48

Fifteen months later---

"And this is me," Shelley said, "pointing to a picture in the family album, and that's my sister Danielle. Wasn't she pretty?"

"She still is," Gary said, squatting on the floor next to Shelley, "and don't you think it would be better if you sit on the couch?"

"You mean this?" she said, smiling and patting her stomach.

"Won't he suffocate, you being all doubled up like that?"

"No, *she* won't, especially not at four months," she said, carefully turning another page.

Shelley's mother came into the room. "Dinner will be ready in a few minutes," she said, picking up an empty glass. "You can set the table."

"Mom, who's this man?" Shelley asked, holding up a photo of a man wearing a handlebar mustache and a homburg hat.

"That's your great-uncle on Daddy's side, Uncle Jacob." She handed back the picture. "Come on now. You can bore Gary with the family album later."

"Oh, I like looking at old photographs," he said, "but only of the family," he rushed on, avoiding his wife's sharp look.

A small photo fell out as Shelley closed the album. "Who's this girl?" she asked, handing it up to her mother.

"Her? Oh, that's your grandma, my mother. She was about ten or thereabouts in that one," she said, handing the picture back. "The other side should tell."

Shelley took it and turned it over. "I thought Grandma's

maiden name was Channing."

"Oh, it was, but my grandfather—her father—changed it about the time of that picture. In those days it was easier to get work if you had a name that sounded less ethnic."

Gary peered over her shoulder to look. His blood chilled.

Shelley turned it at an angle to read the faded writing. "Her name was Dolly,

Dolly... what?"

"Czarnowski. Now do you see why they changed it?"

Epilogue

Today, Gary and Shelly are the doting parents of three children, one girl followed by two boys. All seem happy with things as they are and not as they were, much to the relief of both parents. But the children are still young, and only time will tell in which direction they will go. Gary has recently landed a job at the local university and is an authority on early Twentieth Century America. Shelley is a homemaker and tries to find time for some social networking via the computer. Shelley has not gotten completely over Gary's experience and they rarely speak of the past anymore.

After months of being coaxed, Gary's grandmother finally agreed to move in with Gary and Shelley. Reassured she wouldn't be in the way and would have her own private room, she was looking forward to babysitting and the joy of having little ones around again. Unfortunately, she suffered a stroke and passed away a week before moving day.

Theodore Blocker has not been seen since his last meeting with Gary at Mount Calvary Cemetery. Occasionally Gary senses his presence and looks quickly around, but it is only a passing sensation. Gary is forever grateful to him for helping Sarah and settling accounts with those he left behind in 1939. Gary has checked and learned that the crash of a Cesna airplane with Sam and his family in the Pennsylvania hills no longer appears in newspaper records.

Gary has accepted and reconciled in his mind his vision of Sarah in her youth, with her death as an elderly woman, but he is still troubled by his memory of Sarah's— and his— daughter, Maria, at Sarah's gravesite. The gradual realization that she was and is his daughter still leaves him numb with wonder and disbelief. Indelibly stamped in his mind is the look of shock and bewilderment on her face and the emotional turmoil reflected in her blue eyes, when the knowledge dawned that the young man less than half her age standing before her was actually her father.

From the bits and pieces and fragments of information Marie's mother had told her—especially during her last days when Sarah was hallucinating— Marie was able to solve much of the mystery in her life. She understands the logic behind her mother's clothing and cosmetic company name, SaGar, although she doesn't know how she was able to know which fashions would prevail. Then there were all those little things: The Mickey Mouse watch; the photo of Gary and her mother; Gary's intimate knowledge of the people in her family; her birth in January 1940, which would make her conception coincide with the time of Gary's arrival in the past. She could also understand the reason for Dexter's humiliation and sudden enlistment in the military.

Although the puzzle is partially solved, Marie cannot fully understand or make herself believe the mystery and the circumstances of her mother's life and of her own birth. Sometimes Marie doubts her sanity, but then she remembers the face of the man in the photo with her mother, unchanged from the face of the young man standing before her, and her resemblance to him, and she believes again. She has tried tracking Gary down, but with his surname no longer legible on the photo, the search proved hopeless. When she visits Sarah's grave, she is always looking and hoping Gary will appear again. She knows he has visited because of the fresh flowers placed there. She feels certain she will meet him again. She is determined to meet him again.

Gary has never contacted Marie and is always wary when he occasionally visits and leaves flowers at the base of Sarah's beautiful marble monument with the dates April 5, 1921 – April 28, 2007 chiseled into its ornate base. Because he has never told Shelley about Marie and his relationship to her, he is unable to resolve his inner conflict. He has looked up Maria's address in the telephone book, and has often been tempted to call and speak to her. So far he hasn't. Though he would like to, he's not sure that he ever will. It will depend on Shelley.

End